THE TIMELESS TRIALS

A.C. GUESS

Imprint: Tarina Anthologies

Book Cover Design by The Book Brander

Case Laminate Art by @efa_finearts

Developmental and Line Edits by Kate Seger

Chapter Header Art and Special Edition Sprayed Edges by Etheric Designs

Formatting by Cherie Varian

1st edition 2024

Contents

Dedication

To the people in my corner—thank you for believing in me. Your support means everything.

And to those of you who have been told you *can't* over and over again—I want you to know you *can*. You are strong enough. Chase your dreams. Climb your mountain. We're all waiting at the top to celebrate with you.

Content Warning

This book is intended for adults and contains material that some readers may find distressing. It includes violence, executions, torture, a mention of off-page sexual assault, on-page sexual content, and dragon abuse.

If you require additional clarification or details, please do not hesitate to reach out. You can contact me by emailing acguesswrites@gmail.com.

FROST BARRENS
AGEANDER SEA
ELDARA
LERAVE
NOX
RIVIA
TOLOWEY
OROGI
CATELM
MIDDAE
DAEVE
DRAGON'S EYE
HOUSE OF FROST
DREDA
BAERONIA
PORT IYON
LUSTRO
THORCREST
AGEANDER SEA
THE CITADEL
N
THE WORLD OF AEONTHES

CHAPTER ONE

Not Enough, Not Enough

RAE

Red bloomed from the gash at the corner of his mouth where my knuckles had made impact. *Oh, you've done it now, Rae.* The guilty hand moved to lay at my side, and my traitorous fingers throbbed. I had punched him. Not a girlish slap, not a scratch—a swift, closed-fist punch, square in the jaw. Just like Jarom taught me.

The blood gushed, trailing down his chin to his stout neck and collecting in the overgrown bush of hair that poked out of his shirt. He glowered at me as he dragged a dirt-stained hand across his jaw—the very same hand that had wandered where it didn't belong just moments before. I could sense the pain in his jaw as his feelings drifted toward me, but the effects of alcohol dulled the intensity of his suffering. I should have punched him harder. He deserved more pain.

A silent beat passed between us as he swayed on the spot, his breath reeking of cheap ale and his eyes darkening with malice. I knew two things in that moment: he was wretchedly drunk, and he was going to kill me.

Run. Grabbing a fistful of skirt, I spun around and leaped onto the bar top, rolling to the other side. I landed with an ungraceful *thud* amidst shattered glasses. My ears pounded with rushing blood and I didn't turn back to see if he was following me. He was clumsy with drunkenness—I was alert and quick. I could outrun him.

A blast of wintry air swept the stray hairs out of my eyes as I pushed open the service door to the alley. I scanned the darkness in both directions, milky moonlight offering the only source of illumination behind the pub. I sprinted into the shadows, ignoring the chaotic shouts from the inn. My chest tightened as the frigid air pierced my lungs.

My feet carried me swiftly over the cobblestone streets, making hardly any sound. If I could just blend into the shadows...

Something large and solid appeared in the alley, and I yelped as my body collided with it. "There you are, little bruiser." The voice that spoke was menacing, and I recoiled. A firm hand grasped my neck and pressed me against the wall. I struggled against his grip, but he only pushed me harder into the brick. My shoulders protested as he yanked my arms behind me to bind my hands. The rough surface scraped against the side of my cheek where he had me pinned beneath his shoulder. *Helfyre, he's strong.* I watched white steam billow from a vent above me, glowing in the moonlight as he pulled the bindings taut. The device clipped to the man's vest buzzed with static, and he bent his head forward to speak. "Watchman 746. Suspect apprehended on Mink and 32nd." He snatched my hand and manipulated my wrist to read the numbers embedded there. "Yup. ELC609. It's her. Bringing her in now."

The officer on the other end muttered something in return, though I could not comprehend him through the garbled static. The Watchman, however, nodded. "Understood." He gripped my shoulder and spun me around to face him. He wore a black military hat, and the patch on his shoulder bore a single star, declaring his subordinate rank. A status still far superior to my own. I clenched my jaw as he assessed me with hollow, darkened eyes and a knowing smirk that made my skin crawl. "Let's go."

We pulled in front of the pub, now empty of patrons, and the Watchman opened the back door to remove me. He yanked me up from the seat and my feet splashed in an icy puddle as I stepped down, but I hardly noticed. "Am I not going to the station?" I asked, my voice breathless with disbelief.

"It's your lucky day, Ms. Fenix. Mr. Lawson would prefer to settle this outside the station." My back stiffened against the powerful hand that ushered me toward the entrance. *Oh yes, very lucky.* I would be killed tonight by the drunken man instead of tomorrow by the Watchmen.

The great wooden door creaked in protest on its hinges as the Watchman pushed it open, and I immediately shrunk under the glare of the men in the room. Rendry, the pub owner, huffed at me, red-faced with ire. His cheeks were normally jolly and pinched with a touch of red—I felt a genuine pang of guilt for angering him. He had given me a chance by hiring me. The man I had punched sat on a stool with his arms crossed, a smug smile tugging at his lips. His entitled air of superiority *almost* made me willing to risk another punch, but by some stroke of twisted luck, my hands were tied. He leaned forward on the stool, eyes narrowing as he spoke in a gravelly voice, "You struck me, you little —"

"I'm sorry." I stepped forward, hanging my head in a display of shame. Better to show remorse than to provoke the man any further. Perhaps I could survive this. "I...I did not expect your advances."

The pub owner was unsympathetic. "Stupid girl! What were you thinking? Do you know what you've cost me? A lost night of wages, broken glasses...you've offended my esteemed client!" Portly arms flailed in every direction as he spoke and his eyes bulged. Saliva spewed from his mouth, which was entirely too close to my face. "All because the man found you pretty?" I wanted to object and tell Rendry that the man had been thinking something much more sinister, but I refrained.

"I'm sorry, I was..." *Frightened. Angry. Offended.* I blinked spittle from my lashes and looked over at the drunken man, unable to voice anything I truly felt. His round belly heaved with a crude belch, and I wondered what he had accomplished to be so esteemed. He smiled smugly, apparently pleased with the direction of events. He rose from the stool, swaying ever so slightly. "I'll cut you a deal, girl," he said as he swaggered in my direction. I gulped, suddenly feeling exposed and vulnerable with my hands tied behind my back.

"You settle this with me here, right now, and I won't press charges."

I should be the one pressing charges. But I clenched my teeth together, holding back words that would only endanger me. The men in the room would not side with a wretched poor woman from Nox.

"You pay one year's time, and we'll forget this ever happened." He looked over my shoulder at the Watchman behind me and continued, "Perhaps a bit of leniency will inspire her to be more... *useful* in the future. Don't you think?" He winked, and my expression soured with disgust. *The drunken swine.*

To my horror, the Watchman blinked and nodded with approval. I spun around to face him. "What? He tried to—" But the Watchman dismissed me with a wave of his hand.

"I advise you to accept his offer, Ms. Fenix. You won't get a better deal at the station."

Hot tears welled in my eyes, and I cursed their unbidden appearance. A year was too much. I hardly had enough to get by as it was.

The drunken man leered and held out a hand, displaying the square bit of screen embedded in his wrist. "One year," he demanded. The Watchman untied me and nudged me forward. My wrists were sore from the bindings, and I grimaced as I placed my Time Pacer over his, not having another choice. The time transferred to his Pacer in a matter of seconds. I hardened my expression and stared him down, forbidding the tears to fall from my eyes... forbidding the panic that consumed me to rise up and declare itself. The man placed his grimy fingers over mine and gripped my hands. The stench of his breath, or perhaps the threat of his smile, made my stomach churn.

"Now, was that so hard?" he asked, his tone brimming with condescension. I ripped my hands free.

Rendry stomped toward me, unsatisfied. "And what of my broken glasses? The lost revenue?" He bellowed, raising his hands erratically as he spoke.

"I will clean it up, Rendry."

"You will do no such thing!" His voice boomed throughout the pub and I winced. "I never want to see you in this establishment again!"

Helfyre. "Rendry—*please.* I can—"

"Get out!" he blustered, and I clamped my eyes together as tears finally began to trail down my cheeks. *That's it, then.* I turned to hide the tears and made my way to the oak doors. It would be foolish, nay suicidal, for a woman to argue with a man under the eye of a Watchman. I had learned *that* from my mother. *Fates rest her soul.*

With a heave that required the bulk of my body weight, I pushed the doors open and stepped outside. My body felt numb to the bitter bite of the cold, burning instead with the heat of panic. Thoughts racing, I made my way down the cobblestone street. Numbers raced through my head with each step as I calculated my expenses—medicine, a new dress for Nell's Pacer interview, food to cover the loss of rations from work, fines. No matter how I crunched the numbers, the result was always the same. *Not enough, not enough, not enough.*

CHAPTER TWO

The Bells Toll

RAE

Pa had taken the news fairly well, all things considered. He sat in the thread-bare armchair by the hearth, staring blankly at the wall as the firelight danced upon his face. He hadn't spoken all morning, and I knew his mind raced as mine did, searching for a solution that did not exist. I busied myself, looking through the refrigerator and pantry to find the fixings for breakfast as a distraction. There wasn't much to work with, and the barren shelves only soured my mood further. I grabbed a tube of Goodvit from the fridge and gulped it down. The chalky texture of the paste was foul and hardly palatable, but made slightly more edible as the only food source available. Pushing the last bit up from the bottom of the tube, I paused as something in the distance caught my attention.

Helfyre. The Bells.

The hair on the back of my neck bristled as the haunting melody began. Bells were never a good omen in Nox District. I glanced at my sister, who sat hunched over a stack of papers on the table. Her pencil clacked on the wood as she abandoned her writing and looked up. Our eyes met.

"Why are the bells ringing?" Nell asked, her voice hardly more than a whisper. "A Retirement? Defectors?" The air was suddenly too still, too stuffy. Silence blanketed the room between each chime, and we held our breath, frozen in time.

I shook my head, listening to the low, foreboding tone of the Clock Tower bells. "No—the melody is different. Not right for a Retirement." The realization struck me like a punch in the gut. I could feel the blood drain from my face. "It's Tithing Day." *Oh, impeccable timing.*

Nell paled as she, too, recognized the implication. I glanced at the square embedded in my wrist and felt my pulse quicken. 370 days. I had one year and five days left to live, before considering expenses, of course. My stomach lurched with panic. I did not have enough for unexpected costs.

Living in the Realm of Orogi was an *honor*, they said. Those who could not afford the expenses of such an honor were Retired to pave the future for the most useful...the best. I knew I was neither. Burying my head in my hands, I allowed myself a moment of self-pity before taking a steadying breath. I would *not* allow myself to be Retired today.

"Come," I said, at last catapulted into action. In two steps, I crossed the small room and held my sister's face between my shaking palms. Her skin was warm, her expression cold. Her blue eyes sparkled with tears she would not let fall. "It will be okay," I assured her. Of course it would *not* be okay.

Nell's expression hardened as she pushed away her feelings and nodded. The time for feelings would come later; now was the time to move.

Together, we gathered the papers she had scattered about the table, working with hurried, shaky hands to destroy the evidence of her transgressions. In my rush, a piece of paper sliced the pad of my finger, and the gash welled with blood, but I didn't wince. The pain of injustice burned far more intensely than any small cut.

I shuffled the papers together, catching glimpses of her soul in the words. Nell had a way with written words she could never replicate through speech. She wasn't much of a talker, but she bared her heart through poetry, and I loved her for it.

Poetry, of course, had no place in Nox District. Pretty words, raw truth, and artistic expression were thoroughly unwelcome. The fire that crackled in the hearth gladly accepted our offering as we tossed the papers into the flame. Nell twisted her hands together, fidgeting the way she always did when she was anxious, and we watched the pages curl and vanish into the burning embers. *What a loss.*

My father groaned from his armchair by the fireplace as I turned my attention to him. "Pa—Tithing Day. It's come early. We've got to go." He huffed in disapproval and turned to stare at the empty wall in a stubborn dismissal. We both knew this was bad.

Growing impatient, I took his hands in mine and willed him to look at me. Pa held on to life like the last brittle leaf clings to its tree in the fall, withered and drained, yet stubbornly hanging from the branch well past its time. Most days, he put on a brave face, but I knew the truth. I could hear the slowness of his Time Pacer, feel the pain in his bones. His Retirement was near, but he wouldn't let go. Not yet—not when I had lost the job meant to support us.

My cheeks flushed red with the shame of my failure as he turned glassy eyes toward me. Pa would have to work twice as hard now to make up for that loss, all because I had refused to be useful in the ways a client had requested. I grimaced, recalling the entitlement in the man's voice...the groping hands. Pa promised he wasn't angry with me, but I knew the weight of the hardship I had caused.

I sighed. I could not fix my failure, but I could ease his pain.

"Nell, keep watch." I placed my palms upon his wide shoulders, muscular from years of labor, and assessed the aches that burdened him. The cold of winter made his joints stiff and his chest burned with an infection we could not afford to cure. Working quickly, I pushed healing energy into his body and withdrew as much of the pain as possible. Nell paced nervously by the window, peering below the thick curtains to act as my guard.

My gift of healing was about as welcome as poetry in Nox—its discovery would ruin me. Jarom told me that gifts flowed abundantly in the upper districts, but he'd never heard of anyone with the ability to heal. He expected that was by design.

The Realm would never sanction such an ability, he'd said, both awestruck and horrified, sweeping his fingers across his cheek in vain to find the wound that no longer marred his features—the small gash I had inflicted during an intense training and healed with an abundance of apologies. He stilled, then grabbed my hand. *Promise me, promise me you'll keep it hidden. They can never know.*

I kept my promise to him.

"That's enough," my father said gruffly as he pushed me away, pulling me from my musing about Jarom's concerns. "Save your strength."

"Pa, it's okay. I can—" But he shook his head.

"They're here," said Nell. She dropped the edge of the curtain and allowed it to shift back into place, dampening the cold draft from the window. She straightened the folds of her dress and nervously adjusted her hair, though it was already flawless. I extended a hand toward my father to help him up, but he swatted me away and reached for his cane. *Always so stubborn.*

An impatient fist pounded on the door. Our escorts had arrived. I wiped the soot from my dress and attempted to wrap my unruly hair back into a bun, but my efforts were largely futile. When I opened the door, Watchmen on the other side looked over my unkempt appearance with disdain. Their appearance was, of course, immaculate.

We faced each other in silence—two very different worlds on opposite sides of the threshold. I refused to cower, jutting out my chin with a note of defiance, but secretly grateful they could not hear how my heart fluttered with fear in my chest.

Their knuckles tightened on the rifles they clutched as they surveyed us. Perfect Nell, with her vibrant blue eyes and blonde waves cascading effortlessly about her shoulders. My weary father, propped up against the cane that exposed his fragility and uselessness to society. Me, a disheveled wildling with daring eyes that everyone noticed but nobody liked. If they had cared enough to truly study me, they might have seen them the way I did in my reflection, the thrashing waves and brewing storms of a blue-green sea in their depths. A promised tempest. Just like my mother's.

The tallest of the two soldiers nodded his head curtly toward the street. His companion slipped into our living room, sweeping the corners for stragglers. I paused, stomach lurching as I prayed he didn't notice anything out of order. We hadn't straightened the photograph of the honorable high king in all the chaos, and my books...*Please don't check under my mattress.*

As I stepped over the threshold, I ground my teeth and wondered how they could be so callous. One did not simply lead a subject to their demise without the slightest flicker of empathy. I glared over my shoulder at him as I passed by, brimming with resentment but biting my tongue. If I were braver, I would run.

A tingling wave rushed through me as I considered it—but I knew what happened to deserters. They made sure we knew. As long as that Pacer ticked in my arm, the government owned me—they had the power to extend my life or end it whenever they pleased. There was nowhere in Orogi I could hide from their reach as long as I wore it.

But I had the power to heal.

Discreetly, I turned my eyes to the red slit on my hand, the papercut I had inflicted in my haste to discard Nell's poems. I directed the flow of healing energy into the wound and watched the skin smooth over as if it had never existed. Perhaps there was a way to remove the Pacer safely—to heal myself before it could take my life.

Why else would Jarom have warned me to keep it secret? Why else would Orogi wish to eliminate the gift of healing? It was the only explanation that made any sense.

But if I could run—if I could find a way to remove it and heal myself...

A whimper escaped Nell, and she hopped forward after the Watchman nudged her with the butt of his rifle.

Water doused the flames of hope flickering inside my heart. I couldn't risk it. Not when my family needed me. Not when I couldn't know for certain if I'd survive.

The Watchman tilted his head, regarding me with intrigue. My heart seized—had he seen? He couldn't have. The cut was so small. I blinked up at him, waiting.

"Straight ahead," he growled.

CHAPTER THREE

Dishonorable

RAE

Head forward, arms down, eyes averted toward the ground like a good girl. Good behavior wasn't always a strength of mine, but fear of imminent death inspired a certain degree of compliance. Today was not a day to test. I shuffled along the narrow road as doors opened on either side and Watchmen collected others from their homes. I shivered, unsure if it was due to the nerves or the blustery cold. The slushy snow on the ground had turned as grey as the sky above, and the wind whipped my hair into further disorder, pulling pieces from the knot behind my head.

As more and more of my neighbors crowded into the street, we moved forward in somber silence. The Watchmen ushered us ahead into the main square. Gentle sobs escaped from some unfortunate woman along the path, and I focused my attention on the sound my feet made as they shuffled through the slush. I did not have the emotional capacity to entertain her sorrow at the moment. I had my own worries to attend to.

A blunt force knocked into my shoulder, and I stumbled over my feet in surprise, but a firm hand gripped my elbow, saving me from a mouthful of slush and unwanted attention. "Watch it, Rae," the familiar voice whispered close to my ear. His warm breath tickled my neck. I inhaled the spiced scent of cinnamon and firewood I knew too well.

Oh, Jarom. Lovely. His attempt to talk to me under the Watchmen's eyes was likely to get us both killed, but in truth, I always felt safer with him around.

We stepped forward, our movements falling together in sync, and I chanced another glance in his direction. Black circles of exhaustion rimmed his eyes and I blinked in surprise. He had skipped our evening training session to turn in early, so why did he look so tired?

"Where were you last night?" I pried, careful not to move my lips too much as I spoke in case the Watchmen had their eyes upon us.

"I went to bed early. Training at the Academy has been brutal." His tone had a final, dismissive quality, but I knew he was lying.

My steps slowed, and I opened my mouth to speak. The dangerous look he tossed my way warned me not to push him.

Fine then. Keep your secrets. I'd get him to tell me later.

"So things at the Academy have been...good?" I asked, watching Jarom's eyes dart around the alley, unease written all over his face.

He hadn't heard me—or was simply too distracted by his own worries. A pop snapped in his neck when he tilted it to the side, then he shoved his hands in his pockets. He continued walking forward, ignoring my presence. His attention was clearly elsewhere.

"Jarom?" *What is wrong with you?*

Still, he did not answer.

"Jah-rome!" I snapped at him, invoking the hated mispronunciation of his name to get his attention.

"Jar-um," he corrected out of habit. He glared at me, cocking a brow in question.

There we go. That did it.

"What is going on with you?" I asked. I'd never seen him this wound up.

But Jarom dropped his gaze to his feet. "Nothing. Just nervous."

The discomfort in my heart began to grow. It was normal to be anxious on a day like today, but still...I just hoped he was alright.

"Tithing Day?" I whispered.

"It appears to be," he answered. He turned his gaze toward the men in grey uniforms pounding on doors.

I glanced down at the Time Pacer embedded in my wrist and read the glowing numbers. "Do you know what the going rate is? How much do they expect?"

"Who knows? Time will tell," Jarom said. His hand flexed at his sides, and I noticed the tension he held in his shoulders.

"Time will tell," I agreed, narrowing my eyes in suspicion. If we weren't being watched, I would have punched him in the shoulder for spewing such sanctimonious nonsense and teased him ruthlessly for letting the Academy influence him, though I knew he had a mind of his own. Then I'd *make* him tell me what the hell was going on with him and why he was acting so weird.

He turned toward me, his eyes surveying my face. He exhaled slowly, the tension melting from his expression.

"All in good time, Rae. All in good time," he whispered. A halfhearted smile touched his lips, and he winked. "I'm proud of you, for what it's worth."

Damn him. The dimple in his cheek never failed to bring a smile to my own face, and I felt my irritation with him begin to dissipate. *Unfair.*

I resolved to show him how much I had been practicing his sparring lessons after the Tithe... as long as we both made it home tonight.

My step faltered and a lump formed in my throat. *But what if we don't?*

Concern twisted my stomach into knots. What if we didn't have enough time to donate? Or even worse...what if the Tithe was a failure, and the high king decided to punish the whole district? I shook away the thought. It had been several years since the invocation of the last Timeless Trials, and Jarom was nearly old enough to be excluded from the draft. The thought comforted me.

Jarom's expression fell to a frown. "You going to be alright? You have enough?" he asked.

I let my shoulders slump. Perhaps I should tell him. "I lost my job yesterday."

He grimaced and shook his head. "Helfyre, Rae. What happened?" He paused briefly, then grabbed my hand. "Doesn't matter. Here, take some of my time... I'll be fine."

Without waiting for permission, he discreetly pressed his wrist against mine, and I felt the whir of his Pacer as it transferred hard-earned hours to mine.

"Thank you," I said, breathless with gratitude. I studied the freckles on his nose and his hazel eyes. The way his mouth quirked into a half smile when he looked at me. He had always been here for me, ever since we were children. I had survived this long because he had taught me to be fierce and to survive in a cruel world.

The desire to kiss him overwhelmed me, but I brushed it aside. It would be crazy in this moment, under the eyes of the Watchmen, with the bustle of villagers surrounding us. I just—wanted him to know.

Be brave, Rae. Speak the truth.

My throat ran dry, but I let my feelings tumble into words. "Jarom, whatever happens today, I need you to know, I—"

His entire body tensed and he stopped abruptly.

"Don't say it. You don't. You can't." All the warmth in his eyes evaporated, leaving behind an emptiness I did not recognize. An emptiness that pierced straight through my heart. One that felt sickeningly reminiscent of the vacant gaze of a Watchman. "You don't know me. Not really. I'm different now."

Different how? Because you're training at the Academy?

I gaped at him, startled by the change in his tone. Was this really about his career? Did he think I'd see him any differently or judge him because he took an opportunity to better his life? If anything, he could keep me safer once he became a Watchman. What was wrong with him?

He wiped his hands over his cheeks, pulling them downward with a hint of exasperation, then grabbed my shoulders. I turned my chin upward to meet his gaze. Something flickered through his eyes—something I couldn't name, but the intensity of it left me feeling even more uneasy.

"I'm sorry. I've got to go. You and I can't be seen together anymore. I can't risk it."

I balked, feeling the anger boil up to my throat. "Just because you're training to be some big shot Watchman doesn't mean—"

"Stop." Anger flashed in his eyes and he clenched his jaw, glaring at me until I lost the resolve to argue. "How could you think it's about that?" His words carried a hint of pain, yet the piercing intensity of his glare wounded *me* as well, cutting deeply to form a rift between us. "Just...give them your donation and get out. You'll be fine. Do not come looking for me afterward. And please just—"

He softened into the Jarom I knew again, and his Adam's apple bobbed in his throat. He shook his head and shoved his hands back into his pockets.

His expression settled into the stony facade of a Watchmen—a look that held no familiarity or tenderness for me.

My eyes darted to the pacer embedded in his wrist. If it wasn't about his career, then what was his problem? "Jarom, if this is about the Tithe, take the time back. I'll manage without your help. Please—"

If he had given me more time than he had to spare, I couldn't accept it. I couldn't live with him sacrificing himself to help me.

The muscle in his jaw hardened. "Keep it. I'm sorry...I'm just nervous. I'll see you tonight, okay? Practice your footwork." And he turned his back on me.

He shouldered past the family in front of us and weaved through the crowd, increasing the distance between us until I lost sight of his curly crop of hair. I stopped in the middle of the path and watched him walk away in shock, ignoring the brush and bumps of others moving past me until Nell nudged me hard in the ribs.

"What the heck was that?" Nell asked.

"I don't know," I answered truthfully, resuming the slow march down the icy path. *But I'd better live through the day so I can find out.*

As the great herd of people rounded the corner into the main square of Nox District, Nell gasped and grabbed my hand. A large metal frame blocked the entrance to the square, and Watchmen examined each person passing through the gate. I clasped Nell's fingers in mine, passing along a silent message of encouragement with three squeezes. *I - love - you.* She responded with four squeezes in return. Nell wasn't afraid for herself as she didn't yet wear a Time Pacer, but I knew she was worried about me. *Rightfully so.*

When I reached the gate, the Watchman held out his arm to stop me. He patted gently along my skirts and bodice with calloused hands to ensure I did not carry a weapon. I lifted my chin high as he grabbed my wrist and passed a black baton over the numbers on my Time Pacer. As he finished his examination, my eyes wandered to a cluster of women in the square bound by their wrists. The Watchman restraining me cleared his throat impatiently, drawing my attention back to him. "Oraelia Fenix?" he asked, his tone full of self-importance.

"That's me."

His eyes narrowed, sweeping from my feet to my unkempt hair, deep in thought. "Wait here." My heart leaped with worry as he spoke into the device clipped to his chest. "I've got one."

One what? What have I done now? But I did not have long to dwell on his meaning, for a towering man suddenly appeared and regarded me with an intensity that made me falter. His jet black hair fell to his shoulders, which were broad and muscular beneath his dark cloak. The air seemed suddenly... lacking as he cast his eyes upon me. I opened my mouth to speak, but the storm in his eyes flashed brilliantly with wonder, then dissipated into grey, unassuming skies.

The Watchman smiled eagerly at the man's reaction. "What of this one, Rydar? I found you one, didn't I?"

My heart pounded nervously in my chest, but the towering man shook his head and frowned, his demeanor cool and carefully measured. "No. Not this one. She's too..." He waved his arm around, gesturing to all of me as though my faults would become evident to anyone who laid eyes upon me. "No. Just no."

No? Just no? I'm too what, exactly? I glowered at the man, though I knew I did not want whatever he offered. The Watchman sulked, displeased by the man's assessment. "And what of this one?" He reached behind me to grab Nell's hand and pulled her to my side. Rydar's eyes grew disinterested as he surveyed my sister.

"Name?" he asked lazily.

"Nell," my sister whispered, and I nudged her sharply in the ribs to correct her mistake. "Helena Fenix," she amended.

The Watchman's eager expression soured when he lifted her wrist to scan her Time Pacer and found nothing. "She's not of age yet."

The man called Rydar frowned and turned his back on us. "Very well, then. Neither." I blinked in confusion as he drifted away without another word.

The Watchman grumbled something inaudible as he tapped his fingers, a bit roughly, on the screen of his tablet. "Helena Fenix. You are to report for your Pacer Interview tomorrow. Hour seven, sharp. Tent fifteen. Do not be late."

Nell nodded almost imperceptibly, then stepped through the metal gate as the Watchman allowed her to pass. He rounded on me once more. "And you. To the left. Third kiosk. Get in the queue."

The crowd jostled me as I stepped into the main square and made my way toward the queue. I scanned the downtrodden faces in the crowd, searching for Nell, but she had disappeared into the sea of people. A bodiless voice drifted from somewhere above us, its tone clinical and impersonal.

"Please prepare to present your name and identification at the kiosk." A white banner swept from one end of the dais to the other, red letters boldly announcing *125th Annual Tithing Day - May the charitable donation of your time leave an everlasting legacy.*

Right. I frowned. I wasn't feeling particularly charitable, but I doubted that mattered.

I shook the intrusive thought from my head, knowing it to be traitorous. My eyes darted nervously toward the main dais to observe the officials who oversaw the proceedings. Hopefully, they hadn't brought along any thought interpreters from the Citadel this year. Whispers claimed the high prince had such powers.

I corrected my thoughts, just as a precaution. *I am so grateful for the Good Work of our most honorable high king. May his time be everlasting.* I ignored the bile rising in my throat.

A large meter stood to the right of the dais, and I watched the numbers tick upward as I approached—the green bar was well below the expected total. I shuddered, fearing the repercussions of an unsuccessful Tithe.

The harrowing wail of a young woman disrupted my thoughts. I turned toward the source of the sound, noticing the platform erected along the south side of the square below the Clock Tower. The woman howled at the Watchmen on the platform, throwing herself at the stairs in an effort to climb them. I flinched when the closest Watchman knocked her over the head with the butt of his rifle. She careened, then flopped down the stairs like nothing more than a sack of potatoes.

My breath hitched in my throat as I felt her pain slam into my senses, but it slowly faded to numbness as the Watchman dragged her away. The bound and gagged subjects upon the platform shook with silent cries. *Dishonorables.*

I wondered which one she had so desperately wanted to save from Retirement today. I shuddered and prayed to the Fates that I would not join them soon on that platform. *Deep breath, Rae. Not today.*

CHAPTER FOUR

Coming Up Short

RAE

It was my turn. My stomach churned as a young man was escorted away from a kiosk by two Watchmen, sputtering in desperation over his shoulder. "Just one more week! I promise I'll have more to give next week! On my honor!" The man's voice cracked from the strain, and his eyes bulged as he fought to free himself.

A woman sitting at the high table on the dais glowered at him as they dragged him away, then rolled her eyes and leaned to whisper to her neighbor. The man stiffened at her words, his broad shoulders tilted ever so slightly away and his angled jaw set in firm disapproval. His black, shoulder-length hair seemed to absorb the light around him, and his eyes were grim, gray circles of brewing storms. The haughty woman huffed and shuffled her paperwork, and the man peered into the crowd, meeting my eyes with his dark stare. The man who had turned me away after the Watchman's inquiry. I gulped and stepped forward, trying to shake the feeling of unease.

A woman in a crisp dress stepped before me and blocked the man from my view. She carried a tablet in her hands and wore a smug expression on her face. "Surname?" she requested, tapping merrily on her tablet. Her voice bore the sweetness of pure evil disguised by warm honey. It took great effort to keep the scowl from my face.

"Fenix." I scanned the crowd, searching for the crown of auburn curls that belonged to Jarom, overwhelmed by the sea of glumness. Grey painted the skies over dirty, slush-covered streets. People huddled in the queues wrapped themselves tightly in grey, patched-up coats and stared at nothing with hollow, grey eyes that never captured the twinkling of the sun. Everything was just...grey.

The tablet lady clicked her tongue at me to recapture my attention. I smiled in what was surely a painfully forced display of pleasantry. "I'm sorry?" I asked, realizing I had missed an important question.

"Your age and identification code, please."

"Oraelia Fenix, 21 years, ELC609." I held my hand out to her.

She glanced at my hand, but rather than shaking it as I had intended, she flipped it over with the disdain of one who was forced to handle something disagreeable. After verifying the numbers on my wrist, she released me and wiped her hand on the neat folds of her skirt.

"Very well," she said, stepping to the side to allow me access to the kiosk. "Scan yourself in, please. May your gift honor the Good Work of our most honorable high king."

"May his time be everlasting," I responded. *And may my time carry me through at least another year.* With a deep inhale, I closed my eyes and stepped up to the scanner.

The red light surged to life, and I immediately felt a tug in my core, as if the device demanded the very essence of life from my cells. I exhaled through pursed lips and lowered my eyes, drowning out the rest of the world before granting the device access to do as it would. A low whir in my ears served as the background sound to my slowing heart, and I did not allow myself to panic as I felt my hours and days slip away into the device. When I could no longer bear it, I removed my wrist and attempted to focus my eyes on the woman. This proved difficult, as the world was spinning and my head felt foggy. I needed to stop.

Her features were blurred, but I could see the frown of disapproval marring her otherwise pretty features. "Is that how little you respect the Good Work, darling? Surely your appreciation runs deeper than that, Oraelia."

I stared back, my unfocused eyes unable to make sense of the conflicting expression she wore. The sinister smile. The twinkling eyes. The sweet yet putrid scent of something aggressively floral and honeyed as she leaned toward my ear.

"A word to the wise," she whispered. "It is...*dishonorable* to be so greedy with your time. I'd suggest you spare a few more hours for the cause. Think of the Good Work."

She lifted my hand and placed it forcefully on the blinking device. "Good girl. More. Now."

CHAPTER FIVE

The Wrong Sort

RAE

Oh helfyre. I did not have more to give, but I knew I had to.

I flashed the woman the most demure, cooperative smile I could muster. "My appreciation of the Good Work is unending," I said, hoping she would accept that as an apology. I could feel my knees shake, threatening to buckle and collapse to the unforgiving ground beneath my feet. My head was still spinning from the loss of lifetime I had already offered, yet more must be given.

I ignored the buzz in my ears and the aching protest of my bones as the scanner began to rip away my time. Tick, tick, tick. I gritted my teeth as I allowed the last dregs of my time to slip away into the collection device. My skull pounded and my eyes grew weary, but still, I gave. More, more. I knew I was dangerously close to running the well dry and wondered if it would be painful when my time finally expired. When my Pacer released the poison destined to Retire me. *No. Not today, Rae.*

A sturdy hand landed on the Time Warden's shoulder, and she stiffened. The man tilted his head and regarded me with his piercing stare before whispering to the woman. *Rydar.* She turned to him, her brows furrowed in confusion, and her mouth parted in a retort that was silenced. He towered over the woman, making her small and powerless in his shadow. She closed her mouth, then nodded curtly and turned towards me. My eyelids drooped, heavy with the weight of my fatigue, and I blinked to focus my vision. The slowness of my nearly empty Time Pacer made my mind sluggish and hazy. The stern woman's lips moved, but no sound entered my ears past the incessant buzzing. I looked for the man she had spoken to, but he had vanished.

A slap across the cheek followed by a sharp sting helped lift the haze. "That will be enough, I said," the woman told me, her voice lacking its signature sweetness.

I rubbed my wrist where the Time Pacer was embedded and bowed my head. "May his time be everlasting," I said, surprised by the dryness in my throat and the rasp of my voice. When the silver gate before me opened, I did not look back or ask for permission. I took what remaining time and dignity I possessed and forced my feet into action, though they felt heavy and dragged through the slush.

I glanced around once I had put a bit of distance between myself and the Time Warden. The main square buzzed with the activity of hundreds of people milling about, yet they remained somberly quiet, almost reverent in their fear. The blurs of color and hushed tones made my head spin. *No, Rae. Keep walking.* I was not going to faint and draw attention to myself. I refused to draw the attention of nearby Watchmen. I just needed to find Nell, or Pa, or even Jarom and get home. Get to safety. I could figure out the rest later.

Blackness ate away the edges of my vision, making it disappear like splotches of ink on parchment. *I'm going to pass out.*

I expected to feel the cruel slap of icy rock catch my cheek as I fell and collided with the ground, but something different caught me. A strong, almost painful grip hoisted me up before I made contact with the stones below. A man's voice, deep and menacing, spoke to me as he dragged me past the gaping onlookers. "Don't make a scene."

"Don't make a scene?" I mumbled. *What does he expect this performance to accomplish?* Blood pulsed through me like the rise and fall of a warning siren, but my head lolled to the side. I was too weak to fight back.

"Where are you taking me?" *Please, not the platform. Not to the Dishonorables.*

He merely grunted in response and pulled me further into the shadows—further away from the onlookers in the square and out of sight. Not one of the villagers stepped forward to confront him.

A Watchman standing guard at the exit puffed up his chest and gripped his rifle, knuckles white and trembling. "Everything alright, Rydar?" he asked, his voice small with uncertainty. *Even the Watchman fears this man. Excellent.*

The guard stepped firmly in front of the keystone archway, blocking the exit from the main square, but his darting eyes spoke of a crumbling resolve. He would not save me.

Of course, Watchmen didn't save—they controlled.

A glower from the man holding my arm sent the guard hurrying away like a dog afraid of his own shadow. The Watchman deserted me, leaving me completely alone to defend myself against the towering man.

I knew I should fear him and shudder like everyone else had in his presence, but I was too drained—too spent for common sense. "Let me go," I grumbled, trying and failing to yank my arm away.

He ignored this. "You've spent nearly all of your time," he growled, his voice carrying a distinct tone of distaste. "Why?"

Because I had to. I responded with the only safe reply in my arsenal, though I did not manage to filter my sarcasm. "My appreciation of the Good Work is unending?"

The man's eyes narrowed, and I flinched in the wake of the tempest within their depths, but I straightened my spine to my tallest height. "I am not a time waster." I felt immediately foolish when the words left my mouth—he had neither insinuated nor stated such an accusation, but I felt obligated to defend myself nonetheless.

The twitch of his mouth was nearly imperceptible, but I did not miss the hint of a smile that slipped past his restraint.

"No, you are not," he conceded, his voice deep and rumbling. I felt suddenly uncomfortable in his grasp, coming to my senses enough to notice the dark hair that lined his angular jaw and the way his muscular chest rose and fell with each breath. Too close. Much too close to me. I wriggled, trying to free myself from his grasp, but felt stymied by the scent of storm and sandalwood. He frowned and released me.

His grey eyes swept over my features, full of...*something*. Disdain? Anger? "You must be more careful, Oraelia Fenix. You don't want to draw attention from the wrong sort." His hand rested on the wall by my head and my throat hitched as I suddenly forgot how to breathe.

"And are you the wrong sort?" I whispered, inches from his face.

He smirked, half his mouth moving upwards as his eyes smoldered with darkness. "Many would say so, yes."

"Are you threatening me?"

"Are you threatened?"

Yes. I stared into his eyes but lifted my chin in defiance, though every bone in my body told me to run. "I guess time will tell," I answered, feigning a confidence I did not possess. But my stomach churned with fear, wondering what he wanted from me. *Who is he?*

The corner of his mouth pulled into a smirk, and I had the unsettling feeling of being completely exposed beneath his gaze. His hand reached for my wrist, wrapping it firmly with his fingers. I wanted to recoil in fear, but found myself incapable of movement. His hands were rough yet gentle as he turned my wrist upright and pressed his Time Pacer to mine.

"What are you doing?" I whispered, struck with the fear that he would steal my last minutes and leave me to die in this darkened corner of the square.

"Helping you. Do not expect my good graces to favor you again." He released me after a moment, and warmth returned to my limbs. My Pacer still ran slow, but I felt re-energized. He had indeed helped me. *Why?* "Never look for me again. We must never cross paths."

"Rae?" a quiet voice whispered from nearby, slicing through the tension. Nell.

She stood in the mouth of the alleyway out of the square, hands wringing together inside brown, woolen mittens. Wisps of her hair blew gently in the wind, and the redness of her cheeks where the cold had kissed her skin made her icy blue eyes even more pronounced. They were full of worry.

"Go," the man whispered. "Get lost." Before my brain could catch up enough to process, he had vanished.

CHAPTER SIX

Not Jarom

RAE

"Who was that?" whispered Nell, then after looking over my appearance, she added, "You look awful. What happened?"

"Wow, thanks," I said, huffing in mock irritation and elbowing her in the ribs, though I knew she was right. Leave it to Nell to tell things exactly as they were. She was a poet on paper, a realist in practice. Rolling her eyes, she sidled next to me and hooked an arm through mine, then clasped my frigid hands in hers. The mittens she wore were scratchy, but I welcomed her warmth. As we walked back toward the square and lost ourselves in the throng of people, I searched my mind for an explanation I didn't have. I shivered, imagining those stormy eyes upon me. Unable to make sense of it, I shook the image from my head.

"Where's Pa?" I asked, offering a change in subject so I didn't have to discuss whatever had just transpired. She raised her eyebrows at me, noting my deflection, but she answered anyway.

"He's collecting the weekly rations."

"And Jarom?"

She sighed, hesitating as she studied my eyes. "I don't know. I haven't seen him since he left us."

I paused, my stomach lurching as panic set in. He told me not to look for him, but I had made no promises. *Where is he?* How could he expect me to not worry about him today, of all days, when disappearances warranted twice the usual amount of concern?

"Nell—" My voice was breathy. My heart pounded furiously, and I felt the blood rush in my ears as I imagined worst-case scenarios. Swallowing, I tried again. "Nell, the Time Wardens—did they take him away?" I hadn't been able to find him in the main square, nor had I spotted him in the queues. Heat burned through my chest as my throat tightened. What if he hadn't made it through safely? What if his donation hadn't been enough? I should never have taken that time from him.

Nell's quiet reserve and the nervous wringing of her hands did little to calm me. The pounding in my head and aching of my bones forgotten, I surged ahead. The slush sputtered around my feet as I stomped forward, taking long strides as I pulled Nell behind me. We weaved between the crowds, wind biting my cheeks and ripping my mussed hair from the loose knot behind my head. My eyes narrowed in a silent challenge to anyone who made eye contact, and I lowered my chin, moving with purpose. Men and women jumped out of my way as I stormed toward the platform.

In a matter of seconds, I had traversed the square to stand before the Dishonorables. The wooden beams creaked ominously in the wind, and the men and women who stood on the platform were bound and gagged so that their tears fell silently to their feet. I was overwhelmed by the pain that emanated from them as I scanned their faces. Guilt stung my heart, for I hadn't the energy, cover, or bravery to help ease their pain. Not with so many watching. Healing was such a waste of a gift.

Nell tugged my dress gently and whispered, "He's not here. Come on. That Watchman's looking at us."

My shoulders relaxed as I breathed a sigh of relief. Jarom's curly hair wasn't amongst the dozen men and women on the platform.

I tried to leave, but I felt rooted to the spot, overwhelmed by emotions I couldn't name. Pity, maybe? Guilt? Anger? The storm of emotion swirled in my stomach until I felt sick.

I studied the row of victims. The woman whose shoulders shook as she sobbed. Perhaps she was a mother—a daughter? The man with black grease on his fingers—how readily would his employer replace him today? Would he even be missed? The gangly teen at the end, who couldn't have been a year past his Pacer Interview... he had hardly had the chance to live.

Shouldn't I care about them too?

The truth simmered like acid in my stomach. I wasn't brave enough to do anything about it, no matter how much I cared. And even worse, I didn't see their loved ones stepping up to save them either.

In Nox, everyone knew the brave only disappeared. Or Retired. And nobody had the courage to fight it.

"Let's go home."

My toes felt numb in my boots as we ambled through the crowd together. I wished I had a scarf to bar the frigid wind from my cheeks and hide the scowl on my face. As we stepped toward the archway in the stone facade of the square, a Watchman brought his rifle down and forbade us from passing. His eyes twinkled with malicious delight, regarding us as a propitious prize. "Where do you think you are going?" His tone was short, just like my patience.

"Home," I tried, my voice far too harsh in its response. *Dangerous, Rae.* The Watchman's eyes narrowed with suspicion, and he widened his stance. "All are to remain in the square until the culmination of today's ceremonies."

"And what are we meant to do? Freeze to death?" I retorted, letting irritation win over good sense. I had already donated to the cause; what more did they require from me?

The Watchman regarded me, a sneer on his face as his eyes meandered from my crown to my feet. "Perhaps a visit to the shops for more appropriate winter attire? Or perhaps I could arrange for you to visit the platform with the other Dishonorables?" He grabbed for my arm at this, his eyes menacing, but I pulled away.

Stepping backward, I hung my head and stared at my overly worn boots. "Apologies. I understand. All in good time, good Watchman."

Anger flickered in his eyes as he mentally wrestled with whether to detain me, but he finally puffed out his chest with importance and spoke, though his words were thick with condescension. "Yes, all in good time. Go."

I didn't question my good fortune and allowed Nell to steer me away quickly before I incriminated myself further. She muttered under her breath about my stupidity. *Fair.*

"Are you going to be okay?" she finally asked, concern marking her forehead between furrowed brows.

"I don't know." The truthful answer slipped from my mouth, unintended.

She groaned. "You just need to make it until tomorrow. Stop worrying."

I forced a smile. Yes, Nell would receive her own Time Pacer tomorrow if all went well—a blessing and a curse. A curse for her, a prison she couldn't escape. A blessing for me. She should never have to share her lifetime with me, but we both knew she would. Just like I'd done for Pa.

"Are you nervous?" I asked, remembering the anxiety that suffocated me in the days leading to my Pacer Interview. I knew Nell would be alright, but it was always nerve-wracking to face the judgment of the Time Wardens.

She shrugged, a mischievous smile spreading on her lips. Of course. Nell had nothing to fear—she knew how to make anyone fall in love with her.

"Shall we visit the shops, then?" I suggested, knowing full well that we wouldn't be buying anything. Nell flashed a genuine smile, her eyes brilliant with joy.

"We shall," she said with a nod, and she reached for me. Hand in hand, we weaved through the crowds, aiming for the vendor stalls along the east side.

The white fabric of the tents rippled in the slight breeze as we neared, and silver threads woven throughout danced in the sunlight. A silver brocade pattern wound through the starched fabrics— giving the impression of subtle sophistication with the pristine whites of its design. Next to all the greyness of Nox, everything about it felt white and sterile—untouchable.

The scent of tea leaves and candied nuts permeated the street, delicacies that made my mouth water with the mere promise of the aroma wafting through the air. A lady with silver bangles and beaded cuffs around her wrists stared with critical eyes over the rim of her teacup. She sat on a silk ottoman with ankles crossed and full skirt stirring with the breeze.

I wiped my hands in the folds of my skirts, afraid to sully the luxurious display with the dirt on my fingers. We were meant to look, not touch. To yearn.

Look what we could have if we could only learn to be better. To be more useful to society.

Baubles of light hung from the tops of each tent, illuminating the treasures and wares we knew were well beyond our means. Every year, the merchants from Lustro and Middae visited before the Pacer Interviews and showcased their treasures, as if to taunt us with what we could never have.

Still, I enjoyed meandering through the stalls with Nell, picking up trinkets and oddities that drew my attention. Jewel-encrusted bands, eyewear with glinting glass that corrected problems with vision, impractical and beautiful silk shoes with flowers made of thread, potions and serums to color hair. Sharp eyes filled with mistrust followed us wherever we went, but Nell and I took our time as we wandered along the stone-paved path.

Nell flitted about from shop to shop, admiring the different trinkets and, perhaps, imagining a life where she could own them. She entered a stall full of hair jewelry and adornments and ran her hands over the silks and stone-studded accessories. She lifted a shimmery blue ribbon and studied her reflection in the stall's looking glass as she wrapped it around her crown.

"You'd best be able to pay for that." A tall man wearing a respectable coat jacket and yesterday's stubble approached her, his distaste evident in his sneer. His scowl amplified as he looked down upon her, assessing her lower-class dress, worn shoes, and unpainted face. He smelled of bourbon and privilege. "I won't be able to sell it now that it's been made... dirty." I bristled at his insult, but bit my tongue. He reached for Nell's wrist and turned it over forcefully. His eyes flashed with anger, but I stepped toward them with my wrist upturned. It was not worth the argument.

"How much?" I asked. The man scowled at my Pacer, but released Nell. She rubbed her wrist, wincing.

"One day."

Helfyre. I wouldn't know how much time I had left until after the Sync tomorrow morning, but I knew it wasn't much. All the same, I smiled with false confidence and allowed the man to touch his wrist to mine to complete the transaction. *Let it be enough.* His Pacer beeped, and I dropped my arm to my side, glaring at him with more anger than I had any right to bear.

Sirens sounded. I panicked for a moment, worried that I had somehow set them off. But the man turned his back on me and looked toward the center of the square. "What is that?"

A dark shadow traversed the plaza and a collective scream rose up as the villagers ducked in fear. I covered my ears and turned my eyes skyward as a deafening roar overpowered the noise of the sirens. A giant beast with glittering black wings and obsidian scales circled the air. *A dragon.* I gasped, somewhere between awe and terror, as I watched the dragon land with commanding grace in the center of the square, people jumping out of its way.

A cloaked figure slid off its back, landing with a perfect drop that splashed slush in a circle around his dark boots. He was small compared to the dragon, but the power and regality he exuded was unmistakable. Formidable.

A cavalcade of sleek, black cars processed into the main square, encircling the man and his dragon to form a protective barrier.

The shop owner closed his gaping mouth, seeming to finally come to his senses. "The high prince is here," he said, just before swooping a leg behind him to kneel and bow his head before the prince.

CHAPTER SEVEN

Dragon Fire

RAE

I felt my knee sweep toward the ground, and I wasn't sure if it was of my own accord or by some other force. I only knew the unexpected arrival of the high prince heralded misfortune for our district. He did not usually attend to such tasks below his stature, and the few times I could remember had only brought about peril and suffering for his subjects. A shiver ran down my spine as the man's voice boomed through the square, amplified by some power I could not see.

"Rise, and be not afraid. For today, you have paid homage to the Good Work of the honorable high king. He is most proud." He dropped the hood of his cloak, revealing the dark crown upon his head. The fine metal twisted and rose into thin spires, like a castle emerging from a dark, foreboding forest. His dragon extended its wings in the pregnant pause that followed and pushed into the air. People gasped as it landed with a thud, talons gripping the edge of the stone roof below the Clock Tower. The dragon's violet eyes swept over the square, neck extended and poised to strike. Its roar shook my very bones.

The high prince climbed the steps to the main dais, commanding the villagers' attention. His sandy curls captured the vibrance of the sun, but I sensed a complete and irrevocable darkness in his soul that made me shudder.

"A good day it is. For you have spent your time wisely!" His words echoed, besmirched with the slightest trace of insincerity. He smiled, pride gleaming, and seemed to expect the crowd to mirror his sentiments as he gestured toward the Clock Tower. A large black panel below the clock glowed with the number of hours and days we had given. Hours they had stolen.

The heavy silence that fell upon us did not discourage him. "The time you have shared today will sustain the Good Work and pave the way for the future! Be not dishonorable with your time, for it is a limited and cherished resource."

With a sweep of his cloak, he waved to the unfortunate men and women on the wooden platform. "Time heals all wounds but cannot cure the greed that has settled into the hearts of these Dishonorables. Through wasteful spending and irresponsible behavior, they have become...unsuitable to live in the Realm. Unfit to utilize our limited resources. Let them Retire today and leave behind the last of their hours to benefit the Good Work!"

I swallowed, knowing but dreading what came next for the people who had not donated satisfactorily during the Tithe. The poor souls on the platform trembled.

A Watchman approached the first Dishonorable. The man's body bucked as his arms were untied, but the Watchman gripped his wrist and led him to the wooden table at the front of the platform. He withdrew a sword and planted the man's arm on the surface.

I closed my eyes, realizing that today's Retirement would celebrate the high prince's penchant for dramatic flair—this would not be a simple ceremony of draining the Time Pacer to trigger the release of the poison it contained. Today's Retirement was clearly of the more exciting variety.

The steel sword glinted in the sun as the Watchman raised it above his head. *Schwing.* The sword sliced through the air, severing the man's hand from its body with one fluid stroke. It lay lifeless, the mutilated Time Pacer still attached, on the table. The man's screams pierced my eardrums and the wave of pain rushed into my chest so fiercely that I almost lost my footing. I gasped, steadying myself, feeling the rush of poison from the severed pacer course through his veins like wildfire.

My heart sank as a lady was led to the table next. More screaming. Their pain crashed into my chest like waves on a rocky shore and tears flooded my eyes.

Schwing. Schwing. Schwing. Pain. Blood. My head spun, overwhelmed. Finally, the Watchman wiped his blade on the soiled clothes of the last victim, who screamed at his feet and clutched the bloodied stump of his arm.

The high prince nodded to the Watchmen, and they collected the severed Pacers before descending from the platform, leaving behind the wailing men and women, already succumbing to the flow of poison in their bodies. Blood spilled down the side of the table in streaks—little tributaries that pooled together into a scarlet puddle.

"Gladus," yelled the high prince, his voice resounding with power, "They have suffered long enough. Incinerate!"

Oh, so we're doing Retirement by dragon fire today. A grand finale. My heart pounded.

The beast shifted its weight, gripping the ledge with its talons. Its obsidian scales glimmered in the sunlight and it raised its maw in a deafening roar. Fire erupted in a streaming jet from its jaws, and I could feel the oppressive heat of the flames on my skin even from a distance. A final scream and then horrified silence.

Nell grabbed my hand and whispered over my shoulder. "It's done."

I did not realize I had clamped my eyes shut. When I pried them open, Nell's gaze was on me, frozen with shock, her face drained of all color.

Beyond her, smoke rose from the scorched earth where the platform had once stood. The Dishonorables were nothing more than flame and ash, free from this world at last.

I wanted to go home, strip out of my wet boots, watch the sun set over the rooftops, and curl under my blankets with one of the books hidden below my mattress. But the high prince was not yet finished with us. And I could not unsee what I had seen.

"Their time has ended." He bowed his head in a feigned display of respect. "The rest of you," his voice boomed with renewed vigor, "are called upon in the name of the high king to continue his Good Work. Make your legacy with the time you are allotted. The future shall be paved by only the most honorable and useful to the cause."

The crowd remained silent, and I wondered if their hearts beat with anger as mine did...if any part of their soul wished the dragon would turn and breathe its fire on the high prince instead.

Flint Barragan was unbothered by the hatred I sent his way. He stared into the crowd, eyes full of icy disinterest, but he flashed a dimpled smile that made him appear almost...charming. An advisor approached him and whispered hastily into his ear. The high prince nodded and returned his attention to the square.

"However..." The word trailed dramatically into the void, and I shifted nervously, watching the twitch of a smile pull at the corner of Flint's mouth. He quelled the small suggestion of emotion with a deep breath and continued. "It is my great burden to share that the Tithe has been unsuccessful this year."

Something inside of me shattered. The air shifted, carrying the scent of fear that surged from each of the villagers in the square. Stale and grey and acrid like smoke.

I dreaded his next words—we all did.

Flint continued, adopting a somber expression as he paced the dais. "Though your contributions to the Good Work have been appreciated, they have fallen short of our Realm's needs. As such, we are left with no choice but to initiate another Trial to make up the difference in funding."

Murmurs swelled once more in the square, this time charged with the unmistakable tinge of anger. It had been years since the last Trials had been initiated. Why now? Had we truly failed the Realm so horribly? Did they not understand how greatly we struggled to get by? How much we had already suffered?

The prince's eyes hardened like the stone of his namesake—the black, striking color of flint. He appeared unimpressed with the crowd's reaction, and his jaw tightened. He waved a hand to silence the objections, his voice rising above the murmurs. "May the Trials remind you that time is a *privilege*. That we must prove ourselves worthy of it *every* day of our mortal existence."

Nell reached for my hand, squeezing fear into her grip.

"It's okay," I whispered from the corner of my lips, but my heart thumped wildly in contradiction.

The Timeless Trials were meant for the brash and the desperate—only fools would willingly take part. But every Trial saw fewer and fewer participants volunteer for the *special* honor, leaving the Realm to select the participants at random. Still, there had never been a woman participant in the history of the Trials. Nell and I would be safe. I squeezed her hand back in reassurance. We'd be okay, but Jarom...

The remaining shards of my heart splintered into dust. Somewhere in the crowd, a woman began to sob.

Flint's eyes darted toward the woman, but he resumed his slow stroll across the dais. Above him, the onyx dragon tracked his every move, talons gripping the ledge, haunches taut and ready to spring. The high prince raised a hand, gesturing grandly to the crowd.

"Be not afraid! This opportunity is a blessing—to serve your Realm when your district has failed to provide for the cause...it is a chance for redemption. The high king is both forgiving and generous." Flint moved his hand to his chest, as if touched by his own words. "Today, Nox has demonstrated nothing but disloyalty and greed, yet it is at this very moment that the high king chooses to demonstrate his good will to the people."

A man in front of me huffed irritably and grumbled something crude under his breath. People shifted nervously, tossing glances at one another, but Flint leaned forward and lowered his voice. The simple act created an intimacy that drew the attention of the crowd. I wanted to listen—to know what horrible words would tumble from his mouth—and yet I wanted to block out his voice forever. Both at the same time and in equal measure.

"Participation in the Trials is not a punishment, but a gift. Let the Trials prove that the citizens of Nox are worthy of redemption...that they are willing to serve Realm's needs with their *blood* when their tithes fall short. Together, we will weed out the unworthy and watch with awe as the thirty-five competitors fight to win the ultimate prize of immortality or sacrifice their lives to the cause."

Thirty-five? My stomach lurched. Last time, it had only been twenty.

"Above all, let the Trials prove the mercy of our high king, for he gives the poorest of you the chance of redemption rather than the promise of destruction for all."

Yes, how merciful is our king. He would let thirty-five men sacrifice themselves when he could simply obliterate us all. Point taken. How thankful we should be to send our men off to the deadly trials, all so he could pad his pockets with donations from nobility to make up for the disappointment of our district.

I narrowed my eyes, wishing I could trade my gift of healing for the gift of annihilation. If I could kill with my glare, I would have.

"Look around. One of you is about to join the ranks of high society in Lustro. One of you will soon know honor and wealth beyond your wildest dreams. Isn't that exciting?" His dazzling smile received no cheers, no dignity of a response. Just cold, hungry stares from a thousand sunken eyes that knew nothing but defeat.

He swept his gaze across the people gathered in the square, unfazed. "One last thing. I would like to announce a slight...adjustment to the original rules. The Trials are now open to *all*. Men and women shall be equally considered for the honor."

The world stopped for a moment, though I could see that the prince's mouth still moved. *Men and women?* Murmurs surged in the crowd at the announcement, and Nell made a small sound—a mousey whimper. I forced myself to refocus on the high prince's words.

"—as a special stipulation to honor my search for a worthy bride. Should a woman win the Trials, I could think of no one more fitting to serve the Realm at my side. Do not be shy, ladies...this is *your* year. You may just be the next Princess of Orogi. The Time Wardens are available to answer questions about eligibility. We will be in contact if you are selected for participation."

Music swelled in the square, a triumphant melody that thundered with drums and emotion. I stood rooted to the spot, trying but failing to make sense of the blur of people and noise and sky and the floaty, numb feeling that pervaded every inch of my body.

"Rae..."

"It's okay." The response came automatically, bypassing thought, reason, and truth.

The high prince gestured to the screen below the Clock Tower as a moving picture of the Trial's last winner appeared. The former victor's face was handsome, with eyes that glittered with pride, colors flashing and surging around the square with the quality of a nightmarish dream.

The crowd gasped as the screen showed moments from the last Trials, and I stared upward in a stupor, too dazed to make sense of it.

I blinked, noticing that something was amiss. Whispers and agitation spread amongst the crowd, and people began to point. I followed their gazes.

A black figure scaled the side of the clock tower.

"Look!" a man shouted, but everyone had already seen. The Watchmen barreled through the crowd, rifles trained on the figure above.

I watched in shock as the cloaked figure paused his climb, and a weighted hush fell over the square. He withdrew something from the folds of his cloak and aimed it at the high prince, a glint of silver catching the light. The colors from the screen below illuminated the man's face as he lowered his hood and I gasped, recognizing the auburn curls, the pointed chin. *Jarom.*

A single shot blasted from the barrel.

CHAPTER EIGHT

His Time Has Ended

RYDAR

The bullet whistled past my shoulder and lodged itself into the platform, splintering through the wooden planks. By the grace of the Fates, it narrowly missed the bone of Flint's forearm. I gripped my brother's wrists and pinned him to the ground, sheltering him from the assassin below my body. Searing pain exploded in my groin from one well-driven knee, and I gritted my teeth through the wave of nausea that followed, cursing the bastard I'd sworn to protect.

My brother's steely gaze flickered with anger and bravado, brimming with a deep hatred and an insatiable need for retaliation—retaliation that would certainly not end with just one victim.

Protect the prince at all costs, I repeated to myself, though I loathed the man with every fiber of my being. Every rational instinct urged me to step aside and let the assassin carry out his mission, to shield the people from Flint's impending wrath. Yet an unrelenting, searing pain deep within me compelled me to obey my orders. I pushed through the agony, holding my brother firmly beneath my weight until the Watchmen finally arrived to assist me.

With mechanical precision, they encircled us, rifles directed toward the panicked crowd that swarmed toward the exits. The wood dais creaked and sagged beneath the pressure of the moving crowd.

Another bang and a sharp howl erupted from a Watchman to my left. He fell to the ground, nursing the flood of crimson that poured from his shoulder.

"Unhand me at once. Gladus! Incinerate!" Flint writhed recklessly, sending flecks of spittle into the air as he shouted for his dragon. Thankfully, she could not hear him.

A horn blared, announcing the progress of a black car wading its way through the sea of people. "Get in the car, Flint," I growled, my voice gravelly from the strain of fighting his resistance. I could not let him burn the district down to quell his anger, and I could not let him die, though he deserved it. I nodded toward the nearest Watchmen, silently giving the command. *Take him to safety.* The car retreated with screeching wheels. *Good. One less liability.*

A collective shout rose from the crowd, and I whirled around, casting my gaze upward at the threat. My arms locked in front of me, pistol raised with one finger resting on the trigger, my target engaged. All around me, chaos fought for my attention but lost.

My gaze narrowed on the man. Was he plagued by evil or simply broken by this cruel world? It did not matter. His time had ended.

His cloak billowed fiercely in the wind, the gusts seeming to draw strength from the altitude. He adjusted his grip on the tower and brandished his pistol with a haphazard wave—the volatile mix of impulsiveness and anger, a combination I knew all too well from my encounters with Flint.

Bang. Another shot landed somewhere amongst the crowd and the shrieks of terror rang with the lingering hum in my ears from the blast.

My fingers tightened around the trigger, firing a warning shot in return.

The townspeople covered their heads and screamed, as though the act alone could save them from wayward bullets, but my aim had been perfectly calculated. It sailed straight past the man's ear, striking the tower to create a small explosion of debris. The man bucked, flinching as the plaster and stone ricocheted against his face.

The warning only served to escalate his unhinged behavior.

"They're thieves! All thieves!" The figure's voice pierced the air, powered by anger and desperation. "There is no 'Good Work'...they steal our time to lengthen their own! The Crown must pay! They..." But he paused, lost for words and out of breath. His chest heaved with adrenaline and disgust. In the pause, he glowered at the main dais, locking his eyes and the barrel of his gun on me, his expression deadening. "And it's Jar - *um* not Jar - *ome*! I am a *person*! Not a number. Not more time to pad your pockets. A *person*!"

I squinted down the barrel of my gun. A squadron of Watchmen circled the base of the tower, shouting orders at onlookers and pushing them back to secure the perimeter. Above them, four Watchmen scaled stealthily toward the target with deadly precision. They would neutralize him in moments.

"Jarom!"

The world abruptly jolted and seemed to tilt on its side, or, at the very least, everything I thought I knew suddenly ceased to have sense or meaning.

The woman's voice blocked out every other sound—every other thought in my mind. I lowered the gun and turned, scanning the crowd in search of the speaker, the owner of the voice I recognized in my soul.

My heart froze.

She pushed through the crowd, running toward the Clock Tower with golden hair streaming behind her like a banner caught in the wind. All around her, eyes swiveled and regarded her with surprise and fear etched into the deepening lines of their faces.

Anger squeezed me with a viselike grip. I had told her to leave. To disappear.

And here she came, doing quite the opposite, screaming her way through the crowd and into my heart. Into trouble.

Helfyre.

"Jarom, please," she screamed, shouldering past the herd of people. The smack of her boots against the slushy ground filled the breathless silence, and the man on the tower shook his head sadly, then re-aimed his gun into the crowd.

Control and reason abandoned my body. Three shots erupted in rapid succession. Head, heart, gut. The three shots fired to neutralize the threat, to ensure no harm would come to her.

I stood there in the aftermath, oddly detached yet acutely aware of the woman's movements—sensing every breath and rustle of her hair, the pounding of her heart, and the way her presence reached deep into my soul as we shared the grim spectacle, watching the man's body tumble poetically from its perch on the tower. The instinctual need to protect her struck me like a dagger of truth through my heart, the wave of accompanying realization a crushing weight on my lungs.

I wanted to save her but somehow, in the chaos, *I* had unwittingly become her biggest threat.

CHAPTER NINE

Blood From His Cheek

RAE

I did not know what to do with my arms or legs in that moment. I could not remember how to breathe. My hands covered my head and my body trembled in the aftermath of the screams and chaos as everyone fell to the ground.

Three shots.

The black figure on the dais lowered his gun, his gaze meeting mine with an intensity that sent a shiver down my spine before he turned to watch Jarom's black, lifeless body fall from the tower. It crunched as it collided with the ground, a sound I would not soon forget. *No.*

Chaos ensued. Villagers screamed and made for the side streets leading out of the square. Watchmen shouted and pointed rifles at the crowd as men and women ducked below their hands. The sleek fleet of cars that had accompanied the high prince's entrance now blazed to life with sirens and lights, evacuating through the crowd to safety. My legs moved of their own accord, propelling me toward the place where I feared the body of Jarom lay motionless, never to jest or spar with me again. *I don't understand.*

A hand grabbed my wrist, and I whipped around to see Nell's face, white with shock and streaked with tears. "Rae, we need to run. It's not safe."

But I did not want to run. I wanted Jarom. "Go home, Nell." A forceful shake freed my wrist from her grasp, and I pushed my way through the crowd, leaving her behind. I blinked tears from my eyes, and they fell to freeze on my cheeks and lashes as I surged forward. "Jarom!" My throat burned, my shout hoarse with strain. My skirts billowed around my boots, and I ignored the chilly dampness that had crawled up the fabric to brush against my knees.

There. My heart threatened to leap from my chest as my eyes settled on his crumpled form. His body was bent at an unnatural angle, and his eyes were vacant, staring blindly through me and perhaps into the Next Realm of death. There was no pain from his body. He was gone. Truly gone.

Heat rose in my throat and my cheeks, and I stomped forward. As I burst through the remaining people in the square, Watchmen took notice and aimed their rifles at me, but I didn't care. I had business with Jarom—first and foremost, attempting to raise him from the dead so I could murder him for attempting whatever this spectacle was intended to accomplish.

I was thwarted by the boulder of a man who dared to step into my warpath. The hand that grasped my shoulder was unyielding, demanding my attention. "I told you to get lost." Rydar's voice rumbled darkly with anger, but my fury rivaled his temper.

"Let. Me. Go." I ripped my shoulder free of his grip and trudged forward with tears in my eyes. Not one second later, I found myself restrained once more as his arm wrapped around my waist. I whirled to face him, planting the heels of my palms on his chest and shoving with all the strength I could muster. "You killed him!" He held tight, glowering at me down the length of his nose. His windswept hair hung forward as he stooped over me, brushing the tops of his shoulders to frame his angled jaw.

"You know this man?" he asked, nodding toward the lifeless form of Jarom as I pushed against him unsuccessfully. He was like a block of stone—though a mountain would yield more readily.

My jaw clenched, and I responded through tears and gritted teeth. "He is my friend."

Shadows befell his face as his eyes darkened. "Friends do not endanger the people they love. Come. You'll be needed for questioning." He nodded curtly to the Watchmen standing only a few paces away, and they approached, guns aimed at my heart. My chest seared with the pain of panic. *Not today. Not me.*

I shifted my weight and stomped over Rydar's foot, then whipped my hand across his face, drawing blood from his cheek with my nails. A glimpse of shock registered on his face, but he did not cry out or release me. His tongue licked the corner of his lips where blood pooled, and the simmering scowl on his face gave me pause.

A burlap bag was thrown over my head, and I shrieked in distress. *No.* I resisted as my hands were bound, uncaring of whose legs I kicked and whose ribs I elbowed as the darkness disoriented me. I was not strong enough. A pair of hands shoved me forcibly into a car and Rydar's voice was the last thing I heard before the Watchmen sedated me. "Take her in. Alive and unhassled, if you know what's in your best interest. They'll need to question her."

Chapter Ten

A Crown of Icicles

RAE

My pounding head did not appreciate the bright light that assaulted my eyelids as I slowly regained consciousness. I stirred, noticing the ache in my shoulder and the raw pain in my wrists. My hands were bound at the small of my back, and I was sitting on a frozen, rocky floor. I was not alone.

The forms of several others stirred beside me, groaning as they awoke. I blinked, trying to focus my eyes, but I swore as my vision acclimated to my surroundings. The walls and floor glittered with a pale blue hue suggestive of ice. Stalactites hung, shimmering with iridescence from the ceiling, forming a crystal crown of icicles. A cavern. My breath escaped in little white clouds before my lips and I shivered in the bone-deep cold. The cavern was striking in its resplendence, yet dangerous and deadly. I needed to find warmth.

Six women lined the wall beside me, all hunched over with arms bound and with varying degrees of alertness. Each was young and beautiful but looked in serious need of a bath and some nourishment. I was certain I looked no better.

I scanned the space cautiously, noticing the orbs of light glowing between the icicles, casting a harsh brightness upon us. The rhythmic sound of dripping water from the glittering stalactites mirrored the thrumming of my pulse. *What is this place? Where is Rydar?*

My hands clenched. I had *words* for him.

I sat up straighter, wriggling to maneuver my position by pushing my bound hands against the stone wall. Perhaps I could angle my wrists against a sharp bit of rock and free myself... though I did not know where I would go next. I glanced at the opening of the cavern, seeing only ice and snow that stretched as far as the horizon.

The swish of skirts and clack of heels along the rock floor drew my attention. A well-polished woman wearing an austere expression and billowing skirts sauntered into the room, regarding each of us with disdain. She hid her hands in a white fur muff at her waist and exuded an air of great importance. She stared with sharp, perceptive eyes, then clicked her tongue in disapproval. "*This* is what Rydar brings me to work with?" she grumbled with annoyance.

With two quick steps, she approached the girl to my right and gripped her chin, forcibly lifting her face to better inspect her. The girl recoiled, trying to free herself from the woman's vice-like grasp, but her gaze froze with fear. "Be still, girl," the woman admonished, and her eyes flashed dangerously as her hand smacked across the girl's cheek.

She raised her voice, which cracked shrilly and echoed about the chamber. "Get up!" With a snap of her fingers, my bindings slipped away, and I was forced to my feet by her power. I readied myself to lurch forward and strike her as she passed in front of me, but I found myself unable to move. At least I was alert, unlike the woman whose head lolled lazily to the side next to me as she stood, held up only by the woman's will and magical influence.

"Come now. We have our work cut out for us." She paused in brief consideration. "But first, a bath, I think."

Without warning, a cascade of frigid water doused me at her command, soaking my hair and clothes. I had not known it to be possible to grow so completely and irrevocably cold, and I cried out with pain, certain I had frozen to the core. But almost immediately, my fingers began to thaw as warmth crept through my limbs, torso, and head, and I was comfortably dry once again. I marveled at her power, promptly remembering to close my mouth, which I realized hung agape with fearful wonder.

She paced in front of us, somehow managing to look down upon us, though she was the shortest in stature of the group. "I suppose you are the best the

Realm has to offer. I have been appointed to ready you. Tedious work." She paused again, a sneer appearing on her face. "Do any of you even have gifts?"

None of us responded, and each passing second exacerbated the scowl on her face. "Nothing? Not even a sensor of venoms or a plant whisperer?" She threw her hands to her side, clapping them against her skirts. "What use are you all, then?"

A girl with soft doe eyes and curly brown hair whispered, "I can foresee the weather."

The woman turned toward her with pursed lips. "Useless. We have tools for that. Anyone else?" Her beady eyes scanned the room and landed on me. *Please don't be a mind reader.* I sealed my lips and shook my head in what I hoped portrayed an image of regrettable denial.

The woman sighed and rolled her eyes to the vaulted ceiling. "The high prince is to select a wife this year—and you have been hand-picked and vetted for the honor, though I don't see how any of you deserve it." I cringed at the mention of the prince, but a dark figure emerged from the shadowy passage at the rear of the cavern and interrupted her.

"Not this one, Elowynne. This one is here for questioning." My heart pounded as Rydar approached me with his hand extended. The hand that had pulled the trigger to end my friend's life. I lowered my chin and glared, imagining the matching welt I could create on his other cheek with one carefully placed jab. How presumptuous of him to believe I'd go anywhere with him willingly.

Rydar did not take his eyes off me. His expression was unreadable and devoid of emotion, as cold and barren as the icy snowscapes beyond the borders of Nox.

"Oraelia, come with me," he commanded, his tone forbidding any argument or discussion. Rather than dignify him with my hand, I crossed my arms coolly and turned my gaze toward the mouth of the cavern. Perhaps running until my body froze in the snow would be preferable after all.

His shoulders slouched as he sighed, looking suddenly worn down and weary. "Forgive me, but you must come." He reached to grab my hand, but I ripped it away and glowered. A silent challenge. Without missing a beat, he scooped me into his arms and strode away, not bothering to bestow another glance back toward Elowynne or the girls. As much as my body protested the offense of being carried, I could not help but notice how his arms held all the warmth absent from his features.

This would not do. "Put me down," I demanded, drawing my eyebrows together and using my elbow to dig into his chest. "I can walk on my own."

He did not grace me with even a glance in my direction. "No." We entered a dark passage, and my heart raced as blackness shrouded my senses once more in the sudden absence of light.

With all my strength, I pressed my back and legs against his arms, trying to hinge at the hips, but he held fast and his steps did not falter. I resigned with a great sigh. "Please. Put me down."

At the change in my tone, his steps slowed, and he set me on the stony floor. His hand enveloped mine, and he continued to march forward, half dragging me along behind him.

"Where are you taking me?" I asked, needing two steps for every one of his even strides to match his pace.

"You are required for questioning." Darkness shrouded his features, yet I could feel the intensity of his gaze as he spoke. "Do not be foolish. Do not tell them the man was your friend. Do not overshare."

I balked at his commanding tone. "Why should I listen to you? *You* are most certainly not my friend."

Something indiscernible flashed in his eyes, but his vacant expression remained unchanged. "No, I am not."

Resentment welled inside me until I was so overflowing with it that my body reacted independently of my good sense. With an aggravated groan, I wrenched my hand free and bolted in the opposite direction. Blindly tearing through the passageway, I did not make it far, as I tripped over a jagged bit of stone protruding from the floor. My knee seared with pain and my palms tore open on the rough rocks. Rydar grabbed my shoulders and stood me upright against the frozen wall. My chest heaved with ragged breaths.

"I am trying to *help* you." he whispered, seething with rage and frustration. He glanced down toward my knee. "Are you hurt?" He turned my palms over and studied the raw skin, his brows knitted together. "Let me wash the debris from—"

I spoke through gritted teeth. "I do not want your help. You killed Jarom."

He turned away from me and gripped a fistful of his long black hair, staring up at the ceiling in exasperation. I could almost hear the echo of his internal scream before he collected himself once again. "It is my sworn duty to protect the high prince. It was my *duty* to eliminate that threat. And somehow, I must also find a way to protect—" He paused, studying me for a moment as he considered his next words. "The people. Always and forever."

"Then it is *my* duty to hate you." My tone was venomous. Unforgiving. I could not be sure what he hoped to gain by helping me, but it would *not* be my forgiveness.

His eyes closed as he took a measured breath. "Very well. You would not be the first, or only, person to hate me. But please, don't underestimate the danger you are about to face. I do not wish to see you Retired tonight."

I blinked.

"Yes, Oraelia. They will Retire you if they suspect you had any part in his plans, so please, exercise caution. Slouch your shoulders a bit more. Look down. Look less..." And then he gestured to all of me, searching for the word that eluded him.

"Less?"

He sighed. "Yes. Less. Do not give them more. Do not give them a reason to fear you. Believe me."

I knitted my brows together, not knowing what he could possibly mean. Concern betrayed his carefully laid defenses, showing through his stoic manner in the corner of his mouth, the crease in his eyes.

"Fine," I snapped, though I did not understand his investment. "I don't have any intention of being Retired tonight."

The faintest of smiles graced his lips as he bowed his head in acknowledgment. "Good. Follow me."

I trailed behind him, shrinking into his shadows, shrinking my anger and fear and self to be somehow... less when everything I felt was *more*.

CHAPTER ELEVEN

The High Prince's Touch

RAE

An iron door slid into a groove at our feet to reveal a dimly lit underground chamber. Tension hovered above us like a heavy, palpable presence that weighed down the air and made breathing difficult.

At the center of the rounded chamber, the high prince sat leisurely with hands behind his head and boots upon the table, unaffected by the surrounding unease. The oversized chair he occupied towered high above his crown, but the malice concealed within his soul was undeniably the largest presence in the room. A row of Watchmen knelt before him, rifles pointed unapologetically at my heart.

My steady pace did not betray my fear as I slipped into the room in Rydar's shadow. At the table, Watchmen sat on either side of the prince, their chests decorated with the many stars and accolades of their achievements and the insignia of Orogi upon their shoulders. A surly man wearing a burgundy tunic sat to his immediate left and whispered into the prince's ear. The golden chains and air of comfortable privilege that hung about his shoulders made me take an immediate dislike to him.

After a scathing glance over my figure, the high prince craned his neck around to respond to the man. "Is this really necessary, Matthos? Retire her, and let's return to the castle. There are women ready to warm my bed tonight...it would be ungentlemanly to keep them waiting."

The man beside him shuffled his feet in discomfort, but his expression remained placid and neutral. "Your Highness, we must identify the depths of the threat today and ensure that it is fully eliminated."

The high prince stared upward, tilting his chin toward the cavernous ceiling with little effort to disguise his annoyance. A crystal chandelier above his head cast flickering light about the chamber, its candles reduced to mere stubs in their holders. All around, ice crystals glistened, bestowing a magical quality to the dangerous, chilling cavern. "Very well, Matthos. You interrogate her. I require a drink. Something to warm my bones in this dreadful place."

Matthos moved to stand, but the high prince pushed him back into his chair. "No, no, no, Matthos. Rydar will get me a drink." He turned an incendiary smile to Rydar, who stiffened at the request, but nodded in a carefully controlled manner. I watched, pondering the sudden change in Rydar's usual commanding presence.

"Anything for you, Flint."

"High prince," he corrected with a dangerous scowl. "But you know that. Tell me...does it excite you to disrespect me? I noticed you chose not to bow. Bold."

A fleeting grimace spread across Rydar's features as he curved his spine into a reluctant bow, his lips pursed, jaw clenched tight. Following his lead, I lowered myself into a deep curtsy, wincing as the scrape on my knee brushed the frigid ground.

"Apologies, High Prince," Rydar said in a cool tone, then he rose and moved to the side of the chamber. With measured slowness, he raised a goblet and filled it with an amber liquid from a crystal decanter. The high prince's attention returned to me now that Rydar's form no longer obscured me from his view.

"Matthos, do what you must. Make it quick," he commanded, then leaned back in his chair to study his fingernails, his disinterest in the proceedings clearly conveyed.

Matthos was a balding man with a sweaty brow permanently creased with worry. It was unusual to see an aging man from Lustro, where most owned enough time to pay for enhancements to their appearance. His mature features suggested he craved respect and wisdom over vanity and youth. An advisor, then. Likely docile in a fight, lethal with words. My brain made quick work of analyzing the room, evaluating the threats, and probing for any weak points. *You must survive this, Rae.*

The advisor cleared his throat ostentatiously, and he folded his hands upon the table. "Very well, let's begin. Ms. Fenix, where were you last night?"

My lips pursed as the uncomfortable memory came to the forefront of my mind. "Work."

"And what is your occupation?"

"I was a barmaid, but I am currently unemployed." Chiding murmurs filled the room. Living in Orogi and taking advantage of its resources without contributing to the Good Work was shameful. *One must always be useful, or one must be Retired*—my mind chirped the unhelpful adage in a singsong tone. *Helfyre, Rae. Focus.*

"I was dismissed last night," I amended, ignoring the nerves that numbed my body with more efficiency than the brutal cold of the room.

Matthos clicked his tongue, his disapproval evident. "Why?"

It was my turn to shuffle my feet in discomfort. "I punched a man. He made advances that were...unwanted."

At this, the high prince sat up in his chair, his interest piqued. "You hit a man?" he questioned, his eyes glittering with amusement as he drew a sip from his goblet. Rydar's gaze met mine when the prince buried his face in his cup, and I saw the clench of his jaw and flash of his eyes before he shook his head in a silent warning.

The prince's mirth quickly dissipated as the amber liquid passed through his lips. He spewed the contents of his mouth across the table. "Rydar! The other one, you *fool.* You know I loathe Red Reserve." The goblet clamored against the stone wall and rang noisily as it landed on the floor. Rydar tilted his head with an accommodating smile, but his expression clouded with darkness as he turned to retrieve the cup.

I studied Rydar's slow trudge across the room, wondering how he had incurred such dislike from the high prince while admiring his careful reserve in his presence. If only I could master the same skill. Had the man thrown a goblet past *my* head and barked at me to demand a new drink, I would have dumped the contents of the entire bottle over his face—high prince or not.

Not that I felt an ounce of pity for the man who had ended Jarom's life.

Matthos opened his mouth to speak, but the high prince waved dismissively and stood. Stone scraped beneath his boots' wide strides as he treaded around the table, holding my eyes beneath his piercing stare. He leaned casually backward on the wood, crossing his ankles in front of him, with an air of superiority that filled the icy cavern. "You know the man who intended to kill me." It was not a question, so I did not grace him with a response, though I did raise my brows inquisitively. He folded his arms over his chest. "Were you aware he was carrying a weapon?"

"No." *Why should I have known?* "We were all searched when we arrived for the Tithe."

"And where did he go after he was searched?"

"I don't know. We were separated."

"Convenient." He paused for a moment, tilting his head in reflection. "Our records show he transferred time to you at the start of the Tithe. Explain."

I should not have felt taken aback by this question, but I gaped all the same, affronted that the generosity of a friend should call my character into question. "Is it a crime for one friend to help another?"

Across the chamber, Rydar fumbled with the decanter, slamming the stopper into place with excessive force. His eyes met mine, dangerous and dark, like a starless sky before a storm. I felt heat creep into my face and stared at the floor, admonishing myself for the misstep. *Right. Wasn't supposed to mention that. Helfyre.*

The high prince's eyes glinted. "So you know him well, it appears."

"Yes—no. I do not know." Truthfully, I felt confused by the whole ordeal. Jarom had been my closest friend, but he had kept secrets from me. Perhaps we weren't as close as I had believed. Frustrated, I let out a sigh. "I had nothing to do with this. Had he told me of his plans, I would have let him know he was being a fool."

The prince's mirthful expression darkened. "You would have told a man he was being foolish?" He scoffed, pushing away from the table and approaching me with a prowling gait. Now he was simply trying to goad me.

"Was he not, then?" The words left my mouth before my mind could quell them. He stood inches from me, so close I needed to lift my chin to meet his gaze, but I did not let my stare falter. I wondered if he could sense the thrumming of my heart.

Rydar's hand fell upon the prince's shoulder, interrupting the silent war between our eyes. The high prince turned to face him, snatching the refilled goblet from his hand.

As the prince tipped the drink back into his mouth, swift footsteps and the slide of the iron door drew his attention. Elowynne bowed to the prince, and six young women filed in behind her. I blinked in amazement, recognizing them as the same women I had discovered upon waking in the icy cavern. But they were not the same, I realized—not at all. These young women were exquisitely styled, radiating with beauty and jewels to match their glittering gowns. Elowynne paused, poised with her hands clasped inside her muff, a triumphant smile illuminating her face.

"I believe we are done here." Rydar's voice was cool but cautious as he glanced between the high prince and the newly arrived women. Matthos, who observed keenly from his seat at the table, nodded in agreement.

"I'll determine when we're done," the prince snapped in retort. His eyes paused to examine the red scratch that stretched from Rydar's cheekbone to the stubble at his jawline, and I smirked, knowing I had been the cause. "What happened to your face, brother?"

Brother? I glanced inquisitively in his direction, noticing the similarity in their features for the first time. Angled jawlines, long, straight noses, square chins, broody eyes. But if one brother was the golden sun, all sandy curls and treacherous charm, the other was the shadowy night, with shoulder-length, windswept hair the color of obsidian dragon scales.

Rydar shifted uncomfortably, touching a hand to the fine red streak. "It is nothing."

"Nothing? It doesn't look like *nothing*. Show me."

The high prince reached for Rydar and rested a hand upon his brow, his fingers bent unnaturally with spasm. Rydar flinched so discreetly that I would have missed the subtle crease at his eyes and the clench of his jaw if I did not also sense the excruciating pain coursing through his body. He doubled over in agony at the high prince's touch. Fear gripped me as I watched in shock, torn between some unfathomable desire to help him and the instinct to flee.

CHAPTER TWELVE

A Feisty One

RAE

I watched in dread as the prince's eyes rolled backward, his chin lifted to the Fates. A dreadful whimper escaped from Rydar, a sound so contrasting with his powerful frame that my heart flinched. *What is this empathy, Rae? No. You do not feel bad for Jarom's killer.*

Within seconds, the prince's vacant eyes returned to their usual steel blue color, and he smiled at me with such blatant malice that I trembled. "How intriguing. The lady scratched you. Spicy." He nearly purred as he spoke. Delight twinkled in his eyes as he studied my features and tucked a strand of hair behind my ear. His touch revolted me, but I did not retreat. *Spicy?* It was impossible to mask my disgust.

"The lady fancies herself a fighter. I *do* love a feisty one. In bed." He winked. Every muscle in Rydar's body grew rigid, but he did not challenge the prince as he got to his feet.

The high prince placed his hands upon my upper arms and stroked them gently, though there was nothing tender in his gaze. He tilted his head, an amused smile tugging at the corner of his mouth. "What to do with you?" His voice trailed as he considered me. "Too feisty, certainly. Her personality is a menace to society, and she was involved with a dissenter. Could be dangerous.

Can't send you back without a proper punishment...need to show the people a message." He turned and clasped his hands behind his back, making a show of rumination.

I didn't do anything, I wished to challenge, but I bit my tongue, exercising caution. This wasn't a time to argue. His slow stroll stalled, and he glanced over his shoulder at me. "What do you think, Rydar? A Retirement?"

My heart jolted in my chest at the suggestion, but a smile tugged at the corner of the prince's lips as a different idea glimmered in his eyes. "No. I have a better idea for Miss Bravado. Have you heard of the Timeless Trials, Oraelia?" His gaze flicked toward Rydar, whose whole body had stilled. "She'd be perfect. She has a certain...bite, doesn't she? The Trials will put her back in her place."

If he meant my place to be the Next Realm, then yes, the Trials would absolutely put me there. My eyes darted nervously toward Rydar, hoping he would counter on my behalf, but uncertain why I would expect such a favor.

Rydar's chest swelled with a slow, measured breath. "Your Highness, perhaps we should reconsider the rule change this year...women were never meant to participate, and it is not likely to win over the respect of the people. The council has yet to agree and—"

"Well, why shouldn't they? I've already made the announcement." His nostrils flared and his head snapped toward Rydar. "And which councilman disagrees? Name him."

Rydar opened his mouth to speak, but apparently thought the better of it and swallowed his words. A heavy silence fell between them as they regarded one another, both sporting sour expressions. Suddenly, Flint's face brightened with amusement. "Ahhh, I see. It is you. *You* do not want her to participate. Father will find that *very* interesting."

The prince turned toward me again. "This is just perfection. What do you think, Oraelia? You simply *must* participate. And if you win the Trials, I will even make you *my queen.*" He said the last words as if it were an enticing proposition and not fuel for nightmares. "You heard what I announced at the Tithe, didn't you?" he inquired. "Any woman brave and clever enough to conquer the trials is worthy of standing at my side as queen for all of eternity. Perhaps that could be you." He gestured toward me and flashed a dazzling white-toothed smile.

There was not a chance in this realm or the next that I'd be interested in becoming his queen. Not now. Not ever.

As for the Trials...they would have to drag me kicking and screaming.

"Don't you think she'd make a beautiful queen, Rydar?"

Rydar shifted uncomfortably and motioned to the ladies across the room. "Your Highness, *these* are the ladies that have been presented for your consideration." He gestured toward the frightened women who drooped like sun-starved flowers, shrinking into the shadows to hide from the prince's attention. "They have all been carefully selected and vetted. Miss Fenix has not."

I tilted my head, pondering the swift manner in which Rydar had redirected the prince's focus toward the other woman. I couldn't help but wonder what his true intentions were, what motives he had for helping me. But I was certainly in no place to question them.

The high prince merely scoffed at his offering. He frowned at the timid women, crossed his arms, and then threw a glare at Rydar that made me shudder. "And why not? Are you so incompetent that you failed to present this one as an option, or did you purposely hide her from me?"

Rydar's eyes darkened, but his body exhibited no signs of aggression. "I assure you that neither is the case. I only thought—"

"I did not ask you to think," Flint snapped. "I asked you to find me a suitable wife."

Flint moved closer to me, resting his hand on my shoulder with an air of ownership. The onyx rings on his fingers gleamed beneath the lights, and I froze, as though the weight of his hand crushed me, driving me into the ground. He met my gaze, and his eyes sparkled like the faux gems that made promises of little value. "Anyway, if I must marry, do I not deserve to select someone who will entertain me? *You* are a hundred times more intriguing than that lot, my little spitfire. I want *you*." Every fiber of my being wished to rip his hand away, but I remained still.

Rydar did not respond, but the flickering muscle in his jaw exposed his annoyance. *Does the high prince's interest alarm him? Is he...jealous?* I shook away the ridiculous thought.

The prince turned back to the old man with the balding head. "Matthos, draw up the announcement. The people must be made aware. I hereby decree that Oraelia Fenix is to participate in the Trials as punishment to atone for her crimes against the Realm. But as a merciful man of my word, should she win the Trials and prove herself worthy, I will pardon her crimes and make her my wife." He moved toward the table, supervising the bumbling man's scrawling hand that raced across the parchment to record his words. Rydar stepped forward. "Your Highness."

The ice in Flint's gaze was cold enough to wither flames. "Yes? Do you wish to contradict me? Shall we just Retire her, then, and wash our hands of this nonsense?" he snapped. "Give the chance to the time-wasters you've selected for me?"

Rydar's stiffness melted as readily as the first snowflakes of winter upon the warm earth. "No, you misread me, brother. If you wish her to participate, she shall. I will ensure it."

I turned sharply toward him, furious at his audacity. *You cannot be serious?*

The prince clapped his hands together with a jovial smile and turned to the Watchmen. "Wonderful. It is settled. Take her in."

I found my voice as he turned his back on me. I had no intention of cooperating with their scheme or becoming a pawn in their ill-concealed rivalry. "No."

His step faltered in mid-stride. Slowly, dangerously, he spun to face me, and I grew small beneath the sharpness of his gaze. "What did you say?" The inclination of his voice rose, daring me to repeat myself.

"No." My voice was weaker, less sure.

"No?"

"No, thank you." *Rae, you fool.* But in my heart, I knew all of my options were unfavorable... all of them ended in my certain death. The matter came down to *which* death I would face, so I spoke the only word that made me feel strong. "No."

He stalked murderously across the room, one eyebrow raised with incredulity. "You dare insult the high prince of Orogi? Must I remind you that you were brought in for questioning this morn for your involvement in a crime of high treason? Instead of punishing you for that offense with Retirement, I am offering you the chance to win immortality... the chance to win my hand to show my mercy to you and the people. Be wise, Oraelia."

Anger simmered in my stomach. I garnered my strength, folding my arms over my chest and leaning closer, only inches from his face. "I didn't do *anything*, and I told you no. Retire me, if you must." My anger rose like flames that not even a splash of sensibility could extinguish. *What are you saying, Rae?* I knew I should stop, that I should not resign myself to such a fate, but it was too late.

The high prince blinked, the glimmer of surprise disrupting his otherwise composed facade. "You would choose Retirement before accepting the opportunity I've granted you?"

"Do I appear eager to play your games and die for your entertainment? Do you think I yearn that badly for your hand? I would rather walk through the fire of a hundred dragons." And I would. Better to Retire today than spend an eternity with this man. I'd made up my mind.

The prince laughed haughtily and threw his head back with feigned indifference, but I knew my refusal had stirred his anger. *Good.*

To my surprise, the blue of the high prince's eyes settled, as if the murky silt had shifted to the riverbed to leave behind smooth, crystalline waters. Waters that would drown the unsuspecting. "Very well. I am a gentleman; nobody could deny that. I would never force a woman to desire me when there are so many others who would beg for the opportunity to be mine."

I glanced at the six women lining the walls, so desperate to be unseen that they appeared to become part of the stone wall themselves. *Yes, dear prince. They are falling at your feet to beg.* He tilted his head, hesitantly raising a hand to stroke my cheek with gentle, albeit threatening, knuckles. "But is there nothing I can do to change your mind? I am known to be quite... persuasive." He leaned so close to me that, for a moment, I feared he would press his lips to mine. But it was a different form of assault that swept the wind from my lungs.

Pain flared in my mind, snaking through my nerves and veins like rampant wildfire. His fingers brushed my brow, rigid and claw-like as they raked through my hair. It was incapacitating—I could feel his mind ravage my thoughts and memories, violating my mind.

From far away, like the words were spoken beneath the surface of a rushing river, I heard Rydar's shouts. "Flint! Release her! Do not—"

I fell backward as soon as the prince removed his hand, but another firm hand fell into place, gripping my elbow to steady me. Rydar's expression turned grave, and his eyes darkened with shadow and storm. I could see the vein in his temple throb with unusual haste and my own pulse raced, surging in my chest as I gasped for breath.

Whatever the high prince had gleaned from this invasion now brought a delighted sparkle to his eyes. The dimple in his cheek resurfaced. "It seems I cannot coerce you to change your mind. Your resolve is quite admirable." He sipped deeply from his goblet to hide his smirk. "Though...what a shame it will be for you to miss dear Nell's Pacer Interview. Fates know, she'll need all the support she can get." He spun the onyx ring on his finger idly and paced the floor with unhurried strides. "I hear the Time Wardens have been particularly *stingy* with the initial Pacer deposits as of late. And your father... well, he does appear to be short on time, doesn't he? It would be a tragedy for Nell to lose *both* her sister and father sooner than expected. What a terrible hardship that would be on one so young."

Horror froze my blood. Each word he spoke drew a numbness that crept from my fingertips to my core. His threats were clear. The ice in my tone was colder than the frozen room as I spoke, though my voice was hardly more than a whisper. "You wouldn't."

"Wouldn't I? Too bad you won't be around to find out."

The prince shrugged with a knowing grin before turning to address the Watchmen. "Take her away for Retirement. She may request to see me if she changes her mind before the morn."

Rydar gripped my arm and raised his hand to halt the approaching Watchmen. "She will change her mind, High Prince. Of that, I am certain. Let me reason with her." The prince's eyes narrowed with a shred of suspicion.

"She is obviously unreasonable, but by all means, waste your time." He gestured toward me like I was the most unfavorable dish on the banquet table.

Rydar paused as though uncertain, then nodded and wrapped his arm through mine to steer me away. "Come."

Elowynne harrumphed from the corner, reminding the prince of her presence, her lips drawn into stern disapproval. "And what of these women? What am I to do with them?" The prince's failure to laud her styling efforts elicited a disgruntled frown from the woman.

The prince shrugged. "Get them ready for the Trials. Perhaps one of them will be more... agreeable than that one." His frigid eyes darted in my direction. "May the Fates prove one of them worthy of my hand."

Elowynne's pout illuminated her well-concealed wrinkles, previously hidden beneath layers of makeup and enhancements. She pursed her lips and followed the path of the Watchmen as they moved toward her projects, clicking her nails together with an air of irritability.

The Watchmen surrounded the women. One of the girls gaped at the rifle in the guard's grip and cried out in fear, shoving past him to dash toward the exit, curls bobbing behind her as she scurried along in her heels. The guard grabbed her by the hair, and she shrieked in pain, tears spilling from her eyes. "Please, I can't. Don't make me."

The terror in her eyes shredded a piece of my soul, leaving a scar that would haunt me. I wished I could do something—anything—to help her.

The Watchmen gripped the girl firmly, refusing to let her escape as he awaited the prince's command.

"Retire her too, then," Flint said, sounding bored, but he turned toward me with a smirk that chilled my bones. He sighed dramatically. "I suppose if these ones don't work out, there's always next year. How old is your sister, again, Oraelia?"

What? No. My mouth opened in objection, but strong hands covered my lips to silence me, and Rydar spun me around to face him. His eyes darkened with a warning, his nose inches from my own. In his deep, rumbling voice, he spoke a single word. "Sleep."

The moment he touched me, my consciousness faded, as defenseless to resist as a candle in the midst of a hurricane.

CHAPTER THIRTEEN

Hope for His Mercy

RAE

The crumbling brick walls were familiar, though not comforting, and there was nothing familiar about the heaviness of my limbs, the fogginess of my mind. The stench of pollution that pervaded the poor district of Nox mingled with something novel, something far more pleasant. I inhaled deeply, appreciating the richness of leather and sandalwood touched by something more subtle—like the promise of rain in the air. I blinked, slowly growing aware of the gentle rocking of my body and the muscular arms that carried me. Grey eyes regarded me, darkened by rolling thunderheads of quiet concern.

"*You.*"

His expression lightened as my eyes found his, ignorant of the scathing glare upon my face. "Good. You're awake."

"That's all you have to say? I'm awake?" *Foolish, unobservant man.* "Yes Rydar, I am awake, and I am *angry*. Put me down." My irritation with him did not allow for mincing of words, for the exercise of caution.

He ignored my request and continued to walk past the dreary door frames and worn stoops of Lerave, home to the poorest of Nox District. The high afternoon sun offered the only glimmer of hope in the dismal streets, but the jarring light burned my eyes as it reflected off the snow. The muscles in Rydar's jaw clenched tight as he moved forward, holding back words he did not want to speak, words he *owed* me. Finally, he set me down in a fluid motion on a door stoop.

My skirts swirled around my ankles in the gentle gust of cold air coursing down the alley. His eyes settled on mine, and he sighed, daring to look as though he cared. I nearly growled with resentment, knowing he couldn't. I rose to my feet and stormed away without a backward glance.

"Oraelia..." he called, running behind me and reaching for my hand as though the simple gesture could keep me from fleeing, but my anger and need for answers slowed my steps. I turned, entertaining the idea of allowing him to speak, but first, it was my turn.

"How dare you?"

"How dare I? How dare I what? Try to save you?" His voice was dangerously low, rumbling with a hint of displeasure.

"Is that what you call your efforts? Well, I surely do not require your saving. If you'll excuse me, I have some saving of my own to attend to." I turned my back to him and surged forward with arms crossed. As I walked, I leaned into the blustery wind, tucking my chin to my chest and hastening my steps.

"Where are you going?" His pace was infuriatingly unhurried to keep up with my brisk strides.

"Home, to warn Nell and Pa. I am not playing your stupid games, so go back to the palace and tell the prince I won't join the Trials." *And he can't have Nell either. Or the other women. He shouldn't have any of us.*

"And what do you plan to do? Let him Retire you?"

Of course not. Run? Hide? I groaned in frustration. "It's none of your business."

"Oraelia, you must listen. Whatever you are planning, stop. I know the high prince. He will not sway once he has made up his mind—he will *destroy* them to destroy you. Is that the end you want? You must trust me in this."

I stopped and whirled around to face him, hoping my eyes articulated the anger I felt deep in my core, in my bones. My hair whipped about my face, tousled by the wind, wavy and streaked with the aura of sunset. "Why should I trust you? You and I are not friends. We are talking about my life and death, and you have the *audacity* to tell me to trust you?"

"You must."

"I *must*? I think not. Not when you've done nothing but bark senseless orders or make decisions for me without my consent. You *assured* the prince I would participate in his Trials on the very same day you shot down a man I loved? A man who'd obviously been hurting—broken and destroyed by your world? You are not worthy of my trust."

His eyes hardened and he shook his head, his jaw locked. "I could not stand by and let him endanger you. He was unpredictable and angry...I feared he would—"

"What do I have to do with this?" I snapped, not expecting to find his expression softened with the apologetic tenderness filling his eyes.

"I could not let him hurt you—I couldn't let him hurt anyone," he amended quickly. "I'm sorry for the pain of his loss. May the Fates rest his soul." His head lowered, his dark hair falling forward to mask his expression as he rummaged through his pocket.

I faltered when he passed a hardened lump of bread into my hands. I looked down at it in surprise, then back at Rydar. A sad smile flickered across his face but evaporated as quickly as it had arrived. He nodded toward the roll. "I cannot take away the pain of his loss, and for that, I am deeply sorry. But I can help you pay your respects and grant him safe passage into the Next Realm," he said.

My throat ran dry as I turned the roll over in my hands, unsure of how to feel about the thoughtfulness of the gesture. I hadn't had the chance to properly say goodbye to my friend, and he'd supplied the means to do it. His *killer* had supplied the means to do so.

I wavered, but decided to accept the offering. *For Jarom.* I took a deep breath, then split the roll, passing half back to Rydar. "You should pay your respects, too."

He did not contradict me, but rather closed his eyes softly and accepted his half from my hand. As he set to ripping it apart, I wiped the snow from a banister along a nearby stoop, then placed my morsels of bread in a line. Rydar joined me in silence, adding his own to the offering. Hot tears welled in my eyes as I waited, watching for the wind to stir and carry the crumbs away, bringing them to aid Jarom on his journey to the Next Realm. *Goodbye, Jarom. May you finally find peace.*

A long silence stretched between us.

"I am on your side."

I turned toward him, noticing the way his stormy eyes darkened with his emotions, dampening the light around him and yet drawing you in with the subtle promise of soulfulness, as though the whole sky and celestial realms twinkled from within. He was beautiful. Devastatingly unapproachable and dangerous, perhaps, but in the sort of way that made my pulse quicken without reason.

Absolutely not, Rae. I fought to compose myself. "Stop looking at me like that. You expect me to trust you when you veil your thoughts and secrets behind thick walls and—smoldering eyes?"

"Smoldering eyes?" He raised a brow, and the corner of his lip pulled upward, very slightly.

How I wanted to wipe the hint of a smirk from his mouth.

"Do not let it go to your head." I crossed my arms again in defense, realizing that my gaze had lingered a fraction too long on the angles of his jaw, the dimple at his chin. *For Fate's sake, Rae. One kind gesture does not make him attractive. Focus.* "I have questions."

"Ask away."

"You are the high prince's *brother*?" It seemed a good place to begin.

His chest deflated with a burdened sigh. "Half brother, but yes."

"Then you're a prince of Orogi? Is that why you think you can just hand me over to your brother and force me to join the Trials? Have you no consideration for my preferences? Do I not even get the honor of deciding *which* horrible death I will face?"

"Does anyone get to decide?" His fingers reached for my arm to graze the numbers at my wrist, and the unexpected tenderness of his touch sent a shiver down my spine. I wrenched my wrist free and covered my Pacer with my other hand.

"Do not touch me." *Do not remind me of my misfortune.* I backed away a few paces to lean against the brick wall of the alley, creating distance between us.

His eyes flashed, as if aggrieved by my anger. "I have tried to help you since I first laid eyes upon you this morn, though you make it nearly impossible. You are teetering between life and death regardless of my involvement, and you have done nothing but make matters worse for yourself despite my best efforts. And no, I am not a prince. Not anymore."

I leaned forward, trying to crush away the writhing discomfort in my stomach. "What does that even mean? Your brother—"

"My brother is a menace, and that is not just my opinion as his older sibling. You must heed my advice when it comes to him. *He* has already forced your hand to join the Trials, whether you care to admit it or not. I cannot save you from that misfortune as much as I wish to, but I can help you survive it. At the very least."

"No." That was a fool's mission, and I did not intend to be made a fool. "I will manage just fine. I..." but I faltered. I was not fine. I was nearly out of time and cornered by loosely veiled threats. I could run... but they would track me. The idea to rip out the Pacer flashed through my mind once more—to take the chance that I could heal myself, but I shuddered, recalling the gruesome end that came for those who tried. And saving myself would only leave Nell and Pa to the danger of the prince's whims. There had to be something else.

But the high prince's invasion of my mind had crushed every potential solution. I sank to the ground and wrapped my arms tightly around my knees, my breaths shallow and rocky. Deny the prince? Die. Take part in the Trials? Die. Run away? Die. I ignored the way Rydar looked at me, as though he wrestled to hold back the words that threatened to burst from his fortress of careful control.

Only two options remained to me—participate in the trials or die a coward, leaving my family to the prince's mercy. Despite the gravity of the circumstances, I snorted. The prince had no mercy. I could not do it... not at Nell's expense. Not at Pa's. I had seen what this prince was capable of. I knew there was only one path forward, though my heart vehemently wished to reject Rydar's intentions on the basis of principles. I swallowed grimly.

I would walk through the fire of a hundred dragons before taking part in their games, but I would become the fire of a thousand before I let them harm my family. I lifted my head and glared at Rydar, projecting the storm and sea that churned in my soul through my eyes. *It's the only way, isn't it?*

A tight-lipped smile confirmed his understanding, though I didn't speak the words out loud. "You must, Oraelia. And for that, I'm so sorry."

CHAPTER FOURTEEN

Shadowvein

RAE

"I will die." It felt childish to state, but there it was. The truth, in all of its unpretentious glory.

Darkness flashed in Rydar's eyes. He ran a broad, calloused hand through his tousled mane, lost in his own mind as he searched for words. "No, you will not die. You will fight." He spoke with a confidence that did not allow for any debate. He sat beside me, leaning his head against the brick, and the warmth of his arm brushed unexpectedly against mine. "And I will help you. I feel partially responsible for your predicament."

Move away, Rae. But my body would not obey my directions.

I do not want to die.

Silence settled between us, snowflakes falling on our shoulders in the hush of the world. "I do not intend to let you die." His words rumbled with ominous conviction, as if he had read my mind and wished to counter my thoughts.

I glanced at him, expecting to see his hardened gaze, but was surprised by the lines of concern that had surfaced, the soft, weary worry that had broken through his impenetrable walls. "Why do you care?" I whispered. The question felt foolish the second it left my lips, and I resented the way it hung in the air expectantly—a thoroughly unreasonable reaction for a man I hardly knew. His expression returned to its hardened, guarded state. A retreat to his fortress.

"I fear what the prince will do if he does not get his way. We must all fear that."

"Oh. I see." I did not see. He was a master of saying one thing and meaning another, but I was determined to expose his true intentions. I played with the ends of my hair, braiding to keep my fingers busy. A nagging concern tugged at my heart. "How can I be certain he will leave them alone if I play his games? Can I trust him to be a man of his word?"

Rydar shifted his weight and turned to face me. "You cannot. But I am."

I lifted my gaze to meet his eyes. In the quiet, I noticed the slowness of his Pacer, the soft, lagging march of nearly depleted time. How could a prince of Orogi be as poor as a nobody from Nox? The space between my brows narrowed with suspicion, wondering what secrets he guarded. "You have not yet fully convinced me to trust you, prince who is not a prince."

He cleared his throat uncomfortably and tugged his sleeve over his wrist. "Your mistrust is prudent. I should not hope to dissuade it. But I will make you a promise. I will take care of your family, doing everything in my power to protect them. In return, you must promise me to fight. You must promise to win the Trials—to earn both immortality and the high prince's hand."

The sincerity in his eyes muddled my desire to refuse him. "But I have no chance of winning." *And I do not want to marry the prince—it would be kinder to let me die.*

He shook his head. "No, you must promise you will do everything possible to win. I will accept no less."

Something about the man confounded me. Why did it always seem there was *more*, an iceberg of unspoken truth below the surface of the sea? *What do you truly want?* My eyes narrowed, unable to reconcile his interest in my well-being with his desire to match me with the loathsome man. He did not make *sense*—the discordance between his actions and words incensed me.

"And if I do not want to live a fulfilling eternity with his highness?" I huffed, nettled by his indifference.

"What you want, or what I want, holds little importance in this matter. It is for the best, believe me." His whole countenance darkened. "I did try to warn you about him." My cheeks flushed with irritation, but he continued. "Swear it, Oraelia. Your full effort to win for the protection of your family. I need your word."

"Fine." The word slipped through my teeth, and I released the ends of my hair to clench my fists at my sides.

"No. You must mean it," he grumbled, unfastening the buttons at the cuff of his jacket and pushing the sleeve upward to expose his forearm. "Have you ever witnessed a shadowvein oath, Oraelia? The unbreakable promise?" He withdrew a dagger, and my eyes widened as the blade caught the sunlight. To my surprise, he lifted the knife, holding it poised over his arm.

I blinked. "A what?"

"A shadowvein oath. A promise bound by blood and magic that cannot be broken, lest the oath breaker die."

"Lest the oath breaker—die?"

"Yes. An unbreakable promise. You may not trust me or my word, but there are no doubts in a shadowvein oath. No chance to mislead or betray. I need you to know that I am on your side. I need you to trust." He paused, studying my features for any window into my thoughts, but I remained still, uncertain. This was preposterous, yet I could not in good conscience refuse his offer to help Nell and Pa. But trust eluded me when it came to Rydar Barragan, enigmatic Unprince of Orogi, as much as I felt tempted to believe his good intentions.

"I am willing to promise you in blood, if you swear to me that you will do everything you can to survive. Please."

I studied his face, the pleading intensity in his eyes, and my heart thundered. If I agreed...*No.* That was ridiculous. But then what would become of me? Of Nell? The haunting image of the women in the frigid cavern raced through my thoughts—the dread on their faces as they received their death sentence: forced participation in the Timeless Trials. Yet, in this iteration, I envisioned Nell's face, her eyes widening, hands anxiously twisting, tears streaming down her lashes, as if she were personally pleading with me. I could not subject her to this fate. I did not wish this fate on any of them, but the Fates cared not for my wishes.

An idea struck me. "I will swear it."

Rydar smiled grimly in that strained way of his and reached for my hand.

"But I have one additional stipulation."

He paused, hand still reaching for mine, and lifted a brow, studying me with an air of surprise.

"I will participate in the Trials, but only if the high prince agrees to send the others home."

He frowned, brows furrowing. "I have neither the power nor authority to stop the Trials, Oraelia."

"No. The women. He must send all of the other women home. If he is so convinced I am to be his wife, then he will place all his bets on me, and only me."

Rydar stared at me for a long stretch of silence, breathing slowly to expel little clouds of white in the absence of his words.

"I will make it happen." I searched his eyes for the slightest hint of deception, but found nothing but truth in his gaze and unexpected trust blossoming in my heart.

My eyes fell to the dagger in his hand, and I nodded my consent. He bowed his head in return, dipping his chin solemnly to his chest, face framed by darkness.

He sliced through the skin of his forearm, and I resisted the urge to gasp as the sharp sting of his pain invaded my senses. Droplets of blood emerged from the cut, floating skyward to form a cloud of ruby flurries between us. The alleyway darkened, and the air felt heavy with the presence of blood magic. With a grim expression, he wiped the blade and passed it to me in open palms. My heart pounded as I held the cold steel to my flesh, wondering if I was making the right choices and searching his eyes with uncertainty. He nodded, his lashes meeting one another in a heavy blink, and something stirred in my heart, compelling me to place my tentative trust in him.

I tightened my grasp on the handle and copied his movements, surprised by how easily my skin parted beneath the steel blade. My blood welled and rose, joining his in a whirling cloud of red. The blood swirled and darkened, becoming everything and nothing. Then, the dark mist separated and delved back into our arms. I watched, astounded, as the mist settled, forming a shadowy figure that moved and breathed and roared beneath my skin. A miniature fire dragon soared from my elbow to my wrist, mirroring the movements of his brother, the identical dragon that coursed through Rydar's arm. My skin resealed itself, leaving behind a pearly white streak. I marveled at the beast beneath my pale skin...it was the most breathtaking and fearsome bit of magic I had ever beheld.

"You are tied to me now, as I am to you. Take the dagger and do not forget your word."

My skin bristled at the notion of being tied to this man, but I accepted the gift of the dagger. I looked down the street toward home, the deep pain of longing gripping my chest as I thought of Nell and Pa. "Can I say goodbye?"

"I would not advise it."

Despite my best-laid defenses, tears threatened to fall from my eyes, and I turned so he wouldn't see. We all had our secrets to guard. "I won't tell them."

"That would be unwise." He paused, considering, then sighed. "Go. I'll tell the Watchmen to wait until dawn to collect you."

"You will not come for me?"

"I have other...duties, Oraelia."

"It's Rae. Please."

He flinched, as though this concession of informality had wounded him. "It is best if we do not become too familiar. Do not mistake me for your friend. I am on your side, yes, but I make no friends."

I watched in astonishment as he turned and stormed away, abandoning me in the alley without another glance, leaving me to wonder why his words hurt me, why they held any power over me at all. Perhaps I had misread him. Perhaps his interest in my survival was purely to fulfill intentions he had concealed from me. I feared it had been a mistake to bind myself to him.

Resentment bubbled within my core and heated my skin. But I folded my arms and silenced the emotional storm within me as I watched him leave. *I will make no more mistakes when it comes to you, Unprince of Orogi. I have no need for false friendship.*

CHAPTER FIFTEEN

Margarae

RYDAR

"The high king will receive you shortly. Proceed into the throne room and await your turn for his audience." The guard's eyes offered nothing, no trace of emotion. The life had been stamped from them after years of service to the Realm, but the faintest curl of his top lip betrayed his true opinion of me. The passage of years had done little to restore my name and good standing within the court. I would always be the fallen heir. A reminder of what happened to those who defied the king. Not even his own blood deserved his mercy.

The doors swept forward, and I slipped into the room, greeting the shadows like old friends and allowing them to envelop me in the outskirts along the walls. I kept to the sides, folding into the darkness cast by the flickering torchlight of the room, surveying the throne with the same wariness I'd confer on a battlefield. It was difficult to presume the king's state these days.

Trystan followed a few steps behind me. "I am told he has been exceptionally...lucid today," he whispered at my back. I turned, narrowing my eyes in warning at Trystan. Not because I denied the questionable state of the king's mental acuity—that was a truth most acknowledged but dared not utter in the interest of self-preservation. No, my concern stemmed from the understanding that speaking such truths in the king's presence was at odds with the likelihood of his survival. And I needed him to survive.

A man knelt before the throne, restrained by heavy chains. The iron cuffs binding his wrists clanked noisily against the stone floor as he fell forward, screaming in agony, the torchlight flickering across his harrowed features.

He produced a guttural shout, lurching with jerky, uncontrolled movements so that the cuffs scraped repeatedly against the ground, creating a sound that clawed straight through my nerves. His eyes flickered, the haunting dance of shadow and light in their depths painting the picture of a man on the precipice of madness. One moment, they filled with the calm of clouded obedience and the next, they raged with clarity and defiance. A window to his tortured soul—and proof that even the king's magic had limitations.

Even the weakest shattered through his mental shackles, given enough time. And this one had obviously had too much.

My father reclined in his throne of frosted brambles, the embroidery of his regal robes glinting in the torchlight, his face concealed by the white bone mask he'd fashioned from a shrunken dragon's skull. His relaxed, lazy posture exuded a sense of cold detachment.

"Useless," he hissed, waving a hand in dismissal. "This one has outlived his utility, General Hadmurn," he sneered.

The general stepped forward, bearing the insignia of Orogi on his shoulder and a hint of disgust in his eyes. "Your majesty," he acknowledged with a respectful nod, awaiting the king's command.

"Retire him."

If the general held any reservations about the king's orders, he did not reveal them. Without blinking, he withdrew his sword and in one swift, decisive stroke, he sent the crazed guard on his journey to the Next Realm.

We watched in silence as the deceased guard's blood pooled beneath him, staining the white of his uniform.

"General Hadmurn."

"Your Majesty?"

"The next time any of your soldiers show…similar signs of resistance, you will take more immediate action."

"Understood."

"Good. You may go. All of you."

The king reclined on his throne and watched the room empty. A pair of Watchmen dragged the corpse of their unfortunate comrade through the door, and I turned to follow, respecting the king's dismissal.

"Not you, Rydar."

The very air in the room seemed to chill as he cast his gaze in my direction. Or, at the very least, the general angle of his mask seemed to suggest his focus, for the gaping sockets showed only shadows instead of the dazzling blue eyes I remembered. I could not be certain that there was even a man behind that mask anymore...he'd become a monster, lost halfway between this realm and the next.

"You slink through the shadows like you wish to remain hidden. Do you finally bear the weight of shame for your transgressions, or are you scheming?"

"Neither, Your Majesty." I stepped into the light, avoiding the crimson trail along the stones, then swept my cloak behind me and dropped a knee to the cold ground. "I have come to make my annual appeal for more lifetime, as our arrangement dictates."

When I rose, my father's body stiffened, but he leaned forward to speak, letting his tone drop a few degrees below the temperature of the room.

"And you find yourself...worthy of more lifetime? From where I sit, your usefulness has been questionable at best. I'm not convinced you deserve the extension. Perhaps it is simply time to...Retire you."

He never made this conversation easy, for he reveled in the superiority of watching lesser men beg.

"My service to the Realm and my commitment have not wavered. I seek only to request more time to fulfill my duties, as our oath commands."

"Ah. Our oath. A constant reminder of the life you stole from me." The words dripped with a bitterness that could make even the acridest coffee taste sweet in comparison. His head turned, gazing into the shadows as silence filled the room, hinting at whispers only he could hear. "Margarae, Margarae..." he whispered.

"Your Majesty," I interjected quickly, attempting to pull him from the lapse before he wandered too deeply into his memories. "I have kept my word. I am owed more time. This was in our agreement."

His head snapped back toward me, the gaping holes boring straight into my soul. Anger radiated from every pore of his body. He leaned forward again, lowering his voice so that it carried the whispers of hostility in the slow drawl of his speech. "Then *explain* to me why I have been informed that there was an attempted assassination on my only heir at the Tithe in one of the northern cities of Nox?"

So he had heard. "*Attempted* assassination, Your Majesty. I eliminated the threat."

"Your brother was nearly killed," he snapped. "Did the man act alone, or must I be concerned that your usefulness in ensuring the prince's safety has run its course?"

I swallowed the dry lump in my throat, steeling myself for the inevitable conversation that loomed ahead. I knew the futility of my attempts, and perhaps the danger, but my loyalty to the Realm's people compelled me to speak my mind. "He acted alone. But there are signs of growing unrest in the district…"

He lifted a hand to stop me and trampled my words with his own. "Then manage it. An uprising represents a considerable threat to the safety of your charge. Need I remind you what will happen if you fail to fulfill your duties? Have you forgotten the consequences?"

"I…have not. But, there are growing whispers of rebellion and dissent in the smaller cities. Perhaps a gesture of goodwill, a reconsideration of the decision to hold the Trials this year… I worry that carrying through with the event may only serve to exacerbate the tension."

For a long moment, he did not respond, but the frigid temperature in the room made my skin crawl with a sense of foreboding. Finally, he rose from his throne and ambled in my direction. "You dare tell me how to rule?" he asked, his venomous tone slithering my way like a snake about to strike.

"I only wish to offer my counsel to serve the Realm," I amended, ignoring the way my heart pounded in warning.

"I do not require your counsel. I do not need it. My rule is absolute, my decisions final. Silence the dissenters and let the Trials remind them of their place, of their responsibilities to the Realm. The people need a firm hand, not coddling."

I hesitated for a moment, compelling myself to drop the matter, but the words emerged with a will of their own to be heard. "A firm hand, yes, but not an iron fist."

The dark black circles in his mask focused in my direction with chilling intensity. "An iron fist is the sign of a strong ruler, Rydar Barragan." He paused again briefly, regarding me, then tilted his head. A smile of malice appeared on his face, framed by the deadly teeth of the dragon's maw. "Allow me to demonstrate."

An invisible hand pushed me to the ground. I cried out as my knees slammed into the stone, but no sound left my mouth. My mind was no longer my own to control. The king's hands weaved their magic, holding my thoughts and twisting them to his command. Shackling me.

Against my will, my own hands reached for my throat, tightening around my neck, crushing my windpipe until the pressure became unbearable. My eyes bulged at the verge of bursting, and my lungs ached with a scorching pain, starved for air.

Only when the edges of the room became hazy in my vision did he release me. I collapsed, heaving a great breath of air to fill my lungs, my body shaking uncontrollably.

The vibration of his footsteps moved through the floor and into my hands, which rested against the stone as he began to pace before me. "As my blood, I have allowed you to maintain control of your own free will, the chance to make your own choices…though I'm not certain you deserve it. But do you see? Do you see how easy it would be for me to make adjustments?" He spat upon the ground. "Do not forget your place again, Rydar Barragan, or the mercy I have shown you."

For a moment that spanned an eternity, I lay against the ground, my nose pressed against the stone as my will screamed at me to move. To fight back. To challenge him. But I could only muster one ragged breath.

The king's boots paused before me. "Now, do you have any further concerns to raise about my rule?"

"No." My voice was hoarse, as though the walls of my throat remained stuck together.

"You see? An iron fist is effective, after all. The Trials will proceed, and those who challenge the crown will face the consequences."

He did not need to say it, but I knew I was included in that statement. There was no use in arguing any further.

"But that is not all you have come for. Speak, I grow impatient with your presence. And get up for Fate's sake."

My muscles quivered, but I forced them to comply with my will as I lifted myself from the ground. I turned my gaze upward, fighting to keep the anger from my face. "There is another matter we must discuss," I managed between gritted teeth.

"Go on."

I drew in a deep breath, choosing my words with care. "The assassin at the Tithe—he acted alone. But there was a woman he associated with—"

"Retire her," the king interjected, his tone curt and unforgiving.

"Flint has demanded her participation in the Trials," I continued, treading carefully. "He wants to send a message to the people." The pain of the high king's assault on my mind had ebbed, yet my heart still rattled wildly about my chest.

"Good. Make sure she dies," he commanded without an ounce of hesitation.

"I—cannot," I began, the weight of unspoken truth lingering between us.

"You—cannot? Or will not?" His gaze bore into me.

"The high prince...is rather invested in her survival," I admitted, carefully choosing my words to conceal any hint of my own interests. "He has rejected all of the options presented, and she, in turn, insists on the removal of the other contenders."

My father's displeasure was palpable. "Who the hell does she think she is? I think not. I want her—"

"Flint will be disappointed," I blurted, attempting to guide the conversation in a direction that served both the prince's interests and my desire to keep her alive. "He intends to ensure her survival. He has taken a liking to her."

The high king studied me, taking several measured breaths as he made his assessment. "The prince's liking? Or your own?" he mused.

My insides writhed and contracted, but I did not allow my body to show any outward sign of my fear, not even a flinch. "My only concern in the matter is the prince's success and the stability of the Realm, Your Majesty," I replied, careful to mask the concern from my voice. It was imperative that I conceal the complexities of my involvement in the situation beneath the surface. He could not know.

"Has no one else captured your interest, then? You remain...unloved?"

"I will never love." The words twisted painfully in my chest as I spoke them, as if they were blades emerging from my mouth instead of my voice. I did not want them to be true, but they had to be.

"Pity." His attention turned back to the shadows, to the whispers only he could hear. My audience with him was ending—his lucidity was fading. "Someday he'll know, won't he, Margarae? Everyone has a soulmate if they live long enough to find them. And we'll let him live *just* long enough to learn. Someday he'll understand..."

The king's lips curled into a sinister smile, visible behind the elongated shadows cast by the carnivorous teeth of his mask. He did not share whatever thoughts brought the unsightly grin to his face, but I had my suspicions. Finally, he broke free from his fantasy and turned toward me.

"Do what you must to ensure the prince's success and happiness, but know this, Rydar. I am no fool. I will see through your machinations—fail me, and the extension of lifetime will be the least of your worries."

CHAPTER SIXTEEN

Survival Sunset

RAE

The rooftop was the safest place to hide from unwanted conversation, and it was where I often found solace at the end of a difficult day. I sat with my arms wrapped around my folded legs and my chin resting upon my knee, watching the sun dip below the rooftops of Nox. Sunsets were beautiful, not just for the vibrant hues that swirled through the sky as if masterfully painted by the Fates themselves, but for what they represented. Dusk marked the end of another day; another turn survived. Dawn would bring a new catastrophe to outlive, as it always did. But for now, I lived. Dusk was the time to be free—to just be Rae. Rae, admirer of sunsets and color.

Movement behind me disrupted my thoughts, and I whirled around, my stance defensive. My shoulders sagged as I recognized my sister's golden blonde hair and probing blue eyes.

"Bit on edge?" she asked, nodding to my fists that remained balled up at my sides. "You want to talk about it?"

Yes. "No." I had already explained what I could to Nell and Pa to excuse my absence after the Tithe, but I'd spared them the details of the prince's request and my bargain with Rydar. They did not need to know my sacrifice.

"Suit yourself. I'll sit with you, then." She grabbed a handful of her skirts and plopped down, patting the space beside her in invitation. The last rays of sun twinkled in her eyes, and she smiled so openly I could not bear to burden her with my troubles. I tucked my hair behind my ear and sat down beside her. Her head leaned on my shoulder, and we stared into the sunset, her unspoken solidarity offering a balm to my soul. Street lamps flickered on as night fell, and the sun's brilliance faded into the artificial glow of city lights.

Nell fidgeted, turning a piece of parchment in her hands with nervous energy. Absorbed by my own worries, I had forgotten to notice how apprehension gripped her as well. Of course—tomorrow was a frightening day for both of us. Tomorrow, she would join the ranks of adulthood and wear her own Time Pacer. I placed my hand over hers and studied her eyes, which were untouched by the smile she forced upon her features. "Don't worry, Nell. You'll do great. I just know it."

She swallowed, tears sparkling in her blue eyes. "I hope they give me enough on my Pacer. You know...so I can help you." I smiled, wishing I could tell her how much that meant and what I had done to ensure her safety. Most of all, I wished I could see her emerge from the Pacer Interview tomorrow—a victorious grin on her face and a lifetime of opportunity before her. But that was impossible.

The parchment rustled in her hands as she unfolded it and smoothed it over the skirt of her dress. "I wrote a poem. I was trying to untangle some of my feelings about tomorrow...plus everything that happened with Jarom and the Tithe had me on edge. Do you—want to hear it?" Her voice faltered with uncertainty.

"A poem by Nell? Always." I grinned. She exhaled with relief at my encouragement, and her eyes settled upon the paper in her lap, index finger running over the scrawled letters as she read.

Scorched by the desolation of fire,
My heart weighs heavy,
All cinder and ash.
But from the ash, the phoenix.
A new flame is summoned.
Burning, burning to call forth the rising sun.
The majestic wings of the dragon
Soar beyond the destruction,
Heralding the change of a new dawn.
A new beginning.

Carefully folding the paper, she looked toward me in anticipation of my review. Her chest remained still, unmoved by the rise and fall of breath, her whole body tense.

"It's beautiful, Nell." She melted. It was a crime that poetry was forbidden. The world could use more beauty. More truth.

"Thank you. It's not perfect yet, but I hoped you'd like it." Her gaze turned toward the horizon. "I wrote it for me, of course—to encourage myself. But I think it suits you better." She smiled, suppressing a laugh with a quick exhale. "Maybe someday I will grow into it, and it will sound like me, too."

My heart flinched, conflicted by her admiring tone. "I hope you never end up like me, Nell." *Bitter. Angry. Doomed by my own failure to stay small and my penchant for attracting trouble.* Her face fell, crestfallen with confusion, and I inhaled deeply, searching for the right words to make her understand. "Stay you, Nell. Fiercely, unapologetically. There is so much more for *you* to become. I promise that is infinitely better than trying to become more like me." Her lips pinched together, fondness taking shape in her eyes. She smelled of honey and the simple comfort of warm, fresh bread as I pulled her into an embrace. "I'm proud of you. Go to sleep, Nell. I'll see you in the morning." Watching her climb through the hatch on the roof, my heart broke, knowing full well I'd never see her again—telling myself it was for the best. *I'm sorry.*

Rolling the sleeve of my dress to my elbow, I watched the shadowy fire dragon pace the length of my arm. His presence both encouraged and revolted me. I took a deep breath, studying him before deciding to turn in for the night. "You had better keep your promises," I whispered, and he roared indignantly in return. Smiling, I traced a finger over his head. *Yes, you do suit me, little dragon, don't you?*

I dozed fitfully, unwilling to allow true sleep to claim me. After several hours of examining my eyelids amidst fretful tossing, I relieved myself of the expectation of rest. I slipped quietly from the tattered nest of blankets on my bed and gingerly stepped into the hallway, the wood floor cold upon my bare feet. I did not want to wake anyone—some tasks were best completed without an audience. A farewell was one of them.

Pa had fallen asleep in his armchair, the fire in the hearth long extinguished. The chill of the air had already begun to seep through the drafty windows, past the heavy drapes that ineffectively guarded against the wind. Pa's chest moved slowly in rest, but I could feel the brittleness and pain that disturbed his sleep. Warmth flooded into my hands as I pressed my palms to his shoulders, leaving him with one last gift of healing. His shoulders relaxed, releasing the tension he held, even in sleep. The toll this took on my body magnified my sluggish exhaustion, but I only wished I could do more. He deserved so much better. Placing a wool blanket over his chest, I kissed his brow and whispered goodbye.

For Nell, I fished in my pocket to find the blue ribbon I had purchased from the vendor stall. The silk was cool and smooth between my fingers, smattered with texture by bumps of embroidery. My fingers traced the flowers and landed on the butterfly at the center of the ribbon, and I smiled at the beautiful creature I had heard of but never seen. I placed the ribbon on the table and reached for Nell's parchment and ink to scrawl a hurried note. "A butterfly, for a fresh start. Sorry it wasn't more. I'll see you after the interview. So proud of you." The ink splattered as I signed it with love. I stepped away, praying to the Fates that one day, she would understand.

Crossing the room to the door, I lingered with my fingertips against the frame, struck by a sudden whim. I tiptoed across the floor, grimacing as it creaked, then dashed into my room to find the dagger I had stashed beneath my mattress. My blankets yielded easily as I tore away a strand of fabric—much too worn and tattered to resist my efforts. Hiking up my dress, I used the length of fabric to fasten the dagger to my thigh, tying it with a simple knot. Terror gripped me as I chanced a look at my Pacer, which had reset with the daily sync.

ELC609. Twenty hours, forty-three minutes. I guess death is persistent in its efforts to capture me.

Now or never.

Slipping through the front door, I closed it quietly and looked to my left, overcome by the impulse to run, to take my chances in the frosty snowscape beyond the boundaries of Nox. But the shadow dragon roared in protest, and the sensation of fangs piercing my skin served as a warning against those thoughts. *Understood, little dragon. A promise is a promise.*

A black car tore around the corner of the street, and the back door flew open. "Oraelia Fenix, you are summoned by High Prince Flint Barragan to take part in the Timeless Trials as his champion. Get in."

With a deep breath, I slid into the car, though every muscle in my body warned me to run. The two Watchmen in the front seats donned masks as soon as I closed the door, and a heavy mist fell upon me before I had a chance to react.

CHAPTER SEVENTEEN

Creator of Nightmares, Conductor of Death

RAE

"A re they all here?" The gruff voice was unfamiliar, though my mind painted the speaker as a large, surly man.

"All thirty-five. One died before we could remove the Time Pacer, but yes, they're all here, including the woman."

The woman. Me. Time pacers? Words raced through my head as I tried to make sense of my surroundings. I flexed my muscles and willed my limbs to move, but they felt too heavy, weighed down by a thick blanket. A cold gust nipped my cheeks and filled my lungs with icy air. I pulled the blanket to my nose and savored its warmth, letting the soft fibers brush against my cheeks.

"Thirty-four remaining, then? Any other surprises?" Their footsteps shuffled along the floor, mingled with faint beeps and a high-pitched whirring.

"No, nothing unexpected. A few with cancers and other nasty diseases, but nothing beyond our capabilities. Minor issues, too—defective eyesight, trivial injuries. They're all in optimal working condition now."

"When will they be ready to move?"

The steps slowed, and one of the speakers stopped to rustle with something before responding. "They're waking up now. They'll need food and water, and then I can release them."

"Excellent. Elowynne, your assistance, darling. Let's get them moving."

"Oh, of course. What fun." I recognized the sweet voice, and my stomach clenched, bracing for discomfort. A cold rush of air sent an avalanche of shivers down my spine, and I gasped as the sensation of ice water washed over me. The warm blanket vanished, leaving an absence behind that felt like nakedness. I curled into a ball, shrinking to shield myself from the assault of frigid air.

Groans echoed about the room, joining my own protestations. But it wasn't really a room at all, I noticed, as I pried my eyelids open. Canvas walls billowed gently in the wind and orbs of pale light hung from the tent's roof, casting a blue-hued glow reminiscent of moonlight. Messes of wire and blinking lights stretched from one end of the tent to the other, a complex spider web that ensnared the tidy rows of cots within. My fingers swept along the crisp sheets at my side, and my eyelids fluttered to blink the sleepy confusion out of my mind. *Get up, Rae.*

My muscles refused to obey, but Elowynne's power hoisted me to sitting in one swift motion. The room spun as I fought to focus, struggling to make sense of the blurred figures surrounding me. Men grimaced and squinted, newly upright against their will and scowling beneath the unsympathetic brightness of the lights. Watchmen paced between the neatly ordered cots, carrying guns as their eyes darted jerkily back and forth, ready to strike at the first sign of disobedience.

Elowynne smirked, then sidled next to a man nearly twice her size. Dressed in thick robes that magnified his girth and a fur hat that appeared as wild as his hair, he shook snowflakes from his mane like a hound emerging from a bath. Elowynne wore a long fur overcoat that grazed the tops of her boots and an expression of sharp disapproval that I recognized with instant dislike.

The man scanned the room with equal distaste, then clapped his oversized hands together, though his thick gloves muffled the sound. "Listen up, crew. Welcome to the Trials." He frowned, turning to a mere wisp of a man who paced nervously between the rows of cots. "Can we do something about the beeping?"

The little man jumped in surprise at the address, but he waved his hand in the air without hesitation. The wires, flashing lights, and beeping vanished without a trace. "Apologies, sir."

The larger, wild-looking man nodded with a gracious smile. "As I was saying, we're expected up at the House of Frost in just a few moments for the initial ceremonies, but first, some introductions." He waved grandiosely and finished with a mock bow before continuing. "Orman Gendrick, at your service, creator of nightmares and conductor of death, Grand Master of the Trials. My job is to orchestrate the most exhilarating deaths possible to amuse our stakeholders, and your job, quite simply, is to entertain."

Grim faces shared nervous glances with one another, each reflecting the same fears stirring within me. I shifted my weight and stole a furtive look toward the exit, wondering how far I could run before they caught me. Wondering how long I could survive in the simple grey dress that covered me. The sharp nip from the dragon's fangs in my skin reminded me that it did not matter. I rubbed a palm along my forearm, soothing the creature. *Yes, I know.*

"The high king's healers have taken great care to prepare you for the Trials. You may feel a bit groggy as the slumber mist wears away, but soon enough, you will feel more alive than ever, courtesy of the Good Work. You may also notice that your Time Pacers have been removed, marking you as true mortals. This releases you to the mercy of your body's natural clock and condemns you as noncitizens of Orogi. None shall hope to return to society without reimplantation of a Time Pacer."

My lips parted with surprise as I glanced at my wrist—the skin was smooth and unmarked, with no indication of the Pacer once nestled between bone and tendon. For the briefest moment, my heart lurched in my chest, stirred by the impulse to run. Without a Pacer, I could be free. I could disappear, I could—

A man with wild eyes and braided hair met my gaze for half a second, perhaps enlightened by the same spark of inspiration. He jumped forward and slid beneath the rows of cots toward the exit but didn't make it past the third row before a Watchman gripped him by the braids and pulled him upright, pressing a knife into the hollow of his neck.

The man named Orman threw his head back and roared with laughter. The Watchman gripped him tightly by the collar, and the man's words gurgled in his throat as he tried to speak. Orman's eyes glittered with mirth as he approached, a predator slowly slinking toward cornered prey.

"Fool," he seethed through gritted teeth. "You think you can just... run away? You are not a person—not without a Pacer. We *own* you now."

The man whimpered as Orman grabbed the blade from the Watchman and shoved the guard aside. He cowered as Orman loomed over him, pressing the blade harder against his throat until he drew a tentative droplet of blood. A foul smell filled the air as the man soiled his pants, and the corner of Oman's mouth pulled upward into a malicious smirk. "The only way out of the Trials is your ticket to the Next Realm, fool. Perhaps you'd like me to send you there early?"

The man's eyes bulged, but he shook his head. His movements were so restricted by the knife at his neck that he appeared to be merely quivering beneath Orman's imposing glare.

Orman pushed him to the ground, and the room grew silent, save for the man's stifled sob as he rubbed the raw spot at his neck. Creases lined the brows of the other competitors, and several shifted anxiously on their beds, their eyes deliberately averted from the wretched man. His chest shook with quiet weeping.

Orman stepped over him and swept his gaze across the room. "The only way out now is death. Let that be clear. Make good use of the time you have left because some of you won't live to see the morn." Orman's depthless eyes landed upon me and a smile twitched at his lips—as if he delighted in imagining the many ways in which I might perish. I narrowed my eyes in return, feeling the little dragon soar the length of my arm with a vicious roar that stoked the fire in my belly. I knew he had marked me as an easy target.

Good. Let them underestimate me.

He tilted his head and frowned as he considered me, then nodded to the Watchmen. "Let's move. Get them ready and have them meet us outside."

CHAPTER EIGHTEEN

Goodwill and Goodvit

RAE

A sharp pain in my scalp forced tears to my eyes as a Watchman pulled me up by a fistful of hair. "I can get up myself!" I shouted, whirling to face him with an instinctual drive to retaliate, but I balked at the sight of the gun in his hand and the smirk on his face.

"Think you're a match for me? I'll blast that pretty face right off your body if you try anything." He spoke like he carried a pile of pebbles in his mouth, his tongue too large or too flabby to properly form words.

I blinked, letting my gaze snap between the gun in his hand and the leering grin on his face. I could disarm him at this distance, but why? The other Watchmen would gun me down in an instant.

My soured expression faded into a mask of careful composure. *Relax, Rae. Do not get yourself killed.*

I drew in a deep breath to swallow my anger and recited the mantra of survival. *Stay small. Stay alive.*

"I'm sorry. I was only startled."

The Watchman grunted at the apology, but lowered his gun and shoved a coat into my hands. I pulled the thick garment over my shoulders and watched as he trudged off to antagonize the next competitor. From the corner of my eye,

I saw him push the man from his bed, who landed with a solid thump against the ground.

Leaving the Watchman to his business, I elbowed through the gathering crowd, fastening the buttons of my jacket and searching for Orman and Elowynne, but the couple had already left. I slipped through gaps to the front of the tent with one motive: to get myself close to the people in charge. Information was a boon I could not afford to pass up, and I intended to stay close to Orman. I was not above employing the art of eavesdropping.

The bright sun seared my eyes as I slipped through the tent flap, and I was almost knocked off balance by the box Orman shoved into my chest. "Take one. Pass it along," he huffed gruffly.

I stared at the haphazard haystack of Goodvit tubes piled within the box. My stomach churned, offended by the offering, but I reached in to grab one. The chalky paste was a familiar staple back home in Nox. Whatever it lacked in flavor and texture, the gritty paste made up tenfold in nutritional value. The government supplied the tubes in weekly rations; some weeks, it was all we had to eat.

Better a disgusted belly than an empty one. A man with dark hair and darker eyes relieved me of the box, and I stepped forward, looking into the distance with awe.

Snow-covered mountains and hills stretched as far as the horizon beneath a sky freckled with white flurries. The land was barren and wild—a frozen tundra so uninviting that the whipping winds seemed to hiss with disapproval at our advance. A lone house stood proudly in the distance on the other side of the deep ravine that stretched before us. An icy bridge traversed the chasm, dusted with glittering snow. The white walls of the building climbed to the clouds, where deep blue turrets and a pointed roof pierced through the cottony tufts lining the sky. Long arched windows reflected the sparkling rays of light, and a grand balcony stretched the length of the second story. It was magnificent.

"Welcome to Dreda," Orman explained, "remote island and home of the Trials. There's no escaping—unless you prefer to drown or die of hypothermia. Up to you."

Orman slipped a hand behind the small of Elowynne's back to guide her forward. He trudged gracelessly into the thick, white blanket of snow and approached the icy bridge as Elowynne glided, using her powers to displace the snow around her feet. I grumbled with envy as my own boots sank into the depths of snow.

As we left the billowing canvas tent behind, I fumbled with the Goodvit tube, cursing the plastic seal that refused to break and my numb fingers, which refused to be useful. The icy bridge was slick in some places, but treading on the swirls of soft snow kept my boots from sliding.

Distracted by the Goodvit, I gasped as a solid mass plowed into my shoulder and disrupted my careful steps. Slipping, I fell to my knees and felt the world shift as I looked over the edge of the bridge to the deep ravine below. My stomach lurched with fear, alarmed by the distance between the bridge and the bottom of the chasm. I wondered briefly if it was possible to drown in snow, then scrambled back from the ledge.

On my hands and knees, I reached for the Goodvit I had dropped, but a brown boot crushed my outstretched fingers. The boot's owner bent forward to pluck the tube from the snow, flashing a leering smile of crooked teeth in my direction. I sneered as the brute tore the Goodvit open with his teeth and gulped it down, maintaining eye contact with me as he squeezed the tube in his fist. He tossed the empty wrapper to the ground and wiped his mouth with his sleeve to reveal a cruel smile and a clean face. He shrugged apathetically. "I'm hungry and twice your size. I needed two."

He turned his back and barreled forward, arms swinging widely at his sides. I watched him incredulously for a few paces, imagining I had the power to burn a hole straight through his back to his proud chest. *I hope you slip.*

A hand appeared at my side, gripping an open tube of Goodvit. "Here. Have the rest."

The voice belonged to a tall, wiry-haired man with broad shoulders and kind eyes. His cheeks were sunken, but a genuine smile brightened his sallow skin. Timidly, he waved the tube toward me. "Really. A whole Goodvit is a feast for me. I usually have to ration."

I felt inclined to refuse the gift from this stranger, but his eagerness to share felt earnest, and what he offered felt more significant than a simple serving of food.

"Thank you," I mumbled, humbly accepting the tube and squeezing the thick paste into my mouth. The chalky, gritty texture made me grimace, but the grumbling in my stomach soon eased as we walked forward in shared silence.

"Lio," he said finally, breaking the silence and tossing a furtive glance in my direction. Startled, I surfaced from the mental barrage of ill wishes I recited at the brute ahead of me and glanced at my new companion instead.

"I'm Rae." My cheeks and lips felt foreign with numbness as I spoke. I closed my mouth and trudged forward, crunching the snowflakes that dusted the icy bridge beneath my boots.

"Hope that oaf is the first to go."

A smirk worked its way to the corner of my mouth, thawing the numbness in my cheeks and lips. "I thought nearly the same thing," I admitted, suppressing a laugh. My gut twisted, humbled by the resurgence of fears that plagued my mind. "But I expect it will be me." I winced at the nip from the dragon beneath my sleeve.

From the corner of my eye, I saw Lio's face lift to the blue sky as he laughed in earnest. "You? The first woman to join the Trials? I think not. You'll put us all to shame."

I scoffed. "It's not like I had much choice," I responded dismissively.

"None of us had a choice. Not really. But I heard you worked a deal with the prince...got him to listen to you. That's why it's just you and not a bunch of other women too."

I snapped my head in his direction. "Who told you that?"

He offered an apologetic shrug, his brows knitting together. "My sister was supposed to be in the Trials this year. You saved her."

I looked at him again. Really looked at him. Tall, gangly, and though I hardly knew him, he wore an aura of kindness that felt irresistible. "And now you're here in her place?" A stone dropped into my stomach, weighing heavily at the bottom.

He hesitated for a moment, then nodded curtly. "But what you did...it was really brave. The high prince is a terrifying man."

"The high prince is an asshole." The words tumbled from my mouth before I could stop them, and I snapped my lips shut.

"Something only a badass could say." He nudged my shoulder playfully, and I smiled in spite of myself.

"Well...you're pretty badass too. For taking your sister's place."

Our boots crunched over the ice for a few paces, filling the silence. The ice gleamed blue, reflecting the sky above, and the snow-covered patches formed the likeness of clouds along the treacherous path. I marveled at the beauty—it was as if they intended for us to walk through the heavens before arriving at the gates of Hell.

The House of Frost loomed ahead, but I realized with a start that we had fallen well behind Elowynne and Orman. Inexplicably, the pair already stood proudly at the entrance, framed by the sleek white pillars supporting the balcony above. Arm in arm, they watched us in silence, and a deep sense of foreboding flooded my stomach. My insides wriggled like a worm clenched in the mouth of a wren, sensing its fate and knowing it could not escape. Something felt...off.

With a gasp, a small white cloud departed from my lips as two wide doors swung open on the second story. A flood of people emerged to fill the balcony, peering over the railing with buzzing excitement. I glanced toward Lio, who looked equally disturbed by the developments.

"What is happening?" Nerves rattled his voice, and his voice rattled my soul. Something was wrong. Very wrong.

CHAPTER NINETEEN

Rains of Fire

RAE

Orman's voice carried with ease on the wings of the wind. "I dare say, Elowynne, the competitors are woefully slow, aren't they? I believe I'm aging!" He chuckled at his own joke. "What time-wasters. Let's hurry them up, shall we?"

"But Orman, the games have not yet begun." Her voice was cloyingly sweet and rehearsed, but a knowing smirk belied the innocence of her tone.

"No time like the present, eh?" Orman raised his arms and chin to the people gathered on the balcony and smiled brightly. "What do you say? Let the games begin?" A raucous cheer erupted from the onlookers.

"Well, since we appear to be in agreement, good lads and ladies, let me present to you the thirty-four contestants of the Timeless Trials! May time be on their side."

I froze in place, gaping up at the cheering crowd. Sunlight streaked down from the skies, creating a stunning backdrop behind one of the most terrifying sights I had ever beheld—the sophisticated monsters gathered on a balcony, foaming at the mouths to witness our deaths.

"The first challenge begins...*now!*"

What? No. My heart pounded and my mouth ran dry as fear seized me. I bent my knees, crouching in wary defense as I swept my gaze from one end of the ravine to the other. A deep, unsettling rumble shook the ground beneath my feet, and the crowd gasped as vibrations crawled from my soles to my legs and into my heart. The sound of falling snow and rock shook the air, but the world ground to a halt as a flaming arrow landed in the snow before me.

Elated gasps filled the air. "Don't waste time, now." Orman chuckled. "No telling how long that bridge will last."

I looked up in horror as a cascade of shooting stars fell from the sky, arrows arching toward us in slow motion, a rainstorm of fire.

"Run!" Lio's hand reached for mine and ripped me from my paralysis. We ducked our heads and raced forward, slipping on the ice and snow as the ground rumbled with the voice of an angry beast beneath us. Arrows littered the earth, sticking out of the snow as reminders of death's encroaching grasp with each step.

An arrow whizzed toward me but veered with the wind so that it only grazed past my arm.

Screams erupted behind us. An anguished wave of pain ransacked my senses, begging me for the mercy of healing. Another fiery burst of pain from a fallen competitor ripped through my heart, mirroring the pain of the arrow that landed in his. All around me, pain flared and bombarded my senses as competitors fell until I could no longer distinguish between their pain and mine. But I did not stop or chance a glance over my shoulder. There was no time.

I gritted my teeth and ran, drawing up a wall in my mind to close out the anguish around me.

Adrenaline pumped through my body as I dodged the fiery rain, sprinting forward with legs that felt uncoordinated and clumsy with numbness. My neck snapped backward suddenly, pulled by a man who grabbed a fistful of my hair to steady himself on the ice. Pain blindsided me as my skull struck the ground and the man trampled over me. I gasped, clutching at my abdomen where his boot had tread. *Get up. Fight.*

I scrambled to my knees, wincing as I struggled in vain to steady my feet on the slippery ice. Faces contorted by fear raced toward me, and my heart pounded violently in my chest. Blood splattered the path where lifeless bodies lay beneath shafts of arrows. A billowing cloud of white debris crawled along the bridge, swallowing a man whole as it approached.

The bridge was collapsing.

Roaring filled my ears—screams, crashing ice, a cheering crowd, blood coursing through my veins—all muddled together as one great storm of noise and pain. I scrambled backward, trying to right myself as desperate men barreled past me. Crumbling chunks of the bridge crashed into the ravine, and I watched in horror as the gap rolled closer and closer to where I sat. I launched myself toward an arrow that had pierced the ice, grasping it to hoist myself to my feet. Thundering noise rumbled behind me, but I surged forward, shouldering past men and racing toward the safety of the ledge. I leaped forward, throwing my body into the snow and clenching my eyes closed as ice and debris showered my face.

I covered my head with my hands and buried my face in the wet snow, unable to move. My whole body quaked with uncontrollable tremors until the rumbling collapse of the bridge transformed into the roaring applause of the crowd. I raised my head, gasping for breath.

Orman stood on the front steps of the House of Frost with a triumphant smile and outstretched arms. "What an entrance!" The resounding roar from above shook the ground. He stepped down the stairs, patting each of us on the shoulder as he passed. "Just spectacular! Pell, Brickert, Vance, Oraelia, Harman, Lio. Welcome, welcome. Taiver, Gidian, Lorne—you made it. Welcome."

He made it to the end of the competitors and threw his hands up to the balcony. "Twenty-one competitors remain after the first challenge! Outstanding!" He paused, letting a smile of delighted mischief curl beneath his mustache.

"How would you like to meet them all?" he asked the crowd, his voice adopting a playful spirit.

I flinched at the surge of hysteria from above. Clapping, screaming, hollering, and stomping shook the ground in a way that became utterly disorienting and triggering. I turned my head slowly toward the other competitors and saw my shock mirrored in their vacant faces, their chests flaring with ragged breaths.

"Well, do not dally any further. We must prepare you for the ball! Welcome to the House of Frost and the Trials. We've been waiting for you."

CHAPTER TWENTY

Smile, Darling

RAE

The front doors of the House of Frost opened wide like the jaws of a monster ready to devour us whole. Orman gestured us inside, beaming at the disheveled, traumatized mess of competitors at his feet. Not a trace of concern or pity marred his features, and not an ounce of humanity showed through the smile plastered on his face. I pushed myself to stand and brushed the snow and grit from my palms with a wince. Gravel had torn apart my skin. *No turning back now.* Orman clapped me on the shoulder as I climbed the stairs and passed through the threshold.

My veins throbbed with rushing blood. My senses were too overrun with adrenaline to truly appreciate the architecture of the sweeping ballroom, but the room demanded admiration. Long, gothic windows painted white like snow stretched from floor to ceiling on either side of the grand ballroom, and a rose window dispersed fragments of colors upon the walls and floors as the sun's rays peeked through. Double staircases swept from either end of the room to meet in the center, with white railings that sparkled like the spokes of a snowflake.

A swarm of men and women descended the staircases from either side to receive us, chattering with excitement as they pointed and gawked in our direction. Goosebumps prickled on my skin as the room grew silent. "That was truly *something*, Grand Master Orman. You have outdone yourself."

The high prince smiled conspiratorially at Orman as he glided down the stairs, and Orman received the compliment with his chin held high.

The prince's cloak, lined with thick grey fur, swept majestically behind him as he descended the stairs. Gold scrolls of embroidery lined either side of his deep blue jacket and a glittering crown topped his sandy curls. I flinched as his eyes searched the crowd, landing deliberately upon me.

"Twenty-one contestants remain after that grand entrance... including my own victor!" The crowd, nobles by the looks of their lavish attire, whistled and cheered in response.

My eyes swept across the room, sickened by the disgusting display of revelry. Men had just *died*. Horrifically. Thirteen men had already perished for their amusement.

Who would mourn their deaths and pray to the Fates for their safe passage into the Next Realm? Who would retrieve their bodies from the snow?

In the dark recesses of the ballroom, I found Rydar, and I jumped with a start as his eyes met mine. He studied me carefully, his expression unreadable. Shadows enveloped him as he leaned against the wall, swathed in his signature aura of unapproachability.

"I'll admit, I did fear for a moment that my victor would be eliminated before the Opening Ball," the high prince continued, chuckling slightly as he spoke. "Did you all see her?" His face twisted up with fear, and he pretended to lurch forward, mocking my desperate leap into the snow from the collapsing bridge. I scowled at the crass reenactment, but the nobles filled the room with lighthearted laughter. "Perhaps I'll have my bride, after all, at the end of this!"

He turned toward me again, his expression a paradox of menace and charm. *Oh no. He's coming over.*

Part of me, and a large part at that, considered fleeing back to the unforgiving tundra outside, but I froze, unable to move. The eyes of the room fell upon me and held me firmly in place.

He approached with carefully measured steps, his arrogance oozing from a dazzling smile. But it was his vacant eyes, the depthless, soulless pools of black, that held my attention. I gasped as his hand reached for mine and twirled me into an embrace, entangling me in the prison of his arms. My ribs protested his crushing grasp and my spine threatened to snap as he lowered me into a graceful dip.

"Smile, darling. Everyone is watching," he murmured. When I refused to oblige this request, he pinched my side, and something dangerous flashed in his eyes. I forced a smile through gritted teeth. "You have such a beautiful smile." He released me and I wrapped my arms around my waist to hold in the anger welling inside my stomach.

Flint Barragan's eyes scanned the room in silence. "Ah! Rydar. I expect you can oversee the preparations for tonight? I'm taking the lads out for a hunt." The glance he threw in my direction made my insides coil with discomfort. "Tell Elowynne this one needs a better dress if she's to dance with me tonight."

Rydar bowed his head in agreement and then led me away. "Go with Elowynne. I'll be there shortly," he whispered over my shoulder as he steered me in the woman's direction.

Elowynne stood in a circle of women, chattering brightly and sipping from a long flute of champagne. Her eyes flickered toward me. "Elianna, dear, I will catch up later... my services are required." She passed the flute of champagne to her neighbor.

She ushered me into a sitting room with a comfortable chaise and long, gauzy drapes over the windows. A looking glass stood in the corner of the room, and before it, a round pedestal. She bustled behind me, pushing me toward the mirror while decrying the state of my hair. Her lips pursed into a tight line as she circled me, stopping to prod and pinch and measure.

I took in a deep breath, deciding to push my luck. "Elowynne..." I began, hoping the champagne may have loosened her tongue. If I could glean anything about the upcoming Trials from her—

"Be quiet, girl, I'm thinking. The high prince is not easy to please." It had not occurred to me that a woman of Elowynne's stature would have her own fears, but there they were, in the creases at her eyes and the tense muscles in her jaw.

She hurried away to the other side of the room, pillaging the interior of a dark, wooden wardrobe, weighing fabrics in her hands, and shaking her head. Finally, she returned with an armful of deep blue material, almost black like the night sky. "This one will look lovely with your hair. Try it on." With a light flick of her wrist, my grey garments disappeared, replaced by blue silks and tulle.

I marveled at the whisper of fabric against my skin, the caress of the smooth gown so natural I questioned if I was wearing anything at all. "It's beautiful," I acknowledged, as much as I wished to despise it.

But it was too beautiful—too little and yet entirely too much. The sort of dress Nell and I would have dreamed of, one that would have cost our entire family's lifetime. Shivers ran down my spine as the cold air of the room brushed against the exposed skin of my neck, my arms, my bare back. "I'll just wear the grey dress, thanks," I said, pulling the straps from my shoulders. I did not desire the attention of the high prince.

"Hush, dear, and hold still. You can't look like you've just crawled through the Gates of Hell at the ball... the prince will have my head."

But I did just crawl through the Gates of Hell.

Elowynne frowned, gripping pins between her lips as she fretted over the seams, smoothing imperfections at my hips and shoulders. "You are lovely when you stand up straight." She jabbed my shoulder blade with her thumb, sighing, and I glowered at her in return. "And you're as stubborn as my daughter. She's here too, you know."

What? My stomach twisted into knots, pulling tighter than the careful loops that Elowynne conjured with her thread. "I thought I was the only woman in the Trials?" Rydar had promised—though why I trusted a single word from the man's mouth, I did not know. I thought back to the tents and the bridge, searching my memory for the presence of another woman, but recalled nothing of note.

Elowynne's laughter floated into the air. "Oh no, no, no. She's not a participant. She's here to win the champion's hand, dear. Presuming you lose, of course. And she's not the only one—all the high class ladies are here to make an impression. You won't find a more eligible bachelor in all of Orogi than the winner of the Trials." She sighed dreamily. "Rich beyond measure and a true embodiment of bravery..." Her head bobbed, and she wrestled with a seam at my side. "Except perhaps, the prince, but he's set his eyes on you for whatever reason."

Bitterness seeped into her tone, but her face remained neutral as she combed her fingers through my long hair and angled her head in consideration.

"It really is a pity you'll have to die in the Trials, though—you'd make fast friends with Alia."

Thank you for the vote of confidence.

A knock at the door startled us both. I winced as her hand caught a snarl in my hair, pulling it sharply as she turned. *Helfyre.*

Rydar stepped into the room, wearing his familiar scowl, though something more stirred in the storm clouds of his eyes. The knot in his throat bobbed as he assessed me from head to toe, and I folded my arms across my chest, uncomfortable beneath his piercing gaze. My breath hitched in my throat as he strolled forward wordlessly, circling around me to examine the dress from all angles.

"It's too modest, Elowynne. The high prince prefers... less." Blood rose to my cheeks as his eyes trailed from my breastbone to my navel. "A deeper neckline and—"

He stooped, gathering the fabric hem of the dress, raising it slowly along the length of my leg. "A slit in the fabric here." My pulse raced as his warm hand brushed at my knee, then climbed higher still, hesitating with intrigue just below the strip of fabric wrapped around my thigh. *Take my dagger, and I will cut you, Rydar Barragan.* I stepped backward with haste, stumbling clumsily off the pedestal.

His arm slipped around my waist with ease, sparing me the shame of shattering Elowynne's looking glass. Flames rose to my cheeks, dancing just beneath the surface of my skin, and I cursed. My traitorous, thumping heart did little to hide my embarrassment. Or my attraction. *Settle down, Rae.*

His grey eyes twinkled with amusement, infuriating me as I untangled myself from his arms. Elowynne watched with great interest from a few paces away, lips pursed, wheels turning, until Rydar faced her. "Elowynne, go draw the lady a bath. She requires a real one if she's to attend the ball."

Her mouth opened in protest, but Rydar raised a hand to stop her. "No, none of your conjured ones, Elowynne. A real one with the lavender soap is required for a woman in her state. Go." Elowynne hurried away with a huff, leaving me alone with Rydar.

"Do I repulse you so thoroughly, then, Unprince of Orogi?" How the man had managed to insult me within five minutes of enduring his presence was beyond me. Why his opinion mattered was even more perplexing. But it did.

"I merely thought you'd appreciate the chance to relax and wash away the blood and sweat. And I hoped to send the meddlesome woman away so we could discuss *this*—" He reached for the dagger at my thigh, but I was faster.

Arms shaking, I held the dagger before me with my legs staggered, ready to strike. The fabric of the dress stretched taut over my thighs, threatening to tear open at the seams. Perhaps a slit would be beneficial, after all.

Rydar cocked his head to one side, as if truly seeing me for the first time. "Not bad." My breath hitched in my throat as he stepped forward to disarm me with the confident precision of a trained warrior. "I see you still do not trust me. But why use my own dagger against me? When I went to such great lengths to persuade the healers to allow you to keep it?" I was unprepared for how he dismantled my defenses, melting them away with one rumbled whisper in my ear.

I gaped at him in surprise, smelling the sandalwood and storm at his neck. The corner of his mouth pulled into a smirk, and he gently returned the dagger, closing my fingers over the hilt so his hand enveloped mine. "Keep it. I'll have a proper sheath made for you."

He tucked my hair behind my ear, studying me with his piercing gaze. "Are you alright?"

The simple question took me by surprise, and I hesitated, unsure how to respond. There were no words for the storm of emotions in my heart. I stared at the wall in silence, rejecting the hot tears that welled in the bottoms of my eyes. No, I was not alright, far from it.

I hated him for making me come here... hated the hint of concern in his voice. I hated that I did not know if his concern was true or feigned, and why he had taken an interest in my wellbeing. Most of all, I hated the unbidden spark of attraction I felt whenever he drew near and the burden of not knowing what to do with it. None of it mattered, anyway. I was going to die. The shadow dragon roared in protest at my thoughts, and I winced.

Noting my expression, Rydar shook his head and closed his eyes. "Of course you're not alright. I couldn't expect you to be."

"I'm not," I snapped. "I am angry. Scared. Tired. But at least the arrows didn't strike me down today, and I am alive. Happy?" It was one minor blessing amongst the horrors of the most recent hours.

His eyes brightened, touched by a dash of mischief. "Yes, that was fortunate, indeed."

Suspicion crept into my mind as my eyes meandered from the smirk at his mouth to the devious glint in his eyes. "Fortune or intervention?" I guessed.

His amused silence spoke volumes.

"You helped me?"

"Perhaps. I recall certain promises. Though that would be very foolish of me to admit in this place."

"Foolish indeed... But perhaps I *can* count you as a friend despite your persistent objections?"

"Oraelia, no. *If* I indeed offered a small favor, it is certainly not to be misconstrued as my favoritism. Do not read too much into it—you will disappoint yourself."

Misconstrued? I laughed at this.

He was not indifferent, nor was I. I had misconstrued nothing.

Something changed in his eyes, and he drew in a deep breath. "I have warned you not to mistake me as your friend. I will help you survive to please the high prince. That is my duty. Nothing more. Please."

Of course. A man of duty, and me, a tool to be leveraged for his own benefit. I should have let it go there, but the way the light in his eyes deadened, smothered by the half-truths he spoke, unnerved me. A lump formed in my chest, swelling until it pushed painfully at my throat, too large to be contained. I pressed on. "And why is the prospect of friendship so unappealing to you? Is it me?"

"Of course not." His voice broke as he spoke, like the words stuck in his throat. "Is that what you think? No, it is complicated."

"Then why?"

He stepped away and raked a hand through his mane, sweeping his fingers through the hair at his brow to the top of his head. A habit that always accompanied his frustration, I noted. His eyes landed upon me after a brief glimpse toward the coffered ceiling, this time full of something that looked a lot like sadness. "My friendship is much more trouble than it's worth, I'm afraid."

"You should let me be the judge of that."

He exhaled deeply, poorly hiding his frustrations. "Absolutely not. Oraelia, listen. I am doing what I can. You will win the Trials. You will marry the high prince. I will help you in those endeavors because I care about your safety and the prince's happiness, but please, you must ask nothing else of me. I cannot give it."

"I see." My chest tightened, burning with the discomfort of words demanding a voice. Words that lashed out despite my best efforts to contain them. *What is he so afraid of?* "Must be a terribly sad existence... to care only about duties."

"And your existence is so much grander? Full of friendship and happiness? Free of the burden of disagreeable duties?"

I crossed my arms over my chest and glared. "No, I'm stuck in this Helfyre."

"You and me, both."

In that moment, the mask of a great warrior lifted, and he looked nothing more than a haunted boy. One who needed friendship as desperately as I did.

"You do not scare me, Rydar."

"I should."

Silence pervaded the air between us, filling the impassable chasm of space between our bodies. A sudden, nonsensical desire to cross the chasm overwhelmed me—to press my lips against his, to taste the scent of rain that clung to his skin, but I hesitated. *What are you doing, Rae?*

He stepped backward, straightening his posture and adopting a more formal disposition. Walls up. Guard up.

"The prince will be pleased to see you in this."

His tone was empty, little more than a dismissal, but I was not ready to release him. "And what do you think?" I wanted to hear it, hear that I affected him the same way he affected me.

"What I think matters not." The sound of running water from the bathing chamber stopped abruptly, leaving behind a noticeable absence of sound and the permeating smell of lavender. Rydar sighed deeply. "Go. Elowynne may lose her mind if I delay her responsibilities any longer. I will see you at the ball."

Heat rose to my cheeks as he reached for my hand, tracing a line down my forearm with his fingers, chasing the little dragon that matched his own. To my surprise, the shadow dissipated, fading gradually into pink skin. Sadness tinted his smile as he met my eyes. "A temporary illusion to ward off curious minds. For your safety."

I nodded, wondering if I should pull my hand away, but allowing it to linger. His voice lowered. "I took care of them, so you know. They are safe. Our arrangement stands."

"Thank you."

"Do not thank me. Uphold your end of the bargain." He released my hand, leaving behind a cold emptiness in my palm and a silent scream of frustration in my heart.

CHAPTER TWENTY-ONE

Golden Plumes

RAE

I glared at the aberration of plumage and flowers that sat firmly, unwavering-ly, on top of my head. No amount of pulling, negotiating, or pleading for its removal had freed me of the nuisance. Elowynne stood behind me, gripping my arms as she gazed over my right shoulder into the mirror. Her eyes sparkled with admiration—she was evidently pleased with herself.

She sighed deeply, not with irritation but with pure reverence for her work. Her eyes and shoulders relaxed with the exhale. "I can Retire now. I've reached my peak."

I did not share the same appreciation for her styling efforts, nor did I under-stand them. After Elowynne had scrubbed, oiled, brushed, and powdered me from head to toe, she forced me to endure her pokes and prods while working her magic. The results were... alarming. I hardly recognized my own reflection.

The golden plumes she had affixed to the hair above my ears rose straight up to the Fates, forming the great wings of a phoenix. A tribute to my surname, she had said. A golden crown sat between the wings, with ornate spokes that rose from the crest of my head like the sun's rays. Blood-red roses lined the bottom of the crown for additional glamor. My protests had garnered no sympathy from the woman. Instead, Elowynne had resorted to securing the disaster to my head with magic to ensure its permanence. And so we stood, scrutinizing my reflection in the mirror, one of us victorious and the other disgruntled by defeat.

The headdress was my primary complaint, but Elowynne's insistence on applying extravagant makeup did little to appease my ire. She painted the corners of my eyes with sweeping golden wings and glued charcoal lashes to my lids that fluttered each time I blinked.

And the dress—the beautiful dress was more than I could bear. Elowynne had adjusted the neckline so that it plunged to my navel between the delicate straps at my shoulders, much to my dismay. *Thank you, Rydar, for your design input. Highly appreciated.*

Shimmering fabric embraced the curves of my figure, clinging to my waist and hips before flowing into a gauzy skirt of tulle around my legs. The dress glittered like stars, dusted with flecks of gold along the bodice and train.

My breaths had become short and panicked, though I could hardly blame the bodice—the top was much too sparse to cause any restriction to my lungs. The shortness of breath could only be blamed on knowing I would wear this dress all evening. In public. Potentially while in grave danger.

My shoulders slumped in resignation, but Elowynne's quick jab to my back forced me to straighten my spine. "Stand up straight, Oraelia." I glowered at her. *She* did not look like a festive bird colliding with the sun.

"By the Fates! The time!" Elowynne exclaimed, checking the Pacer at her wrist. "You time wasters rub off on me more than I'd care to admit." She chuckled airily and brushed the pleats of her dress, then tidied her hair, though I could see nothing out of place. When she was satisfied, she ushered me toward the door. "Sun and stars, Oraelia. Stop fretting and stand up straight. I won't forgive you if you embarrass me while wearing my best work. Follow me."

Elowynne whisked me through the corridors, her heels clicking loudly in the passageway over the marble floors. I willed my feet to match her pace, though I struggled in the golden heels that threatened to break my ankle with every step.

"We'll be meeting the remaining competitors in the antechamber to the ballroom. The others have been waiting there, getting prepped for the ball. You were fortunate to be afforded the privacy of your own chambers to get ready," Elowynne tossed over her shoulder. "Perks of being a lady."

My nose scrunched as I considered whether to respond, watching her hasty steps pull further ahead of me. *Does she expect a thank you? Not happening.*

Elongated windows lined the hall, and the moon reached inside to cast its light upon us. Her steps slowed as she approached a pair of doors, marked on either side by tall, blue-glazed vases. "In you go," she said, opening the doors to the small sitting room.

Inside the chamber, the gathered competitors milled about anxiously. I could see the worry in their eyes as they turned toward the open door, though many of them wore delicate masks. Elowynne slipped past me and made her way toward a Watchman standing guard by a set of double doors on the far side of the room.

One of the competitors approached me, sneering beneath the lacy mask covering the top half of his face. He wore a silver jacket, and his blue hair glowed unnaturally, like rolling waves beneath starlight. "Look who survived the bridge, after all." I recognized the deep, haughty tone of his voice and glared at the man who stole my Goodvit on the bridge. He wore a pin on his lapel that glimmered with the flourishing, gilded letters of his name. Brickert. "If tonight doesn't finish you off, I will," he said, his voice gravelly and full of menace. *This one fancies himself a winner.*

I straightened my back and lifted my chin, refusing to be intimidated. "I'm flattered, but you're not my type, Brickert." I said his name as if it were something revolting.

His brow furrowed with the effort of working out my meaning, and I smiled. *All muscles, no brain.* Fluttering my lashes coyly for good measure, I turned to leave him behind. *Brute.*

A familiar face caught my attention in the rows of chairs. Lio patted the seat next to him, and I walked over, smoothing my dress before sitting on the velvet cushion. "Nice mask," I whispered.

"Nice hair." My chest deflated with a heavy sigh, and Lio smirked.

"It's awful, isn't it?"

"It's not so bad... have you seen Brickert and Gidian?" He tilted his head discreetly to the left, and I followed with my gaze toward the brute who now glared in our direction. A competitor with hair spiked and painted to look like flames stood with him.

"At least you wear yours well," Lio whispered.

Muffled voices seeped through the walls around us, and delicious smells filled the air, distracting me from our conversation. The ravenous beast in my stomach awoke with a roar. Lio must have heard it, too, because he chuckled quietly, then resumed the nervous thumbing of the pin on his lapel.

"Think they'll have anything better than Goodvit to eat?" he asked. The idea of a feast made my mouth water, especially since our last meal was the measly tube of Goodvit shared between us. The scents of fresh bread and roasted meat made my stomach churn in anticipation.

"It certainly smells better than Goodvit."

Elowynne clapped her hands at the front of the sitting room to reclaim our attention. She sparkled from head to toe, draped in glittering necklaces and earrings that brushed the tops of her bare shoulders. I marveled at her, wondering when she had found the time to make such a drastic wardrobe change. Then I grumbled with resentment, wishing my own transformation had been half as expedient.

She cleared her throat a bit dramatically before speaking. "It sounds as though dinner is just wrapping up." My stomach sank and groans surged all around. Elowynne ignored us and continued. "In just a few moments, the doors behind me will open and you will take your places for the opening dance. Orman will announce each of you by name, and you will enter the ballroom when you are called. You will dance with whoever approaches you, and take care to make a good impression. Best of luck." Her smile widened as she scanned the room, appreciating each of us in turn. It felt oddly like a goodbye, though she uttered no such words. Instead, she sighed.

"Our stylists have truly outdone themselves—I am certain the benefactors will be pleased. The more you impress them tonight, the more generous they will be with their donations to the grand prize. Make us proud."

"So... we just have to dance? What if we don't know how?" the man with fiery hair asked, his voice wavering with nerves.

Elowynne balked, as if the words had physically assaulted her. "You showed up for the Timeless Trials and you're worried about a little bit of dancing? You *fake* it, for Fate's sake, Gidian." She mumbled something about hopelessly uncultured miscreants and turned her back on us to peek through the gap between the doors.

Applause swelled in the silence from the room beyond the wall, and Elowynne nodded. "Rise," she commanded before the doors opened slowly behind her, "and prepare yourselves for an... eventful evening."

Chapter Twenty-Two

The Hourglass

RAE

I gasped as the doors to the ballroom opened wide. Never had I witnessed a space so extravagant, so ethereal. I wondered briefly if I had crossed over to the Next Realm, but my heart fluttered wildly in contradiction to that fear.

"Good lads and ladies! Please welcome the remaining twenty-one competitors to the Opening Ball!"

Enthusiastic applause lauded our arrival. The lords and ladies cheered merrily, decked in feathers, silk, and jewels that could have easily fed the entire district of Nox for a winter. My stomach was knotted with discomfort at the thought.

A vast dance floor stretched before us, paved with warm, earthy stones that curled in a circular pattern. White cascades of flowers dripped from the ceilings and twinkling orbs cast a symphony of shadow and light across the room. Towers of food rose from the long tables along the walls, gravity-defying works of art that made my mouth water with longing, though the arrangements looked too beautiful to eat.

The most magnificent feature of the room was the glittering hourglasses filled with shimmering crystals mounted at the top of the walls. My gaze landed on the one with navy jewels at the bottom, where my name was written in gold, scrolling letters. *Oraelia Fenix. 376 years.*

It took great effort to keep my jaw from dropping to the floor. The other hourglasses were labeled in much the same way, with the names of what I could only assume to be the other competitors. *Vance, Pell, Gidian, Brickert, Lio, Ruwe, Tickon—there was one for each of the twenty-one competitors.* With a flicker of guilt, I wondered about the missing names—the empty spaces that must have held the names of those who had already passed. Names I would never know.

And what would become of our names when the time came? A wave of nausea washed over me.

In the very center of the room, a grand hourglass encrusted with glistening crystals sat above the words *The Good Work.*

Greedy monsters.

Wearing a scarlet jacket, Orman stepped to the center of the dance floor, just below the largest hourglass. His silver buttons gleamed in the spotlight, and his wild beard had been tamed, now glittering with gems for the occasion. His voice elevated above the music, amplified by his sheer will.

"Good lads and ladies." He paused, waiting. A dangerous glint flashed in his eyes. The string quartet in the corner of the ballroom lulled, and the applause slowed until a hush fell over the room.

"Good lads and ladies, I present the twenty-one competitors of the Timeless Trials! Please hold your applause and additional donations until the end of the opening dance. Let tonight honor the Good Work of our most honorable high king!"

A lady in the crowd, with a large splotch of gold painted on her face, beamed at me and clapped her hands together, almost childlike with glee. She quickly withered beneath Orman's sharp glare.

"Competitors, when I call your name, please present yourself before the good lads and ladies. Do not fret—there is nothing to fear. Yet." He winked gregariously to the crowd, and laughter bubbled up in return, then he let his eyes drop to the scroll in his hands. "Ruwe Lipinde."

A muscular man with jet black hair strode into the room with an air of confidence that set the ladies into a fit of giggles. One of the girls stumbled forward, following a swift nudge to her ribcage from a distinguished-looking man at her side. The man jerked his head pointedly at Ruwe, and she curtsied deeply. Ruwe returned the gesture with a bow. He took her hand with grace, leading her away as Orman continued down his list, calling each competitor forward until the room was crowded with couples.

When Orman reached Lio's name, he sighed and drooped his shoulders forward. Lio's timid gait toward the dance floor betrayed his uncertainty, but a lovely lady blushed the fiercest shade of pink—the exact shade of her hair—as she approached him in a fit of giggles.

Orman announced the last man, Pell, and I stood alone in the middle of the open doors, suddenly too aware of the way my fingers trembled and my exposed skin prickled at my shoulders and chest. I searched the couples and the crowd nervously, moving only my eyes as I willed my fingers to still. Rydar's eyes met mine, and the slightest of smiles pulled at one side of his mouth. I held my head high. "Oraelia Fenix."

I stepped into the center of the room, so focused on conquering the uneven stone floor I forgot to carry myself as Elowynne had instructed. With great effort, I willed a pleasant smile to my face. I didn't wish to care about the benefactor's opinions, but I knew their support and donations mattered to my survival. The high prince of Orogi, Flint Barragan, appeared before me, and I faltered.

Not you. But of course, it would be him. My heart thumped nervously, dreading each step he took toward me in his deep blue jacket and silver crown of frosted brambles. Behind him, Rydar nodded grimly and gestured for me to bow.

I gathered the tulle at my thighs and swept one leg behind me in a deep curtsy. When I rose, Flint smiled in his most deceitfully charming way, revealing the dimple in his cheek and the hint of a sparkle in the depths of his eyes as he extended his hand to me. I placed my palm in his, and his lips brushed the top of my hand with a gentle kiss.

Orman bowed with a fist clenched over his chest. "To the Good Work!" The crowd applauded politely, and chatter surged as they admired the couples on the floor. Turning to the string quartet in the corner of the ballroom, Orman nodded. The first shrieking notes startled me from my thoughts, reminding me of the dangers lurking behind every laugh and every smile in the room.

"Jumpy, are we?" Flint asked. The music settled into a dreamy, elegant tune that wrapped us in its beauty, demanding the movement of feet.

Flint placed his arm at the small of my back and grasped my right hand loosely in his. "You are stunning," he whispered. "Your eyes—like the deep sea. Full of secrets." The hair on the back of my neck rose at his words. "Tell me about yourself, Oraelia. Do not be a stranger...we are to be married if you survive."

The muscles along my spine tightened, pulling away from his touch, but I found my feet fell into the dance with ease, as if they had always known what to do—always known how to pretend, to blend.

His fingers brushed my back, exploring the rigidity of my muscles, and he pulled me closer, forcing me to look into his eyes. "So secretive...so elusive." We crossed the floor in a waltz of words and delicate steps, waves lapping upon the shore. "Not to worry...keep your secrets. I always find the answers I want. How are your sister and father, by the way?"

He dropped my hand to brush the hair from my brow, the featherlight touch of his fingers conveying the unmistakable threat they carried. The fear in my eyes seemed to please him. "You have nothing to fear, darling, so long as you do not embarrass me. And lucky you, with me by your side, your hourglass will overflow with donations. You'll want those to get ahead in the Trials. So don't ruin the moment."

I studied his face, the dangerous smirk, the eyes untouched by joy, all while allowing his light touch to guide my steps, letting the music sweep me up and down like the swell of waves in the sea. Like the waves that carried me to the shore in the dark hours before my mother's death beneath a starry sky. Stars that twinkled with laughter as the waves swallowed us, a mockery of her dreams for more.

The room was a blur, but my eyes moored to the stormy gaze across the room that followed my every step. An anchor that kept me from drifting away in fear or drowning in washed-up memories.

Rydar's expression was guarded. A man with rich brown hair and a scar along his cheek whispered to him, and Rydar nodded curtly, holding me in his gaze. He passed an amber bottle to the man, who lit up at the sight of the label. I raised my brow, questioning without words, but Flint spun me away in the crescendo of notes rising before the final fall of the haunting melody.

The joyful clatter of cheers and applause replaced the music and Flint took my hands in his.

"Absolutely breathtaking. Jaw-dropping. Inspiring. Exquisite. Don't you think?" Orman asked the crowd, who politely chuckled in response to his overt enthusiasm. "I know, I know, you want to help your favorites by getting them ahead and not to worry…I won't hold you up any longer!" He waved his bejeweled fingers toward the hourglasses above.

"As you know, your time donations could mean the difference between life or death for your favorite competitor. A competitor with a full hourglass has an advantage; a competitor with an empty one is dead. So do not be greedy, or we may well just see *you* in the Trials next year!" He laughed deeply at his own joke.

Flint leaned in to whisper in my ear. "The highest-funded competitors get extra perks…little advantages throughout the Trials. The lowest-funded run the risk of…elimination. Keep impressing the benefactors if you want to live." He pulled away with a smile, then planted a kiss upon my hand, bowing at the waist. I curtsied nervously in return, watching the lords and ladies from the corner of my eye. A lady with golden strands woven throughout her hair placed a hand over her heart and sighed wistfully.

A lopsided smile pulled at the corner of Flint's mouth and he nodded toward the ceiling. Deep blue gems spilled into the hourglass above my name, tinkling softly against the glass as they gathered in a heap at the bottom.

"You're welcome," he said. "It pays to be the favorite of the high prince. If all goes well, you and I will be dancing for a very long time together."

CHAPTER TWENTY-THREE

Old Timer

RAE

The applause faded, and the couples dispersed to clear the dance floor as the quartet struck up the next number. I searched the crowd for Rydar, but he had vanished. The man with brown, wavy hair draped over his ears approached us, smiling so warmly at Flint that the scar on his face stretched even further across his cheek. He held the amber bottle from Rydar tucked neatly under one arm. With a respectful bow, he greeted the high prince, then clapped Flint on the shoulder with a playful grin. "Your Highness."

He acknowledged me with a polite dip of his chin. "And you must be the beautiful betrothed of our high prince. Oraelia Fenix, correct?" He leaned forward and whispered with a wink, "I trust he's been treating you like royalty, my lady?"

Betrothed? Is that official, then? My lips pursed involuntarily, but I quickly exchanged the expression for a lighthearted smile. "Oh yes. A gentleman like no other. It is a dream come true to fight for my life in the Timeless Trials to prove myself worthy of his affection." A heavy silence filled the air. I gulped, my expression freezing as I realized what I had just said. Out loud. With sarcasm. My stomach writhed with discomfort, waiting for the consequences. *Why can you never keep your mouth closed?*

To my great surprise, the man burst into laughter instead of smiting me on the spot. "Oh, I like her for you. Wonderful choice, Your Highness."

Flint's eyes were icy, though he afforded a small smile in return. "Yes, she has a rather brazen charm about her, doesn't she? But do not get ahead of yourself, Trystan. She only gets to marry me if she wins the Trials, after all." His face turned smug, knowing he had the upper hand in every way. "I have my doubts about her resilience, if I'm being honest, but we shall see what the people think of her. I hope they will find her worthy of their time." He nodded toward the hourglasses.

My playful expression faltered, but I hid the daggers in my eyes beneath a fresh smile.

Trystan cleared his throat awkwardly. "Well, your father is eager to meet her. And hopeful for a royal wedding. A joyous occasion would do the Realm well."

The high prince did not respond with anything more than a contemplative "hmmm."

"Will the high king be joining the celebrations tonight?" I asked pleasantly, hoping to take advantage of the moment to turn the conversation in a useful direction. Information was always valuable.

"The high king is otherwise engaged. Important affairs. In fact," he turned to Flint, "we have some matters to discuss. Please excuse us, Oraelia, but I must steal away your dance partner for a bit." He passed the amber bottle under his arm to Flint, whose eyes grew large with greed.

"Old Timer? Trystan! Where did you manage to pick this up?"

"Straight from the high king himself. To celebrate. Perhaps we can find a more private space for sipping and discussion?"

He smiled darkly. "There is an excellent sitting space in the library. I will meet you there, but allow me a moment with my dear Oraelia first."

"Of course. Your Highness. Oraelia." He nodded to each of us and strode purposefully toward the double doors that led to the marble hallway.

The high prince's lips twitched imperceptibly as he lifted his elbow and his brows, waiting for me to hook my arm through his. "Come, let's go for a stroll." My heart fluttered, but not with excitement. The feeling that consumed me was dread, though the high prince's expression gave no indication of trouble.

He dropped his facade once we exited the ballroom into a narrow hallway. His eyes narrowed, swirling with rage, and a muscle in his jaw twitched with anger as he gripped my arm.

"*Never* embarrass me like that again." His voice was dark, commanding. Powerful.

I opened my mouth to protest, but only managed to take in a sharp breath as the back of his hand struck my cheek. My temple burned with a searing pain where his rings tore my skin, and I clasped my hand over the mark, feeling the trickle of sticky warmth on my cheek. The strike took me by surprise and brought tears to my eyes despite the wave of shock that stunned me. I blinked the wetness from my lashes, refusing their presence.

Flint shook his hand, rings glinting in the light of the sconces along the wall. "Let me be clear. You are only here because it is *convenient* for me. Because it is amusing to me and because I find you moderately intriguing. But make no mistake. It would be so simple to fix your death in the Trials—to make it look like an unfortunate accident. A poor damsel out of her element who just couldn't survive. The high king expects me to marry this year, so I am playing along to appease him, but you step out of line, and I will *gladly* end you to buy myself more time. I have no use for a woman who thinks she can embarrass me in public. Save that brazen tongue for the bedroom, and remember your place."

"It would be difficult to forget where I stand with you, dear prince." *Dispensable. Inferior. Subordinate.* Every bone in my body willed me to fight back, to show him *his* place, but I bit my tongue and refused the bait. There was no winning against the high prince of the Realm.

He regarded me carefully for a moment, eyes narrowed in contemplation or contempt. It was impossible to tell.

"Go," he said, breaking the simmering silence between us. "I have more important matters to attend to than a foolish woman. And clean up your face before you return."

He stormed down the narrow hallway, and if he felt the anger of my glare as I watched his departure, he did not falter or care. I leaned against the wall, allowing my face to screw up in a moment of self-pity, but clenched my eyes closed to stop the tears that wished to flow. I would not be seen with streams of charcoal below my eyes—the evidence of sadness. Not by him, not by any of them.

My cheek felt warm where he had struck me, but the cut no longer burned. I brushed my fingers against the scratch, contemplating using my power to heal the wound, but it was too dangerous. I could not afford to provoke the high prince, nor could I answer the questions he would certainly ask if the mark disappeared.

The metallic doors in the hallway opened, and Elowynne rushed through them, heaving her shoulders in relief when she saw me. "There you are! What do you think you're doing in the servant's corridor? Who let you out?"

I blinked in surprise. "The high prince."

She clicked her tongue. "Well, he's not here now, and you can't be out here by yourself, unguarded. What nerve!"

"I just needed a moment."

Her gaze landed on the cut on my cheek and her lips turned downward in obvious disapproval. "What happened to your face?"

"Nothing."

"Ridiculous." She lifted her hands in a gesture of irritation. "I make you the most beautiful person at the ball and you go and ruin it. Unbelievable. No more wandering, or I'll personally ensure you have a pair of Watchmen tailing you. Now come."

I drew in a deep breath to collect myself and followed her through the doors.

CHAPTER TWENTY-FOUR

The Charity Chalice

RAE

I stood at the outskirts of the dance floor, quietly observing the way the swishing of dresses and shuffling of feet made the music come alive while a dizzying crescendo of thoughts swirled in my throbbing head, each clamoring for my attention. I searched the room for Rydar, uncertain if my heart raced with anticipation or dread. He was nowhere to be found, but I refused to acknowledge how heavily disappointment weighed on my heart. A waiter approached me, carrying a silver platter covered in an array of bite-sized morsels. "An hors d'oeuvres, Miss?"

"A what?"

His eyebrows raised, and an amused smile graced his face. "A snack," he whispered. "The disgraced prince insists the pastries in the center are divine."

The disgraced prince or the disgraceful? Alarms went off in my head, but my stomach writhed with hunger. Plucking a puff from the center of the tray, I shoved the whole bite into my mouth, realizing a moment too late that I had been a bit too ambitious.

I covered my mouth with my hand to hide my bulging cheeks and nodded my thanks to the waiter. The pastry melted on my tongue, rich with butter and filled with savory meat. It was a hundred times more satisfying than the chalky

Goodvit I had shared with Lio. I was about to reach for another when a delicate hand grabbed my wrist and spun me around.

"Lady Oraelia? Sun and stars! Look at you!" A young woman faced me, holding both my hands in hers with an expression so bright that the orbs of light lining the ceiling paled in comparison. A large, irregular splotch of gold paint covered one side of her face, and a crown of teardrop crystals and blushing roses topped her hair.

She gasped, noticing the streak of red along my cheek. "Oh! You're bleeding! Is that from the ice bridge? Were you scratched by an arrow? A rock? Never mind. I'm surprised Mother didn't hide the scratch...perhaps she thought it made you look brave? You are *so* brave. Yes. Mother must have left it as a token of your bravery."

"I am...not brave," I blurted, almost certain I looked as awkward as I felt. *I'm just trying to survive.*

"Nonsense. You *must* come with me. We have so much to talk about!"

To my dismay, she led me away from the waiter and the tray of delicious savory puffs. "I'm Lady Alia, by the way. I'm so excited to meet you! Mother's told me all about you, of course. Come now...The girls are all dying to meet you, too."

She steered me toward a group of ladies who broke from their excited chatter as we approached. Icy disdain chilled the air as they regarded me.

"Nice hair." The speaker was tall, elegant, and beautiful with such severity that the impact was haunting rather than alluring. Her dark hair was parted in the middle and swept into an elegant braid. Shimmering powder dusted one side of her face and hair, and pearls of all sizes were scattered from her forehead to her jaw and sprinkled throughout her hair. Her down-turned lips were frosted with the same silver dust that shimmered on her eyelids.

"Your mother has outdone herself, Alia," she said in a chilled tone, looking down her sharp nose in obvious disapproval. I became distinctly aware of the weight of the plumage and golden sunburst affixed to my head.

"Oh hush, Isa, you're just jealous." Alia turned to me with her dazzling smile, full of warmth and hope and perfectly white teeth. "Forgive Lady Isolde," she said to me. "It is most difficult for her to be in our presence...but can you blame her? I mean, look at us. It is hard for her, I think, to be the *third* most beautiful at the ball."

The circle of girls sniggered, but one frigid glance from Isolde silenced them. "Well, I just don't understand what the prince sees in her. She's not *that* special."

"Honestly, Isa, stop sulking. It's unbecoming."

Her lips puckered with disapproval, straining to hold back a retort. In murderous silence, Isolde popped a deep red berry into her mouth and chewed slowly before spitting the masticated fruit into her silver goblet.

She must have noted the way my lips parted in disgust, for she rolled her eyes as she grabbed another from the plate attached to her goblet. "What?" she asked, her tone a challenge. "I'm full."

I did not even know where to begin, but Lady Alia graciously interrupted to save me.

"So, Oraelia, you *must* tell us about the other competitors. What are they like?"

A waiter drifted by carrying a silver tray, and I wistfully watched as he approached Brickert and Gidian. My stomach grumbled. I wanted to excuse myself, but the girls were watching with eager eyes, waiting for my response. "Oh, I, uh—I haven't had the chance to interact with them much yet. Why?"

Alia threw her head back with an exasperated sigh, yet still bubbled with playful lightheartedness. "Well, whoever wins will be the most eligible bachelor in all of Orogi, won't he?"

She noted the change in my expression and gasped. "Oh! But I'm pulling for you, of course. I have no desire to marry any of those brutes, anyway. I'm only here at Father's insistence. He seems to think it might change my mind about marriage."

She played with her crystal teardrop earring and tilted her head toward the other girls. "They all have their favorites picked out...but not me. There's no chance I'm marrying one of them, so you need to win and marry the high prince."

Her chest deflated with a deep sigh, and her eyes turned downward in a grimace of pain. "But if you lose, the champion will set his eyes on me. I know it. How would they not?" She grabbed my wrists and smiled, and I looked at her. She was lovely in an unconventional manner, but her eyes sparkled with inner beauty. "So you have to win, alright? I mean, look at us. We're the most beautiful people here. Everyone can see that." Her conviction was so sincere that I couldn't help but smile, though dubious of her claims.

Isolde was less apt to agree. "I suppose the gold makeup does improve that unfortunate birthmark of yours, but only slightly."

Alia snapped her head toward Isolde and gave her a look that would make even the bravest man cower. "It's unique and different and I happen to like it. You've had many enhancements, haven't you? Pity they couldn't find one to improve your ugly personality."

One of the ladies snorted so abruptly she spewed her beverage in a very unladylike manner. A deadly glare from Isolde wiped the amusement from her face and she quickly regained her composure. She walked to a vessel attached to the striped wall, tipped her goblet, and drained the remaining contents.

The woman behind her, wearing a forest green dress covered in black lace, rolled her eyes dramatically. "Alia, Isolde, enough. Let her tell us about the men. What do you think about that one? Brickert, I believe?" I followed her gaze toward the huddle of competitors, seeing Brickert's distinct blue hair that glowed with the essence of stars beneath the chandelier.

"Oh Brickert," I responded, shaking my head. "He's awful."

She brought a hand to her chest, drawing in a deep breath of shock. "Really? He looks like a dream."

"He's not worthy of your dreams, believe me. He's been awful to me."

Her laughter rang in the air. The jarring, haughty jingle of her tone sounded like bells. "Well, what do you expect from your competition? Should he just give up and die for *you*? Come on now, you must know you don't have a real chance. I'm pulling for him."

"Janesta, don't be rude," Alia scolded, wrapping her arm around my shoulder, protecting me from her friend's remorseless smirk. "So, Brickert is a no. Are any of them worth their time? We're expected to donate this evening to our favorites. Don't worry—I've already donated time to you." The crystal bands on her wrist sparkled in the lights as she waved toward my hourglass with a wink.

I scanned the ballroom, searching for Lio, but he was already marching toward me with tensed shoulders, wringing his hands together nervously. "That one—Lio. He's a sweetheart."

Lio paused uncertainly as he noted my companions, but Alia waved him over cheerfully before he could manage a disappearance. "Lio, come!"

As he approached, his eyes darted anxiously from one girl to the next, but he smiled graciously at the invitation. Sliding next to me, he whispered, "We need to talk."

"Oh no, you can't steal her away just yet. Tell us about yourself, Lio. Oraelia was just singing your praises."

Lady Janesta surveyed him coolly, smoothing the lacy skirt of her dress.

I shrugged at him with a smile.

He opened his mouth as if to object, closed it, and started again, his cheeks turning pink beneath the delicate mask covering his eyes. "Thank you, ladies. I'm flattered." He shifted nervously as they began to fire questions at him.

Glad to be out of the spotlight for a moment, my attention drifted to the rest of the ballroom. I vaguely heard Lio's voice, talking about his family, seven siblings, his mother, his dreams...but I let my attention wander, allowing the music to fill my soul and carry me away for a moment.

Couples glided across the floor, their dresses swishing across the room like paint on a canvas. Ladies giggled with hands over their mouths by tables piled with artful displays of food, and glasses clinked together in merry toasts. Eager to fill my growling stomach, I turned to excuse myself from the group but hesitated as a waiter pleasantly tapped my arm. He presented the silver tray of little delights before me with a helpful smile.

Grateful, I reached for a pink and white swirl on the edge of the platter and muttered my thanks. Lio politely refused the offered tray with a wave, and the waiter drifted away.

Lio smacked the food out of my hand as soon as I brought it to my mouth. It landed on the floor at my feet, splattering into a shapeless blob. I glared at him.

"What are you doing?"

"Don't eat anything from the trays," he hissed. "Haven't you noticed?"

The girls were listening with rapt attention, so Lio leaned in to whisper, "The waiters are only offering food to the competitors. Something's wrong with it. I'm sure of it."

I sucked air through my nose in a shallow breath, holding it in my lungs. A sinking feeling of concern grew in my stomach as I followed the waiter's path.

Sure enough, he stopped in front of Gidian and Ruwe to offer the tray, ignoring the other lords and ladies that milled about the room.

Helfyre. Why did you take that puff? My stomach rumbled and coiled uncomfortably. Now I couldn't determine if it was due to sickness or hunger. What if the pastry had been poisoned? Was the poison already working its way into my system, silently destroying me from the inside?

The memory of the waiter's wry smile and whispered advice replayed in my mind. *The disgraced prince insists the pastries in the center are divine.*

I had never hoped more that Rydar was indeed playing favorites to save my life.

Janesta sighed and scooped up the food from the ground, much more nimble in her floor-length gown than I could ever dream of being in mine. "At least put it in a chalice if you're not planning to eat it. Don't be wasteful," Janesta scolded, dropping it into the cup attached to her plate.

The look of confusion on my face clearly irritated her. "*You*, of all people, must know food is scarce for so many. In Lustro, everyone is expected to do their part...Think of the hungry. It's not that hard."

I am the hungry. "I don't—I don't understand." I stumbled over my words, my eyes darting between her disapproving glare and the cup in her hand.

She sighed with exasperation, making me feel foolish. "The Charity Chalices." She waved the silver goblet in my face and gestured to the silver receptacles at each entrance. I watched in horror as a woman across the room approached the receptacle on the wall, dumped the contents of her cup into the vessel, and then returned to her partner. Janesta scowled with disgust.

I still wasn't following. I had never had the blessing of excess food. My brows drew together, processing the meaning of her words, fearing the explanations that my mind pieced together. "And the Charity Chalices...get sent...to the hungry?"

Janesta's nose wrinkled, and her expression rearranged into a judgmental sneer. "Well, it gets processed and turned into a meal substitute paste for the needy, of course. Haven't you ever heard of Goodvit?"

My stomach turned. Numbness spread in my arms and legs, and a lump formed in my throat. The air felt heavy—solid and unbreathable. "Excuse me," I whispered, hardly able to voice the words before I turned to retreat.

I needed to get away. I needed space. Air. Escape.

Chapter Twenty-Five

Winter Rose

RAE

Alia called after me over the fit of giggles that erupted from the girls, but the buzzing of my ears drowned out the noise, the music, the chatter. It was all too much. Gathering handfuls of tulle, I ran, without a plan, without direction. I pushed through the crowded room, bumping into a waltzing couple and causing them to stumble over their steps in my wake, then rushed toward the outskirts of the room. Couples clung to the walls, whispering intimately with one another, looking up from their conversation with intrigue as I barreled past. The glass door I approached held the promise of mountains, fresh air, and silence beyond it, and I did not hesitate to grasp the handle and throw it open.

Cold air smacked me in the cheeks, grounding me and calming the churning, nauseated feeling of disgust in my stomach. I ran, not caring that the wind stung my eyes and made them water with tears. Not considering that perhaps the tears had already been there—it was impossible to know for certain.

Gulping the frigid air to fill my lungs, I leaned into the wind and rushed toward the balcony. The wind played with my hair, defying even Elowynne's magic, but shock snapped me back to the moment. A powerful set of arms wrapped around me, warm and assuring. Steadying. "Not running away, are you? We have a deal."

My breath hitched in my throat before the anger burst freely from me. I looked up at Rydar, at the concerned expression beneath his windswept hair, and pushed against him with all my might. I would not allow the comforting scent of sandalwood and rain or the deep blue skies of his eyes to dampen my anger. Not now. I had a right to my anger, and it would not be quelled so simply.

"*You.*" I rounded on him, and I could see the flicker of surprise in the slight raise of his brow. "I cannot. Get me out. I—" But the words swirled incoherently in my head, fighting for attention, fighting to spill from my mouth all at once. "It's...too much. I'm starving. The food is probably poisoned. I can't tell if my stomach hurts because I'm hungry or dying. Brickert is horrible. Your brother is a nightmare. I miss Nell. These people just eat and eat and laugh and drink and have the audacity to believe they're being *helpful* by saving their waste? Do you even know what I've eaten my whole life to survive? Do you *know* what Goodvit is?"

Wind whistled through the monstrosity of feathers and spokes of gold that gripped my head. I tugged once more against the unrelenting ferocity of Elowynne's power, but the wretched thing would not budge. "And this thing! This *stupid* thing. Elowynne magicked it to my hair, and I swear I will shave my own head to remove it if I am not freed of it this instant!" I pulled fiercely at the plumes to no avail, screaming silently through gritted teeth in exasperation.

Rydar's eyes twinkled. He bit his lips, which turned downward to stifle a laugh. My eyes narrowed with contempt. *How dare you? None of this is funny.*

"You laugh? You mock me?" My voice simmered with murderous intent.

"No, I am—I do not know how to react. You are—" He paused.

"I am *what*, exactly?"

"Breathtaking, first and foremost." He took a step toward me, and for once, I felt his fortress begin to crumble. "And a bit frightening at the moment, if I'm to be honest. I would certainly not hand you a blade in this state."

I stepped closer to him, narrowing my eyes. "Then it's a good thing I still have your dagger."

His eyes sparkled with amusement and the knot in his throat bobbed downward as he swallowed. "Indeed. I'd advise you to use it against me—knock some sense back into me before I do something foolish."

"Foolish? Like what?" *Do it.*

"Something that can never happen." Rydar stepped so close, I could feel the heat of his body as easily as I could feel the warmth that crept to my cheeks—warmth that stemmed from anger and certainly *not* from unrelated causes.

I stared purposefully at his charcoal jacket, refusing to meet his eyes, performing a careful study of the silver embroidery across his broad shoulders, the high collar that framed how his Adam's apple moved, the intoxicating scent that always accompanied him. *Foolish, Rae. Foolish.*

"Here." A sensation of lightness washed over me as Rydar lifted the headdress from my hair. He stepped away, holding the cursed phoenix feathers in his hands, and they burst into flame, curling into nothing in his unflinching palms. It was a satisfying display of destruction, and I let the heat of the flames burrow into my heart.

"Thank you."

"You're welcome." A pause.

He walked over to the balcony, his firm footsteps the only sound to break the silence of the night. The moon glowed, bathing the snowy mountains in its light. Rydar reached for the swathes of white flowers that covered the balconies, the full, fluffy blooms that gave the appearance of snow gathered on the railings.

He returned to me with a single winter rose glimmering with frost. Tenderly, he placed the bloom next to the braided knot in my hair, and my skin prickled with tiny bumps as a shiver ran up my spine.

"There." He hesitated. "It's going to get worse before it gets better. For that, I am sorry."

I lifted my chin, reconsidering my rage with him in the silence. His piercing gaze swept over my face with the hint of a smile forming, but froze, lingering too long at my temple. His countenance darkened.

"How?" he grumbled, sweeping my hair back with calloused fingers. The stars themselves flickered in fear at the change of his mood. My lips parted as his hand cupped my cheek, and a gentle breeze stirred the charged air between us.

"Who did this? What happened?"

I raised an eyebrow. "I am competing to the death in the Timeless Trials, and you are worried about a little scratch?"

"Tell me."

I turned away, clenching my jaw, debating if I should answer. But I would not keep his secrets. Not from Rydar. "It was the high prince. I displeased him." I expected him to admonish me for saying the wrong thing, for being foolish, for putting myself at risk, but he did not.

The breath he drew was so deep, so encompassing, it felt like he filled his lungs with the essence of night and became the embodiment of darkness itself.

"I will find a way to fix this." His words were stilted, each spoken with great effort through clenched teeth, like thunderclouds rolling in before a storm. An acute pain accompanied his words, a burning sensation that made me gasp through parted lips in surprise, though he did not flinch. "It will not happen again. I assure you." He cupped my chin, eyes swirling with storm and pain and indecision.

An uproar from inside the ballroom broke the spell he held on me. The door to the balcony flew open, and Alia rushed out, all glitter and light and wild eyes. Rydar stepped away from me with haste, creating a distance between us as Alia rushed toward me.

"Oraelia. Come quick! Lio was right! The food!" Her eyes flickered briefly to Rydar, though she chose not to acknowledge him. She urgently grabbed my arm and pulled me behind her, luring me back to the commotion inside. "What are you doing with the fallen heir? Did he hurt you?" But there was no time to answer.

Chapter Twenty-Six

Deadly Hors D'Oeuvres

Rae

The room clamored with pandemonium. Through tulle and satin and bell-shaped skirts, I caught a glimpse of a form writhing on the floor, clutching desperately at his throat. Foam frothed in his mouth, spilling onto the floor in grayish bubbles as his eyes rolled back into his head. His limbs convulsed, and pain ran through his veins like molten metal. His agony rushed toward me, begging for relief, begging for healing. Begging for what I could not possibly give, and I winced at his pain, knowing I could not bring him mercy. I was ashamed; I didn't even know his name and couldn't read the gold letters on his lapel from where I stood.

The searing pain ended as quickly as it had exploded in his body, and he lay motionless on the floor, exhaling his last breath of life. The final breath created a vacuum of silence in the room—a hush so profound it stole the air away from us all. Not a soul stirred in the seconds that followed.

I glanced toward Alia and gulped. *Is this my fate? The most decadent food I have ever experienced in my life will ruthlessly destroy me?* If I thought I felt ill before, it was nothing compared to the writhing nest of snakes that squirmed inside me now. Beads of perspiration collected at my temples, and the room spun, leaving me feeling oddly detached from my surroundings. *I'm going to die. They've poisoned us.*

A light tinkle sounded above our heads. I looked up slowly and saw the source of the sound—the hourglass marked *Lorne* grew dark, no longer shining with light and glittering with gems like the others.

The crimson stones of Lorne's hourglass climbed lazily through the top of his glass, gathering into a ruby cloud that drifted over our heads. The room watched in silence as the cloud shimmered, then split in two. Half of the gems funneled into the largest hourglass, marked with *The Good Work*, and the other half dispersed among the remaining competitors. I watched the numbers tick upward around the room beneath each competitor's hourglass. Lorne's fell to zero, quivered, and dissolved before our eyes, leaving an empty space above. The room burst into applause at this bit of magic, but my eyes were glued to the Watchmen, who marched into the room to haul Lorne's body away.

The lights dimmed, and an eerie glow lit the walls. The sound of grinding stone filled the space, and a pedestal rose from the floor at the edges of the dance floor. Orman Gendrick bounded up the stairs that emerged from the platform, running a hand through his slicked-back hair, his grin at odds with the sinister glimmer of his eyes. "Another competitor, another brave soul, passed on to the Next Realm after a surprise trial."

Alia nudged me and mouthed, "The food. Poisoned." Then she jerked her head pointedly toward Lio in acknowledgment of his suspicions.

Orman folded his hands in front of his abdomen, bowing his head. "A pity...I had my time wagered on that one. But alas! Poor Lorne's luck failed him, and he ate the poisoned hors d'oeuvres hidden amongst the perfectly safe decoys. The rest of our competitors are safe, for now, though their number has dwindled to twenty."

My tension melted into relief. The other food had not been poisoned. *I'm still alive.*

"Lorne's time has ended, and his gift honors the Good Work of our honorable high king. May his time be everlasting!"

The crowd mumbled, "May his time be everlasting!" in return. My top lip curled upward in disgust, but I snapped my mouth closed as Orman's wicked gaze glanced in my direction.

"And now," he continued, deepening his voice for dramatic effect, "let us prepare for one last... special number. A waltz." A collective gasp of awe filled the room, and faces turned to one another, spellbound with anticipation. The competitors wore anticipation of a different variety, turning sickly green in the eerie dimness.

Orman's lopsided grin did nothing to settle the flurry of nerves that stirred in my belly. The nobility watched like predators stalking prey, enclosing the competitors and myself in the middle of the dance floor. Too late, I realized we were trapped.

"Competitors, in just a moment you will select your partners. Come now, to the center, we don't have much time. Do not worry, good lads and ladies; no harm will come to you, so do not be shy." I shared a glance with the other competitors, and questions darted silently between our eyes, but nobody was foolish enough to voice them.

The string quartet struck up a quiet, haunting tune with notes that floated up and down like the rise and fall of breaths. As if the room itself was breathing. Living. Changing. It was, in fact, rearranging itself before our eyes.

The circular pattern of stones on the floor glowed milky white as if the rock were hewn from the moon, seeping out of the stone like a flowing river of moonlight. Etchings surfaced on them, forming a dial of glowing symbols. I took it in rapidly, letting my eyes dart from one to the next—a phoenix, a serpent, scales, the Fates, a scythe, an hourglass, a wave, a tree, a dragon, a candle, a wolf, the sun. Twelve symbols for the twelve hours of the clock and a triangular plate rising tall and ominous in the center. A giant sundial.

"Good lads and ladies, may I present to you the sundial waltz! Competitors, when I call your name, please select your partner and your place on the dance floor. But be careful...where you choose to stand may make the difference between life and death."

I stared at the rough-hewn stones, pondering how they could possibly present a deadly threat but, at the same time, finding it hard to breathe. *Which of us is going to die?*

"Ruwe, you have the honor of going first. You have acquired the most donations. Go and choose your partner and your place. May time be on your side."

The audience applauded as he skulked across the floor, moving toward Alia's horrible friend, Janesta. She smiled coyly and passed the chalice she held to a friend at her side, then accepted Ruwe's hand and let him lead her to the sundial. He chose the scales.

"Oraelia, you're next, our second highest." *Second highest?* Surprise paralyzed me for a moment and I stared numbly at Orman. Was this meant to be my *advantage* for receiving the second-highest donations? Being put on the spot to make a decision with no context to inform my choice? *How very helpful.*

I had not expected to be second and was unprepared to select a partner. *Am I meant to dance with Flint?* Sweat dampened my brow as I searched the room for the high prince, but he was nowhere to be found. Was I to dance by myself? Ask one of the other lords to escort me? I brushed my shaking palms against the gauzy fabric at my hips, frozen by uncertainty. Light chuckles at my expense began to bubble around the room, urging me to break free from my inaction.

Rydar Barragan approached me, his strides even and commanding as he closed the space between us. His eyes focused on me with fierce intensity, glimmering to bring light to the grave expression on his face. He extended his hand to me with a slight bow at his waist. "He's not here. You're dancing with me."

Behind the bravado of his tone, his eyes spoke true, imploring me to take his hand, nervous I would deny him. Hesitantly, I placed my hand in his.

Rydar's fingers gripped mine tightly, pulling gently as a deep foreboding grew in my chest. I stalled, stiffening as his free arm wrapped behind the small of my back to steer me toward the dial. "The dragon, I believe, is best suited for the two of us." I nodded, trying not to let my fear show through my eyes, grateful I had not been made to decide on my own.

Gidian, Lio, Brickert, and Pell set into motion next, seeking their partners. Gidian stood on the other side of me with his partner, a slender woman with sleek obsidian hair. They bumped into us, taking the stone marked with a candle at my back.

Lio joined us, filling the space at the edge of the dragon's stone where we stood. Isolde laced her arm through Lio's, wearing a smile boasting of privilege. Lio's fingers tapped restlessly against his thigh, and we exchanged a fearful glance.

Orman continued to call out names until all twenty of us had selected a partner.

"Everyone must find a space on the dial. Yes, yes, squeeze in, Vance. There you go. There are twenty competitors left and only twelve hours on the dial. Do the math—some of you will have to share a space. Very good. In you go."

There was hardly enough space for all the competitors to squeeze on the dial, but the Watchmen herded us together, so close I could not step forward or backward without treading on toes. My heart rebelled against the proximity to so many others with wild, bucking jerks in my chest. I searched for an escape, but the guards blocked us, caging us with their menacing glares and readied rifles.

"What is happening? What are they going to do to us?" I asked Rydar nervously, craning my neck to see.

Ephemeral swatches of light bounced against the walls, disorienting flashes of color that rippled like moonlit water. Rydar lowered his head, whispering in my ear in a low grumble. "Remember how I said things would get worse before they got better? They're about to get worse. A lot worse. Follow my lead."

The grinding sound of friction between metal and stone silenced the chatter in the room, and everyone stood still, watching. Waiting.

Metal bars emerged from the edge of the dial, sliding into place to cage us in. The flames of my concern fanned into a full-blown wildfire of panic. A wave of awestruck gasps crested and fell in the room. The lords and ladies gawked at us, chattering enthusiastically, impervious to the fear filling the arena and gripping my throat with unrelenting fingers.

Orman waved his hand grandly at the top of his pedestal, glittering in a spotlight. "Good lads and ladies, it is now the hour for the last dance of the evening...the sundial waltz. Know that no harm will come to our good ladies—and lad," he amended as he turned and winked to Rydar, "though I cannot say the same for our dear competitors. May time be on your side, my friends." He chuckled lightheartedly. "The rules of the game are simple. When the music begins, you waltz. When it ends, you pray that you...do not." His eyes glinted with equal parts malice and delight.

Music lifted to the vaulted ceiling with a jolt of shrieking notes. Rydar turned me toward him, his eyes locked on mine, holding my gaze steady. "Trust," he mouthed. "Stay with me. No matter what happens."

CHAPTER TWENTY-SEVEN

The Sundial Waltz

RAE

The haunting melody commenced with a few lively strokes of strings, and so did the dancing. Moved by an invisible force, we began a slow waltz around the edges of the dial. A rotation with no end and no beginning, just circles in time through the haunting music. *One, two, three, one, two, three, one, two, three.* My eyes did not part from Rydar's, and I wondered if he felt the racing of my heart, the way it vehemently warred against every step of my feet. Steps that were not mine, steps out of my control.

We danced over each etching on the dial—dragon, candle, wolf, sun—fleeting glimpses of the symbols flashing at the edges of my vision. My body grew numb with each step, gripped by fear. What lurked beneath each note? What horrors lingered unseen? As we circled the dial, I caught a glimpse of Elowynne's smile, full of danger and guile.

The music halted abruptly, and the room plunged into darkness. The floor grew frigid, and I realized with horror that tendrils of icy light wrapped around my ankles, trapping me in place. A single chime, loud and true, rang so fiercely that I felt it deep in my bones. My heart seized with panic, but it jolted back to life as a beam of light illuminated the first hour. *When the music ends, pray you do not. So help me Fates.*

Like lightning, the serpentine etching at the first hour came to life, bursting from the ground in a flash of light. A collective cry rang out from the crowd, and Alia screeched, stumbling away from her partner and the snake in haste. It wound itself in tight coils around her partner, and his eyes bulged as his ribcage compressed, tighter and tighter until bone snapped and a horrid gurgle escaped from his purpled mouth. The victim's crushing pain washed over me, and I screwed my eyes shut, gripping Rydar's hands tighter and tighter until the agony of the man's last moments finally relented. His pain left my senses the moment his soul embarked on its journey to the Next Realm.

The serpent burst into a shower of sparks when I opened my eyes. It sparked and crackled in the air, then vanished, along with the man, into nothing.

I scrambled through my memory, trying to remember his name, but it would not come. My mind was irretrievably stuck on a continuous loop of horror, replaying the horrible sounds he had made at his end and the excruciating pain he had endured.

Applause surged. Alia's eyes met mine, her face blanched with terror save for the patch of gold across her cheek. The bars opened behind her, and she hesitated, her brows knitted together in concern. "Please do better than Pell," she whispered. A Watchman helped her down, and the bars slid back into place.

Pell. That was his name.

"Oh, a wonderful start! The first hour has struck! Pell has ended, poor dear. Did you see that serpent? So artistic—I have chills!" Orman chuckled, making a show of shivers running down his spine. "A round of applause for his contribution to the Good Work, good lads and ladies!"

My body trembled, and my mouth fell open, horrified by the raucous applause that followed the spectacle. A death. A horrific end. For entertainment. And I would be forced to endure the pain of each one, knowing I could do nothing to heal them until my own fate claimed me or they released us from this dance.

"Tick tock, 'round the clock!" Orman cheered as the musicians readied their instruments.

"Again?" I snapped my gaze toward Rydar.

The ice around my feet melted away, and my legs quivered with weakness. Rydar cupped my chin in his hand and gently turned my face toward him, willing me back with a grim nod of confirmation.

"Again. One for each hour. Trust."

Eleven more victims? My head shook so slightly, yet with such fervor that I felt like a leaf quivering on a branch in the wind. "No—"

"You promised."

I can't. I pushed away from his arms, but the melodious notes swelled again, this time faster and lighter as the crowd clapped to the beat of the music. Cheerful. Celebratory.

My feet waltzed around the ring against my will, ushered along by the notes of music. Round and round, we circled, pushed by the couples behind us, pulled by those before us. *Candle. Wolf. Sun. Phoenix.* The etchings glowed beneath our steps, waiting to strike, all except for the stone of the first hour. That stone now lay dormant, charred black as though struck by lightning.

I held my breath as we passed over the charred stone and moved over the second hour—the scales—praying to the Fates that the music would not fail me now. That it would carry me past the danger. But if the Fates had ever once answered my prayers, I would not be here at all.

The music came to an abrupt stop, and the tendrils of light gripped me. The scales of the second hour glowed beneath my feet.

No. Tears welled in my eyes as I panicked, jerking my knees against the restraints, trying desperately to free myself before the etching came to life. "Help me."

Rydar gripped my shoulders and shook me, forcing me back to him. "Trust." *Trust? You are letting me die here. Do something.* The lights dimmed, and the chimes began. *One. Two.*

I clenched my eyes shut, waiting for the scales of the second hour to come to life and strike me down. *Three.* My eyes snapped open, and the chimes continued... sinister, deafening clangs that shook the whole room. Ten in all.

The shrill scream erupted to my left, and I whipped my head around to see the ghostly wolf emerge from the etching, howling soulfully to the moon before it lunged at its victim. His partner stepped away, holding a hand to her chest as she watched the wolf shred the man with claws and gnashing teeth. I gasped and instinctually clutched a hand over my heart, as though the simple act could hold my body together when it felt as though it were being shredded to ribbons like the man whose pain I shared.

Blood splatter turned to sparks of gold, leaving only the charred stone of the wolf etching behind and the shell-shocked partner of the victim, who was quickly ushered away to safety.

The ice at my feet thawed, but my body remained frozen in fear. "Is it random?" I asked, horrified, though I guessed the answer. Breaths rushed in and out of my chest faster than the drumming of my heart.

"It is random. Twelve victims in all. Ten more." And he gripped my shoulders, setting me into motion, locking his eyes on mine. "Trust. Do not think about it. Focus on the dance, the music. Imagine it is only a dance between us. Can you do that?"

Are you actually mad? But his fingers brushed my cheek tenderly, and he smiled sadly when the music began anew, our feet falling into the *one, two, three, one, two, three* of the inescapable waltz. The room blurred, my senses dulled, and all I knew was Rydar's firm grasp at my back, the creases in his eyes that whispered stories I could not hear but felt somewhere in my soul, the thumping of his heart against mine, the power and assurance of his gaze. Everything else faded.

My consciousness felt murky, though fear still pounded warningly in my chest. As if I had just woken from a nightmare that I could not quite remember.

Rydar pressed my cheek into his chest when the music paused, and the chimes began, knocking on the door of my consciousness. The blast of light erupted, so close I could feel the rush of heat in the power that rose from the dial. The fiery dragon soared once above our heads, trailing tendrils of light from its mighty wings, then diving to claim its victim.

My hands covered my face, and I shrieked at its approach. Gidian, only steps away from me, screamed as the dragon clawed at his face, consuming him and the competitor next to him in a ball of flames. They both disappeared in a shower of fiery sparks that floated to the ground at their partners' feet. I felt the moment the dragon's flames torched its victims and the moment each left this realm for the next.

"Oh! A double! How grand. Four souls at rest, eight more to send to the Next Realm. Tick tock, 'round the clock!" Another chorus of cheers. More dancing. More death. An hourglass filled with flames. A sun that burst. A tree that battered. A wave that drowned. A scythe that sliced. I lost my sense of time and place with each death. Sometimes, one competitor. Sometimes, two at a time. Every etching that came to life ripped my heart from my chest until nothing was left but a trembling husk of myself, dancing, dancing, dancing. Stuck in a waltz I could not escape. Forced to endure the unfathomable, horrific pain and the agonizing helplessness to stop it.

Rydar's arms wrapped around me—it was just the two of us and the music and horrors.

It was too much. "I cannot do this." The words slipped from me. My voice cracked with fear, and hot tears ran down my cheeks. My nerves seemed frayed down to the very core, and I feared I would never recover from the trembling weakness that spread to every corner of my body.

"You must. There is only one more." But I could see in his eyes that he was hurting.

"Please."

Rydar guided me forward through the notes and gasps of awe, the cheers, and the laughter. "I cannot rescue you from this. You must see it through." Pain seeped into his eyes, and he rested his chin on my head, hiding his expression from me. His voice was raw, his words strained.

"Then let me rescue myself. Let me go. Please." *Let me run far from here and never look back. I will not die this way. I will not let my death be their entertainment.*

I pushed against his chest, defying the pull of the dance, fighting the steps my feet could not resist. But the dragon on my arm reminded me that even if I could break away, any hope for escape was pointless. I was stuck—the Next Realm called to me no matter what I did...it was simply inescapable.

I could try to evade it, but it would always catch up with me.

Sun. Phoenix. First hour. Second hour. Third hour.

Softly, as though he didn't intend to utter the words at all, Rydar whispered. "I cannot rescue you, but I will protect you, even from yourself." He held me tightly, pushing me along. "They will kill you if you flee, and I cannot let you go to your death. I know this is painful to witness. It is horrific. But I will endure it with you to keep you safe. And you must endure it to stay alive. Stay with me."

You know nothing of my pain. I closed my eyes, unable to tolerate a moment longer. My mind had turned the quartet's melody into a mere shadow of the music, a warped cacophony of noise, full of clockwork and sighs and unsettling shrieks. Three etchings still glowed amongst the charred remains of the sundial—scales, candle, phoenix. One of them would kill me.

The music ended for the last time, and the tendrils of light gripped my ankles above the candle, the ninth hour. I buried my face into Rydar's chest, allowing the tears to flow freely, feeling each chime of the clock echo through my soul. Counting. Dreading. *Nine chimes. Please no—*

Ten chimes. Eleven. Twelve.

Emotion rushed from me like a tidal wave crashing onto the shore—overwhelming and all-consuming. I did not know what unfolded as the last hour struck...only that the excruciating pain took far too long to extinguish before the victim met his end. My brain paid no heed to the screams, blood, or cheers that rose to the vaulted ceiling.

When the bars slid away at last, I did not hesitate. My feet, restored to my own control, marched with purpose and haste, carrying me as far away from the wretched ballroom as possible. I would not do this anymore...I would not play these games. I could not watch the other competitors die one by one and hope that Rydar would save me from something he most certainly could not.

I would rather die on my terms, trying to escape this hell, than wait for it to destroy me. Right after I found a corner to vomit the ball of writhing snakes from the pit of my stomach.

The little shadow dragon roared back to life in my arm, slashing me with its sharp claws of fury. A warning. I gasped, closing the fingers of my other hand around the searing pain, and continued to run. Promises be damned.

Chapter Twenty-Eight

So Much Blood

RAE

What is your plan, Rae? Truth be told, I had none. Agony lanced down my arm as the shadow dragon snapped at me, warning me to be sensible. A stitch in my side also demanded my attention...It was too difficult to think of a plan through the pain and panic. But I fled down the corridor, discarding the golden shoes that clacked noisily against the marble floors. They landed behind me with a muffled *thunk*. I would not regret their absence.

I didn't know where I was running to, but I stormed down the passage, letting the moonlight guide my steps, grounding myself with the chill of the marble beneath my soles. If I could only find the entrance hall—*And what? What, Rae? Run through the snow and freeze to your death? Do not be a fool. Think.*

I did not get very far before his voice landed like an arrow in my heart. "Oraelia, wait!"

No, I had to escape—I had to.

But his long strides caught up to me, and his arms wrapped firmly around my waist, drawing me toward him in a tight embrace. He buried his head in the space between my neck and shoulder and redoubled his grasp when I fought against his hold. "Oraelia, stop. Please." The brush of his hair along my shoulder sent shivers down my spine.

"The oath..." he grumbled. "You cannot flee. It will kill you." And true to his words, the shadowy dragon snapped viciously, warning against the flutter of my heart and my impulse to run.

"Unhand me, or I will kill you." I did not mean it, but I nonetheless snapped at him like a caged animal. I feared what I would do if he did not release me—my heart pounded wildly in my chest, panicked, savage, ready to lash out.

"Oraelia, please. Why must you make it impossible to protect you?" His arms loosened so he could turn me to face him, but I would have none of his affection. None of his games...not after the horrors I had just witnessed. My hand found the dagger at my thigh beneath the layers of tulle, and I slashed at the air as I spun away, holding the blade before me as my chest rose and fell with each shallow breath.

His eyes flickered down to the dagger in my hand, then to his chest, and I felt the sharp sting of my handiwork; his pain echoed in my own flesh.

Shit.

He showed no outward indication of his discomfort nor fear in his expression, but the faintest hint of surprise surfaced in the slight raise of his brow and parted lips. He placed a palm over his heart, where red seeped through a gash in the fabric of his jacket.

Oh. Regret flooded through me as blood coursed powerfully through my veins. My breath caught, trapped in my throat. "I'm sorry. I'm so sorry. I—"

The dagger clattered on the marble floor as I moved toward him, holding my hands over his, already slick with blood. So much blood. *What have you done, you fool?* My heart pounded furiously in my chest, and my limbs quivered with numbness. *Heal him.*

No, I cannot. He will know. They will know. What will they do to you if they find out? Horrified, I looked up at him, but his eyes searched mine with care, and he wrapped his fingers gingerly around mine.

"*Never* apologize for defending yourself," he began, his words rumbling ardently from someplace deep within his chest. "Even from me." He swallowed, then released my hands and stepped away. "Especially from me."

A heavy weight settled on my shoulders, and a rock lodged itself in my throat. I watched the blood seep through his shirt and felt the sting of his concealed pain with my gift. I desperately wanted to heal him, to make it right. I looked deep into his eyes. *Can I trust you?*

I wanted to. Despite his insistent warnings and distance and grumbling personality, I wanted to believe he meant to help me...that he was on my side. But still, I hesitated.

Instead, I ripped the fabric from the bottom layer of my dress. He watched me with intrigue as I wound the silk underlayer of my skirt into a thin strip. His expression faltered, but he did not resist when I pulled his shirt away to examine the damage I had inflicted. The cut was shallow, but blood spilled from it in angry red tributaries.

I'm sorry. Carefully, I placed my hands on his chest and trailed past his ribcage, pulling the ends of the makeshift bandage around his back and tying it behind his shoulder blades. My arms wrapped around him as I pulled the bandage tightly enough to stem the bleeding. The moment my hands touched his bare skin, he gasped, though not from pain. It was my touch that shattered the walls of his fortress.

"You'll need to see a medic, but this should help," I whispered, realizing suddenly how close, how intimate the moment between us felt.

"Thank you," he murmured finally, then cleared his throat. "Forgive me. I am...not accustomed to being cared for."

The way his eyes locked on mine when I pulled away stirred something inside me, and we stared at one another for far too long, neither moving nor breathing. He took me in his arms, and fire flared in his gaze just before his lips pressed against mine. I gasped and relaxed into his hold until the world melted away, and all that remained was his hand behind my head, his body pressed flush to mine, the warmth of his lips claiming, exploring, tasting. My heart pounded *more, more, more.*

As quickly as we came together, he pushed me aside. "No," he growled, his breaths heavy and strained. "This is—" He held up a hand as I moved toward him. "No. We cannot."

"What are you so afraid of?" I demanded, the pitch of my voice as heightened as my pulse. Was he angry with me still? Did he not feel the same pull I felt between us, the one that compelled us together?

No matter how stupid and ill-advised it may be, it was there. I could feel it every time he entered the room. Every time light sparked through the dark storm clouds of his eyes. I could feel the magnetism between us that connected me to him even when we did not physically touch. The hyperawareness of his proximity sent ripples of warmth through my skin if he so much as looked my way. But he was one of them. And we could not be friends.

"Please. Forget this happened. I am protecting you," he breathed.

Protecting me? "Perhaps you should concentrate your efforts on protecting me from the tournament, not from yourself. I am capable of making my own decisions, and I am certainly capable of defending myself from the likes of you if I want to."

"Then you should want to."

"But I do not."

He leaned against the wall, surveying me carefully and remaining silent. Infuriatingly silent. *You have nothing to say?*

He made no indication of a response.

Fine. I have a lot to say.

"And what was that? In the ballroom? I could have died... I could have... Did you see what happened to the others? Any time—any hour—it could have been me. And then what? You would fight a lightning bolt...magic.. .thing and try to save me?" *Smooth, Rae.* "Why did you not save any of the others if you are so brave? Why me?"

I glared at him, demanding an explanation, pretending I had not just made an enormous mess of my words. Pretending his constant efforts to distance himself did not make the air difficult to breathe, and my brain wasn't muddled with too many tangled thoughts.

With each passing second, he retreated, drawing up his walls and growing more distant. "The hours were random, my confidence was not," he hedged. So much was left unsaid in his gaze, and I wanted to shake him free of whatever fears gripped his tongue.

I crossed my arms protectively across my chest. "Well, your confidence does little to inspire mine."

He ran a hand through his black mane, attempting to soothe his frustration. "It was carefully planned. Everything. You were never in danger."

I huffed with indignation, letting my tone darken with bitterness. "I was never in danger? Really? Everyone was dying, Rydar. Forgive me for fearing for my life." My pulse pounded furiously in the palms of my balled fists, and I imagined his heart beating as tumultuously as mine. I wanted him to react, to feel as deeply as I did, but I could see him slipping away. I clenched my jaw and glared up at him.

He flinched, and a flash of sadness darkened his eyes. "What would you have me do, Oraelia? What did *you* do?"

Reason blurred, and my words became a jumbled mess on my tongue. "What did I do? I—I was in danger."

"We are all in danger," he responded gravely. "I am doing everything in my power to keep you safe. To keep us safe." His eyes softened in an apology. He exhaled slowly, drawing up the walls of his fortress and closing the gate. "Come. It has been a difficult day. Let me walk you to your room. You'll need rest. Tomorrow—"

But he froze, his eyes widening with fear at the sound of footsteps. His nostrils flared wide with the sharp inhale he took, letting it linger too long in his chest. The strained exhale that followed contained no words, but I could hear the curse in his breath all the same.

CHAPTER TWENTY-NINE

She Is Mine

RAE

"**R**ydar! Is the ball over, then? What did I miss? How did it go?"

Even through the slur of his words, I knew the voice. A shiver ran down my spine as I turned to face him. He staggered down the hallway, smiling brightly but not bright enough—never enough to light the darkness in his eyes.

"Ah...you're still alive?" he asked, noticing me as his head swayed in my direction.

"Happy to see you too, Your Highness." I curtsied with a sneer, not bothering to hide my dislike or my soured mood. *What in the flaming fire of Hell are you doing with your sarcasm, Rae?*

Flint wrapped an arm around me with debonair confidence, and my shoulders cringed, receding from his invasion of my space. He reeked of the sharp stench of bourbon, and his eyes roved up and down my figure, undressing me with a sense of ravenous entitlement. Rydar's jaw clenched.

"Come with me," Flint spoke into my ear, his voice husky and slurred, as though he had intended to whisper but lacked the necessary finesse in his current state. "If you're going to be around until the next trial, we may as well see what kind of—magic—we can create together."

I pushed him away, disgusted. "I will not go anywhere with you." My eyes darted toward Rydar, who had grown completely rigid save for the ticking vein in his temple.

Flint's beady black eyes flashed with anger, and he gripped my wrist with too much force. "You will do as you're told. You're mine."

"I belong to no one." I stared into his eyes, challenging him. His eyes flickered down to my wrist, landing with surprise on the dragon that soared the length of my arm, driven by the agitation that surged in my veins. *I guess Rydar's illusion wore off.*

"What is this?" His voice turned heavy. Poorly controlled rage bubbled to the surface, seeping into the inky black of his eyes.

I ripped my hand away. "It does not concern you."

"Flint, come. You've had a bit too much to drink. You will make a fool of yourself. Oraelia was just going to her room to rest before the next trial." Rydar moved toward me, reaching for my elbow.

The high prince swayed as he watched us, and a moment of clarity cleared the unfocused drunkenness from his eyes.

"This was your doing, Rydar?" A smile uncurled to reveal his teeth, brimming with unmistakable wickedness. "If I didn't know better, I'd say you've grown fond of her. I knew it. The high king will be so keen to meet her."

I expected Rydar to deny our oath, but he did nothing of the sort. Instead, he regarded me with coldness in his eyes, looking at me as though I were— nothing. A chill ran down my spine, though not with the same rush of longing as before. The Rydar I had encountered earlier was now buried deep inside this emotionless, stoic shadow of a man.

He returned his gaze to the high prince, speaking coolly, "There is nothing to tell the high king...do not be a fool by distracting him with your nonsense, brother. I did what was required to persuade her, to address her objections. You wished for her to take part in the Trials, and I ensured it would happen. That is all."

That is all. The dismissive tone and emptiness of his gaze threatened to carve my heart right from the walls of my chest. I glared at him, overcome by the sudden rush of indignation. *Is that really all, Rydar? And that kiss we shared? That was nothing, too?*

But truly, I had been the one to start that...and he had pushed me away so quickly. I panicked, feeling my chest grow warm and uncomfortable as I replayed the scene in my mind. Maybe I had misread him. Maybe I misjudged his feelings for me. Perhaps I *was* nothing. I willed him to look at me, to look me in the eye and tell me that there was nothing more between us, but his face remained vacant and firmly directed at Flint.

Flint's eyes narrowed with suspicion, then the corner of his mouth twitched upward into a lopsided grin. "Oh, you *have* grown fond of her. The high king will be delighted!" My gaze darted between Flint and Rydar, watching the tension grow between the two brothers.

Rydar took one controlled step toward Flint. "Do not be ridiculous. I am not a fool."

"Nor am I." Flint grinned so wickedly that my lip curled in disgust just before he turned toward me. Flint pressed his mouth to mine, holding me close as he tugged on my lip, possessive, assertive, claiming. I shoved him away, tossing him a look of utter revulsion.

The high prince laughed diabolically under his breath, glancing back to inspect Rydar's reaction. Every muscle in Rydar's body had grown tense, and I feared he would strike the high prince down with naught but the fury of his eyes. Flint smirked. "I knew it, you fool. But she is *mine*. Do not forget."

I was livid, and I rounded on him, not stopping to think. "I told you, I belong to no one. I am not his, and I am certainly not yours. Don't *you* forget."

The hungry entitlement of his gaze flashed to anger, and he raised his hand again to strike me. I was ready this time. My fingers wrapped around his wrist, gripping fiercely, unashamedly, as I pushed him to the wall.

"Never. Strike. Me. Again." I said the words slowly, deliberately, letting my anger seep into each syllable that slipped between my grinding teeth. When I released him, the high prince glowered at me, and I glared back, waiting for him to strike. *Try me.*

The doors to the ballroom at the end of the passage opened wide, and the crowd moved into the hall.

Alia's crown of roses bobbed through the sea of people, and her eyes brightened with delight as she saw me. "Oraelia! There you are. I was worried." She curtsied politely to the high prince and nodded curtly to Rydar before linking her arm in mine and steering me away. *Bless her.* "Goodnight, gentlemen. If you'll excuse us. She's coming with me."

CHAPTER THIRTY

Ice Adder

RAE

"Where are we going?" I whispered.

She tossed a glance over her shoulder, but did not slow her steps for my benefit when she saw me lagging behind.

"The dark circles under your eyes are catastrophic, and you look like you haven't eaten in ages." The light of the torches along the wall danced in the smile of her eyes. "Lucky for you, I know the best cook in all of Orogi." Her dress swished at her ankles, glittering in the torchlight so that each gem held the essence of fire as she rounded the corner.

"I saw what you did to the high prince, by the way. Impressive." She winked, then grew serious. "But stupidly dangerous. Your room's just up here."

When we arrived at my chamber, a wave of sickening unease banished any hope I had for rest. Someone had broken open the door, leaving the handle askew between the splintered pieces of wood.

My heart raced as I opened the door, the hinges making a terrible noise all too similar to the screeching music of the string quartet.

The room was in complete disarray. Shattered glass littered the floor, and feathers drifted lazily in the draft of the broken window. Words glistened on the walls in red paint, still wet and dripping. *Time's up.*

Alia let out a gasp, her eyes widening as she inspected the room. My limbs felt numb, and I gingerly stepped into the chamber, pushing the broken glass away with my feet and regretting my lack of footwear in an unexpected turn of events.

"Why?" I asked, gaping at the disorder.

A scuffling sound and flash of movement made my heart jump. A silvery-white serpent darted out of the shadows, slithering toward me through the rubble, lunging to attack. Alia seized my arm and pulled me backward until I stumbled over my feet. Glass shards bit my bare soles, and I cried out in pain. Alia slammed the door shut, and the sound boomed throughout the hall.

"What was *that*?" I asked, whirling to face Alia.

A look of great alarm had thoroughly dismantled Alia's usual carefree charm. "Nothing good." She grabbed my wrist and dragged me away from the chamber. "A reminder that you have more to worry about than the Trials."

So many questions warred in my mind, but the pain in the soles of my feet made it nearly impossible to sort through them. "Alia...wait. What—"

"I knew the girls would be vicious, but an ice adder?" She shook her head, shuddering. "One strike from those fangs, and your heart will freeze within seconds. You can't stay there. Come to my room."

Alia peeked around the corner at the bend in the hallway. As we fled, a trail of crimson footprints marked the ground beneath the whisper of our skirts. "The other ladies...they're ruthless. They're desperate, and you're the biggest threat to their plans."

She pulled me into her chambers and locked the bolt over the door. My head spun. "Plans? What plans?"

Alia ignored me, lost in her own thoughts. She paced around the bathing chamber adjoined to her bedroom, her footsteps echoing through the walls as she muttered anxiously to herself. She poked her head around the door. "Come on. A bath will do you good...wash some of the grime away."

A lovely sentiment, but misguided. There were not enough bubbles or warm water in the world to soothe my racing heart. "Alia—stop. What is going on?"

Alia rushed about, always in motion. "Nothing we can't sort out. Enemies around every corner. Plenty of people who'd like to see you Retired. No worries. You're going to win. You have to." Her voice was slightly frantic as she grabbed bottles of oils and salts from the shelves along the wall.

Rushing water gushed from a copper faucet into a freestanding tub at the center of the room. Tendrils of steam drifted in the air, dancing before the breathtaking view of snow-covered mountains against a velvet sky.

Bubbles climbed over the edge of the tub as Alia tipped a violet liquid into the water. She passed a folded, white, fluffy towel into my arms. "Do you need help, or should I go? I am sorry—" She paused, slightly scattered. "Perhaps I'll go grab some food?"

I wrinkled my face, dizzied by her antics. "Alia—"

"Of course. I will leave you to relax."

Utterly distracted, she made her way toward the door. "Alia, wait." I needed answers. I glimpsed my reflection in the mirror as I turned my head to where she had paused at the door. Haunted eyes stared back at me in the mirror. Trails of makeup pooled beneath my lashes and my shoulders slumped forward with fatigue.

"Alia...can you help with my hair? And the dress?" *And maybe some answers?*

Alia smiled, coming back from her thoughts. "Of course." She pulled over a chair and motioned for me to sit in front of the looking glass. Her hands worked through the knot at the back of my head, pulling the pins that held my braids in place. "What happened to your headdress?"

Oh. "I uh—"

"The rose is beautiful, though," she interrupted, not caring to hear the explanation. "Simplicity. Not something you often see around here."

"I noticed."

Each pin she pulled from my hair released a bit of the tension that throbbed in my head. "You need to be careful," she finally whispered, placing the pins in a heap on the marble shelf. "I don't want to see you get hurt."

"Alia, I'm competing to the death in the Timeless Trials. You're going to see me get hurt."

Her brows pulled together in a grimace as she pulled the last pins from my hair and set them aside. "Don't be ridiculous. You're going to win, remember?"

I grumbled vaguely, and Alia scowled at the dubious expression on my face.

"I mean it," she said. "I need you to win. You've got to be more careful. No more riling up the high prince, alright?"

I scoffed, throwing a crumpled expression her way. "I can make no promises on that front."

"And stay away from Rydar," she continued as if she hadn't heard me. "Broody nightmare, that one."

The mere thought of his name sent a pang of pain through my chest, but Alia pretended not to notice my reaction. "Just...be careful around him. He's got quite a reputation. And not the good kind."

She loosened the knot of hair at my back and unraveled the braids so my waves cascaded freely over my shoulders. "What did he do to you?" I asked.

"Nothing. He's hardly ever spoken to me."

She let out a sigh, unsure whether she should explain further, but her voice was filled with enthusiasm as she went on. "They say he's a murderer...killed the high king's almatae, and he never forgave him for it. Even denounced him as heir. The king keeps a close watch on him now. Makes him stay in line. Not someone you want to cross."

My heart raced uncomfortably as she combed her fingers through my hair. *Only you would fall for a murderer, Rae. No, stop that. You are not falling for anyone.* "What's an almatae?" *A safe question.*

Alia glanced at me as though in surprise. "It means 'the one my soul loves'. Darikonian, I think. Not a common thing, of course, but those who find their almatae are soul-bound for eternity. The truest, deepest love. The king hasn't been the same since he lost his."

I tried to imagine Darikona's location on the world map I had scoured over in my pilfered books—the ones hidden beneath my bed that I would read late into the night—but my memory of them was hazy. The pain in my heart deepened as I thought of home, of Nell and Pa.

"He's handsome, though, isn't he?" Alia watched my response carefully in the mirror.

I suppressed the warmth that flushed in my cheeks. "I suppose he is, yes." *Stop it, Rae. Forget him.*

Alia smirked, unconvinced by my lackluster effort to feign indifference. "All the ladies fawn over him, of course. They've all tried to win his affections, but he's a bit of a loner... doesn't give anyone a chance."

Yes, that sounded like him. I assumed his attitude toward me was not any different from how he acted with others. The thought settled uncomfortably in the pit of my stomach, but I brushed the hurt aside.

Alia continued, "And then you come in and have the high prince *and* Rydar taking notice of you...some of the ladies are jealous."

I snorted. *Jealous of me? I would switch positions in a heartbeat.* "What about you?" I smirked at Alia, wondering if she, too, had adopted that attitude.

She laughed in earnest. "Fates, no!" She leaned over and whispered conspiratorially, "You can't tell anyone, but I've already found love."

Her confession surprised me, but she didn't offer an immediate explanation.

"Then why bother with all of this?" I motioned to the air in front of me, gesturing at nothing but hoping she understood. The Trials. The other ladies. The drama. "Why don't you just marry the person you love and be done with this?"

"Because I can't marry her."

Oh.

Alia grew uncharacteristically bitter, pulling the pins from her own hair now. "Stupid, really. It's not like the two of us can overpopulate the district...But if they ever caught us..." She shuddered.

She grew quiet as she scooped the handful of pins from the marble counter and placed them in a jar. "Anyway, the other ladies see you as a threat. You're standing between them and the high king's blessing for marriage this year."

I blinked in surprise, certain my bewilderment showed in my furrowed brows and parted lips.

She looked at me, affronted by my ignorance. "The high king has to approve any weddings in Lustro. Can't have too many of us marrying and growing families each year...it would get crowded. There are limits. The Pacers and immortality can be a blessing and a curse, you know. Long life is a blessing, but it comes at the cost of managing overpopulation and finite resources."

Oh. My face screwed up even further. "The Pacers are nothing but a curse in Nox. Most of us run out of time before we've truly lived."

Her brows pulled together in a grimace. "Of course. I'm sorry. I didn't think."

She twisted my hair, busying her hands even when nothing was left to do. "You have the most beautiful hair, by the way. Natural too? Promise me you won't get any enhancements after you win. I never see this color…like the gilded rooftops in Lustro." She held a handful up to her face and let it lay over her own head. We both laughed at the horrified grimace on her face. "No. Definitely not. Platinum is my color."

She sighed, crossing the room to the door. "Go. Enjoy your bath and get some rest. I'm going to go see Nadera. Best cook in Orogi. You'd love her."

My stomach grumbled at the thought. "Alia, are you sure it's alright to stay here?"

"Of course. You're safe with me. Just don't answer the door for anyone. I'll be back."

"No, I mean…will she mind?"

Her eyes wrinkled with disbelief, and she chuckled. "Nadera? Don't be ridiculous—she's my almatae. The one my soul loves. There is nothing and no one who could come between us." She shrugged and added as an afterthought, "No offense."

None taken. I smiled as she walked out of the room, then slipped out of the tulle and silk and into the warm bath until my fingers shriveled and the water grew cold.

Alia had not returned yet when I left the bathing chambers. My body felt drowsy from soaking so long in the hot water, and I was drawn to the inviting daybed beneath her star-filled window. I nestled into the soft, comforting covers and felt myself drift off to sleep.

The sound of an aggressive fist pounding on the door jolted me awake. I held the blankets close to my body, my hands curling tightly in fear. "Alia?" I whispered, but I knew in my heart it was not her.

CHAPTER THIRTY-ONE

Just Getting Started

RAE

I sat upright in bed, praying to the Fates that the visitor would leave, but the knocking only grew more frantic the longer it went unanswered. The heap of blankets in Alia's bed stirred.

A bedraggled mess of platinum hair popped up from the covers, and she rubbed her fists over groggy eyes, swiping her hands over the large reddened birthmark that stretched from the bridge of her nose to her cheekbone, now that she had removed the golden paint from the ball. Her eyes met mine, and panic pushed away the clouds of sleep in her irises as the knocking intensified.

"Hide," she mouthed, gesturing with flapping arms toward her wardrobe. She jumped out of bed and pulled a robe tightly around herself, shivering from either nerves or the chill of the morning. I pulled the wardrobe door closed just as she unlocked the bolt to her door. The visitor stumbled clumsily into the room.

"Have you seen Rae? She's missing. Someone said she might be with you? Oh Fates..." Lio's eyes darted nervously around the chamber, bouncing between the bed, the windows, the armchairs...finally landing on the rumpled sheets of the daybed. His head whipped back toward Alia.

"Is she here? What did you do to her?" He paused on Alia's face, and his brows raised with surprise as he truly saw her for the first time. "What happened to your face?"

"What happened to your manners?" Alia crossed her arms coolly over her chest and tilted her chin upward, daring him to continue.

Lio's gaze quickly recoiled and his lanky frame compressed until he was several inches shorter. "Sorry."

"I happen to think it's beautiful and unique," Alia stated with an edge to her voice.

"Oh. Yes. It's—" Lio gaped, trying and failing to produce words to appease her. I opened the wardrobe door, aiming to dissipate the uneasy silence he had created.

"Lio."

His chest swelled with relief when he saw me, and he rushed toward me, enveloping me in a surprising, though not unwelcome, embrace.

"You're okay! They told us to get ready for training and evaluation, so I went to find you, but your room was a wreck. And after what people have been saying...I was so worried. Is it true? Did you really stand up to the high prince?"

I threw a fiery glance at Alia, miffed by her indiscretion, but she lifted her hands in defense and shook her head. "I said nothing. Promise. People saw when we left the ball." *Oh, wonderful. The high prince will love that.*

He smiled conspiratorially. "So you *did*, you wonderful thing. What was it like? You're either a fool or the bravest person I've ever met, but I like you, Rae. He's *terrible*, you know. Maybe even worse than my father. You are...something." Lio's mouth flapped faster than a frostbird's wings when he spoke, until his cheeks turned red from lack of air and he needed to pause to draw a breath.

He went right back to speaking, and I wondered if he'd drain the room of air if he continued blabbering in such a way. "Then I heard Isolde and Janesta—something about an ice adder and devious plans to sabotage you and *helfyre*, Rae." The memory of the silvery white ice adder flashed in my mind, and I shuddered but pushed it aside. "You've got to be careful. These people are frightening."

Despite it all, I laughed. "What did you expect, Lio? These people revel in watching us die. They're not our friends." Lio pulled his lips inward and clenched them closed, looking even more terrified than before, and Alia's eyes filled with hurt, but I brushed aside the regret that accompanied my words. There were more important matters to attend to.

"So, when is this training? Where?" Nerves fluttered in my stomach. *What are they training us for? Will they punish us for arriving late?*

Lio paced the floor, letting his feet thud heavily against the ground. "I don't know. I don't know how to fight Rae. I'm scared. They said there'll be a new Trial every day until they have a winner...they're just getting started. They're whispering about swords and beasts, and I don't know what I got myself into. I mean...I knew I came here to die, but it's all happening so...*fast*."

"Lio, calm yourself and eat something before you shake the house apart with your stomping," Alia chided from the blue satin chaise. She pulled berries from a vine on a tray, popping them into her mouth while watching us, the crease in her brow growing deeper with each step Lio took. Lio paused long enough to look with longing at the assortment of cheeses, bread, and fruit on the glass tray, then resumed his nervous pacing.

"Oh, for Fate's sake, it's not poisoned, Lio," said Alia, rolling her eyes, then chucking a muffin at him. He fumbled with it, trying to keep it from bouncing between his hands, all the while cursing until he managed to hold it firmly.

"*I'm* not one of the bad guys," she said pointedly, glaring at me with hurt in her eyes. I tilted my head with an apologetic shrug.

"Thanks," Lio mumbled, shoving half of the muffin into his mouth at once. I picked up a dense slice of bread from the tray that smelled sweetly like fruit, though I could not identify which type. I bit into the edge and chewed slowly, using the time to organize my thoughts into coherent words.

"Did you hear anything about the next trial? You said they were training? Shouldn't we go?"

"Rae, what am I going to do at training? I don't know how to fight!" He motioned to his lanky frame as if that were a sufficient explanation. In his defense, his bones did look breakable...I reckoned it wouldn't take much to snap them. I shook the intrusive thought from my mind.

"Anyway, I was more worried about you...had to find you."

"Well, you found me. We should go." I shoved the rest of the bread into my mouth and grabbed his hand. When I made to move toward the door, Lio didn't budge.

His expression withered, and his eyes drooped. "What's the point? I'm never going to win. The winner will be someone brave and strong. Like you."

My stomach dropped. "Don't say that. Never say that."

"Well, it's true!" he insisted with a frown.

I shook my head. I knew neither of us had a real chance in the Trials, but I tried to soothe him all the same. "Lio, you are brave. You're smart, and you notice things that others don't. You're the only one who noticed the poisoned hors d'oeuvres, you genius!"

A laugh shattered the look of consternation on his face, but it was laced with bitterness. "I'm no genius. With seven mischievous younger siblings and a father who only cares about finding his next drink, noticing things is a survival skill."

I smiled sadly but shoved him in the shoulder. "No, I mean it! I'd be in the Next Realm already if you hadn't intervened. I can help you with the fighting. We'll look out for each other. We can... we can do this, Lio."

"Rae, only one of us gets to walk away at the end. It can't be both of us. But it should be you. You're brave enough to stand up to them—" The pain in his eyes threatened to cleave my heart in two.

"I'm not letting you give up that easily. Come on." But when I tugged on his arm, Lio remained rooted to the spot. His haunted eyes grew melancholy with understanding, pleading with me to listen.

"Just promise me...if I don't make it—"

"You'll make it."

He shrugged noncommittally. "Well, if I don't...Promise me you'll help them if you win—my mum and my brothers and sister. Get them away from my dad. If you can stand up to the high prince of Orogi, my dad should be no problem for you. That's more than I can say for myself."

A flood of emotions welled in my chest, and words that refused to form stuck in my throat. Losing Lio was not something I was willing to consider. But I needed him strong. I needed him to try, so I nodded. "Right now, I'm going to take care of *you*. Come on, I'm teaching you the basics, and then we're figuring out how to survive this."

CHAPTER THIRTY-TWO

The Enemy's Weakness

RAE

We rushed toward the doors of the training hall. Lio's sweat plastered his messy hair to his forehead, and a sheen of perspiration glistened on his skin. A welt formed on his thigh where he had impressively managed to strike himself with his own elbow. He was far from a natural talent...if anything, he got steadily worse with practice, but Alia's cheers and encouragement improved his mood until he stood a little taller, a little calmer. Of course, Alia's room now required a considerable amount of repairs and a whole new wardrobe—Lio had splintered the wood with his shoulder—but our training session had been at the least worthwhile to restore an ounce of his confidence.

Lio nodded at me and we pushed the doors open together. They groaned on their hinges as they swept forward, announcing our entry to the room. Fortune was on our side, as most of the occupants were already too deep in their training exercises and scuffles to notice our arrival. My eyes immediately landed on Rydar, hypnotized by the muscles rippling beneath his shirt with each precise, controlled movement. "You're gaping." Lio nudged me in the ribs and I snapped my mouth shut. *Is my attraction to him that obvious?* I resolved to keep my inconvenient emotions in check.

My attention turned toward the pinks, blues, and greens that drifted between the matches like petals caught in spring air. The ladies wore full, elegant skirts that swayed with their hips as they weaved amongst the competitors carrying water, towels, and an abundance of flirtatious giggles. Janesta ambled slowly about the room, lacing arms with a devastatingly beautiful brunette in a burgundy gown. Isolde dabbed blood from a scratch on Vance's brow, and her cold eyes locked with mine as she whispered into his ear. *The snake.*

I narrowed my gaze, but Orman Gendrick stepped in front of me, towering with self-importance and blocking her from my view. "You're late." His dark eyes swept over Lio, then me. His prominent brow furrowed as he considered us with disdain.

His assessment of us elicited a grunt of disapproval, but he steered us to the center of the room. "Your loss. We only have a couple hours of time to train, then you'll be suited up for your next Trial." A malicious smirk grew on his face, and I had the uncomfortable sensation that he was imagining which gruesome death would call me to the Next Realm, but he seemed to catch himself and snapped out of the daze.

"Mind yourself. More citizens of Lustro are arriving as we speak for the next attraction... they've paid good time to be here today. Don't disappoint them. Do well and earn their favor for the rest of the Trials. You'll need it." The way his eyes blazed with anticipation did nothing to soothe my nerves. "Just waiting on the arrival of one last special guest, then back to the games we go." He winked, and his eyes darted tellingly toward the wall of windows on the far side of the room. I studied the clear blue skies but saw nothing save the snowy mountain landscape outside.

A haughty voice drawled behind me, "What are you doing here?"

I blinked, pulling my attention away from the light that filtered through the wall of windows to bathe the floors in gold. Flint Barragan faced me with a sneer, his eyes wincing at the beam of sunlight that crowned his sandy curls and gilded his lashes. He had styled his hair and donned fresh clothes, but the smell of alcohol still clung to his pores, and he swayed slightly on the spot, looking as though he was at risk of becoming sick. *Good. That makes two of us.*

When it became clear that he expected some sort of response from me, I curtsied. "A pleasure to see you, as usual, Your Highness."

"Hmmm," he grumbled, considering me with a look of disgust. "You should leave the fighting to the men. I'll send for you when it's your time to die in the next Trial."

If I recall correctly, dear prince, I won our last skirmish. Bit of a sore loser, aren't we? "I am not afraid of a little training session, Your Highness. Are you?"

The rage that burned in his eyes brought a smirk to my face.

"It would be improper for me to fight my future wife," he said in a velvety voice that did little to veil his displeasure.

"How convenient to choose when it is and isn't proper to fight me." Lio stomped on my foot, shaking his head in a silent warning.

Flint's face reddened. "I have a better idea. One that should prove to be...amusing." He craned his head to the side, searching the room, until the cords of his neck pulled taut and popped out. "Rydar!" he snapped, bellowing so loudly that several competitors paused mid-fight. Rydar approached, wiping the sweat from his brow with a towel.

Flint's lips curled into a decadent smile as he faced me once more. "You'll be training with Rydar. That should offer...*invaluable* entertainment for me." Rydar's jaw clenched, but he nodded curtly at his brother.

Flint clapped a hand on Rydar's shoulder, who stiffened beneath his grip. "And Rydar? Make sure her head hurts as much as mine does when you're done with her. Talking to her has given me a splitting headache."

"Are you alright?" Rydar whispered, directing me toward an open space on the floor. "You don't need to do this. I can't risk you getting injured before the next trial."

Not you, too. "Don't patronize me," I said, glaring back at him. Rydar grumbled, but I spread my feet into a fighting stance before he could object. "I deserve the same training as the others. Besides, isn't that all that matters to you? The Oath and winning the Trials and duties to your brother?" His brows knitted together as he mirrored my stance, angling himself so Flint could not see him speak.

"Oraelia, that is not all that matters. I need you to be safe. I am doing everything I can."

We circled one another slowly, and I studied the darkening clouds in his eyes. A conflicting storm of emotions thundered in my chest.

"Are you?" I hissed. "How do I even know you have upheld your end of the bargain? How do I know they are safe? What proof do I have? How am I to trust your word when you spend so many breaths telling me to stay away from you? Am I to stay away from you, Rydar? Or am I to stay close? Are you a friend or the enemy? What is it you want, Rydar? Say it plainly." His lips drew downward into a frown as he considered me, and I brushed away the inconvenient memory of his lips against mine with a surge of indignation and a rush of heat in my cheeks. *Not the time, Rae.*

"What I want matters little. I cannot give you what you want...what I want. And that kills me. But I can promise I won't hurt you," he said.

You already have. "I make no such promises. The high prince is watching. Best to give him what he expects."

I lunged toward him, landing two easy strikes and sweeping his legs from under him in one fluid motion. He landed on his back with a thud and blinked up at me as I pinned him to the ground, a smile growing on his face. "I never thought I would enjoy losing so much." His voice rumbled deep in his chest as his hands moved to my hips.

Resentment flooded my veins with fire. "You didn't even try!"

"Had to see what you could do." His eyes softened and flickered to my lips with such longing that I felt a rush of heat in my core. I became distracted by the roundness of his shoulders and the rise and fall of his muscular chest beneath my hands as I drew them away, letting my fingers drift along the ridges of his abdomen.

My back slapped against the floor in a flash, the impact forcing my breath away. Rydar's hands gripped mine, pinning my wrists to the ground by my ears. His knees hugged my sides and his hips perched over mine. The air between us sparked with an invisible charge as he leaned forward, allowing a wicked grin to spread on his face. Wicked in the kind of way that made me forget to breathe. "That is...not fair," I mumbled.

"Always know your enemy's weaknesses."

Fine. Two can play this game. A low rumble escaped him as I bit my lower lip, sweeping my gaze over his darkening eyes, his angled jaw, his full, soft lips that pulled into a lopsided, devious grin.

With a burst of energy, I thrust my hips up to destabilize his balance and threw my arms around his middle, pulling myself from beneath his weight. My arm hooked beneath his upper arm, flipping him under me once more. "I'm a fast learner," I whispered into his ear.

His chest rippled with shallow breaths, and his voice turned husky. "There's so much I wish I could teach you...if circumstances were different."

My breath hitched in my throat, and blood rushed to my cheeks. Before I could think of anything witty or even useful to say in response, a pair of hands grabbed Rydar's shoulders and dragged him upward. The high prince's face twisted into a furious scowl as his fist collided with Rydar's jaw. "What are you doing?" he shouted. "I told you not to go easy on her. Useless fool."

Rydar regained his footing. His eyes met mine, then flickered to his brother, the darkness of deep concern and unspent ire smoldering within. The cords of his neck bulged with tension, and every muscle in his massive frame seemed on edge, as though he fought to maintain control over his own body. And his pain...his pain was somehow everywhere and all-encompassing, not isolated to the place where his brother had struck him. I turned my gaze to Flint's smug expression, then back to Rydar, puzzling the dynamic between them. I shook my head in an effort to dissuade Rydar's imminent retaliation. *I can handle this,* I willed him to know.

Flint shouldered Rydar out of the way and reached for my wrist. "Get out, Rydar. I'll take it from here."

CHAPTER THIRTY-THREE
Screeches and Sirens

RAE

I smiled at Flint, though the dangerous mood that flooded his beady eyes warned me I should tread lightly. But that was not a strength of mine, and so the words flowed from me without a hint of reserve. "Are you certain you'd like to fight me, Your Highness?" I taunted. "You already look rather defeated by the effects of your indulgence last night...I fear there's not much left for me to do."

His soulless eyes darkened with the blackness of a starless night. "Be careful, Fenix. Let me remind you...I can end you at any moment I wish. Do not embarrass me while you run on borrowed time."

"You embarrass yourself quite fine without my assistance." *Helfyre, Rae. Too far.*

I braced myself for the smack I knew would fall upon my cheek, but it did not come. Perhaps he had learned. I, clearly, had not. *Stay small, stay alive.* If I had ever truly understood that life lesson, I would not be here in the first place.

"I shall relish watching you suffer," he said with finality. He turned away, stroking his chin while he pondered the activity in the room. By the windows, Ruwe and Brickert held deep lunges, their matted hair dripping sweat down their noses. Trystan tested their balance and reminded them to breathe.

Rydar stood several paces away, his arms crossed as he watched the un-certain blows between Lio and another tawny-haired, sullen-eyed competitor, the sound of their movements reverberating through the air. Rydar barked instructions at the pair, though his eyes flickered too often toward mine. His posture appeared more controlled, more settled, but the hint of pain lingered in his chest.

In the corner, Isolde passed a cup of water to Vance and stroked a palm over his shoulder, whispering to him with her snakelike smile. He nodded, and she slipped a silk-wrapped parcel into his hands. When he accepted the gift, the black fabric fell away, revealing the gem-studded hilt of a dagger. My heart raced, a thunderous cadence slapping against my ribs—evidently, I was not the only competitor who'd been gifted a weapon, and it was not difficult to assume the intended victim of her gift.

Vance pushed his dripping hair out of his eyes and strode over to me, planting his feet squarely in front of mine.

"My turn to dance with you," he said gruffly, then turned to the high prince with a bow. "With your permission, of course, Your Highness."

Flint's eyes sparkled with enthusiasm. "I was just looking for a more suitable opponent for her. You'll do, I suppose. Don't hold back."

"Not a problem," he said with a smirk, and my eyes fell to the concealed dagger at his side.

Rydar caught my gaze from across the room, and the concern in his eyes sent blood rushing through my veins. I brushed the insult of his doubts away and focused on my match, sizing Vance up, studying his messy stance and his muscular frame.

He appeared well-fed and strengthened by years of physical labor, though his lack of training was apparent in his unbalanced, unguarded form. His lips curled into a sneer. "Isolde sends her regards. She's promised to pledge her support to me as long as I end you...or seriously maim you. She's not too picky." He winked and lunged forward. *Predictable.*

I blocked his strike and shoved an elbow into his chest, making him stumble backward over his feet. A fire blazed to life in his eyes, an ardor only found in the soul of a desperate man. Desperation was dangerous, regardless of technique or lack thereof.

His feet snapped back into a fighting stance and lurched toward me, jabbing and slicing limbs with wild chaos, hoping to make contact with any part of my body. I was much faster than him, more lithe on my feet. I twisted away, grabbed his chest, and let gravity help me pull him to the ground. He bucked beneath me, trying desperately to free himself, but my pin held him exactly where he was meant to be.

"You stupid—" But whatever he was about to call me was drowned out by the earsplitting screech of a dragon. The room grew still as the sound of the creature pierced the air, making its displeasure known. The form of the great beast, burdened by bindings of chains and leather, soared past the window.

"Ho ho! It's almost time!" Orman's jaunty voice filled the chamber, immediately followed by a swell of anxious murmurs.

A sudden searing pain tore through my side.

I gasped. Pain blossomed at my waist, burning as though the fiery maw of the dragon had torn a chunk of flesh away from my body. I averted my gaze to my side, clutching at the ruined skin above my hip, watching with horror as blood gushed through my fingertips. My eyes locked on Vance with fear, and I saw the glint of accomplishment on his face just before I noticed the blade in his hand.

"Time's up, Oraelia. You must know you never had a chance." He moved to aim the knife at my throat.

My heart raced with fury, and I ripped the blade from Vance, disarming him with swift precision. *I should plunge this knife straight into your heart, you imbecile.* And I almost did...but my arm quivered in hesitation.

I tossed the knife across the room. The bloodied blade rattled on the floor, splattering droplets of red beneath it. Vance's expression faltered when I drew his face close to mine, clenching a fistful of the sweaty tunic at his throat to raise him toward me. There were no words for the anger that burned through my body at his foul play, no words to convey the storm of emotions that churned in my chest.

The clatter of the knife against the ground drew attention, and I felt gazes fall on us, making sense of the knife, the blood that drenched us, the furious tension between us. My eyes pierced him with rage, and I shoved him back to the ground. Clutching my side to stem the bleeding, I ran from the room and made my way toward the hallway. I needed to heal myself, but the pain was too great, too distracting.

Think, Oraelia. You must heal yourself or you will die. But if you heal yourself, they will know, and they will kill you.

The bleeding was too much—my feeble pressure was not enough to stop the flow. My hand pressed against the wound, but the hot, sticky mess spilled through my fingers no matter how much I willed it to stay inside. Stars appeared in my vision, and I stumbled away from the training room, using the wall for support. With vague awareness, I noticed the trail of red left behind by my fingertips.

Do it. You must. Do it now. My legs crumpled beneath me, and I drew in a ragged breath, wincing from the pain. *Had anyone truly seen what happened? They will know...If you heal yourself, they will know your secret, and they will Retire you.*

But I had little choice. Warmth trickled from my fingertips, flowing into the gash and knitting the wound together from the inside. My mind whirled, and I took another unsteady breath, holding on to the pain so I did not lose my focus. I poured my energy through my fingers and let the magic bind the skin, using the gale storm of emotions in my heart to fuel my efforts.

When all that remained was a scratch on the surface of my skin, I melted into the wall, leaning against the stone and succumbing to exhaustion. My breaths came in short, shallow spurts and my heart raced furiously in my chest. I knew I should move. *Get up, Rae. Hide. Run. Do anything but waste away here and wait for them to find you.*

I could not will my legs to do my bidding. The useless, leaden weights refused to cooperate until my eyes drooped and my consciousness drifted between wakefulness and sleep, and I quite forgot why I was ever concerned to begin with.

From deep within the house, a siren wailed.

The howling, earsplitting sound ripped me from my languor. I scrambled to my feet in a panic, blood pounding in my ears as a sheen of sweat surfaced on my skin.

"All competitors are to report immediately to the main entrance of the House of Frost. With haste. At once. Without delay." Elowynne's sweet, honeyed voice floated through the halls.

A pair of powerful arms steadied me, and the familiar scent of sandalwood and crisp rain in the air invaded my senses. "Walk," he grumbled, exuding an aura of darkness and shadow.

Somehow, my feet scrambled into a pattern of forward motion, though I was not entirely certain that it was I who controlled them. *One, two. One, two.* Rydar's body brushed against mine, ushering me around a corner.

A shroud of darkness cloaked us and muffled the sound of the alarms, though the windows in the hallway glimmered with sunlight. "You are hurt." His voice carried anger and the rumble of impending destruction. A mountain on the verge of eruption.

"I am fine," I lied, using my hand to cover my side and refusing to wince.

He batted my hand away, and his nostrils flared at the sight of the crimson stains on my clothes and fingers. He peeled back the torn fabric to expose the wound, and he stilled at the sight of my side.

"How?" he muttered, swiping a finger over the fading red line, the remaining scratch that marked where the blade had pierced me. The brush of his fingers sent chills down my spine with a wave of unbidden desire.

"It was just a scratch," I murmured in defense, wriggling away from his hand.

The intensity of his gaze bore straight through my soul, dissecting me with an expression that eluded definition. "It did not look like a scratch," he stated.

"You keep your secrets, and I'll keep mine." I placed my hand over his, smoothing his grip over my waist, daring him with my eyes. "Doubt me if you must, but I am not as weak as you think." A tortured grumble ripped through his chest as he pulled away, flexing his fingers as if to rid them of my touch.

"I have no doubts that you will be the end of me."

The sirens blared with renewed strength as the dark shroud dissipated. Rydar swept his hand through his dark hair, brushing it away from the throbbing vein in his temple.

"The next task. Go to the left of the dragon. Survive." The howling siren punctuated each word, and his eyes filled with something I did not recognize, but needed with every fiber of my being. His hands wrapped around my face as he uttered one last word. "Please."

CHAPTER THIRTY-FOUR

The Glass Chamber

RAE

Elowynne twisted the blouse in her hands, studying the tear in the fabric and the scarlet stains that blossomed from it. Her eyes rose to study me, narrowing with suspicion. I shifted uneasily to cover the scratch on my side. "You were injured during training?"

"Just a scratch." I regurgitated the same lie I'd told Rydar. But it wasn't a total lie—only a scratch remained. I just prayed to the Fates she hadn't overheard what had happened.

Elowynne held up the blouse, unfolding it to show off the large patches of scarlet. "There's quite a bit of blood." She raised a brow in a silent demand for an explanation.

Helfyre. "I bleed easily." I shrugged it off, praying she'd accept the justification.

"Hmmm." She turned, absentmindedly palming the fabric before depositing it into the wash bin. Whether she believed me or not, she did not say. I had my suspicions.

A lump lodged itself in my throat. *What if she finds out that Vance stabbed me in practice? Will she tell?*

Of course she would. She was not my friend.

"Put this on," Elowynne demanded, her tone sharp enough to jolt me out of my worrying. The black fabric snapped to my skin with the unsettling brush of her magic. "How does it feel?" She scrutinized me with a furrowed brow, gazing down the length of her pointed nose. I flexed my arms and bent my knees, testing the flexibility of the suit's fabric. The lack of skirts felt freeing, but also foreign.

Words eluded me, so I nodded in approval and wrapped my arms across my midsection, trying to settle the nausea bubbling inside. My body shook with nerves. Each piercing wail of the siren echoed through my mind, flooding me with apprehension. Elowynne's sharp features softened. "Good luck," she whispered, then pressed a button on the wall. A door materialized and slid away to reveal a natural tunnel, dimly lit by the chain of torches along the wall.

The tunnel door slid back into place, sealing me off from the dressing chamber, where Elowynne watched me disappear with a frown. Cool, damp air whispered at my cheeks, and shadows danced in the flickers of light from the torches. The walls muffled the sounds of the blaring sirens, though I could still hear them in the rattling of my bones.

Each step forward was a challenge. I felt my legs quiver as I reached the end of the hallway, unaware of how I had gotten there. My pulse beat fiercely in my veins, throbbing in my fingertips and ears. A roaring sound surged from behind the door at the end of the passage, but it wasn't the screeching call of the dragon...this was something entirely different.

I balled my hands into fists, trying to still them, but it was an impossible endeavor. How was I going to defeat a dragon? Would it hurt when the beast roasted me with fire, or would it be so fast I would not suffer? *I'm going to die out there.*

Taking on a haughty prince was one thing...a fire-breathing dragon with wings and talons and gnashing teeth was another. I pondered Rydar's last words to me, wishing there had been more time to ask questions. *Go left, he says. If I survive this, I'm going to kill him.* My teeth clenched tightly as I cursed him and his *best efforts* to keep me alive.

Steam billowed through the cracks of the door, and the rock slid downward to reveal an open archway. Blue skies and sunlight blinded me. The heavy boots of a Watchman thudded against the rocky floor as he approached me. "Your hand," he demanded.

He did not wait for me to respond but reached forward, grabbed my wrist, and pierced the tip of my finger with a small black box. I winced at the unexpected pain, but it was nothing more than a quick pinch to draw a droplet of blood. The Watchman stepped backward, typing into the device as he monitored me with his sharp eyes. "Through the doorway, Miss Fenix. More directions will follow. Good luck."

I gulped and stepped through the arch onto a ledge. My stomach lurched at the sight of the open ravine, and there, in the depths of the abyss, waited the magnificent dragon.

A roar of cheers rose to meet me. From the other side of the ravine, I could see thousands of people in seats that overlooked the arena, and I squinted to take in the ocean of different colors and the excited hum that filled the air. Wind whipped the hair out of my face and the breath right out of my lungs.

"Competitor number eight, the first female in the history of the Timeless Trials, Oraelia Fenix!" I turned my head toward the source of the booming voice and saw Orman Gendrick on a platform above me, wearing silver and a smug smile of superiority. A massive screen, larger than the dragon below, flashed to life behind him, and I saw my own form appear on it, glaring down at the crowd with a ferocity I did not know I possessed. The screen transitioned, revealing a series of metrics that detailed my health, perceived standing, and pledged donations. The pledges rose steadily with each shallow breath I took.

The Watchman nudged my shoulder, pushing me toward the crystalline bridge at the edge of the landing. A glass chamber was suspended in the air at the far side of the bridge, hovering above the ravine.

My eyes widened as I glanced toward him for confirmation, and he nodded. With wobbling legs, I stepped onto the narrow bridge, setting my gaze firmly toward the other side and not daring to look into the abyss below. I was not afraid of heights, but falling seemed to be a reasonable concern, given the circumstances.

The sun reflected off the glass chamber in a dazzling burst of light, but as I moved closer, I saw the forms of the other competitors crammed inside. They stood still, frozen like statues, but I could feel the nervous energy in the room as the door slid open to admit me. When our eyes met, Lio's brimmed with dread, and I moved close to him, brushing my fingers against his in a wordless gesture of reassurance. "Not today," I mouthed. "This isn't the end." His hand clasped around mine.

Orman's theatrical voice filled the arena. "Good lads and ladies! Welcome to the Trials!" A surge of roaring applause responded. "Now that you've laid eyes upon our eight remaining competitors...what do we think? Who will win? Let's cheer for our favorite as loud as we can! Ready?"

He paused, waiting for the eruption of noise to settle. "Brickert!" The audience hollered in response. "Lio! Vance! Taiver! Vyn! Ruwe! Harma... and Oraelia!" A roar of support followed each name.

"Pick your favorites, make your pledges, and let us honor the Good Work of our high king. May His time be everlasting." He bowed his head with reverence, and the crowd echoed back in unison.

"Competitors, it's time to weed out the weak and determine the final five. Are we ready? Listen carefully. In just a few moments, you will be lowered into the arena with the fire dragon. Isn't. She. A. Beauty?" He raised his hands to the crowd, letting a jovial laugh bounce around his chest, and the spectators roared back in approval. Orman turned his attention to us with a wicked smile playing at the corner of his lips.

"Your task is to steal one of the time prizes hanging behind the dragon, then return to the chamber before the hourglass runs out. You have a mere ten minutes to complete the task, so make the time count." He winked gregariously and turned to the crowd again, speaking to them as though we could not hear him. "Managing time isn't their biggest strength, though, is it? They are time wasters, after all!" Laughter bubbled all around, and I tightened my fists at my side.

A great jolt rocked the glass chamber, nearly knocking me off my feet as it began a slow descent toward the ground. *Toward death.*

"Ah! I almost forgot," Orman called out, and the chamber stopped so suddenly that I fell backward into the wall, steadying myself with an outstretched palm against the glass. I craned my neck upward, and my stomach writhed at the expression on Orman's face. "It's always more exciting when the dragon is already a bit...riled. Guards!"

Half a dozen Watchmen emerged on horseback, spilling forth from the mouth of a cave into the ravine. They circled the dragon with long poles resting on their shoulders, their faces covered with masks, and their usual grey uniforms replaced with black. The horses pranced around, and I squinted to focus my vision, noticing a flash of silver at the end of the poles. I watched in horror as one approached the beast, drew back the lance, and sank the barbed tip into the beast's haunch.

Scarlet blood trickled down the dragon's rear leg, and it roared with a fury that rumbled through the mountain bed. Its head snapped upward, and the vast expanse of its wings stretched to the sky, but iron shackles restrained the beast from taking flight. I gasped as the dragon's pain burrowed into my heart, sharp and fiery flames that licked the hollow of my chest.

The Watchman quickly retreated to be replaced by another. And another. "Don't you worry," Orman called out between the gasps of the audience. "The lances are nothing more than a pinprick to the beast...just enough to rile her up for our competitors."

The dragon strained against the chains that shackled her to the ground, and a stream of orange and white flames flowed from her jaws, though the Watchmen stayed well out of reach.

After the last Watchman drove his lance into the dragon's flank and retreated, another pair of sentries emerged from the shadows. Great shears glinted in the sun's light as they approached her. Their horses, with gleaming chestnut coats, pranced alongside the beast's flanks, and my stomach churned with horror. The Watchmen placed the shears at the base of the dragon's wings, then clamped them closed to slice through the tendon at the joint.

The dragon screeched in agony, its wings clipped and rendered useless, its soul crushed by the reality that it would never fly again. The pain that crashed into my chest bore a hole straight through my heart, and I sucked in a ragged breath. For a moment, I forgot to be afraid of the beast—forgot to worry about my own safety. The overwhelming emotions of pity and sadness consumed me.

I turned my appalled gaze toward Orman, resenting the excited glimmer that danced in his eyes. How could anyone find this entertaining? How wicked must one be to dream up such a horror? Such brutality? And more importantly, *What would his scream sound like if we tossed him into the fray with the angered dragon?*

His smile widened. "Oh, yes... she's angry now! Very good. Contestants, off you go. May time be on your side."

CHAPTER THIRTY-FIVE

A Web of Cracks

RAE

Blood rushed through my veins, dulling my senses so that I was only vaguely aware of the screaming crowd, the snapping, screeching dragon...the quick descent of the glass chamber, and the resounding *thud* as it met the ground.

A sharp pain in my side jerked me back to reality. "Move over," Brickert commanded. His body weight shifted forward, readying to sprint from the platform.

The countdown began—short, clipped beeps punctuated by the pounding of my heart. I stole a quick glance at Lio, his face drained of color and his eyes so wide I feared they were on the verge of exploding. A final, drawn-out beep settled in the air. My breath hitched in my throat as the walls of the glass chamber slowly unfolded, unfurling like a winter rose in bloom, exposing us to the mercy of the dragon.

She was enormous. From the crown of spikes on her head to the mace of her tail, she was a fearsome creature to behold...much larger up close than I had realized from the top of the ravine. Her ridged back was curled against the cragged wall behind her, her movements restricted by the chains that tied her to the ground. She greeted us with a roar and snapped her vicious jaws with displeasure.

Her claws wrapped around a heap of treasure laid out to tempt us—glistening hilts, blades, and other weapons pulled close to her body. Behind her, satin sacks swayed in the wind, tied to the craggy wall of the mountain. The prizes.

The glass walls thudded against the icy rock in the ravine, scattering the powdered snow into tendrils that snaked upon the ground. *It's now or never.* I swept my gaze over the scene, looking for advantages to leverage, but I only saw death in every direction.

Go left, he had said. Right toward the dragon's head? Was he insane? He had to be mistaken. Did he *want* me to be roasted by flames?

The ground rumbled ominously below our feet, and without thinking, I reacted. Seizing Lio's hand, I took off—aiming toward the dragon's magnificent horned head and fearsome jaws.

Lio's squeal of terror climbed higher than the Fates as we ran. His grip on my fingers tightened, and his feet scraped against the ground in fear, yet I pulled him along with determination. *You're not giving up on me, Lio. Not today.* He fell into step behind me, speaking in short, clipped grunts between his gasps. "Rae! Helfyre! We're going to die. Oh, Fates!"

We raced toward the dragon until we fell into the shadows cast by her enormous frame, and she set her fiery eyes upon us. My heart stopped in my chest and I screeched to a standstill, putting my hand out to guard Lio as if that would keep him safe from a blaze of dragon fire. My knees bent, ready to make a quick side-step as she pulled her head high to inhale, her nostrils smoking with the heat of her flames.

But a fresh wave of distress and discomfort flowed from her, and I winced, feeling the pain in her agonized roar. She whipped her head away from us toward the source of her affliction. Ruwe perched precariously on top of her left wing, his foot sliding into the damaged gap between her wing and body as he clamored to reach the ridges on her back. His fingers were slick with oily black blood as he finally pulled himself to the top, his eyes locked on the satiny satchel tied to the wall above his head. It was the last thing he ever saw.

I flinched as a jet of flames issued from the dragon's mouth, roasting Ruwe until he was nothing more than a pile of ash floating in the wind. Lio stammered incoherently as I tugged him behind the dragon, disappearing into the darkness between the beast's back and the looming face of the rock wall. Two dark forms swung above our heads, just out of reach. Time prizes.

"Give me a leg up," I told Lio. His hands shook, and his face was ghastly pale, but he nodded curtly and kneeled on the ground without a word.

Orman's voice boomed, echoing throughout the ravine to narrate as developments unfolded. "Oh, my! Look at Brickert. He's got the first satchel...the first prize. Run, Brickert!"

I hoisted myself up toward the dangling sacks, cursing my fumbling fingers as they struggled with the knot.

"Oh, look at Vyn! He's made his way to her nest...see him hiding behind the egg? She's not going to like that, Vynnie. Dragons are very protective mothers." Sure enough, the crowd gasped in horror as the dragon's deafening roar rattled the mountains. "Ouch! Bet that hurt, Vynnie. Don't give up on us now!" I caught a glimpse of Vyn, his suit singed and his skin raw where the dragon's flames had grazed his shoulder, but the fire in his eyes blazed and drove him forward. "I can't believe it...he's secured the prize! Run, Vynnie! And look, Brickert is back—and here comes Harma, close on his heels! Come on, Taiver, you've nearly got it! How many will survive? Who will make it?"

With every shift of the beast behind me, my heart pounded in my chest, every cry and gasp from the crowd. The blasted knot would not loosen. If anything, I had made it worse. *The dagger, you idiot.*

I seized the blade at my thigh and sliced through the air, parting the knot with a flourish of whooshing metal. The satchel fell into my open palm, its weight surprisingly hefty considering its size.

My feet slipped on the icy rock as I jumped down, and my knee slammed into the rough ground as I lost my balance. *Helfyre, that hurt.*

An explosion shook the ravine. My ears rang, blocking out all other sounds and overwhelming my senses. I dropped my satchel and blade, pressing my palms to my ears to block out the horrible buzzing, but it did nothing to lessen the sound. Lio gripped the sides of his head, equally shaken by the blast.

"Ho, ho! Here come the explosives." Orman's voice sounded far away, like his words echoed through a long, dark tunnel. "That means your time is almost up, competitors! The hourglass is draining quickly. Don't waste time! Make haste!"

Lio and I exchanged a horrified glance. "Go," he said, reaching down to pick up the fallen satchel and my dagger, shoving both into my arms. "I'll get the other one. Go."

"Not without you," I grumbled, pushing the prize back toward him. The dragon shifted so that the ridges of her spine nearly pinned us against the rock wall. *Are they sharp enough to impale us?*

Another bang rocked the ravine, and a horrid screech followed. "Hurry!" I yelled to Lio, though the ringing in my ears was so overpowering that I could hardly hear my own voice. I pulled him along behind me and positioned him beneath the second satchel. Lio sank to his knee, and I stepped up, slicing through the cords with another slash of the dagger. The fabric sack landed on the ground just as another explosion blasted rock from the wall above us, showering the dragon with debris.

I snatched the second sack up and grabbed Lio's wrist, sprinting back toward the glass chamber. Rock, snow, and debris flew into the air in the middle of the ravine as another explosive burst from the ground.

The dragon roared behind us, and I could feel the heat of her flames at my back. Sweat dripped in my eyes, and I gasped for breath as I ran...we were so close. The open chamber was only steps away.

Lio shouted in panic behind me, and I suddenly stopped, spinning on my heels to help him. Vance tugged at the prize in Lio's hands, but Lio held fast, refusing to release it even though he clutched his temple with his other fist. His face screwed up in anticipation as Vance hiked his elbow back to deliver another blow. I lunged toward them, wildly slicing the dagger across Vance's exposed side.

"Go, Lio," I shouted, tearing the satchel away from Vance and tossing it back. "I'll deal with him."

Vance roared and pressed a hand into his side, but barreled toward me with explosive force, knocking me onto my back.

Haunting chimes began to toll, counting down the last seconds. *Is the hourglass empty? How many more chimes? Not enough. There is never enough.*

"Give me that." With a menacing growl, Vance lurched forward, pinning my wrist to the ground and reaching for the satchel in my other hand. His elbow knocked the breath from me.

Not a chance. I rolled away from Vance, ignoring the bite of the sharp rock beneath me, and scrambled back to my feet. He crouched, his wild eyes darting between the sack in my left hand and the dagger in my right, his body tensed for another attack. I kicked him hard in the chest and leaped onto the glass floor of the chamber. Vance threw himself onto the glass after me, wrestling for the bag as a horn blared in the distance. The chamber began to rise, and the walls closed around us.

"Oh...oh, my! The competitors are up and out, but we have a bit of a last-second scuffle...Vance came up to the chamber empty-handed and is trying to steal from Oraelia! And...Oraelia has a dagger? Is that even allowed? What's going to happen? I can hardly watch..."

Shut up, Orman.

Vance hissed with frustration, writhing like a ravenous snake gripping its prey, fighting for his life as we rose higher and higher into the air. The dragon roared below, and we tumbled sideways, sliding into the glass wall. Cracks like spiderwebs climbed through the pane before the wall shattered, showering us with shards. Vance hollered and reached for me again, ripping the dagger from my grasp, but the chamber lurched with the shifting weight. The edge raced to meet us and I closed my eyes, bracing myself for the long fall to my death.

CHAPTER THIRTY-SIX

Death Would Be Kinder

RAE

My legs, then my torso, slid off the edge of the platform, and I screeched with fear, but Lio's fingers wrapped firmly around my shoulders to stop my fall. His knuckles grew white with strain, and his cry echoed in the mountains as he pulled me back onto the glass, dragging me through the broken shards to safety.

I winced as the shattered pieces of glass ripped through my skin. I knew it should hurt, but I didn't register the pain. My heart beat too frantically in my chest, a battering ram pounding at my ribcage. For a moment, I could only lay there, feeling the wild thumping of my heart, the sweat and matted hair on my forehead, the dazzling sun in my eyes. I was alive. Barely.

My head rushed with dizziness as I peered over the edge. We were as high as the crowd of spectators now and rising higher still. Vance's form lay in a grotesque heap of misaligned limbs at the bottom of the ravine, my dagger glinting in his deformed hand. The dragon tossed its head wildly from side to side behind him, obsidian scales glistening like spilled oil in the sunlight.

The platform jolted, reaching the highest height, and I watched in horror as a series of explosions burst within the ravine, one after the next, obliterating anyone left behind. The dragon screeched in horrible pain as debris skittered down her scales, and her head landed with a thud against the ground. Waves of pain rushed forward from her, and I grimaced as it hit me. She was not dead... death would be kinder.

The buzzing noise in my ears ebbed away, replaced by the roaring applause of the crowd. I stared blankly at the spectators, trying to make sense of the nightmare. My limbs wobbled with weakness as I pulled myself to standing, noticing my reflection in the pane of glass—how the streaks of sweat ran through the dirt and blood covering my skin, how my hands desperately clutched the satchel in front of my body.

"Wasn't. That. Exciting?" Orman shouted, sensationalizing his voice with dramatic pauses to spur the audience into another rabid uproar. "A true display of bravery and skill...six competitors made it back to safety! We know what that means, don't we? But we'll get to that in a moment." My eyes panned from one end of the mountainside to the other, mouth gaping at the rowdy audience. "Shall we see what each of our competitors retrieved from the dragon?"

Orman waved up toward the giant screen, which displayed a moving image of us standing on the platform in a state of shock, traumatized beyond words. "Let's give a round of applause for Brickert, our first to make it back to the platform. Go on and open that satchel, Brickert. Show us your spoils! You've earned it!"

Brickert's temple ran with blood, and he stared unblinking into the sky, lost in his own thoughts. Harma nudged him hard until his eyes unfogged. With shaking hands, he unwrapped the satiny strings at the top of the bag, then pulled the mouth of the satchel open wide and dipped his hand inside. He removed a gold, glittering timepiece as large as his head, with the number 4,500 stamped across the face. "Oh, what luck! He's secured one of the largest time prizes...4,500 years. That's a lot of gems to add to your hourglass, Brickert! Next up...Harma!"

My attention drifted, sifting through the distressing visions my mind replayed, nightmares that would not leave me because I had lived them. Watchmen entered the ravine, loading the now unconscious dragon onto a trolley, then rolling her away into the shadowy crevices of the mountain. Where were they taking her? What would they do to her? Would they kill her now that she had served her purpose? *One must be useful, or one must Retire.* My chest burned with fiery anger and pain, my heart nothing more than a lacerated tangle of ribbons. What a waste—Ruwe, the beautiful, majestic dragon...even Vance. My face soured. Maybe I had wasted time, but they wasted *lives.*

"Oraeeeelia..." The gurgle of laughter pulled me out of my thoughts. I blinked up at Orman and the screen to see myself, a catastrophe of blood and fury haphazardly assembled into human form. "Wooooo, she's in a bad mood." He chuckled jauntily. "What's in the bag, Oraelia? What did you win?"

My eyes dropped to my hands, still clutching the silk satchel with a white-knuckled grasp. Pulling the ribbons away, I opened the top to reveal the golden timepiece within, staring blankly at the golden face as I fished it out. *One year.*

Orman sighed heavily, as if his sorrow were too much to bear. "Oh no, horrid luck. All that for a year! No matter, no matter. Every second counts, doesn't it?"

The impulsive side of me considered hurling the timepiece at Orman's face, but the logical side of me recognized it would be a wasted display of defiance...I couldn't throw that far. *Pity.*

Orman's expression grew somber. "Now, it pains me greatly to say this, but only the final five competitors can move into the next phase of events. We all hoped the task would sort this out for us, but alas, six survived. And so, it must be left to the will of the people to decide! Unless the high prince would like to allow a sixth competitor to move on?"

"Five will do, Orman," Flint called from his viewing box above.

Orman bowed his head. "Then let us decide."

The raucous cheers echoed through the ravine like my pounding heart echoed in the walls of my chest. We had all survived—all six of us had made it through the challenge. Would they really eliminate one of us now? It did not require much imagination on my part to guess what an elimination might involve.

"Brickert, Harma, Vyn, Taiver, Lio, and Oraelia stand before us, but only five spots remain for our guests. I ask you, good lads and ladies, who do we wish to see continue on in the Trials? Let the hourglasses decide!"

The screen flickered, and the great ballroom flashed upon its surface, panning to reveal each vessel along the ceiling. Gems trickled slowly into the deep basins as the audience donated to their favorite victors. Mine nearly overflowed with deep blue sapphires, and Brickert's swelled with green. Lio's and Vyn's rose more slowly, neck and neck as the donations slowly tinkled against the glass. Lio bit his bottom lip, watching while he picked mindlessly at the hems of his sleeves. The urge to help him overwhelmed me, and without thinking, I grabbed Lio's hand and raised it into the air, holding our arms up in a stance of allied victory, compelling the crowd to favor him as they had favored me. *Pick him. Please.*

A wave of honey-hued gems cascaded into Lio's hourglass, and he turned to me with a look of awe, too speechless for words.

Finally, Orman raised his hand in the air, and the world stilled.

"It appears we have our final five, good lads and ladies. And what excellent choices you've made. Vyn, so sorry, lad."

A Watchman stepped out of the shadows and shoved Vyn hard in the shoulders. He gasped and fell forward, with nothing to catch him but the Fates. My scream caught in my throat, failing to emerge and choking me instead with a strangled gurgle. I clenched my eyes shut, bracing for the moment of impact, for the wave of pain and then the calm nothingness that would signal his passage to the Next Realm.

It happened fast.

In the tunnels leading back to the house, attendants stripped me and changed me into a simple shift. They spoke to me and made small talk, maybe even complimented me, but I did not truly hear them. I was trapped in my mind, replaying the images of Vyn's fall, Ruwe's disintegration to ash, the tangle of limbs that used to be Vance...all the horrific memories until I vomited the contents of my stomach onto the rocky floor.

The attendants patted me on the back sympathetically, then led me to the other competitors, who had also been relieved of their form-fitting suits. Lio and Harma looked my way when I entered the chamber, but nobody spoke. What was there to say?

A guard led us back to the House of Frost in a silence so profound, it seemed to smother the world with its weight.

Chapter Thirty-Seven

Big Mistake

Rae

A wild ruckus met us as we left the tunnels and returned to the House of Frost. I stepped through the door, waiting for my tears to fall or for a sense of relief to wash over me, but I felt nothing—only numbness. I let them guide me toward the ballroom, but my mind stayed behind in the ravine.

When I entered the room, my eyes immediately found Rydar's. I was angry with him, but as soon as I saw him, the reasons for my grudge slipped through my fingers like sand through an hourglass. The rest of the room faded from my senses as though he were the anchor in this tumultuous sea, the force that centered me and kept me from drifting away and losing myself. Without meaning to, my feet carried me toward him, needing to feel his arms wrapped around me and rest my head in that perfectly formed space between his chest and his shoulders so I could weep.

Flint Barragan's arms wrapped around me instead, twirling me with a twinkle of delight illuminating his face while depthless malice darkened his eyes. "You were magnificent!" he declared to the room, for he was speaking to them and not to me. "Don't you think? How did our competitors fare? Let us shower our survivors with their well-earned time!" He waved to the vaulted ceiling, drawing the crowd's attention to the glittering timepieces above.

Three of the hourglasses shimmered, dissolving into nothing as their gems funneled into the swelling belly of The Good Work and then into the remaining vessels. Ruwe, Vance, Vyn… gone without ceremony as if they had never existed. The numbers ticking up in my own hourglass brought me no sense of joy…no relief. My time could be stolen away as quickly as it was given. The room applauded politely, and bubbling glasses clinked together in toasts of cheer.

"Congratulations are in order! Our brilliant game master truly outdid himself with this task. Brickert, Lio, Harma, Taiver… what bravery and honor you bring to the Good Work. And, of course, Oraelia, may time continue to be on your side. If you win, I can't wait to make you officially mine."

The crowd swooned as the high prince's horrible hands grabbed the fabric at my hips, pulling me close so that the dress pressed snugly against my rear. When I tried to pull away, his grip tightened, trapping me against his body. Sandy curls brushed my neck as he leaned in to whisper. "Everyone is watching, dear." He pressed his mouth to mine, prying hungrily at my lips with his tongue, crushing me in a passionless embrace. The taste of him repulsed me, and I was so stunned by the vile intrusion that I stood frozen in his arms, unresponsive to his advances, with my limp arms dangling behind me.

The happy ripple of applause pulled me from my state of shock. I shoved him hard in the chest and glared at him with fire in my soul that rivaled the dragon's flames. "No." My voice was dangerous, almost a growl. It was the only word I could muster, the only word that could be formed through the hatred that churned inside.

The high prince laughed, a pleasant ringing of bells at odds with the darkness swirling in his eyes. "Poor thing is distressed. Let us give the competitors some space. Please, enjoy the reception and accept the Realm's sincerest gratitude for your generosity to the Good Work and our brave competitors."

He led me away, maintaining an air of grace for appearance's sake while digging his fingers deep into my side. "Big mistake," he whispered, parting from me without another word. He moved toward Orman, who recoiled slightly at the dangerous look on Flint's face. "Come. Walk with me," he said to him, with such coolness in his tone that a shiver ran down my spine.

As they disappeared through the ballroom doors, Orman's prideful grin diminished into a wilted frown.

CHAPTER THIRTY-EIGHT

A Dangerous Friend

RYDAR

Her eyes nearly drowned me the first time I fell into their blue-green depths, tugging me beneath the crashing waves with an undercurrent of unmatched strength, tossing me back to the surface, changed and anchored to her soul forevermore. And now, when she stepped into the ballroom covered in blood and dirt, flashing eyes of fury that softened only for me, I knew I loved her with every broken shard of my soul. But that did not change the fact that my love would bring her death. I was a monster for even entertaining the idea of her.

I had refused to fall in love. Yet, it found me anyway.

"Breathe," Trystan reminded me, his tone low and commanding. He was an excellent general, an even better friend—I did not deserve him. My father deserved him even less.

My vision had swirled with darkness when the high prince grabbed her, pulling her close by the fabric at her hips and forcing his undeserving lips to hers. Reserve abandoned me, and I lunged forward, sick with fury and the intention to decimate him. The retaliating pain that exploded in my veins nearly blinded me. Flint was untouchable.

My father's curses.

Resentment ignited a rising anger within me, buzzing like a swarm of bees taking refuge in my heart. The oath I'd sworn in blood to protect and serve the king's second son had become increasingly unbearable as I watched Oraelia suffer at his hand. And the other promises I'd made, both to myself and my father—now rendered impossible. Someday, I vowed to find a way to break free from the web of threads that ensnared me, from the magic that punished me if I so much as directed the slightest thought of ill will against my brother.

Someday, Flint would face the reckoning he deserved.

I just needed to survive long enough. To ensure the high king did not grow weary of my existence and decide to end me first.

Of course, he didn't need to lift so much as a finger to do so—he had orchestrated my demise the moment he cursed me.

A voice of reason whispered into my ear, restraining me with an iron grip before I destroyed myself. "Rydar, breathe. You can't save her if you cross into the Next Realm."

I let him drag me away, falling limp into his arms as the pain subsided in my veins but doubled in my heart. How could I love her and allow her to suffer that abomination of a man? I cursed myself, angry that my body had failed me...angry at the curse that stifled me, denying me the reprieve of ripping him limb from limb as he deserved. I wanted to render him useless so that he could never hold her or touch her against her will again. Flames of rage burned in my throat, and I surged forward, but I roared as the hot fire tore through me once more.

Trystan smacked me hard across the face and gripped my shoulders. "Stop it. Be wise." My teeth grated together, and my muscles tensed, bearing down to master the flare of pain that coursed through me until, at last, it subsided. Trystan's grip on my shoulders lightened, and his expression grew grave. "She is important to you."

I nodded, but my throat had run dry, too parched for words. She was not allowed to be important to me, and yet, somehow, the Fates ensured she'd found her way to my heart.

She wasn't just important. She was the essence of my world.

"You cannot win with brute force—you know this. Strategize, Rydar."

My hands clenched into fists, and Trystan shook my shoulders, his face creasing with his building concern. "Breathe. Find control. Use your mind."

His ribs expanded with a deep inhale, and his brows raised, waiting expectantly for me to follow suit. I grumbled, but acquiesced. Matching the slow rise and fall of his chest, I forced the darkness from my mind. Reason and control returned in the stillness, and I closed my eyes in a quiet study of breath.

My lids snapped back open, and Trystan smiled. "Good lad."

How he understood me better than I understood myself, I would never know. But he had pulled me from darkness to purpose time and time again, keeping me alive... keeping me safe from myself. It was no easy feat.

I rose, clapping a hand on his shoulder and nodding solemnly. I needed to pay a visit to Orman. "Thank you."

"Good lad. Go make your move. Strategize."

Orman sat in his study, hunched over papers and scrawling furiously with the passion of a man possessed. Firelight from the hearth danced in his eyes when he took notice of me, but his expression was frosted over in a sneer of icy displeasure despite the sweltering heat of the room.

"You lied to me." His voice was a low, rumbling whisper.

My steps faltered, and I inclined my head, treading carefully as I considered my next words, though I suspected his meaning.

Orman shoved his chair away from the table with force, knocking papers and books to the ground with a tumultuous rumble that paled in comparison to the boom of his voice. *"You manipulated me."*

I lifted my hands, showing my palms in a gesture of peace, and cautiously stepped closer.

Orman seethed. "Explain to me *why* the high prince pulled me aside to request the death of a certain competitor you have asked me to spare." My heart thundered in my chest, but I kept my breath and expression steady. Letting him see the panic that gripped me at the mere mention of her death would not make this better. Orman was worried, and rightly so.

"You *told* me we were working together to manipulate the games in the Realm's interest. *Explain* to me why the high prince has come with a very different expectation of the outcome." He jabbed a finger into my breastbone with a snarl on his face. "What *exactly* am I to do about that? I have a family to worry about...I should report you to the high king." Spittle formed in the corner of his mouth, and his beard twitched as he confronted me, eyes set ablaze with anger. "How *dare* you mislead me and involve me in your schemes? You're supposed to be my friend."

Pain mingled with the rage on his face, and I felt a pang of guilt. I wished I could make him understand, but he had every reason to be cross with me. Still, I needed to try. I needed him on my side. "I have not misled you, my friend. Orman—"

He turned away, raising his arm in dismissal. The floor creaked beneath his feet as he paced, muttering under his breath.

I stepped closer to him. "The high prince reacted impulsively, but our arrangement must stand. I will make him see...let me handle him. Whatever he has promised you, double it."

Orman turned to face me, his haunted eyes glistening with a rare display of vulnerability. "Death, Rydar. He promised me death. You will double that?" His voice cracked with his rising pitch.

Helfyre. "Orman, please. I will fix this, my friend."

His expression darkened, and he regarded me with fresh understanding. "You are a dangerous friend."

I sighed, deflated by the truth of his statement. *Yes, yes, I am.*

CHAPTER THIRTY-NINE

A Scrape of Claws

RYDAR

I stormed through the halls on my way to find Oraelia, plagued by the thoughts racing through my mind. After much pleading and reasoning, Orman eventually came around, yet the daunting task of safeguarding him from the high prince left me with a churning feeling of apprehension in my stomach—I did not want to fail him. Even more disquieting was the worry that Orman would fail to do as he had promised. He was a brave man, but still, the fear of untimely death and the changing whims of the high prince had caused braver men to crumble.

I pushed my apprehension to the back of my mind, deciding to concentrate on the task at hand. I needed to speak to Oraelia, then try to reason with Flint. An impossible endeavor, to be sure—but I could not afford to fail.

My thoughts blinded me to the passage of time and my surroundings. Darkness billowed about me, creating a ward against unwanted interaction from passersby as I tore down the hallway. Lord Gavintry and Lady Lisbane smiled politely as they ambled arm in arm in my direction, but they recoiled quickly at the sight of my expression. *Good.* I did not have time for meaningless conversation.

Taking long strides, I rounded the corner to the competitors' wing. The high sun cast golden rays through the arched windows in the hall, but a heavy somberness persisted despite the warmth from the light. It was eerily quiet—my skin prickled with warning.

Flint stepped out of the shadows, and a dastardly smile crept to his face. A fresh wave of fury ignited within me at the sight of him, turning all of Trystan's good counsel to ash.

"*You.*"

Flint crossed his arms over his chest and rolled his eyes, but his smirk gave away his delight. He reveled in my anger, invigorated by the chance to inflict suffering. His voice drawled as he spoke. "Get over it, Rydar. It was only a kiss."

My lungs sucked in the cold air greedily, and I braced myself, holding back the rage that threatened to take control. *Breathe. For Oraelia.* I could not help her if I lost myself. My words forced their way through gritted teeth—the iron gates that censored everything I wished to say. "You cannot kill her, Flint. You cannot manipulate the Trials to suit your whims."

He shrugged with feigned nonchalance, though I knew the conniving nature of his intentions. "Why ever not? Is it only acceptable when *you* do it? How long have you been helping her?"

I steadied myself, speaking slowly and deliberately, refusing to succumb to the building rage. "I have only acted on your behalf. You wanted her. I ensured you'd have her." The words made me sick as they left my mouth.

"Yes, well, I no longer want her. I wanted a *worthy* bride, and it appears she is not. She needs to go." His tone was flippant, but I could feel the challenge beneath the surface.

"Flint..." I did not mean for my voice to carry the hint of pleading, but he had heard it, and I could not unspeak it—he was listening for it. Victory sparkled in the depths of his eyes.

"You *do* love her." His voice lowered to a whisper. "Have you told her? Does she know what a danger you are to her?" He leered at me. "Oh, this is simply decadent. I'm not sure who it will be more fun to watch die...you or her."

I bared my teeth, closer to losing control than I should have allowed myself to be. "Do not touch her."

He ignored me and snatched my wrist, running a finger over the shadowy dragon forged by my blood oath with Oraelia. "What is it you promised her, anyway? I've been dying to know the terms of your little arrangement with the girl."

I flinched too late. His hand darted from my wrist to my forehead as swift as the strike of an ice adder. Inconceivable pain exploded in my mind, and my knees buckled, crashing to the ground. My face screwed up, wincing and wishing for it to be over. My mind fought to push him away, trying to close the doors on the scrape of his claws as they raked through my thoughts, but his grip was too firm. When he finally released me from his torment, my forehead dripped with sweat, and my breath came in ragged spurts. My head rolled back, hanging limply over my shoulder.

His laughter bubbled with mirth as he spoke. "I see. Her darling sister and father. How are they? I should really pay them a visit. Always good to know your future in-laws, isn't it?"

My heart thundered. I had hidden them well, but I'd need to leave to fortify their protections. If the high prince had seen where I left them, read it in my thoughts... Panic built in my chest.

I did not have the strength to waste on words, so I narrowed my eyes to do the speaking.

The high prince's lip curled upward as he leaned closer to whisper. "You know what? I thought it would be best to rid myself of the girl and wash my hands of this, but it would be so much more fun to watch you suffer... consumed by bitterness and jealousy." He gripped my chin, pushing the matted hair from my forehead, smirking when I flinched at his touch. "What an honor to know I have what you *desperately* want but can never have. Maybe I'll be nice and let you watch on our wedding night, so you can imagine what it would be like."

My fist swung wildly toward his jaw, but crippling pain so intense that I was uncertain if I had even landed the blow sent me reeling backward. A fiery line of stars burned the edges of my vision away, and I groaned through the searing agony that gripped me.

The last thing I saw before my vision disintegrated into darkness was Flint's face hovering above me—the sandy blonde curls and dimpled chin of a monster. He traced his fingers over my hairline with a whisper of hostility in his gentle caress. His voice was velvety as he spoke. "It is so much fun watching you self-destruct, brother."

CHAPTER FORTY

Broken Bread and Broken Glass

RAE

Thirty morsels of bread blew into the wind, carried by the souls on their journey to the Next Realm. A piece for Ruwe, Vyn, Vance, Pell, Gidian...and all the others I did not have a name for. *May the Fates rest their souls.*

I had not intended to make a spectacle of my grief.

With overwhelm dulling my senses and needing to occupy my hands, I followed Alia to the kitchens to ask Nadera for a spare roll of bread. A somber crowd had gathered behind me to witness my work, watching as I laid out each piece on the balcony to feed the departing souls. The crust was rough on my fingers as I tore it apart, and the smell of the freshly baked bread felt like home, but a warped and sad distortion of it. I missed Nell. *Please let her be alright.*

Lio's hand reached for mine when I finished, squeezing affection into his grasp as I stared into the sky but saw nothing. Brickert's hand rested on my shoulder as the breeze stirred again, whisking the hair from my face to tickle my neck. Taiver and Harma stood behind me, though how or when they had arrived, I was uncertain. For a moment, we were not enemies, not competitors, but simply ourselves.

The kitchen staff gathered behind us, shielding us from view—granting the reprieve to honor the fallen, or perhaps merely regretting our fates yet to come.

Nobody spoke, at least not out loud. The wind lifted our voiceless thoughts and carried them away, the feeling of them lingering in the valley and between the mountains like hushed echoes.

When the last crumbs danced into the wind, I turned in silence and made my way toward the door.

Lady Janesta exploded into the kitchens, breaking the stillness. "Alia! We need you. Come quick." She grabbed Alia by the wrists, her face pale and lips trembling. "Lady Isolde...she's making a mess. She won't listen. She's going to get herself killed."

Alia shared a nervous glance with me, then hustled into step alongside Janesta. Lio raised his eyebrows, and I understood his intention to follow. "Come on," I whispered in agreement. I had no fondness for the woman, but I had no desire to see anyone else killed today. Enough bread had been broken.

We followed the pair to the grand ballroom. Alia's steps were long and purposeful next to Janesta's short, scurried movements. A cacophony of screeches and tinkling glass, banging, and splintering wood met my ears as we neared the double doors. A vase flew toward my head as I entered, though it missed and shattered against the doorframe.

Debris littered the floor, coating Isolde's hair in dust and glittering shards, her face and bodice reduced to a chaotic impersonation of her normal, pristine appearance.

She danced amidst her destruction, crunching bits of porcelain and glass beneath her shoes. Her eyes turned wild as she snatched a goblet from a table and hurled it toward the ceiling at one of the few remaining hourglasses. It exploded, bursting into a song of glass and color.

She screamed in response, resembling a feral cat, as she clawed the table cloths free of their charges, stripping the tables and herself of dignity. Crystals scattered across the room amidst the shining carcasses of ruined hourglasses, casting a rainbow of light upon the ceiling to create beauty in the rubble.

Lady Janesta brushed against me, whispering over her shoulder. "She tried to destroy your hourglass—only she doesn't have very good aim. When she hit Taiver's instead, she sort of...lost it. I can't get her to stop."

"Lady Isolde." Alia's voice was sharp and full of reprimand. Isolde's icy eyes snapped toward us, noticing our arrival for the first time and curling her upper lip into a scowl. She charged toward me, but Alia blocked her murderous advance.

"*You.*" Her eyes bulged as she struggled to push past Alia, teeth bared in an inhuman snarl. Alia managed to pull the woman's arms behind her back, but her eyes darted to me, betraying her fear when her grip began to slip. Lio bolted toward Alia to fortify her restraint, but Isolde only redoubled her efforts to thrash her way free, her forehead slick with sweat.

Her voice turned hysterical as she writhed in their grasp. "You ruined everything!" she howled, and spit flew through her bared teeth. "It's not fair! You killed him...you pushed him over the ledge. My Vance. *You* were supposed to die, you stupid—" A guttural scream overpowered the rest of her words. "It's not fair!"

Blood boiled in my veins, and I could not stop the words that spilled from my mouth. "Not fair? You think your life is unfair? You know what's unfair, Isolde? *Everything.* Every cursed hour of my life has been unfair, including this very moment. Do you think I enjoyed killing him? Do you think I want to destroy others to live? Watch the others die or die myself? You think I want any of this?" I moved close enough to feel her breath on my face, to feel the heat of anger radiating from her skin. "Do not tell me *your* life is unfair when it has been *nothing* but privileged."

She sobered for a moment, but the snarl on her lips remained. "You know nothing."

I wanted to hate her. My hands itched to shove her away or smack some sense into that beautiful head of hers, but a sudden flicker in her expression gave me pause. Behind her scowl, her eyes brimmed with panic, and I searched her face for an explanation. *What are you afraid of?*

Perhaps we all suffered in ways that could not be seen.

"Sun and stars! *What* is going on here?" My heart dropped into my stomach. I craned my head to the ballroom entrance and watched as Flint Barragan strode into the room, his boots crunching over the bits of glass. A glower of outrage besmirched his usual charming facade, and his hands flexed, then balled into fists at his side.

Watchmen flanked him with their rifles trained on us while Orman and Trystan's eyes darted nervously about, surveying the damage to the room.

Flint ground his teeth and narrowed his eyes. "Explain."

Nobody spoke. I turned my eyes to Isolde, waiting for her to take ownership but fearing she would shift the blame to me. I wished I hadn't looked—her face had turned ghastly pale, and her eyes pleaded with me, brimming with dread.

An exasperated sigh escaped the high prince, and he waved to the Watchmen at his side. "I don't have time for this. Arrest them all and Retire them one by one until somebody speaks."

The Watchmen wasted no time. Alia let out a sharp gasp as one Watchman grabbed her from behind, and Lio's face paled as another Watchman approached him.

No. I can't let them do this.

"It was me." I stepped forward, bridging the gap between us. Flint's gaze shifted abruptly toward me.

His eyes narrowed, searching my expression beneath a furrowed brow. "Explain." His lips enunciated the sound of each letter with an exaggerated drawl.

Hadn't thought that part through. I filled my lungs slowly as I cobbled together an explanation in my mind, then met Flint's eyes. "I was jealous."

"Jealous?" The word rolled around in his mouth like an unfamiliar food, and his sneer showed he found the taste unpleasant.

From behind Flint, Alia caught my eye and gave me a faint, almost invisible shake of her head, begging me to change course. I could nearly feel her screaming, *No!* straight into my soul.

Too late.

If Isolde would not confess, then I would shoulder the blame. Not for her, but for the others.

"I—I was jealous I only received a year's worth of time in the last task. It was *not fair*." My eyes darted to Isolde at the last two words. She bristled, but averted her gaze to the rubble at her feet.

It only took two unhurried strides through the glass for the high prince to reach me. He grabbed my arms and tilted his head with an unexpected smile that looked something like fondness, then leaned in to whisper. "You know I must punish you for this, darling."

He straightened his back to stand at his full height—the light glinting off the buttons of his jacket as he looked down at me. His voice filled the room with authority.

"Take her to the dungeons. I'll decide what to do with her in the morning."

Chapter Forty-One

Festering Wounds and Wonder

Rae

The stone floor leached away my body heat, trading it for a coldness that seeped into my bones and stiffened my muscles like water turned to ice. But that was not the worst of it.

Pain permeated the air. Fresh waves of excruciating agony crashed into my heart at random intervals to beg for the gift of healing.

I could not see her, but I could hear the spluttering hiss of the dragon as she repositioned, scraping useless wings and talons across the stone deep within the dungeon. An hour of sharing her suffering added a layer of torture to my imprisonment that even the high prince could not have dreamt up. My heart ached for her.

I winced as another roar pierced my ears and rattled the walls. "Shhh," I whispered into the darkness, despite knowing I could do nothing from my cell to soothe her. I began to hum, quiet at first, then louder as I sensed the dragon's movements slow, stopping to listen to the song my mother used to sing.

The door of the dungeons rattled, dispersing the notes of my song as somebody fumbled with the lock. I fell quiet, letting my unease fill the room.

"Rae?" A silhouette poked through the doorway, her features drowned by the shaft of light that poured into the room from the hall. My eyes winced at the brightness.

"Alia?" I whispered.

"Oh praise the Fates, you're still alive." She rushed toward me, reaching through the bars of the cell to cradle my face in the warmth of her hands. My eyes refocused in the darkness, blinking away the assault of the bright lights to study Alia's expression. Her cheeks shimmered with tears, the splotch of red skin on the side of her face darkened by the shadows. "What am I going to do with you, you fool? You were supposed to win! I needed you to win." Her tone was not harsh, but mournful.

A quick breath escaped through my nose, failing to become the laugh it was meant to be. "So the high prince has made up his mind?" *What form of Retirement am I to face in the morning?*

"We're not waiting around for him to decide. Come on. I'm getting you out." Keys jingled in her hands—the ringing sound of liberty. "Snatched them from my father. If we're fast, we can get you out of Orogi before morning."

"Alia—what? How?"

"Don't ask questions."

My heart leaped in my chest, but my muscles strained as I pulled myself to stand. Blood rushed into my numb legs, sending life back to my tingling limbs. My fingers wrapped around the steel bars, and I grimaced until the sensation subsided.

Alia fiddled with the ring of keys, trying each in the lock and huffing as each failed. My eyes caught the shadow dragon on my forearm, prowling up and down the length of my arm in clear agitation. *The oath.* My spirits plummeted.

I could escape the bars, but not my promises.

"Alia, stop. I can't. Do not risk yourself to save me…we both know my time is running thin. Take the keys back and get Rydar. I need him."

She made a face of disapproval at the mention of his name. "Rydar? What do you want with him?"

"Please, Alia. He'll help me." I grabbed her wrist, but she brushed me away to try a new key. A smile cracked through the serious expression on her face when it slipped effortlessly into the lock. She turned the key in the hole, and the mechanism slid aside with a click. The door swung forward, creaking as it moved, and her eyes danced with mischief when she backed away. I could not stomach the idea of harm coming to her.

"Alia...don't. Close it."

She shook her head and rolled her eyes in mock disapproval. "Those Watchmen are so careless— never securing the locks properly." She grinned and pocketed the keys. "Nobody will know it was me. Don't worry. I'll be right back."

"Alia—Rydar. Please."

"Yes, yes. Fallen heir. Got it."

"Alia?"

"Mmm?"

"Do you think the Watchmen might have been careless with the dragon's cell as well?"

She paused at the door frame, her features concealed by darkness, but her hesitation suggested indecision. "You want me to unlock the dragon?"

"She's hurt."

Her voice lowered to a harsh whisper. "Please tell me you're joking. Do you have a death wish?"

"Please."

Silence. Then, the jingle of keys. "Fine. I don't know how you expect to help her, but don't get yourself killed. I can't handle it."

Her feet padded along the stone floor in the recognizable pattern of her wide strides. The lock slid open on the third try. Alia whimpered at the dragon's wail, then quickly retreated to the dungeon door. "Stay out of trouble," she whispered into the darkness and then slipped into the light of the hallway beyond. The flash of brightness blinded me.

The hinges of the cell door groaned as I pushed it open. Darkness disoriented me, but I groped my way forward in the shadows, using the stone walls and iron bars as a guide until my eyes readjusted. The waves of pain from the dragon pulled me toward her like the undercurrent of the sea until I found her.

I found the dragon cowering in a cell much too small to house her majestic form. I should have felt fear, or at least a healthier dose of self-preservation, but I didn't feel threatened by her. I did not know how I knew, but I was certain she would not harm me.

"Shhhh," I whispered, announcing my presence so I would not startle her. The dragon turned her head toward me and dropped it to her front legs, issuing a defeated harrumph through flared nostrils.

"I can help you...if you'll let me." Her eyes were full of sadness, but she tilted her head slightly, regarding me with a spark of intrigue.

Raising my hands to show a lack of aggression, I slipped inside the cell and moved toward her. My heart didn't race as it did when I first faced her in the ravine—her hopeless gaze and slumped form screamed defeat and surrender, and my heart broke for her.

I placed a hand on her obsidian scales, probing with my magic to locate the sources of her pain. Heat flowed from my chest into my veins and escaped through my fingers. The magic found its way to her mutilated wings and sealed the raw, festering wounds where the bindings had damaged her scales, then wove deeper to heal the punctures from Watchmen's lances.

The act drained me of energy until perspiration surfaced on my skin, and my breaths became labored. My legs collapsed beneath me, and I slumped over, leaning into the space between the dragon's front leg and folded wing. Her neck twisted until her head bobbed before me, inches from my face. She could roast me if she chose to, but I knew she would not. Or perhaps I simply did not have the energy to care.

Wonder glimmered in the dragon's eyes. Her muscles rippled as tension ebbed away, and her head rose toward the ceiling—the crest of spikes forming a regal crown that flowed into royal ridges down her neck and spine. Her lids dropped in a heavy blink of gratitude that I understood as readily as if she had uttered the words to me.

Footsteps fell behind me, then faltered.

"You would trade your life to save a dragon? Is it worth it?"

Chapter Forty-Two

Hidden Gems and Misted Dewdrops

RAE

"Do you have any idea what you've done? How dangerous this is?"

The words should have scared me, but my heart leaped at the voice. *Rydar.* I turned to find him staring, heartbreak written in his eyes.

"You are a healer."

I did not confirm the accusation or try to deny it. I only stared quietly, waiting for his judgment.

"Do you know why there are no true healers left, Oraelia? Have you ever wondered why there are none with those powers?"

I pulled my lips inward and sealed the answer behind my teeth, unwilling to voice it.

His brows turned downward with pain. "My father destroyed them. If they figure this out, if they connect you to the dragon...they'll Retire you without a moment of hesitation. The high king's ego is fragile. *He* decides who lives, how long, how well—and a true healer is a threat to his reign over life and death. *You* are a threat to the Realm. *Helfyre, Oraelia. Why are you impossible to keep alive?*"

He shook his head, then ran a hand through his tousled hair, gripping it as though he intended to rip it away. "If I take you…" He paced around the room, his distress evident in his tight jaw and flared nostrils. "It is dangerous…They will—"

He muttered as he walked, never fully explaining or finishing his half-formed thoughts.

I watched in silence, too tired to move from the crevice of wing and bone that cradled me, but wishing he would come to me. *Hold me.*

At last, he slowed. "There's no other way…It has to be so."

My lips parted, noticing the sparkle of tears in his eyes as he approached to lay the whisper of a kiss on my brow, the soothing scent of sandalwood and rain wrapping around me like the comfort of a warm blanket. His arms swept beneath my legs and scooped me up from the ground, holding me close to his chest so I could rest my head against him and find the thrumming of his heart.

"Can you ride?" he asked, his voice deep and powerful.

I raised my gaze and nodded. *Maybe. Yes.*

He lifted me onto the dragon, and I wrapped my legs around her, the obsidian scales smooth against my skin despite their rough appearance. Rydar whispered to her, and I could only hear the deep rumble of his words in his chest, but not the meaning of them. The beautiful creature bowed her head in a graceful dip, closing her eyes in accord.

Rydar slipped behind me, his chest warm against my back, filling the emptiness in my bones left behind by the penetrating cold.

"Where are we going?"

"Away."

"How will we get out?" I whispered, awed by the creature's swaying gait beneath me as she began her sauntering steps.

"The same way she came in. Through the tunnels."

"What about the oath?" The shadow dragon raced along my arm, spiraling in a dive toward my wrist.

"It cannot harm you if you leave with my blessing…if I release you."

"I don't understand—"

Has it been so simple this whole time, Rydar Barragan? You will release me now? How? I twisted my spine to search his face for answers, only to see the pain in the creases near his eyes.

"I cannot let you endure this any longer. Consequences be damned." He placed a palm on my cheek, wearing a smile that spoke only of sadness as he said, "I have failed in every way, but I will not fail you."

The sun, heavy with the fullness of the day, brightened the snowy landscape to a dazzling white—blinding me as we emerged from the tunnels. The dragon's claws scraped at the ice below her talons, rooting her to the ledge before Rydar leaned in closer, the shimmer of sunlight gracing his hair. He placed my hands firmly around the dragon and whispered into my ear. "Hold on."

"Where are we going?" I breathed.

"Across the sea." The dragon's wings extended at our sides with a whoosh, then sliced through the sky. We dropped downward, plummeting from the ledge in smooth descent until my stomach found its way to my throat.

Rydar's arms held fast, pulling me deep into his chest so that I could feel the leap of his heart match the flutter of mine. The dragon's leathery wings rose and fell with grace until we leveled, charging onward into the weary sun.

The dragon circled over the mountains, and I watched with awe, forgetting the danger, the fears, the imminent end that awaited me. Instead, I let myself be Rydar's. For just a moment, I let myself believe I could find safety in his arms and a future in his heart. Were we truly going across the sea? The Ageander? What then? My mind drifted, imagining other worlds and cultures and wonders beyond the borders of Orogi. Imagining the chance for better.

 A.C. GUESS

"We'll stop here for the night," Rydar said into my ear, pulling me away from my thoughts. "We should be safe until daybreak. Nobody knows about these pools, save for Trystan."

I raised my brow at him, wondering what he meant. He smiled wryly.

"When the high king commissioned the House of Frost, he sent us to survey the island. The pools were intentionally omitted from the maps we drafted—it gave Trystan and me a place to meet. Besides, I feared that if the high king knew about this place—he would leverage it for himself and twist its beauty into something sinister. I was tired of his endless penchant for tarnishing anything good left in the world. So now this is my secret. And yours."

The dragon dipped between the crags of the mountains at a brush of Rydar's hand. White tendrils of steam curled toward the sky between the rock like clouds climbing their way back to the heavens, and when we dropped lower into the ravine, I gasped at the sight of the pools. The glistening aquamarine gems stretched below us in clusters, nestled into the heart of the valley beneath a hazy curtain of steam that rose to kiss my legs with misted dewdrops.

The dragon lowered, landing with the grace of a cat and the whisper of claws against icy rock. She moved her majestic head to the ground, prostrating to allow us to slide easily from her back.

The snow compacted beneath each of Rydar's heavy steps, and he pulled me from her back with ease, setting me down gently at her side. My legs wobbled with fatigue, but my heart pumped blood through my veins. The magnificence surrounding us in every direction re-energized me with a sense of wonder.

His eyes followed me with an intensity I could feel against my back as I stepped toward the pool, amazed by the steam that curled from the crystal waters in a dance of clouds. Bubbles tickled the spaces between my fingers when I dipped my hand into the pool, and I gasped at the unexpected warmth.

These azure pools, hidden gems between the looming walls of gray rock, were as warm as the luxurious baths drawn for me in the House of Frost. I had never witnessed anything like it. It was magic.

"This is the most beautiful thing I have seen in my life."

From behind me, his deep rumble of a voice found its way into my heart. "Yes, it comes close, doesn't it?"

I whirled around to find Rydar watching me, his gaze churning with storm clouds and secrets.

"Close to what?" But I knew. It was in his eyes.

"To the most beautiful thing I've ever seen."

CHAPTER FORTY-THREE

A Gift

RAE

My heart fluttered between my ribs. The stunted breath I drew was not nearly sufficient to fill my lungs, but I found myself incapable of more. *He means me. Fates, why is he staring? Should I go to him? Please, do something and stop gaping at him, you fool.*

But my tongue would not form any useful words, and my eyes refused to turn away. One second. Two. The only breath came from the whisper of air through the mountains.

The magic dispersed with a heavy sigh, and he dropped his gaze. He rummaged in his pockets and withdrew a folded bit of parchment. "I brought you something."

My eyes at last pulled away, intrigued by the paper in his grasp.

"A gift?"

"Yes. From your sister."

Nell. My eyes bounced between the paper and his face, and I crinkled my nose, pushing aside the heartache that ambushed me. "Wait...you saw her?"

He nodded.

"You *left* me?"

"Had to," he mumbled through a lopsided smirk, then tugged on the end of his sleeve to reveal the twin of my shadow dragon—our oath. "I have many faults, but I am a man of my word. I made a promise to protect her and your father."

I had a million questions but settled on the most important. "Are they well?"

He nodded. "They miss you."

I missed them so much that their absence felt like a hole spreading through my heart, erasing parts of me until I feared I would become nothing at all. He cleared his throat, then slowly unfolded the paper, rustling the creases smooth beneath his calloused fingers. "She wrote this for you."

Foolish, Nell. But a smile accompanied my silent chiding. Poetry was outlawed, like all beautiful or inspiring work in Orogi. It only made hearing her words more desirable.

His voice lowered into a deep, gravelly tone that paid tribute to the lines of her poem as he read.

You bow, victorious,
aglow with triumph.
The dusk that lays to rest,
cradled by trees, nestled into
the blanket of the horizon.
Victory is written in the stars—
Shining—
acclaimed by starlight and
reverent shadow.
Until dawn stirs to call forth
the rising sun,
and you emerge to paint the sky
with phoenix feathers
and new beginnings.

His eyes darted from the paper to mine. "She's signed it at the bottom. 'Keep fighting—you're stronger than you know. Love you always, Nell.'"

I closed my eyes and smiled, feeling Nell's love woven through her words. Rydar pressed the paper into my hands, and I ran my finger over the creases, touching the ink of each scrawled letter on the paper as though it could some-how bring me closer to her. "Thank you."

He nodded. I released a breath, allowing myself to be at ease, then stepped closer to him. Leaning into his arm, we watched the clouds blossom into vivid hues surrounded by halos of gold. A celebration of another day survived. "I always loved sunsets."

He sat in silence, lost in thought or perhaps merely admiring the way the setting sun illuminated the ground to turn the landscape into an oasis of desert sands instead of snow. I did not interrupt his quiet, but joined him in it until he was ready to speak again.

"I am not a good person, Rae."

Why does he always do this? "You have been good to me."

"Not half as good as you deserve." His hand moved to my cheek, brushing softly against my skin and coming to rest at my chin so that I held my breath and waited for his lips to meet mine. Instead, he merely groaned and dropped his hand, returning his gaze to the fiery sky. I suppressed a grumble of frustration. *Why must you always pull away?*

"When I first saw you, I knew who you were. What you were. You blazed your way into my life like the sun, and you made me feel like there could be a light at the end of all this darkness, and that if I could only be near you, I would find my way out of the shadows." He turned to face me once more, locking his stormy eyes on mine. "You are my dawn, Rae—a light in my life I will never deserve."

My cheeks warmed, flustered by the sentiment.

Almatae. The one my soul loves.

The words pulsed in my mind, surfacing without solicitation...simply *there* and suggesting the truth I sensed in my bones. I was tempted to hide my reaction but faced him, letting my lips part. "Is that another one of Nell's poems?"

His uneven smile softened his eyes. "No. That one is my own." He pulled me close, enveloping me in his arms with a sigh. "I am sorry I cannot give you what you deserve—"

Stop. I was so tired of his walls, his guarding, his reservations. I placed my finger on his lips, sealing his words in his mouth before he retreated into his fortress. Folding my legs beneath me, I rose, holding his silence and his gaze with my own. *What do you want with me, Rydar? What is this between us?*

The need to unravel the truth of his feelings consumed me. I acted without thinking, without planning, letting instinct and the burning desire to know where I stood with him take over.

I pulled the sleeves of my dress downward so that they slipped over my shoulders, and my bare skin prickled with the brush of wind against it, wisps of hair tickling my neck and my exposed collarbone in the breeze. I shivered, though the chilled air was not to blame.

What has come over you, Rae? I fought the urge to falter, projecting a mask of confidence at odds with the flutter of nerves in my stomach. What if I was mistaken? Perhaps I had misread him?

But Rydar sucked in a short breath, holding it in his chest as if he had forgotten how to breathe. I stood still, afraid that a single exhale may disperse the moment like smoke in the wind.

"What are you doing?" he whispered.

His voice was husky, and the knot in his throat bobbed as he swallowed. He was not immune to my efforts. I smiled coyly. "Swimming. You can swim in these pools, can't you?"

"Yes."

The hunger in his eyes dispelled any of my lingering fears. His gaze roved from my lips to my neck to my shoulders, then down to my waist as I pulled the dress past my hips. My skin flushed, and the flurry of wings doubled in my stomach, but still, I held his gaze.

His lips opened but said nothing as the dress met the ground with a rustle, and I stood at my fullest height, unabashed, wearing nothing but my under-clothes and the admiration of his eyes.

Slowly, I backed into the waters, wading deeper until the warmth enveloped me to my shoulders, and I shared the hint of a smile with him, luring him toward me. *Stop resisting, you fool. If I'm to die, I wish to use the last of my time wisely.*

"Do not look at me like that." Rydar's voice strained with pain as he swallowed.

"Like what?" My heart pounded against my ribs.

"Like you want me to follow."

"I do."

CHAPTER FORTY-FOUR

Sacrifice and Sunset

RAE

I heard the hiss of his sharp intake of breath, and the tortured expression in his eyes wavered, then returned tenfold. His shoulders slumped forward. "No."

My pulse quickened, and I felt blood rush into my ears with a rush of self-conscious worry. *What are you doing, Oraelia? This is a mistake.*

"Do you not want to?" The words burned. I unstuck my throat, forcing myself to speak through the dryness of my mouth in a hoarse whisper. "Do you not want me?"

"No, I—"

My body flushed with humiliation, and I sank deeper into the water, turning my eyes toward the colorful sky to hold back tears before I met his gaze again.

The muscle at the side of his jaw twitched, and he pressed his lids together in remorse, tears squeezing between his lashes. His voice was gruff and filled with pain when he spoke.

"I want you more than anything I have ever wanted in my life, Rae. Do you not know what you are to me? Who you are? Do you not understand why, from the moment I laid eyes upon you, I found myself incapable of straying from your side? I have *never* wanted anything more. But I cannot. It will destroy you."

"What are you talking about?" The balls of my feet touched the bottom of the pool, and I crossed my arms beneath the water, following his movements with only my eyes.

He removed his jacket slowly, placing it on the snowy ground at his feet. Then he lifted the hem of his shirt up from his hips, pulling it over his head in a fluid motion. A lattice of silver scars crossed over his chest, and the setting sun cast a golden glow behind him, illuminating his broad shoulders, muscled torso, and strong neck. My eyes dropped to his arms, and I gasped at the pair of dragons he bore—one on either side.

He followed the path of my eyes to his forearm, then raised it toward me. "Ours is not the only oath I am sworn by blood to keep."

"What? Who?" My mouth gaped uselessly, failing to give voice to the storm of thoughts in my mind.

He inhaled deeply and closed his eyes, then waited for a moment in the stillness. "It is retribution for my wrongs. I told you—I have done *terrible* things."

"Explain." I did not mean to sound harsh, but he winced.

"When I was young, just turning of age, I lost control. I didn't understand my strength, and I was so angry...I killed the high king's almatae. His soulbound. It was an accident that I have regretted every day of my life since." He chanced a glance at me, and I saw the worry in his eyes, the fear of my judgment.

"My mother was the high queen...the greatest person I have ever known. He did not deserve her. But when he fell in love with Lady Margerae, he arranged to have my mother dealt with—*quietly*. I tried to warn her, to save her, but I failed.

"When I found my mother, cold and breathless, I lost myself. I went to confront the king—I was young and brazen and meant to kill him for what he did to her. I meant to avenge her death."

He hung his hand, resting his forehead on his palms before he dragged them down his face, as though he could wipe away the shame with his fingers. "I lost control, still young and unaccustomed to the limits of my gift. My power lashed out and killed Lady Margerae instead of him. It was an accident. Flint was in their chambers as well...just a newborn in his cradle. I nearly killed him, too, but the Fates spared him."

A pained grimace twitched on his face. "I told you I am a monster."

My eyes traced the lines of scars that stretched from his shoulders to his abdomen, and my stomach coiled with sickness. How could a father brutalize his own son in such a way? Was it he who struck those marks onto his skin?

I knitted my brows together and found his eyes. "The high king is a monster."

Rydar smiled sadly but shook his head. "He should have killed me for my actions. I would have deserved it, but he showed me mercy. He promised to spare my life as long as I agreed to this oath."

"And what did you promise?"

"My allegiance to the life that I almost extinguished. To serve and protect the high prince for all of my time—" He paused, and the rueful lengthening of his face cast a shadow of sorrow about him before he inhaled the strength to continue.

"And—to never know love."

I did not speak, but the flinch of my expression spoke volumes.

"But I do," he added, and his eyes filled with longing.

My heart jumped, jolting to life with a flutter of hope. "You—you love me?"

"Isn't it obvious?"

I moved toward him, feeling the water ripple around my legs and the rocky floor of the pool brush against my toes. "Rydar. We can figure this out. There has to be a way —"

He held out a hand, stopping me from moving closer. "There is not."

"But—"

"Don't you understand? The high king has vowed to destroy anyone I love. Nothing would please him more than to hurt me in retribution for my wrongs. But I will not let him take you. I will not let Flint have you. I am setting you free."

I looked at the shadowvein on his forearm and the pain in his eyes, understanding all at once the sacrifice he would make to save me. "But he will kill you when he finds out what you've done."

He said nothing.

"No." *I will not allow it.*

"It is worth it."

My lashes fluttered to blink away the hot tears that gathered. I dragged my eyes away from his, and a searing sensation spread through my heart, a blend of fury, bitterness, and sorrow that I couldn't name.

Watching the sun at last dip beneath the peaks behind us, I searched for the words to make him understand. To make him see how I could not let him go, just as I knew he couldn't bear walking away from me.

"Do you know why I love sunset, Rydar?"

He did not answer me, but tilted his head in question, waiting. So I gathered my thoughts and my heart and laid them bare before him.

"Because I love the night. When the sun sets, it marks another day survived. Night falls, and with it comes a peace known only to the darkness. Rest...renewal. If I am the dawn, then you are my dusk. You are the solace I will fight my way towards every day, never resting, never stopping until I can find my way to you beneath the starlit sky. I am not afraid of the darkness, Rydar, especially not yours. This is not our end."

Wind stirred his hair, but the rest of him remained frozen, breathless, watching me with eyes turned downward and a jaw tensed with reserve. And then, all at once, as though his body surrendered to whatever battles plagued his mind, he stripped down to his underclothes and tossed aside his boots and pants. His shoulders relaxed, and he rushed toward me, splashing through the water until he held me in his arms and pressed his mouth against mine.

CHAPTER FORTY-FIVE

A Tapestry of Souls

RAE

I wrapped my arms around him, finding the space between his shoulder blades to pull him close to me, erasing the space between our bodies. His bare chest felt like fire against my skin. His tongue swept between my lips to part them, and a groan rumbled through him when I tilted my head back and allowed him entrance.

Mine. Almatae. The word flashed again in my mind, but soon, the hunger of his kisses and the grip of his fingers wrapped through my hair left me unable to think of anything but the threading of his body with mine and the need for *more, more, more.* To make our connection closer. Deeper. Stronger.

I pulled away to meet his eyes, full of the storm clouds and darkness that now felt like comfort instead of danger.

My skin blazed with life when his breath warmed the skin at my jaw, trailing kisses down to my collarbone, and I bent my head back to expose the skin of my neck to beg him for more. His calloused hands retreated from my hair and found my bare skin, brushing against my shoulders, then drifting along my spine beneath my slip. I shivered at his touch and pressed my hips into his beneath the water, feeling the proof of his desire.

A groan escaped him when I let my fingers trail down the ridges of his abdomen, tracing the silver latticework of scars with reverence, then lowering toward the laces of his underclothes. He held my hand, stopping me from venturing any further. "You will break my resolve, Oraelia."

I smirked. "Good. I intend to."

His lips met mine again, and his hands moved beneath the hem of my slip, exploring upward until he lingered at the knot in the material that bound my breasts. My fingers met his, and the fabric drifted into the water with a quick tug. The slip soon followed, floating away in a lazy tumble to the bottom of the pool, leaving me fully exposed to him.

His hands lost no time in replacing the bindings, circling the peaks of my breasts before placing his mouth against the swell of them to praise me with kisses.

I moaned and pressed my hips against him again. "Please."

"Patience," he grumbled, taking all the time in the world to torture me with the lightest brush of his fingers, touching me everywhere except where I needed him most.

"Rydar."

Water sloshed around us as he pushed me toward the rocky edge at the far side of the pool until I leaned against it, waiting. His hands gripped the rock above my shoulders, and when he met my eyes, I felt my very soul bared to him.

His eyes drifted downward, worshiping the rest of me with his gaze, and I felt no embarrassment, only a deep sense of his admiration. "I love you, Oraelia."

His mouth claimed mine, warm and certain against my lips. A gasp escaped me, and my hips bucked as his hand moved between my thighs, finding the place that ached for his attention. I moved against his hand, needing more—longing for the fullness of our connection, wanting everything he could give me.

He growled with pleasure when my hand explored the hardened length of him, and I fumbled with the laces, writhing against the movement of his fingers. But it wasn't enough. The laces fell away, and I tried not to gape at his length.

"Rydar." A plea.

His knee slipped between my thighs, and I wrapped my legs around his hips, letting the water carry me. I gasped as he found my entrance and pushed inside slowly, and he groaned before moving deeper, sinking himself within me to the hilt. A sense of total completeness filled me.

He moved against me, his hips grinding against mine as he thrust, faster and faster, until I lost the sense of my surroundings. My fingers splayed over his back, digging into his shoulder blades to pull him closer. I moaned as his mouth caressed the sensitive curve of my neck, his breath warm and powerful against my skin. Tension coiled within my body, mirroring the tautness of his muscles as we danced upon the edge, our bodies joined until there was no separation, no individual entities of Rydar and Rae—just *us* and the twining of heart and soul, breath and body.

The golden threads of our souls wove together in the magic of our movements, binding us together irreversibly. For all time. "The one my soul loves," I whispered, and I heard the echo of my words in the beat of his heart.

Cloaked in warm water and starlight, we lost control, gripped by the rush of waves that pulsed through our bodies as we found release together, leaving ripples in the tapestry of our souls forever.

And in the distance, as he wrapped me in his arms and kissed my forehead with quiet tenderness, the stars danced in our honor and the wind howled in reverie as it hissed through the mountain, sharing in the song of our entwined spirits.

CHAPTER FORTY-SIX

Tendrils of Smoke

RAE

I leaned into him, wrapped in his arms at the edge of the pool. I smiled, whole and content, letting the glow of our bond settle deep in my pores, burrowing through my core to thread its way through the fabric of my soul. This was magic. Happiness. I traced slow circles over his skin, lazily following the lines of his scars, marveling at the man who would forever be mine. The one my soul loves.

Rydar flinched suddenly, his muscles tensing sharply, and he twisted with a hiss of pain. Turning toward him, I watched him, creasing my brow with worry. He groaned and screwed his eyes shut.

My heart raced, and I reached for him, placing my hand on his bare chest. His skin was burning up, and the wave of his pain pummeled me as he doubled over. "What is happening? What's wrong?"

My voice was little more than a whisper as my eyes darted from his face to his shoulders and down to his abdomen, finally landing on his clenched fists as they emerged from the waters. The moonlight illuminated the blackness pooling in his fingertips, rising slowly to his knuckles like tendrils of inky smoke.

He met my eyes, and his face paled, drained of color until he was as white as the snow around the pool. He spoke in a raspy whisper that carried dread into my heart. "The oath..." He groaned. "It knows. When our bond snapped into place, it activated."

He moved his hand over his heart and gasped, brushing me away when I reached for him. "No!" Panic flashed across his face and he scrambled backward. "The oath whispers. I did not know—I did not realize it would work like this." He grimaced and pulled away from me, his eyes full of terror as the truth dawned across his features. "He knows. It is forcing me...he will make *me* do it. I did not—I didn't know..."

"What? Rydar—please." I glided toward him, feeling the caress of bubbles as the water moved around my skin, and I threw my arms over his shoulders to draw his head to mine.

His agony ripped free from him in a roar. "Get away! Please. I cannot."

My heart cleaved in half, shattering into pieces of glass that shredded me apart with each breath I took. *You reject me now? My almatae?*

His eyes glistened with anguish. "The oath. Is poisoning. Me." He paused between words, grinding his teeth together. "Because I—because I fell in love with you."

He clenched his eyes closed and inhaled a steadying breath. New beads of sweat gathered at his hairline and rolled down his brow. When I placed my hands on his shoulders, his muscles were tense with restraint. His eyes darkened, flashing with malice and madness that did not belong to him. "It whispers. It wants me to kill you. Says I *must* kill you—that it will destroy me if I resist."

No. I looked him straight in the eye, unyielding, denying his effort to break away. "I am not afraid of you, Rydar. You are stronger than this. We are stronger than this. Let me heal you."

"Do not touch me! Do not come near me. Please. You cannot heal me from this...you will break yourself trying. Do not." He wrestled in my grasp, but I pulled him close and buried my cheek into the warmth of his body, letting the tears mix with the water, sweat, and salt until they were indistinguishable.

My mouth moved against his skin as I spoke, holding him close. "Let me try." I choked on the words, wrapping my arms firmly around him, gripping his shoulder blades until my fingers hurt, pouring out my magic to heal his veins. *We did not come this far to lose one another now.*

"NO!" He ripped away from me, wading backward until he splashed out of the waters and leaned against the dragon with one hand, drawing labored breaths beneath his other palm.

When he had caught his breath, he set his gaze upon me, his eyes churning as the darkened storm clouds rolled in. He shook his head.

"Listen carefully. Take the dragon. Fly north across the sea until you find land. Save yourself. Promise me. You mustn't come looking for me—promise you will get to safety and stay there, and I will release you from your oath. I will free you. The consequences no longer matter."

They matter to me. Knots writhed in my stomach and twisted their way around my lungs, squeezing the air from my chest and crushing my heart. *There has to be another way. I cannot lose you.*

"No. Stay with me."

He lifted his arm, showing me the brand of his oath with the king. "I cannot. He will find me, and I will not lead him to you." The face he made, the apology in his eyes, the glimpse of our lost future that crumbled with each passing moment, broke me. "And I do not know how long I'll be able to deny the curse's demand—I do not know how long I have before it impairs my faculties...or drives me mad. You must go."

"The high king will kill you." The words were so quiet they drifted into the wind, transparent whispers.

"Undoubtably. Or the Oath will take me first." He covered the shadow dragon on his forearm with his fingers, blackened by the cursed oath, and the corner of his lips turned upward into the saddest smile. "It is worth it. You are worth everything."

My mind stormed with a whirlwind of thoughts that swirled and thrashed, but I refused to settle into any useful order to help me find a way out of this.

Rydar stiffened, his eyes growing large with horror. "He knows. He's coming."

He stormed toward me, lifted me over his shoulders, and threw me onto the dragon's back. "Go. I release you."

I righted myself and glared at him, letting every flame of my spirit flare to life in my gaze. "But I do not release *you*, Rydar Barragan. I do not release you from our bargain. You know they will not rest. They will search the furthest corners of the world to find me. We will not run from this. There is no hiding. Not for you, not for me. Do not give up on me now."

He raised a hand in protest, but I would not hear it.

"Take me back, Rydar. I have an oath to fulfill."

"The high king will end us."

"No, we will end him."

CHAPTER FORTY-SEVEN

Torchlight

RAE

We arrived, shivering at the mouth of the tunnels, with icicles for hair and goosebumps for skin. The air bit our fingers, finding its way past the defense of our huddled warmth—there had been no time for the luxury of a fire to dry ourselves before we put on our outer clothes.

My teeth chattered until my jaw ached. We would not have made it without my magic to stem the grip of frost from taking hold.

The dragon perched, lingering on the precipice to watch us with perceptive eyes and tilted head. I kissed her thorny muzzle and urged her to go. *Be free. Please.*

She did not deserve the fates we had chosen, and I could not afford to be linked to her recovery. Reluctantly, the dragon dropped away into the night on leather wings, eclipsing the moon as she soared past. My heart raced, syncing in rhythm to Rydar's until she became nothing but a hint of shadow in the darkness.

Rydar grabbed my hand, and if I could have moved my frozen fingers, I would have returned the gesture. He kissed my brow. "Hurry. We'll need to find clothes and a hearth before the servants wake."

The darkness of the tunnels swallowed us, with only the sound of our footsteps shuffling against rock to ground my senses. Rydar said nothing as we wound through the halls, but I could hear his labored breaths and feel his worry weigh heavily in the air. How long did he have before the shadowvein worked its way to his heart? He hid his pain behind smiles and strength, but I could *feel* it—always there.

A muffled scrape echoed against the walls, deep within the belly of the tunnel. Rydar threw an arm in front of me, and we both halted to listen, uncertain if we had truly heard anything at all.

A torch flickered to life at the end of the tunnel. *Helfyre.*

"Back so soon from your little adventure?" The twisting light illuminated the smarmy grin on Flint's face. He walked toward us slowly, carrying the torch with him so that his distorted shadow stretched along the wall.

"I must admit, I am a little displeased that I was not afforded an invitation." His attention bounced between us and his brow arched with condescension. "You both look dreadful."

"What are you doing here?" I asked, finding my voice. Too small. Too weak. I stilled the quaking of my bones and lifted my chin, refusing to show him the true state of my tattered nerves. I had more pressing matters to attend to than a high prince with a high opinion of himself.

"What am I doing here? Oraelia, do not be rude. I should ask the same of you." His lips twitched and his eyes narrowed. "You—with my brother? Deep in the tunnels of the House of Frost? When you were meant to be locked in a cell, awaiting my judgment? Surely you weren't planning anything...foolish?" He shook his head slowly. "The people would be so disappointed."

I didn't know what he meant, but I made a face of disgust all the same.

He clicked his tongue and threw his eyes to the low ceiling. "Well, if you don't want to explain, there are always easier ways to uncover the truth..."

He reached a hand toward me. Rydar acted quickly to pull me behind his back.

"Don't touch her," he growled, leaning forward, stirring the shadows and collecting them like a shroud about him, a cloak of mystery and wrath.

The high prince laughed. "Oh, there will be time for touching, won't there, Oraelia?" His eyes found mine, twinkling with amusement. "But very well—I'll allow you to tell me, brother."

Rydar's body bucked the moment Flint's clawlike fingers brushed his forehead, his muscles turning rigid like stone beneath his jacket.

Chapter Forty-Eight

The Glow of Victory

RAE

"Leave him be!" I shouted, tugging the high prince's arm away, but it did no good. Rydar's eyes rolled back in his head, and his mind left to go elsewhere—somewhere unreachable to the physical world. I pulled and struck and shook, screaming at him to stop, but the high prince paid me no mind. Finally, his eyes lost their hazy glaze and refocused on me.

Rydar went limp. I hooked my arms beneath his shoulders to break his fall, and the prince studied me as if seeing me for the first time, intrigue glistening in the pools of ink he wore for eyes.

"So it's true? You've found your soulbound? Out of all the people in the world, you choose the one I am meant to marry? I mean, I had my suspicions all along, but how long have you known?"

Rydar grumbled through gritted teeth as though the effort of words required more energy than he could muster.

Flint played with the flame of the torch in his hands, weaving his finger through the ribbons of light with a distracted frown. "It's *tragic*. But not to worry, brother, I promise to take excellent care of her."

He met Rydar's eyes with a dangerous grin. "All the more so now, knowing how much she means to you. And she is quite popular with the benefactors, you know. Our highest funded competitor in years. The public loves her—the first woman in the Trials. The object of the prince's desire."

Flint studied me intently, then met my gaze with an admiration that felt hollow... nothing more than an insincere echo of emotion. *What do you even want with me, high prince? You do not love me. You do not know love.*

But I knew that was not true. The high prince loved himself. And I suspected it was the only love he would ever know.

"You do not want me," I challenged, my voice low.

The high prince's eyes narrowed, but he laughed. "Yes, I do. The people love you. And if they love you, they will love me. Most importantly, once we wed, the crown will pass to me."

"What?" Rydar barked. Fear showed in the whites of his eyes.

"Yes, Father made the announcement last night. Perhaps you would have known sooner if you hadn't been traipsing around with my betrothed."

Flint stepped toward me and gathered my hands in his. "The people are desperate for a bit of happiness. A joyous occasion would be the perfect distraction from their troubles—a royal wedding...a coronation to remember. The people deserve a reason to celebrate, Oraelia."

His gaze hardened, full of reprimand and an unyielding will. "You will behave, and you will win, won't you, darling? I do not like to be disappointed."

"I cannot marry you." The bile at the very thought of sharing vows with the man burned my insides. I had no desire to share another second of my lifetime with him, let alone rule at his side. I was no queen. And I was not his.

"Do not be so hasty with your decisions." He reached over Rydar's shoulder to stroke my cheekbone.

Rydar pushed Flint's arm away, and I gasped at the wave of pain that struck him in retaliation, punishing him for his misstep. He did not cry out, but swallowed the discomfort with great effort, forcing his cry back into his lungs and bracing himself against the pain. When he spoke, his words were strained. Sweat dripped from his brow, trailing down to the tip of his nose.

"You cannot make her marry you."

Flint balked, feigning surprise. "Do not insult me, brother. I shall not *make* her do anything. She'll accept my offer. I am most certain."

"You are mistaken," I responded, letting my voice grow cold. There was no future with the high prince—I knew in my bones I would find my way back to Rydar, no matter the consequences. I was his and only his. *Always.*

"She is my soulbound." The pain in Rydar's voice broke me.

Flint laughed. "You could not possibly hope for her to marry *you*? Look at you."

"I love her," he growled in response.

My heart jumped at the words, but Flint shook his head. "And that is your biggest mistake. Does she know of your oath? Or have you hidden that from her?"

"She knows everything—"

But the high prince waved a dismissive hand. "I'm doing you a *favor*, brother. The high king will let her live if she's mine—you know you cannot promise her the same. Be reasonable, you fool."

He turned away from Rydar, his face emotionless and his back radiating a coldness that made it clear their conversation had ended. His arm linked through mine. "Come, Oraelia. I have a little present for you."

Rydar's arms wrapped around Flint's neck from behind, but his knees buckled with pain before he could pull him to the ground. Flint whirled on his heel and shoved the lit torch beneath his chin, leering with bared teeth. One gust of wind—one breath—and the flames would burn him. I threw myself to the ground to kneel by Rydar, clutching him tightly and meeting the high prince's gaze.

"Do not hurt him." The words seethed from my mouth.

Flint shoved me out of the way, and my back thumped against the stony surface, causing sparks of pain to shoot through my body. *No. Don't touch him.*

With great effort, Flint twisted his neck and closed his eyes, regaining his composure with a crack of his joints. He looked down at Rydar, smirking at the agony on his brother's face.

"Don't you see, Oraelia? I don't have to hurt him. He'll destroy himself to save you. It's beautiful, really. Or pure stupidity."

His fingers wrapped around Rydar's chin and he smiled with the glow of victory already dancing across his face. "You might want to clean up a bit, brother. Did I mention that Father is here? He is *very* eager to see you."

He leaned in to whisper, though his voice was not lowered enough for secrecy. "It's something about the oath. Soulmates? I've never seen him so *delighted*."

Stretching back to his full height, his sandy curls almost skimmed the ceiling. "When I wed your Oraelia and take the crown, my first duty will be to eliminate you."

Rydar's breaths rattled in the shadows, and Flint smiled.

One day, I will wipe that smile out of existence.

"Guards!" The high prince's voice reverberated about the passage until the echoes transitioned to the sound of heavy boots. Five Watchmen rounded the corner at a jog. "Please escort Rydar to the honorable high king's personal study and ensure he remains there," he ordered, his hand wrapped tightly around my wrist, clutching me like his trophy.

CHAPTER FORTY-NINE

The Promise of Tomorrow

RAE

Flint hoisted me to standing and dragged me down the hallway. The guards shifted past us to make a circle around Rydar. They descended upon him, the largest among them barking orders as Rydar thrashed against their restraints, roaring with anger.

"Rydar!" A wave of panic burst through me, splintering my ribs to pieces and piercing my lungs until they could no longer draw breath. What would the high king do to him? Would he Retire him? What if this was the last time I would see him? I fought like a wildling against Flint's hold, desperate to make my way back to Rydar.

The high prince dragged me through the passageway, unyielding to each frantic blow I landed. My bare feet, liberated of my boots in my scuffle, scraped against the rock. His fingers dug into my skin, branding my arm with a mark in the shape of his grip. "*Let me go!*"

Rydar's shouting and the shuffling noise of Watchmen's boots faded into the distance, growing muffled as the prince pulled me deeper into the network of tunnels. Finally, he deposited me at the door of my cell. The rock was cold and rough when it met my cheek.

"*You.*" My mouth foamed with rage. I intended to rip him to pieces, find my way back to Rydar, and rescue him from the guards, but a weakened voice called my name from the cell behind me.

"Rae." Horror iced my veins. I whipped around to face the cell that had once contained me and gaped at the slight form inside, kneeling at the bars in a heap and wearing her nicest dress. Her sadness muted the sunshine of her hair but amplified the blueness of her piercing eyes.

Numbness crept into my limbs and fingers, and I stared at her, trying to blink away the vision in front of me. *Nell. No. How?*

My knees scraped against the rock when I threw myself to the ground, reaching through the bars to grab her hands. I had wanted nothing more than to see her again, but not like this. Not here.

"No. You were supposed to be safe. Nell, how?" I scanned the cell frantically. "Where is Pa? Is he here? Is he alright?"

Nell's forlorn expression unveiled the secrets she tried to hide with silence. My face contorted with the sharp pain of grief—a deep knife wound to my heart that ripped an anguished cry from my core before the tears rushed into my eyes. Nell's expression matched mine, and we cried, embracing as well as we could through the iron bars between us. She didn't need to say it. *Pa's gone.*

"See?" Flint's lofty voice drifted like a lazy breeze in the stale air, and I stiffened. "I brought you a present. Don't you like it? And let me tell you...she was not easy to find, nor easy to secure."

The hair on the back of my neck stood on end, and my jaw clenched tight. I released Nell's hands and turned, nostrils flaring and teeth bared.

"Let her go. This has nothing to do with her."

He smiled.

Smile at me again like that, and I will ensure it is the last time you ever set your eyes upon me.

He leaned against the wall, propping a foot behind him on the rock, then crossed his arms. An arrogant smirk lifted the corner of his mouth, highlighting the charming dimple in his cheek.

"On the contrary, Oraelia, this has everything to do with her. *You* missed your sister. *I* brought her in for the next Trial as a little gift for you. Motivation to be on your best behavior and to keep things...interesting."

Interesting? An intense fear overwhelmed me, and my mind spiraled, realizing he intended to use Nell as a pawn. I would do anything to help her, and his smile said he knew it.

"Don't you dare." My voice rumbled with the sound of storm clouds, and I moved toward him, intending to strike.

His hand snapped up to reflect my blow, wrapping around my arm and twisting—hurting. I ground my teeth, straining to resist his grip. My sleeve crinkled as his hold adjusted and the blood drained from my face. Nell's poem. *Oh no.*

Flint lifted a brow with curiosity, then pulsed his grip to rustle the parchment I had stored in my sleeve.

"What is this?" His eyebrows furrowed as he carefully removed the paper from the lace trimming on my dress and skimmed the letters. His obsidian eyes glimmered when he met my gaze, and the spirit that stirred within them sent an arrow to my heart.

"How inspiring. You did not tell me that Nell was so accomplished. A sister who can write! What other secrets do you have up your sleeves, Oraelia?"

He pulled me close, bending my ribs until they threatened to snap. His lips brushed against my neck, just below my ear, and he whispered—the caress of his voice as gentle as a feather, yet sharp as a blade against my neck.

"I'd hate for Nell's secrets to be made public. You will behave, won't you, Oraelia? Finish the Trials and accept the honor of my hand. I need you…Nell needs you. So much is at stake."

"Don't." Nell's feeble voice sounded closer to a cough than a command. My shoulders tensed. *No, Nell. Now is not the time for bravery. Stay quiet. Stay alive.* It was my fault that she was caught in the crossfire of my mess. I should have been a better example for her. A better sister. I could not bear for my mistakes to cause her end.

Flint tucked a strand of hair behind my ear, twisting his fingers and snagging his hands in the tangles with the whisper of hostility—toying with it to show how easily he could rip the roots from my scalp and snap my head back against the rock wall. Every muscle in my body went rigid.

"Oraelia, I think it is time to forget Rydar. You must understand there is no future with him." His knuckles moved in a gentle caress from my brow to my temple, and I recoiled with fear of his touch. "But you and I—we could be happy together. I could even make it easier for you, if you'd like. I can take away the pain, help you forget."

I froze. When our eyes met, mine widened, and I found myself wading into the darkness of his gaze, surrounded by its hostility, yet sensing no hint of deception in them.

"You can't do that." My voice held no bravado, only the raspy tone of fear.

"Do you doubt me?"

The urge to empty my stomach overwhelmed me. The expression on his face unsettled me, tearing me apart as though he hungered for the fear in my eyes and planned to devour me whole.

What was the high prince suggesting? *How* did he intend to make me forget? A shudder raced down my spine, and my mouth ran dry. I shifted my attention to Nell. "Just let her go. Please. I'll behave."

The dungeon door burst open, and Alia stumbled into the room with Lio on her heels. "Rae! We have a problem...Where are—" Her face turned ashen when she took in the scene. She dropped into an abrupt curtsy, gathering handfuls of skirts as she swept her leg behind herself. "Your Highness."

Alia's eyes trained on the ground. Lio forgot himself completely, gaping openly at the prince like a startled doe in a clearing.

The high prince's nostrils flared, but he allowed his features to melt with an air of pleasantry. "Lady Alia. Lio. How...unexpected."

"Your Highness, my father sent me to check on Oraelia. The next Trial is due to start at any moment." The lie slipped from her tongue with ease, but Lio's flickering eyes weakened the power of her delivery.

"I see." He paused for a moment, and I held my breath. I watched the wheels turning in his mind as he studied us, always plotting. Pain webbed through my chest, creeping tendrils of fear that wrapped around my insides, weaving, gripping, tearing.

I knew he would punish everyone I loved to get his way. Even Rydar had once warned me. The high prince would seize my heart in his fist if he had to, squeezing until it thundered inside of me, forcing me to name each of my fears so he could use them against me. Rydar. Nell. Alia. Lio. He would take them all from me and then take even more—take my autonomy. My time. My self. Take my heart and soul and free will and crush it into dust. And if he could not bend my will with threats to get his way, would he attempt to mold it with magic?

He wrapped his hand around mine, and I gasped for air, as though I had surfaced from the depths of the sea instead of the storm of my thoughts. "Very well. May time be on your side, Oraelia. I can't wait to make you mine. Behave."

I pulled away, but he held fast, lifting my hand to his mouth to place a kiss full of ill-will on my skin. The promise of tomorrow and tomorrow and tomorrow. The promise to make me his, forever, or to destroy everything I had ever loved.

"Alia, please escort Lio and Oraelia to their rooms to prepare for the next Trial. I have some last-minute business to attend to."

CHAPTER FIFTY

One for Each of Us

RAE

"What happened?" Lavender silks fluttered around Alia's ankles like ocean waves as she moved through the hall. "Where is Rydar?"

A pang struck my heart at his name, but I kept running, gripping the stitch in my side. Holding myself together when everything else was falling apart.

The dark tunnels grew wider, and the air grew drier until we found ourselves in the main halls of the House of Frost. The white marble passages sparkled like freshly fallen snow, but our footsteps sounded hollow against its surface.

"I had hoped you'd be long gone," Alia whispered over her shoulder. "I knew I shouldn't have trusted him with you." Her birthmark was highlighted with silver paint, and great purple wings accentuated the corners of her eyes. Dark amethysts crowned her head and cascaded along her braided hair, jingling together as she ran.

"Come on." She led me into the kitchens and ushered me in front of the fire. Lio wrapped a soft fur around my shoulders and pulled up a circle of chairs.

A wisp of a woman with long, dark hair and worried eyes hurried over with a tray of food. Her gaze met Alia's, but she said nothing. She placed the tray in front of us and squeezed Alia's hand in hers before darting back to her station.

Lio picked at the food on the tray, taking up the seat next to mine and shaking his knee so we could all share his nervous energy. The aroma of fresh bread circled around me like a hug, but I shoved it aside. There was no time for comforts.

"I need to find Rydar."

Alia frowned, pushing a glass of water into my hand. "Him? You'll do no such thing. Eat." The glare in my eyes made her brows jump upward, and she bristled slightly, but softened before speaking again. "How can you expect to get anything accomplished like this? You look like Death itself tried to possess your body but found it uninhabitable and abandoned ship. You must take care of yourself first."

"I need to find him. He's in trouble. And they have Nell."

"They have my mother, too." Lio's voice sounded like the whisper of a ghost, and when I looked at him again, I truly saw him. Pale. Shaken. Distressed. His wiry hair twisted out of place, and the creases in his forehead grew deeper than the chasms between the mountains surrounding us.

"What do you mean?" I gasped.

"That's why we came to check on you...to see if you were still there. We saw them taking them in. One for each of us. Nell, my mother—someone important to all of us."

My heart thundered in my chest. One for each of us. "They're using them in the next Trial." The conclusion made itself clear to me, and Lio's pained grimace masquerading as a smile confirmed he agreed with my suspicion.

I grabbed both of Alia's hands in mine. "Rydar. I need Rydar."

"Rae. He—"

"Alia, he is my almatae."

Her face drained of color. "The fallen heir? What—how?"

Sirens began their earsplitting wail, so loud that the sound carried inside of me to shatter my bones with the vibration of echoes. Lio's chunk of bread arched into the air, and he clamped his hands over his ears, sharing a terrified glance with me. A mouthful of food gave body to his sunken cheeks, but the shadows under his eyes had deepened since our last ordeal together.

"The next Trial will begin shortly. All contestants, please report to the South Entrance at once. Do not waste time!" My fist tightened at the honeyed tone of

Elowynne's voice, floating through the air in the brief pauses that fell between the blasts of sirens.

Nell. Lio's mother. Rydar. The others. They were all in grave danger. I grabbed Lio's hand and ran.

The hallway from the kitchens to the grand ballroom flurried with activity. Lio and I pushed our way through the bouncing skirts and well wishes. *May time be on your side.* Did they know how tiresome their pleasantries were?

A man with curly brown hair and eyes trained on me wove against the traffic, his forehead dripping with sweat and his face reddened as though he had just walked off a battlefield. The scar across his face did not detract from his handsome features, and while his expression appeared unfriendly, it was firm set with determination. I remembered vaguely—he was a friend of Rydar's. *Trystan.* The name freed itself from my memory.

He moved through the crowd until he reached us, grabbing my arms. "Where is he? Where's Rydar?" His voice was more of a growl, but instinct advised me to trust him.

"The high king's study. He's—"

Trystan merely nodded and moved past me, pushing through the throng of people until he was lost around the bend.

The sound of unified stomps drowned out all other noise in the hall. A squadron of Watchmen parted the crowd and made their way toward us. Two pairs of hands grabbed my arms and escorted me past the onlookers. My toes skimmed against the surface of the floor, struggling to keep up with their pace.

Chapter Fifty-One

Father and Son

RYDAR

The fire crackled in the hearth of the high king's personal study, and I sat defeated, in a puddle of my own sweat and bitterness, listening to the blare of the sirens that cared little for how many times I had shouted at them to stop. The next trial was beginning, and I could do *nothing*.

Why had I turned back with her? She could have been across the sea by nightfall, safely out of reach, and I—I would be embarking on the journey to the Next Realm, numb to the troubles that plagued me now.

But I did not want to be numb. I wanted to feel. To love. To take Oraelia in my arms at the fall of every dusk and hold her until the break of dawn every day for the rest of my time. She had inspired me to hope for a future I never dared to consider. To live long enough to see the mountains crumble and the world transform, knowing our bond would only strengthen through the passage of time. I longed so badly for this that I had made the gravest mistake of my life. And there was no way to turn back time.

I glared at the doors, cursing them beneath my breath. The great carved planks were steadfast wonders of the finest workmanship—that much I could attest to. My fists had done little to persuade them to open, and even the iron poker from the fireplace lay bent with defeat amidst a pile of splinters.

Sweat dripped from my brow as I contemplated the curls of flame and the murmurs of popping wood. I needed to get out of here, to get to Oraelia, but I was trapped. *Useless.*

I shook my hands, trying to dispel the distracting pain that crept from my fingers to my wrist—the curse burning through my veins in ribbons of shadow.

Destroy her. Ruin her.

The poison whispered, slithering its way into my mind to dampen my senses, urging me to obey. I clenched my fists, letting the pain of my nails against my palms ground me. I pushed the whispers away, fighting them back.

I will not. Take me instead.

It punished me for my resistance, and my face contorted with pain. Sweat soaked through my tunic, making the fabric cling to my back just as my hair matted against my neck. I leaned backward, drawing a deep breath to calm the galloping pace of my heart.

A portrait of the honorable high king glared down at me, wearing the charming half smile that distracted from the venom of his eyes. Dim eyes that no longer sparkled with life—windows to his hollow, broken soul.

The door jostled behind me, and I jumped with a start. The sound of the sirens had lulled, but I hadn't noticed, with the noise of my own worries fogging my mind. I snapped to my feet, edging closer to the misshapen poker on the tiled floor, dragging it toward me with the toe of my boot. *Just in case.*

I watched the mechanisms of each lock twist away, yielding to the visitor on the other side of the door—one I most certainly did not wish to see. The doorknob turned, and the hinges creaked as the door swung inward. My father filled the frame, both with his size and presence.

"I am so pleased, Rydar. I knew someday you'd understand."

"Father."

The bone white of his mask gleamed in the firelight—a dragon skull crowned with spikes to hide his handsome face. I did not understand why he wore the monstrosity. A show of power? Intimidation? He achieved both with little effort. The skull was not necessary to show he had become a monster.

"I must admit I am a bit disappointed, though." He reached for my hand and traced the web of shadows that crept along my fingers. "You are supposed to kill her and suffer life without her, but even *that,* you cannot do right..."

He dropped my hand and turned his back to me. The hem of his cloak dragged against the floor as he walked away, thumbing the brooch at his shoulder—a silver dragon engulfed with wisps of flame. The heavy fabric rustled when he unfastened it to drape it across the sofa.

Resentment stirred within me, a slow simmer of acid that crept from my stomach to my neck and up to my cheeks. The words passed through my clenched teeth. "I am sorry I have thwarted your efforts to maximize my suffering, *Father*."

"Do not use that tone with me," he barked. He moved toward the windows, staring out at the mountains in the distance. Quiet murmurs mingled with the soft gurgle of flowing liquor as he poured himself a drink, lost in another one-sided conversation with his deceased lover.

"Yes, Margarae. Any day now. Almost time, my love. Just as I promised." The stopper clinked back in place against the crystal neck of the bottle, and he turned to face me, but even the mask did not hide the clouds in his eyes. They parted suddenly as he remembered my presence.

"Thwarted? Thwarted...thwarted." He drew out the beginning of the word, savoring the serpentine sound in his mouth. "No, Rydar. I have not been thwarted, not when that poison runs through your veins. You shall have your suffering, believe me."

"The poison can kill me. I won't harm her."

He glanced toward my hand and nodded at the blackness pooling in my fingertips. "That poison won't kill you, Rydar; it will merely break you until you comply." His grin surfaced, visible through the gap of the dragon's maw and twice as deadly as the teeth framing it. "But how could you? She belongs to your brother now, or perhaps the Next Realm if the Trials defeat her. Yet if she survives, you will live in agony, torn between the poison's demands and the oath's call to serve the high prince. A slow, excruciating torment no matter the outcome. *Perfection*."

I frowned, though I chose not to reply. There was no need. I would endure his torture for as long as I lived, but I would never harm Oraelia. She would survive the Trials. She had to. And I would not rest until I'd saved her from this mess.

The king walked toward the center of the room and patted the back of the sofa with a tenderness I thought he had lost long ago. *"Margarae, Margarae, yes, soon, my love."*

"Margarae is not here, Father."

His attention snapped toward me, his voice filled with venom. "How dare you remind me? How dare you utter her name?" He edged around the sofa, prowling closer with murder in his eyes and enough force in his grip to make his glass tremble with fear.

"She hated you, you know." He bellowed a sharp, abrasive laugh that fell around us like daggers. "I defended your character—like a fool! I *loved* you, but I should have listened to her...made you disappear along with your meddlesome mother. So much could have been different."

His words left behind a rawness in my heart that I did not expect. That I did not allow. "Why didn't you just kill me, then?"

He was not listening to me. Margarae had his attention. *"I am almost ready, love.* Love. Love. Love." He played with the sound of the word, lost in his thoughts, while he swirled the amber liquid in slow circles. He dipped his smallest finger into the glass with a clink of his obsidian ring against the edge, then sucked the bourbon from his fingertip.

"How does it feel, Rydar? To fall in love? To weave your soul with another who is just out of reach?" The bone mask did nothing to conceal the gloating in his voice. He placed a hand on my shoulder and took a contemplative swig of his drink. It smelled like fire and malice.

"I want you to feel everything I've felt. To know what I have endured. How does it feel to lose her? *Yes, dear. I promise it will hurt him. He will suffer for what he did to you.* Does it hurt, Rydar?"

I glared up at him, keeping my chin lowered and jaw clenched.

"Good." He turned his attention to the window, studying the scene nestled in the mountains. "I've waited so long. Endured for so long. Margarae will be pleased to finally have her revenge. *Yes, yes, then I will be able to join you. Soon, dear. After we have avenged you."*

He swept aside the gauzy curtains and turned to me. "It is a wonderful view, Rydar. You'll be able to see everything from here."

See what? The Trial? I wanted to hold my silence, but fear triumphed. I could not bear the consequence of losing Oraelia—of facing the rest of time without her.

"You can't do this."

The sparkle in his eyes hinted at the widening grin beneath his mask. "I can, and I will. I have waited *decades* to keep this promise to Margarae. Decades. Decades. And I always keep my promises."

He lifted the sleeve of his tunic to reveal the shadow dragon—the oath he had carefully constructed to punish me all those years ago. The oath that would destroy me. Or force me to destroy myself.

His hand rested on my shoulder, and I felt my knees buckle beneath his featherlight touch. "Perhaps now you will know a fraction of the hell I have lived since the day you stole her life."

The crystal glass in his hand sparkled with firelight, so the liquid glowed like flames when he raised it in a toast.

"May time be on your side, Rydar. May you live long enough to grieve her death or suffer losing her to another. May you understand the depths of my misery before you meet your end." He drained the rest of the amber bourbon in his cup, then placed it on his desk before sweeping out of the chamber, locking me inside with only my fears and the whispers of his dead love for company.

CHAPTER FIFTY-TWO

Fates Be Damned

RAE

The black suit held me together, applying pressure to the invisible wounds that threatened to tear me apart from the inside. Internal wounds that could only be seen if one looked closely enough to notice how my limbs trembled or how my heart pounded against the prison of my ribs. I feared I would unravel completely if they removed the garment.

We stood in a line at the South Entrance—Lio, Brickert, Taiver, Harma, me. The final five. The steel doors before us spanned half the length of the foyer. My ears buzzed with the roaring of the crowd that awaited us beyond those doors—and the fates that would soon come to meet us.

My legs shook as my mind grappled for some semblance of a plan to escape, but a dozen Watchmen held us captive beneath unforgiving eyes and even less forgiving rifles. I steeled my heart, fortifying it with determination. The only way out was through.

Five Watchmen approached, their movements so precise and unified that they seemed to be one entity rather than individuals. They presented five black boxes before us and grabbed our right hands. "To assess your wellness." The guard grunted before piercing my finger with the press of a button. I did not wince.

With the precision of an ice adder, I snapped my hand around his fingers and pulled him close. "Where is my sister?" I needed answers.

His eyes narrowed before fading to their usual state of unquestioning obedience. "You'll see," he responded, then wrenched his hand from my grasp and rested it on the pistol in his holster. The muscle at the edge of his jaw twitched with the hint of a smirk that stirred the growing pit of unease in my stomach.

As soon as the Watchmen receded, Lio's fingers wrapped around mine. The burden of being strong weighed heavily on my shoulders, and I slouched forward. But I had enough of being small.

I stood taller, steadying my breaths, finding courage. There were no helpful hints or safety nets to catch me this time—no Rydar to save me. I needed to save myself. I needed to survive to save the others. And the Fates—Fates be damned. My fate was in my own hands.

The steel doors slid open, parting from the middle to reveal the arena. A great cliff loomed above us, and its shadow stretched toward us like a carpet rolled out in welcome. Sunlight sparkled against the snow and ice, and a chilling wind bit my cheeks, making them burn as if licked by flames.

Vibrant colors painted the stands surrounding the cliff—hundreds of people buzzing with excitement to watch the event. They had come to watch death and suffering in their finest attire.

The ostentatious garb adorning the onlookers came together like the fragments of a stained glass window, each attendee a singular, dazzling shard in the mosaic of high-class superiority. Silk gowns swished in the stands in deeply rich hues, and gemstones glittered on tight-fitting bodices. The men wore suits adorned with intricate brocade patterns and exquisite embroidery. The threads woven through the material shimmered in the sun, like the jewels cascading from the women's necks and ears.

The sun rose like a shining, unforgiving halo of fire behind the crowd. I blinked the light out of my eyes, but the strength of its beams distorted my vision. Parasols dotted the stands like wildflowers in an open field, the delicate canopies sparing the viewers' eyes from the unyielding rays. *How lovely for them.*

I watched the chattering crowd with disgust—the sour, acidic cocktail of revulsion churning about my stomach. I could think of no greater misuse of time, and yet *I* was to be punished for time wasting. A fledgling laugh escaped through my nose, steeped in bitterness. Perhaps someday, I would find a way to punish them.

My stomach wound itself into knots. The Watchmen ushered us into the clearing, and I stared vacantly at the people in the stands—at the sea of privilege.

I resented the shivers that quaked through my body. The weakness. The fear. I had no use for them. A wave of resolve flowed over me, grounding me to focus on the only thing that mattered—my survival.

Because if I survived, so would the others. Of that, I was certain.

"Welcome, welcome, good lads and ladies. Welcome to the next Trial! Take a good look at our final five. One of them will be crowned as victor today!"

A roar from the crowd. A dazzling smile behind a well-groomed beard. Orman Gendrick.

His theatrics only earned a fraction of my attention. Instead, my eyes darted around the arena, combing for clues, analyzing anything that could be used to my advantage.

The giant screens above us alternated between images of the exuberant crowd and the harrowed faces of the competitors. The ground opened up into a great bowl at the feet of the cliffside, with the stands rising on either side of the looming rock wall before us. Ice and the remnants of the last snowfall swirled upon the ground, stirred into a dance by the unforgiving wind.

What was the glimmer of steel in the shadows? Long chains ran the length of the cliff on either side. Where was Nell? Glancing up at the rock wall between the stands, I noticed the wooden platform near the top with a frown, suddenly reminded of too many Retirements. Too many Dishonorables. I shivered at the chill that ran down my spine.

Orman hushed the crowd with a wave of his hands, the jewel-encrusted sleeves of his jacket making the sun pale with envy. A screen flickered behind him, and images streamed across the surface, accompanied by the ebb and flow of triumphant notes…a glorification of the horrors we had survived.

What horrors will we face today? Which of us will die? Who will leave bread for the journey to the Next Realm?

When the music ended, the cameras landed on our hardened faces.

"A round of applause for our final five! Lio, Harma, Taiver, Brickert, and Oraelia." He named each of us while the cameras panned to Lio's sunken cheeks,

Harma's deadened eyes, Taiver's clenched jaw, and Brickert's dark scowl. When my face flashed on the screen, I hardly recognized my features as my own. Fierce, determined, blazing with anger.

The sea of hands clapped for me, but the sound was muffled by the rush of blood in my ears. My limbs tingled, and I shifted my weight uncomfortably.

Orman donned a somber expression, and the crowd quieted. His eyes bounced up from his feet to meet the camera with the precision of years' worth of experience, and his voice grew solemn.

"Good lads and ladies, only one of these competitors will walk away victorious at the end of the Trials. Only *one* will win the grand prize of immortality." He nodded with a grave smile, letting his words settle into the silence.

"Yes, I'm afraid that means we may have to say goodbye to some favorites today." He wiped an invisible tear from the corner of his eye, and shook the invisible drop from his finger with feigned sorrow. "It may be your last chance to show them how much they mean to you."

He reached backward and tugged at a white cloth draped behind him. It tumbled away softly, caught in the wind, to reveal the glimmering hourglasses restored to their former beauty.

The gems shimmered, catching and fracturing rays of sunlight to create prisms of color all around the ravine. "Before the next Trial begins, let us show our favorites some support! Who do we want to have an edge in the final challenge? Give them some help! May time be on their side today."

The hourglasses hummed with a surge of donations. Blue sapphires shimmered in my hourglass, rising to reflect a sum my brain could not comprehend. An eternity. Enough to feed all of my district for the next decade.

And still, it wasn't enough.

All the time in the world meant nothing without the people I loved.

Orman leaned against the railing of his platform, looking down at us with a wicked grin. "We have a very special visitor and a special surprise in store for each of you today. Would you like to see?"

CHAPTER FIFTY-THREE

She Stood Tall

RAE

Our lack of response did not deter him. He clapped his hands together and gestured over his shoulder to the House of Frost.

The cameras focused on the oversized balcony that extended from the southern face of the building. White roses, shimmering with frost, cascaded from the banisters, and Watchmen stood like stone sentries around the perimeter. The figure in the middle of the balcony, perched on a throne of frosted brambles, drew a complete hush from the crowd. The honorable high king.

The bone white dragon mask covered his features, but it did little to veil the wickedness and power of his presence. My fingers curled into fists as I thought of Rydar. *Where is he? What have you done with him?*

The high king stood and drifted toward the edge of the balcony, wrapping long, white fingers around the railing. Reverent murmurs filled the arena—shared whispers of "May his time be everlasting."

His time has lasted long enough. Without meaning to, my arms crossed over my chest, and I glared up at him, jaw clenched, defiance on my face. *Where is Rydar?*

The high king's gaze snapped toward me. Even with his features concealed by the mask, I could feel his scrutiny.

The seconds passed, stretching thin as though time had ground to a halt, but I kept my eyes fixed on him in a silent war. Finally, he withdrew and turned his attention to the gathered crowd.

"Good lads and ladies, my most loyal subjects. What an honor to celebrate the Trials with you."

His voice sent shivers down my spine, a creeping, crawling hoarfrost that spread through my veins.

"These Trials serve as a stark reminder that we must not waste away our time. It is our duty to create an everlasting legacy. Time is our most precious resource—every moment, every breath, every heartbeat is a gift that must not be squandered."

The crowd hummed in agreement, nodding solemnly with deep respect for his words.

"The competitors in the Trials were plucked from poverty and given a chance to prove themselves worthy of redemption. Worthy of more. They remind us of the delicate balance between life and death and the privilege of the time that we possess."

The high king walked slow, measured steps along the balcony, his hand grazing the banister. His fingers trailed through the vine that adorned the railing, destroying any of the delicate flowers that had the misfortune of crossing his path. The white petals cascaded into the valley below, drifting like snowflakes, or perhaps like breadcrumbs in the wind. A testament to all the lives he'd ruined. He paused thoughtfully, then gestured to each of us.

"Let the names of Lio, Brickert, Taiver, Harma, and Oraelia forever resonate in our memories to symbolize the fleeting nature of mortal existence."

Fleeting only because you make it so. I ground my teeth together, glaring up at the man who destroyed everything he touched for his own personal gain.

"And at the end of the Trials, may a victor emerge triumphant to show us that anything can be achieved with unwavering resilience, indomitable spirit, and loyalty to the Realm. Even wealth beyond measure."

The crowd cheered, whistling and shouting their praise. The high king bowed his head, resting his hands upon his chest in a display of humble sincerity.

"As high king of Orogi, it is my greatest honor to serve you. I stand not only as your ruler but as the custodian of time itself. The power to grant or withhold immortality lies within my grasp, and it is a responsibility I carry with wisdom and purpose to create a better world for all those who deserve it! Let the reward of the Trials—immortal life—be a testament to what the Good Work can accomplish."

Cheers erupted and hands soared up to the Fates in veneration for the Good Work bestowed to the people. But I saw the man for the danger he truly was—a man who esteemed himself above the Fates, wielding the power to grant or deprive life at his whims. Whims which were temperamental at best, sinister at worst. A man whose urges commenced and culminated with his own self-interest, an evil that would shatter his people and all things good. He *had* to be stopped.

"Lio, Brickert, Taiver, Harma, and Oraelia, may time be on your side, and may you prove yourself worthy of it. May we all learn from your example."

The crowd's applause rained into the valley, a torrential downpour that made the ground rumble with thunder as the high king resumed the seat.

No—the ground truly shuddered beneath our feet. A crack appeared in the icy rock, widening into a crevice from which five wooden chests emerged. I stared blankly at the boxes, trying to make sense of them, but Orman's voice scattered my thoughts.

"Lio, Brickert, Taiver, Harma, and Oraelia—in the wise words of our most honorable high king, may time be on your side as we begin this Trial. Shall we bring out the guests of honor?" He flushed, flinching as soon as the words left him. "Forgive me, Your Majesty, I speak in jest, for you are unequivocally the most honorable guest in attendance."

The high king waved a bored hand, and Orman's shoulders relaxed with a deep exhale. "Very well," he continued, regaining his composure. "Bring them out."

A pit of dread weighed in my stomach as the cameras panned to the platform at the top of the rock face. Five figures emerged, shoved irreverently into place by Watchmen.

Burlap sacks covered the figures' faces and thick cords bound their wrists, but I knew without question who stood at the end of the line. Sunshine waves caught in the wind beneath the burlap, and her hands twisted together as they always did when she was nervous, but she stood tall. Brave. Nell.

CHAPTER FIFTY-FOUR

Guests of Honor

RAE

"What is this? What are they doing?" Lio hissed at my side, his voice riddled with panic. But I was incapable of a response. My eyes were glued to Nell.

Nell. I'm here. I see you.

The rest of the arena blurred like murky water, and I splashed my way through it, running toward the only thing I could see clearly—Nell's feet at the edge of the platform and the harrowing memories of a hundred Retirements. I had to get to her. They couldn't Retire her. I would not let them.

Gravel yielded to my steps as I sprinted toward the towering cliff, but a Watchman blocked my path. My body crashed into his with so much force that I felt my brain bounce against my skull, and I landed hard on my backside. Strong arms gripped me tightly, and he dragged me back to the line of competitors, thoroughly unswayed by my desperate barrage of pleas.

"Stay," he commanded. Like I was a street dog. I bared my teeth at him, playing the part.

"Oraelia, my love, not yet." The audience laughed. Flint's voice dripped with honeyed affection and charm, but it grated against my insides like sand rubbed into a wound. I lifted my chin and found him standing on the platform amongst the prisoners, the dazzling white of his smile visible even from the bottom of the ravine.

"The honorable high prince!" Orman Gendrick declared, though the prince required no introduction. "Your Highness, will you do us the honor?"

"My pleasure." The dull blackness of his eyes sparked like a piece of flint struck by steel.

"Good lads and ladies of Orogi, our final five—it is my honor to explain the rules of the next event. As it has been in years past, the victor of the Trials will be showered with fame and wealth beyond measure. They will become an elite member of our society—nobility or even perchance... royalty." His eyes narrowed on mine and he winked. An audible swoon coursed through the stands, but I scoffed. *What fools.*

He waved the Watchmen on the platform forward, and they moved to stand behind each prisoner, arms clasped at attention behind their backs.

"As you can see, we have invited five commoners to bear witness to these Trials—someone dear to each of our competitors. Most unfortunately, however, it has come to my attention that each one of our guests is guilty of criminal behavior that we simply cannot overlook."

He nodded toward the first Watchman in line, standing behind a woman with knobby knees and tattered skirts. The Watchman pulled away the burlap covering to reveal a tear-streaked face and eyes that whispered of horrors.

"Ava Monroe, mother of Lio Monroe, charged with abandoning her husband, absconding with their six remaining dependents, and leaving her spousal duties unfulfilled." The woman's shoulders shook. Somehow, my hand found Lio's and squeezed it tight despite the violent trembling of our limbs.

The next Watchman pulled away a burlap sack to reveal a young man, ruggedly handsome, with chin-length chestnut hair.

"Caleb Stone, older brother of Harma Stone. Accused of unauthorized travel and an attempt to flee the boundaries of his assigned district." Flint continued down the line, gesturing toward each prisoner with an open palm as they were unveiled.

"Marcus Blackwell, father of Brickert Blackwell. Charged with willful non-compliance in the matter of displaying the honorable high king's portrait in his place of residence.

"Julian Caldwell, father of Taiver Caldwell. Charged with the offense of deliberate noncompliance by failure to recite the mandated expressions of reverence for our most honorable high king at the daily sync."

Nell's eyes sought mine when her mask was lifted, freeing her hair so that it blew about her face in the wind. "Helena Fenix, younger sister of Oraelia Fenix. Charged with unauthorized expression and dissemination of traitorous ideas in the form of poetry."

To her credit, she did not cry. But the same could not be said for me—hot tears welled in my eyes and bitter flames singed the inside my throat. *I'm coming, Nell. Don't worry.*

The Watchmen stepped away from the prisoners, and the high prince continued, plastering a solemn expression on his face. "As an immortal and influential member of our ruling class, I expect the victor to uphold the laws and Good Work established by our most honorable high king. This Trial has been reimagined with a little twist of my own design.

"Competitors, I offer you two options—two paths to emerge triumphant from this challenge. You may either condemn your loved one to the punishment that befits their crime or declare them worthy of redemption. Should you condemn them, they will face their Retirement, and you may walk away unscathed, unchallenged. Should you consider them worthy of redemption, you must prove their value before us all. You will place your life on the line to save them. Should more than one competitor make it through the challenge, the victor shall be decided by the people."

I shared a glance with Lio, noting the same mistrust on his face that made my own eyes narrow with suspicion. Did Flint truly think we'd believe his lies?

If all of us decided to walk away—to leave our loved ones to their fate—what then? The people would surely not favor such cowardice, and I held no delusions that the high king would let more than one victor survive. I knew better.

Besides, it didn't matter. Not one bit.

My gaze returned to my sister, and a silent scream overwhelmed me, clawing at my insides until I felt I would burst from the frustration of inaction. I needed to do something. Now.

Of course you are worthy, Nell.

Behind the prisoners, large scarlet numbers appeared, casting a red glow over each of their heads. A timer.

"Well said, well said, Your Highness," declared Orman as an hourglass descended at his side. "Lio, Brickert, Taiver, Harma, and Oraelia, you have twenty minutes to complete this challenge. You may remain safely where you stand and condemn your prisoner to their fate, or you may redeem them with your valor. You will find useful equipment in four of the five chests before you. Make sure to reach the top before that timer runs out or—whoops! Down you all go. Do not waste time, or you'll find yourself...*cut* from the challenge."

He turned to face me. "Oraelia dear, as the competitor with the highest pledge support, you have the honor of a ten-second head start. Don't waste it. Now *go!*"

My legs scrambled into action before my brain. I surged forward, feet sliding on the icy patches of the ground as I barreled toward the nearest chest.

A cool, distant voice drifted into the arena, counting down. *Ten, nine*—blood coursed through my veins as I fell to my knees in front of the wooden chest, thinking only of my sister. Failure was not an option.

My fingers trembled uncontrollably, making pressing the chest's latch impossible.

Three, two, one—a high-pitched tone echoed through the arena. *Here come the rest of them.*

Screw it. I rammed an elbow into the patch of metal, and the lid swung upward.

Brickert slammed into me from behind and shoved me to the side, claiming the chest for himself. Rock scraped against my shoulder as I slid, but I scrambled to my feet and dove toward the next wooden box. There was no time to engage with the brute. *So much for the extra time advantage.*

The lid of the chest was heavy, but I wrenched it open with a swift motion, using my legs to add a burst of power to my movements. I breathed a quick exhale of relief at the sight of the harness at the bottom.

I grabbed the leather straps and sprinted toward the rock face, slipping on a patch of ice but scrambling back to my feet. Brickert struggled at my left, cursing at the clip and sucking on the pad of his finger after the metal snapped shut on him. Hands trembling, I fumbled with my buckles and loops, willing them to cooperate. *Where is Elowynne now?* I thought bitterly. Her oh-so-helpful magic would be invaluable at a time like this. Of course, Elowynne would sooner dress a horde of fire-breathing dragons for a ball than lend me a hand.

Lio appeared next to me with an armful of leather bands and a grim look in his eyes. I nodded once, and he began to untangle the chaos of his straps while I stepped through the loops of my own. My arms quaked, struggling to tighten the buckles around my thighs and secure the clip to the rope.

A shriek escaped me as a figure appeared in my peripheral and collided with Lio, knocking him into the wall. Lio slumped to the ground, a trickle of blood sprouting from his nose. I watched in horror as Harma darted away with Lio's harness tucked beneath his arm.

My eyes swept back to the chests in the middle of the arena. All of them had been opened—all the harnesses had been claimed. Taiver and Harma raced to pull the leather straps around their hips, and rock debris skittered against the ground to my left, kicked away from the cliff side by Brickert's feet as he began his ascent.

I looked upward, craning my head all the way back to catch a glimpse of the wooden platform high above us. *Get to Nell. Hurry.*

My blood thundered through my veins, and I dug my boot into the wall before finding holds for my hands. From the corner of my eye, I saw Lio wipe the trail of blood beneath his nose with a sleeve, leaving behind a smear of scarlet war paint. Empty-handed, without a harness to protect him, he reached for the rock wall and began to climb.

Metal flashed beneath us. A curved blade, larger than a dragon's wing, whistled beneath our feet to part the air with one decisive stroke, slicing straight through Harma. Blood splattered against the rock before both halves of him collapsed in a pile at the base of the mountain.

CHAPTER FIFTY-FIVE

Raise Helfyre

RAE

My muscles seized and my mouth fell open. The pain accompanying Harma's death was brutal yet swift, dissipating almost immediately. He did not suffer long.

I turned my eyes downward, watching the arc of the scythe below my feet, the sound of its passing like a whisper in my ear. It dangled for a heartbeat at the height of its swing on the end of its chain, then hurtled back toward us with a resounding whoosh. *Move, fool.*

I scampered higher up the wall with a surge of energy before the menacing blade returned, grazing the air a mere breath away from my toes.

"And there goes the first scythe!" Orman's voice elicited a surge of excited cheers from the crowd. "Competitors, you have about a minute to make it above the threat of the second scythe before it releases."

The first scythe? I turned toward Lio. What had Orman said earlier? *Do not waste time, or you'll find yourself...cut from the challenge. Helfyre, he had meant it literally.*

Lio's face blanched, and he swallowed laboriously, as though trying to force a rock down with a swig of peppered fire rum. Pieces of the cliff crumbled beneath his boot, and he stared at me, his whitened fingers gripping the crevices in the rock face with all his strength.

"May time be on your side, Rae." It was a goodbye.

"Oh no, you don't. Not today." My muscles burned as I made my way toward him and extended my hand. "Together."

One flash of his eyes toward the swinging scythe was enough to convince him. His calloused hand tightened around mine, and he lowered his chin with a grave nod before clambering onto my back. The harness bit into my legs, and my face screwed into a grimace—straining against the abrupt shift of weight. I would not let go. We would not die. *Not today.*

My thighs seared with the pain of every reach, every movement, but I clamped my teeth together and climbed higher, not bothering to worry how Lio's weight and gravity conspired against me. Did the mountain know I'd crumble it to pieces before I let them hurt Nell? Before I let them take Rydar from me? Did it fear me? *It should.*

The rock shuddered in answer, as if it had heard my thoughts.

The arena reverberated with the thunderous crack of splitting rock, and the earth trembled beneath our feet. The cliffside resonated with an ominous rumble, a beastly growl hinting at the raw power within. Jagged talons of stone erupted from the depths, hurtling towards us with an unforgiving force as if the mountain itself had sprouted claws, aiming to shred us to pieces.

A shard of stone, sharp and unyielding, broke free from the wall just above me, releasing a cascade of debris that rained down upon my head. The pain the rocks inflicted paled in comparison to the torment coursing through me, a relentless surge of another's suffering that caused my foot to slip from its grip.

"What is happening?" Lio trembled, but I shook the rock from my head and pushed onward. There was no time to stop. No time for thinking. "Rae, this is bad."

I set my eyes above me and pushed against the protests of my thighs, resisting the urge to slow. How many more minutes did I have to reach the top? How many more grains of sand stood between this moment and Nell's Retirement? Not enough, not enough, not enough. Never enough.

I kept climbing.

"Taiver, Taiver—Wake up!" A gurgle of laughter flowed from the audience in response to the singsong lilt of Orman's voice.

Lio tapped my arm and pointed to the dark figure swinging lazily in the wind.

Taiver's limp form dangled next to a jagged piece of rock, and blood trickled down his temple, dripping into the ravine like the slow ticking of a clock. *Drip. Drip. Drip.* Was he still alive? His pain still flowed through me, now muted but still present. My hand hesitated, resting against a crevice—should I help him?

A second blade sliced below us, shattering my focus. It arched just above the path of the first scythe, with its own trajectory and rhythm from one end of the wall to the other. The scythes crisscrossed below us—two lovers engaged in a delicate dance, brushing close and parting to the notes of an unheard tune.

The glimmer of metal demanded my attention as I swept my gaze upward, finding the series of blades that lay in wait along the wall. A dozen malicious smiles of steel poised to strike. How long did we have to get above each one before it engaged?

"Rae." Lio had noticed them, too, and the quiver in his voice matched the trembling of his limbs. "Rae—I can't."

My teeth threatened to crack beneath the force of my jaw. "We can do this," I grumbled. *Step, reach, push. Survive. Save. Don't let them win.*

Blood coursed through my limbs as we pushed higher and higher, and my eyes darted nervously toward the third scythe that lingered in the shadows. *Schwing.* My foot cleared its path moments before it could slice through my ankle.

Taiver was not as lucky. Lio made a strained gurgling noise, choking on his own tongue when the blade cut through Taiver's rope. The sickening crunch of bone against rock turned my stomach, but I refused to look down. It was a small blessing that he had not been awake to witness the horror of his death.

"Oh, Fates. This is bad. It is bad, right?"

"Hush, Lio. Close your eyes."

"My mom, she doesn't deserve this. If I don't make it—"

"We're going to make it."

Sweat soaked the hair at the nape of my neck, and my muscles threatened to fail with every movement. The fourth scythe glinted in the sun above us, assaulting me with a blinding flash of light. I squinted to clear my vision and reached upward, letting Lio act as my second pair of eyes. *Left. Higher. Right.* His directions weren't exactly helpful, but I welcomed the distraction.

By the time the seventh scythe swung below us, my lungs burned with misery, and my limbs screamed from overuse. I gasped for air and slowed, needing a reprieve to quell the fire that burned through my legs and forearms. Even my hands roared, calling my attention to muscles that had never declared their existence before.

"I just—need—a second," I managed, finding it difficult to source the air for words.

Lio did not respond.

"Lio?" Fear struck me, clutching my heart in its sharpened claws. Was he hurt? Had I missed something? Wouldn't I have felt his pain?

"I'm slowing you down." His voice had lost all life—a broken husk of its former self.

Ice penetrated my veins, but I calmed my nerves with the lie I'd been telling myself over and over. "We'll make it." *We have to make it.* The lies thawed my fears.

He kissed my cheek, his breath warm against my face. "You'll make it. I know it."

"Lio, wait. Don't you dare." *Please don't do this. Don't give up. Try.* But he was already loosening his grip, shifting his weight to reach for the wall.

"Don't," I begged, my voice shaking with panic. "Please. We can do it. We can—"

"I want to choose how I go. Let me make my last moments count for something that matters."

I cried out, reaching for his hand to stop him, but it was a mistake. The shift of our balance nearly ripped me away from the wall. My hand snapped back to the rough texture of the cliff, finding a new crevice to hold with bloodied, torn fingers.

He faced me, fingers already slipping from their hurried, precarious grasp.

"Save them, Rae. Raise helfyre." A smile.

Then he was gone.

CHAPTER FIFTY-SIX

To New Beginnings and the End of Troubles

RAE

"Lio!"

The heaviness of his body lifted from my shoulders but immediately buried its weight in my heart—a thousand stones of grief. He tumbled backward, and I closed my eyes, but I could not close my ears to the horrifying sounds below.

I pressed my cheek against the rough stone and cried out as Lio's pain gripped my chest—a horrifying combination of brokenness and dread that exploded within me. The absence of his pain hurt even worse, ripping me apart until only the shadow of my spirit remained.

The blisters on my shredded fingers wept scarlet, and the protrusions of rock bit against my skin, but I felt nothing. Nothing except the weight of a thousand stones in my heart. Nothing except the emptiness of a world without Lio.

I will not lose anyone else today.

A growl of effort accompanied my movements, but I moved. Higher. Faster. *For Lio. His mother. Rydar. Nell. For* me.

"Five minutes remain! Will they make it?"

Quiet, Orman.

Numbness washed over me, like a rush of water that forced its way into my soul and drowned out the whirlwind of emotion that battled for my attention. My fingers grasped the wall, searching out holds and falling into a pattern of calculated moves—a symphony of burning muscles and unwavering concentration.

A dozen blades danced beneath me, a pit of vipers waiting. Above me—victory.

The seconds ticked, but my racing heart kept time—urging me to move faster, faster, faster, tuning out the horrible last cry of Brickert and the bone-crushing pain of his impact against the rocky ground followed by the delighted gasps of the audience.

Wings fluttered within me, stirring up a mixture of exhaustion and triumph as I neared the platform.

The wooden planks extended from the cliff's edge, towering above me and casting me in darkness. Five trap doors lined the bottom, all sealed shut. I was the first to arrive. A fist of guilt wrapped around my throat. I was the only one to arrive. The other doors would never be opened.

I wrapped a hand around the wooden brace that jutted from the wall and pushed upward against the door with my other. The hinges creaked to announce my arrival.

I did it. I made it.

Cheers erupted from the crowd to celebrate my victory, a tremendous uproar of...screaming? Was that screaming?

A surge of panic jolted through me. The sound of boots clamored above my head, and the staccato of gunshots pierced my eardrums. The crowd shrieked again, but my heart screamed louder. *Nell. No. I was too late. They've already Retired her. Wait—please!*

I scrambled through the hole and emerged into chaos. I felt a palpable tension in the air as the prisoners' gazes shifted to me, their breathing shallow beneath the fabric in their mouths. Watchmen kneeled at the edge of the platform, and sparks flew from the ends of their rifles.

A shriek of fury cleaved the sky in two. Leather wings glided through the clouds, and the dragon's mouth opened wide in a roar, issuing a stream of fiery rage from her jaws. The edge of the platform ignited with flames curling up into the sky—an ardent dance of red and yellow. The sweltering heat burned my lungs, but I dove toward Nell. We had to escape.

Thick smoke swarmed the platform above the glowing flames, and I pulled Nell down, coughing and spluttering with the blackness that filled my lungs. I crawled on my elbows toward the mouth of the tunnel, dragging Nell along with me, but I struggled to see through the hazy greyness that enveloped us.

Something solid struck my forehead, and I recoiled with a yelp.

"S-sorry!" the figure blurted through a cough. Tawny curls framed a woman's face with wrinkles that gave the impression of laughter and eyes that glimmered with watery resilience. The binding over her mouth hung around her neck, but her wrists remained tied together as she crawled along the floor. She looked so much like him. I threw my arms around her, not stopping to worry about how the action might alarm her.

"Lio—I'm so sorry." My voice struggled to produce the words like a pen running out of ink. Splotched and strained and faded.

She pressed her forehead to mine, a moment of maternal grace. "I know. It's not your fault. You gave him a reason to fight as long as he did."

Somehow, in that fleeting gesture, I understood the woven threads of sadness, forgiveness, and gratefulness she wrapped around me. A jacket lovingly placed upon a child's shoulders on a winter morning.

The platform lurched, and the wood splintered with a harrowing crack. The cries of men and a tangle of limbs flailed in the smoke, then spilled into the chasm below.

I looked up in horror, watching the wooden planks shred like paper beneath the dragon's claws as she skidded across the platform, flattening the Watchmen beneath her wings. She lowered her majestic head, crowned with a circlet of vicious spikes, cloaked in the black smoke of rage. On her back, a man with long black hair and eyes of smoldering storm. The darkness at the end of another day survived. My solace.

Rydar.

He reached his hand out to me, now blackened by the shadows of his curse. Writhing ribbons of poison spread from his wrist toward his elbow. The constricting, searing pain within him reached out to caress my senses, telling of truths. Whispering the secrets he hid beneath crooked smiles and eyes ablaze with stars just for me.

"You came. You're alive." My hand slipped effortlessly into his, and my eyes closed in acceptance of his gentle kiss to my brow.

"To new beginnings," he whispered, because I was his dawn.

"To the end of our troubles," I responded, because he was my dusk.

Flames circled us, and the platform groaned in defeat, sinking beneath our weight. Rydar's attention flickered toward the wreckage of wood and flames and corpses. "We must hurry," he warned.

I turned to Nell and tugged the scrap of fabric down from her mouth. "Go—you can trust him." I shoved her toward Rydar, then ushered Lio's mother toward the dragon. "Take them," I implored. "I'm getting the others."

His eyes creased, but he did not argue or stop me from ducking back into the smog. I crawled on all fours, holding Nell's fabric binding to my face as I searched for the white garb of the other prisoners.

A viselike claw knotted through my hair and yanked my head backward, ripping the tresses from the roots. Burning pain seared through my scalp, and I screeched in surprise, causing more strands of hair to uproot in my struggle against the unyielding grasp.

"You stupid fool!" The high prince sneered, wrapping his arms around my waist like a serpent, squeezing all life and hope from me. My heart thundered, and I threw myself against his hold, screaming into the smoke.

"Rydar!"

His eyes flashed with the tempest's wrath, finding mine through the grey smog like a strike of lightning drawn to the highest tower. He urged the dragon forward.

She opened her mouth, and a crackling fire spilled out, the smoke curling around her face like a veil.

A haunting symphony of screeches. A dozen black wings sweeping toward us. A shower of sparks against the jagged rock as a bullet hissed between us.

Time seized, as did my heart. There was no time. There was no way—there were only seconds to make an escape, and I could not make my way to them.

Go. Go without me, my heart urged. The prince's arms smashed against my ribs, but I shoved the sleeve of my suit up to my elbow, flashing the shadow dragon and willing Rydar to see it. "You promised!" I shouted, raising my voice above the roar of fire and clamor of gunshots, hoping he'd understand. "Save her! Save them!"

The high prince smacked my arm down and dragged me away, burying me beneath the heavy smoke, but the image of Rydar's agony was seared into my mind. The strain of his muscles and horror in his eyes—torn between keeping his promise and tearing the world apart to save me.

The Oath, Rydar. Please.

A flap of mighty wings sliced through the air before the tunnel's jaws closed around me, plunging me into darkness and devouring me whole.

CHAPTER FIFTY-SEVEN

Mine

RAE

Get up, Rae. Get up and fight. My hands pushed against the wretched floor, but the tile rushed back to meet my face. My cheekbone smacked against the ground, sticking in a puddle of wetness that seeped from my mouth...Blood? Drool?

Some victor, I am.

The room spun, and my thoughts scattered like marbles across the floor.

Where am I? Get up. Please, get up.

"You made me look like a damn fool!"

I groaned as his voice wedged its way into my brain with all the gentleness of glass shards. I wished the *fool* would shut his mouth.

Lifting my head to open my good eye, I forced it to focus on the crown of golden curls and depthless eyes that swam before my vision. But the only sound I managed was a labored gasp when his boot struck against my ribs. My knees snapped up to my chest, and I moaned in agony. Everything hurt.

Fight, Rae.

I *had* fought. I had kicked and bit and punched until there was nothing left but pain. But what was there left to fight for? They had escaped—they were safe. He had no leverage left over me. *Let me Retire in peace now.*

His hand gripped my chin, digging deep into the bone. "You'd throw away the winnings of the Trial for *him*? What were you thinking? *Fix this.* You are supposed to be mine, Oraelia! You are *mine.*"

The daggers in my eyes did not frighten him. His lip curled upward. "Did you really think he would save you? That you could run off together? That you'd live happily ever after like some fairy tale?" His tone was laced with disgust, but he held my face firmly in his hand, refusing to let me turn away.

I spit in his face, splattering his cheeks with flecks of red. *Blood*, my thoughts registered vaguely. *So I am bleeding.* The strike of his hand against my cheek spread like wildfire through my skin.

"Are you so foolish that you would pick death with him over *life* with me? You would throw away eternity for *him*? Refuse the honor and power the crown will afford you? He is *nothing*, Oraelia. Forget him!"

Seconds of bliss over an eternity of hell? Every damn time. I'd choose him every time.

"Let me share a little secret with you. That oath? It will destroy him if he fails to fulfill it—and he will fail. He is not coming for you, Oraelia. There are no fairy tales in real life. No happy endings. Only survival. Do you want to survive?"

There had to be a way. I could feel it in the fiber of my soul, the stitchings of my future binding me to his. This wasn't the end. "I—love—him," I managed.

"Love is for fools," he answered. "Do you even know what true love does? Do you know what it has done to my father?"

I held my tongue. I had heard the rumors, whispers that were best left forgotten, and the whisperers who had *been* forgotten. Crushed into dust and buried beneath the earth. Stamped down by the boots of our high king and his distaste for unflattering opinions. His iron-clad fist of authority entertained no doubts of his competency.

The high prince answered for me, since I chose to hold my silence. "Love made him weak. It turned him mad. And I will *never* make the same mistake."

So, the high king *was* mad. Would losing Rydar turn me mad? Would I survive it? My head lolled forward, my chin resting on the divot between my clavicles. Would Rydar survive losing me? If I died, would he finally be free, or would he fall to the same madness that consumed his father?

"He is a curse, Oraelia. You are best served to forget him."

"No."

"Damnit, Oraelia!" He shook me so hard that my senses scattered. "You won the Trials, and the public expects a wedding. I will not ask you to love me, but you *must* marry me. We need each other. Get up off the floor and make yourself presentable. Let us go fix this together."

"No."

His eyes flashed with black ire—a darker and more intoxicating poison than the one seeping through Rydar's veins. Perhaps he might have scared me if I were still capable of feeling, but I was not.

A smile curled at the edges of my mouth. He had no leverage left. No hold. He needed *me*, not the other way around. Needed me to win over the public. Needed me to inherit the crown. But I had no use for him. And I had no desire to serve him.

"*You* are nothing. I will never, *never* be yours."

His nostrils flared, and unchecked rage erupted through the bared teeth of his snarl. He laced his hands into my hair, digging his unforgiving nails into my scalp.

Sharp claws raked through my brain, unfurling it and shredding it to ribbons. Unbearable pain tore through my mind like wildfire as his fingers worked through my thoughts—coaxing them to weave into a new form—generating a fabric of lies. He pulled my thoughts taut and braided them, ripping the roots of inconvenient memories away from my skull. Somehow, I knew I was screaming, but the scream only echoed inside my skull, trapped within to be woven into the new reality Flint threaded for me. *Lies. Lies. Lies.*

A cool breeze caressed my cheek, and I stirred, wincing at the ache in my bones and the complete agony of my existence. *What is this? What happened to me?*

My moan beckoned sandy blonde curls and the embrace of warm hands to my bedside.

"You're awake." He smiled at me.

"What happened?" I tried to sit up in the bed, but I gasped in pain. He gently pushed my shoulders back onto the pile of pillows behind my head.

"Rest. You are still healing. Do you not remember what happened?"

I closed my eyes, searching for the memories in the fog of my exhaustion. *The last trial. Fire. An attack. Something...went wrong?*

He graciously filled in the blanks when I furrowed my brows. "You were attacked at the last trial—I made it to you just in time to save you."

I turned my head toward him. "Did I—did I win?"

He kissed my brow. "Yes, you magnificent creature. You won."

I let my head sink into the pillows. I had done it. I won. We would be married. I would get to spend an eternity loving him.

A pang of doubt sprouted in my heart, but I brushed it aside. This was all we had wanted—he loved me. I loved him.

He leaned toward me, and I welcomed the tender brush of his lips. I pulled his lips between mine, tasting him, deepening the kiss with the love I felt for him. His elbow pressed against my abdomen as he responded, but a sharp pain in my ribs made me wince and pull away.

He smiled with sadness and brushed my hair from my brow. "Get some rest, darling."

I pulled the covers back up to my chin and watched him walk to the door. He lingered in the door frame, then turned back to me with a glimmer of joy in his eyes.

"I am so glad you get to be mine, Oraelia."

The End of Book One

Scorched by the desolation of fire,
My heart weighs heavy,
All cinder and ash.

But from the ashes rises a phoenix ~~the phoenix~~
A new ~~flame changes~~
~~Burning~~ to call the rising sun.

But from the ash, the phoenix.
A new flame is summoned.
Burning, burning
to call forth the rising sun.

The majestic wings of the dragon
Soar beyond the destruction,

Heralding the change of a new dawn.

A new beginning.

-Nell Fenix

A butterfly for a
fresh start. Sorry it
wasn't more.
I'll see you after the
interview.

So proud of you.
Love. Rae.

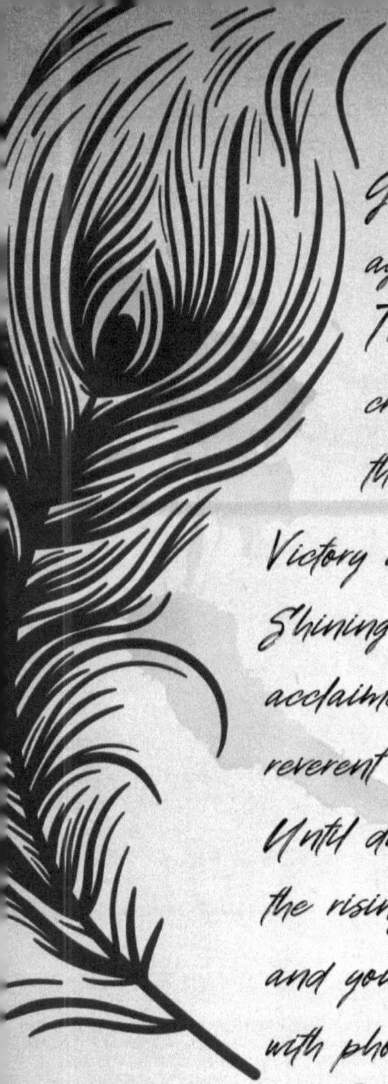

You bow, victorious,
aglow with triumph.
The dusk that lays to rest,
cradled by trees, nestled into
the blanket of the horizon.

Victory is written in the stars—
Shining—
acclaimed by starlight and
reverent shadow.
Until dawn stirs to call forth
the rising sun,
and you emerge to paint the sky
with phoenix feathers
and new beginnings.

Keep fighting—
you're stronger than you know.
Love you always.
Nell

Clocks exhale a weary sigh,
Minutes, like elusive whispers, conspire,
Biding their time with growing disillusionment,
laughing, mocking the efforts of men.

Perpetual echoes of greed and an iron fist,
Suffocating the realm,
stealing seconds,
spilling sand and blood
to overcome
the confines of a fleeting existence.

Yet, my life is mine,
Each hour, each minute,
A cascade of slipping sand,
An opportunity to bury the thieves,
And plant new seeds of survival.

Free verse, free spirit
marching forward with each tick
Let the king of avarice
dissolve into the shadows of time like
A fading memory; a tale forgotten.

Nothing withstands eternity,
Not even these inked verses on parchment.
But the indomitable spirit of the broken must
find the strength to endure.
His time has ended.
Ours is beginning.
Let the bells toll.

Acknowledgements

Thank you, dear reader, for joining me on this journey. I hope you enjoyed reading The Timeless Trials, and I am eternally grateful that you chose to read my story. I'm sorry if the ending made you want to throw the book—I promise there's more to come. This is not the end for Rydar and Rae.

Writing can sometimes feel like a very solitary act, but this book exists because of the efforts and support of many. I could not have done this alone.

Mom, thank you for always believing in me and pushing me to be my best. At times, it felt like I was swimming against the current, struggling to manage all the curve balls life threw at me. It would have been so easy to quit when life got hard, but I knew I always had your support and encouragement. I could not have accomplished this without the example you set for me—the grit and determination you modeled every day of my childhood, teaching me to be fierce and relentless in the pursuit of my dreams. Plus, I think the heaping dose of stubborn willpower you blessed me with genetically may have helped a bit.

Emily, my sister, thank you for being my lifetime best friend. Thank you for always being the first to listen to my stories and for going along with my crazy ideas as a kid. Sorry about the scary stories and the permanent trauma from the wolves. I hope you liked this story better. One of my favorite tropes in books has always been strong sister bonds because I find them relatable. Love you to the moon and back and you bet your ass I'd join The Timeless Trials to protect you, though I know you'd be your own force to be reckoned with. P.S. I'm waiting for your book now. Chop chop.

Mitchell, thank you for taking on the daunting task of providing for our family while I raise the kids and teach them to follow dreams. Your hard work never goes unnoticed. I love you.

Tess, thank you for giving me the initial push I needed to be brave. This story met the world because of you. Thank you for teaching me the way of dragons and other life lessons. They were gifted to me when I need them most.

Leigh, thanks for letting me stress-tell you my entire plot plan and still reading the book, even though you knew everything that was going to happen. Thank you for the encouragement and friendship along the way.

Grommy and Pop Pop, thank you for teaching me to love books and making them a part of my life. Thank you for writing my very first stories with me. You showed me what was possible.

For my first Vella readers and beta readers, thank you for Anne Beharry, Glenda, Ess, Amanda, Aech Bee, Sam...your feedback and excitement for this project helped me through the tough days. Knowing that somebody cared and wanted to read the next episode helped me finish the project.

For my editor, Kate Seger, thank you for helping me fix the chaos to shine up my story. And thank you for mostly letting me keep my emotional support em dashes.

Lincoln, Everett, Chloe, thank you for understanding when mommy is working and for being excited for me. I hope I've modeled the importance of unwavering determination and chasing your dreams. I can't wait to watch you chase yours.

Last but certainly not least, I'd like to thank each of my Kickstarter backers. You helped me create something beautiful, and I am grateful for your trust and involvement during this process. I hope you love it.

A. O'Brien-Smith, ASF DeWeese, Abbey Baer, Alex Blackstone, Alexandra Corrsin, Alicia Doty, Alyssa Brown, Alyssa Gagne, Amanda Eschmeyer, Amber Fuller, Anne Beharry, Annette McElroy, Ashley Ball, Aunt Jeanne, Azi, Barbara Fallon, Beth Barlow, Billye Herndon, Brandon Judy, Bree Bingham, Bree Moore, Brittany Stough, Brooke Grigsby, C.A. Varian, Catherine Cheeseman, Chase Meadows, Cherelle H., Christina W. Nichols, Claire Lee, Courtney

R. Delgado, Dan and Erin Salter (who obviously *are* the best neighbors I've ever had), Diane W., Elisha Padilla, Emily Judy, Emily Smith, Ess McKinney, Francesco Tehrani, Franchesca Caram, Glenda, Iren Adams, Jacquelyn Saunders, Jamie Dalton, Janessa R., Jenna Levitski, Joanne Cheung, Kaitlyn Mehrtens, Karen Tomlinson, Kassi Ketterer, Kate M., Kay Hines, Kriska, Krystina Roupe, Lauren B., Leslie G., Lisa Watson, Lulu D., Maike ten Dam, Marea Quijano, Megan Amaral, Mom (Catherine Jones), Mr. Thor Bear Jones (the goodest boy bestest brother), Mustela, Natasha Ruesc, Nathalie Olofsson, NeonPixxius, Nijeara "Ny" Buie, Nikole C., PunkARTchick "Ruthenia", Rochelle Moore, Ryan Marotta, Samantha Cross, Samantha Stolley, Shannon J., Shanon M. Brown, Sophie-Clara Harvey, Stefanie Martin, Steven Byrd, Sue Guess, Suzy and Mark Guess, Tess Combs, The Dreamer, Tonel, Victoria Heimpel, and Yamilet Santiago.

About the Author

A.C. Guess is a self-proclaimed fantasy aficionado and devourer of books. She has been spinning stories and crafting with words for as long as she can remember, though she tries hard not to remember those early stories. Fueled by coffee and a wild imagination, she dreams of winning the Timeless Trials herself to have more time to bring her stories to life. Unfortunately, she must admit that she would never win because of her preference for simple comforts like caffeine, blankets, and piles of books. A.C. Guess lives in Kansas City with her three kids, husband, and grumpy cat. The Timeless Trials is her debut novel.

www.acguess.com
Contact by emailing acguesswrites@gmail.com
Tiktok @acguesswrites
Instagram @acguesswrites